I Am of Irelaunde

"The author, in her first novel, captures the life and times of Ireland fast in the grip of Druidism. . . . The magical mysteries of the old man make the telling here of such legends as Cumhail and Mac Ronan an unexpected delight."
    —*The Tampa Tribune*

"St. Patrick is the star of this novel that weaves together fictionalized history and legends of the Catholic and pagan religions in their conflicts, but also their shared respect for humanity. . . . The fantasy elements in Patrick's adventures are what give the story its greatest sense of reality."
    —*Dallas Morning News*

"In this historical novel, Osborne-McKnight seeks to tell a more realistic story of Patrick than is normally found, but those who savor the mythical and mystical versions should not despair. The Druids, Irish heroes, and knowledge of the Otherworld are here as well, though in a more realistic context. . . . Author Juilene Osborne-McKnight demonstrates understanding of the Irish in both the method of the telling and in the details."
    —*The Charleston Post & Courier*

"A wonderful, magical story; it whipped me up into the air right from the first page and took me soaring to places I had never visited or imagined before . . . disbelief was utterly banished and I knew exactly how St. Patrick felt, facing the mystical, mythical vastness of Druidic, pre–Christian Eire and contemplating the deeds and the reality of Finn MacCool and the Fenians. The book is an enchantment, nothing less."
    —Jack Whyte

"The characters are as alive and fully drawn as any modern fictional protagonists, yet remain true to their times. . . . Osborne-McKnight's words sweep us along with the surety of a true storyteller. . . . A wonderful new working of the making of one of the most famous and beloved of miracle workers—Saint Patrick of the Emerald Isle . . . You don't have to be Irish to love and be moved by this story, but once you've read it you may wish that you could claim the lineage of Patrick and Osian. This is a superb and special book, one deserving a wide readership."
    —Joseph Bruchac, author of *Dawn Land* and *The Waters Between*

"*I Am of Irelaunde* is a wondrous gift of a novel. It captures Ireland's wild beauty with new eyes. The steadfast, courageous grace of the hero Osian, the awakening inner wisdom of Patrick, and the transformational power of love all join toward spellbinding results. The heroic deeds of both the ancient Fenians and the struggling new Christians are seasoned with the back-pounding humor of the Irish. Not since reading Mary Renault have I been transported to a mythic age brought so vividly to life. It's a treasure of triumphant storytelling."
    —Eileen Charbonneau, author of *Waltzing in Ragtime*,
    The Randolph Legacy, and *Rachel LeMoyne*

I Am of Irelaunde

A NOVEL OF PATRICK AND OSIAN

JUILENE OSBORNE-McKNIGHT

A Tom Doherty Associates Book
New York

I AM OF IRELAUNDE

Copyright © 2000 by Juliene Osborne-McKnight

This book is printed on acid-free paper.

A Forge Book
Published by Tom Doherty Associates, LLC
175 Fifth Avenue
New York, NY 10010

www.tor.com

Forge® is a registered trademark of Tom Doherty Associates, LLC.

Book Design by Lisa Pifher

Library of Congress Cataloging-in-Publication Data

Osborne-McKnight, Juliene.
    I am of Irelaunde : a novel of Patrick and Osian / Juliene Osborne-McKnight.
        p.   cm.
    "A Tom Doherty Associates book."
    ISBN 0-312-87320-4 (hc)
    ISBN 0-312-87567-3 (pbk)
    1. Patrick, Saint, 373?–463?—Fiction.   2. Ireland—History—To 1172—Fiction.
3. Christian saints—Ireland—Fiction.   4. Ossian, 3rd cent.—Fiction.   I. Title.
PS3565.S455 I15   2000
813'.54—dc21   99-089863

First Hardcover Edition: March 2000
First Trade Paperback Edition: February 2001

Printed in the United States of America

0 9 8 7 6 5 4 3 2 1

For
my mother,
my daughter,
and
she who sings in me,
bringer of poetry.
With gratitude for this trinity of grace.

and

For my father,
Fionn to my Osian:
two dreamers in a world
that has forgotten how to dream.

Bail O Dhia ar an obair
(Bless, O God, the work)

Icham of Irlaunde
Ant of the holy londe of irlande
Gode sir pray ich ye
for of saynte charite
come ant daunce wyt me
in irlaunde

14th century anonymous

I am of Ireland,
Out of the holy land of Ireland.
I pray you good sir,
for the sake of holy charity
come and dance with me
in Ireland.

ACKNOWLEDGMENTS

My gratitude goes first to my teachers.

Joseph Bruchac read the book for me, wrote a letter recommending it and has taught me a great deal about the Native American way of giving gifts unseen and unheralded. Wlipamkaani, my teacher.

Playwright Jean McClure Kelty produced and directed my Irish play, read and edited everything I sent her and made suggestions on dialogue, action and pacing that only a playwright could understand.

I would like to thank Father Andrew Greeley, my "parish priest," who understands and loves the storytelling God. Thank you, Father, for the reading, the time and the theology of passionate love.

Jack Whyte, you are my primus pilus; your words were a sword of light; your novels are transport to another time and place. Andrew Pope, my beloved agent, thank you for belief when no one else believed. To Claire Eddy, my editor, I extend thanks for the thoughtful reading and superb editorial suggestions.

My women's circle gave me invaluable advice and support during the long marketing and revision process; thanks go to Eileen Charbonneau, Christine Whittemore, Cindy McPhee, Mitzi Flyte.

Most of all I would like to thank my family, both immediate and extended, Osborne and McKnight, the fian in whose bright circle I have been privileged to be the storyteller.

GLOSSARY

CAST OF CHARACTERS AND PRONUNCIATIONS

Aillen of the sidhe (*al in of the shee*)

Aindir (*an ir*)

Ainfean (*an f'an*)

Benin (*b'an on*) Disciple of Patrick; historical person. Later St. Benignus.

Bodhmall (*bauv al*) Druidess who raised Fionn. Possible historical person.

Bran (*as spelled*) One of the hounds of Fionn.

Breogan (*br' ak an*) Scribe to St. Patrick. Probable historical person.

Caoilte (*kweel ta*) Fenian warrior. Probable historical person.

Conan Maor (*as spelled*)

Cormac Mac Art (*as spelled*) Historical person. King of Ireland 3rd century.

Dhiarmuid Ui Duibhne (*der mut o dub nee*) Fenian warrior. Probable historical person.

Dichu (*di chu*) Chieftain who gave Patrick land for his first monastery.

Finegas (*as spelled*) Druid and teacher of Fionn. Possible historical person.

Fionn Mac Cumhail (*finn mac cool*) Probable historical person. Fenian leader circa 3rd century A.D.

Gilly Dachar (*gil ee dak ar*)

Goll Mac Morna (*as spelled*) Fenian warrior. Probable historical person.

Grainne (*gran ye*). Daughter of Cormac Mac Art. Probable historical person.

Liath (*as spelled*) Warrior woman who raised Fionn. Possible historical person.

Leoghaire (*lie ee*) King of Ireland after Niall of the Nine Hostages. Probable historical person.

Longan (*Lun gen*)

Matha Mac Umotri (*ma ha mac u mo tree*) Chief druid of King Leoghaire of Ireland.

Miliuc (*mil i' uc*) Slavemaster to Patrick. Probable historical person.

Muirne (*mir ne*) Mother of Fionn. Probable historical person.

Niamh (*n'iav*) Wife of Osian. Woman of the Other.

Osian (*O sheen*) Also spelled Oisin, Oisian, Oissian. Son of Fionn.

Padraig (*Par ig*) Later Patrick. Christianizer of Ireland.

Sabh (*sav e*) Wife of Fionn; mother of Osian.

Sgeolan (*scow lan*) Second of the hounds of Fionn.

PLACE AND EVENT PRONUNCIATIONS

Alba Ancient name for Scotland and sometimes England.

Albion Ancient name for England, which was called Britain by Roman times.

Almhuin (*all loon*) The dun or stronghold of Fionn Mac Cumhail and his Fenian warriors. According to all accounts, this stronghold was located in what is now Kildare and could be seen from a great distance by the shining of its white walls.

Crom Cruach According to many old legends, this was a huge stone, surrounded by smaller stones, all representative of the god Crom Cruach and his minions. Crom Cruach was a hungry or sacrificial god who demanded firstborn animals, corn, milk and sometimes humans or human children as sacrifice. Tradition has it that people who worshipped Crom would rub their noses on his stone until the skin was worn down to the bone. His stone stood on the plain called Mag Sleacht, where supplicants would come to prostrate themselves before him. Legend has it that Patrick destroyed Crom Cruach.

druids Druids were the priests of ancient Ireland. To become a druid, a man or woman apprenticed for twenty years with a master druid or ollamh. Druids conducted religious ceremonies in oak groves (see *fidnemid* below) and knew vast amounts of knowledge about science, astronomy, philosphy, history and the natural and metaphysical worlds. Druids had phenomenal memory capacity; all of their knowledge was passed down orally from teacher to student for hundreds of years. Writing was forbidden in druidic practice.

Eire (*air e*) Synonymous with Ireland. A more ancient form of the name.

Faed Fiada (*fade fee a da*) Also known as the Deer's Cry, the Lorica or the Breastplate, this chant (a loose, poetic interpretation can be found in Chapter 15) has been attributed to Patrick and in use by the Irish as a protective prayer for hundreds of years.

feis (*fesh*) A festival or celebration. In ancient Ireland, these would have lasted for many days and would have featured feasting, reading of the laws of Ireland, dancing, singing, storytelling, foot and chariot races, hurley tournaments, oral genealogy and sacred ceremonials.

fidnemid (*fid nem eth*) A sacred grove. In druid practice, the center of this grove was a great oak tree, its arms upstretched in prayer. Often the grove would be ringed by blackthorn bushes. An altar might also be featured in the grove. Mistletoe grew on the oak trees and was sacred to the druids, perhaps for medicinal as well as ceremonial purposes.

Hibernia/Hibernians Roman name for Ireland and the Irish. This is the term for the Irish that Patrick most often uses in his Confession.

rath (*as spelled*) A village of ancient Ireland. Raths could vary in size, but usually contained circular dwellings, a longhouse for the purpose of meetings and celebrations, some kind of surrounding palisaded wall and sometimes a series of exterior ditches filled with sticks and stones.

Sabhal Padraig (*saul Par ig*) Perhaps the area that is now called Down-Patrick, this was reputed to be the area of Patrick's first monastery, church and Christian settlement. He also spent the final years of his ministry in this area.

samhain (*sow ain*) The Celtic calendar consisted of four great sacred celebrations: Samhain (October 31/November 1), Imbolc (February 1), Beltaine (May 1) and Lughnasa (August 1). Samhain was the most portentous of these festivals because it signaled the end of the light season and the turning toward the dark time of the year, with its short days and long cold nights. Much danger was associated with Samhain, for on this night the door between the human world and the otherworld opened; the possibilities for mischief and trouble were enormous and terrifying.

Sidhe (*shee*) Also called the Other, these people were believed to be the descendants of a race of people called the Tuatha De Danaan, who had once lived in Ireland. When the Tuatha were defeated in battle, their conquerors gave them as dwelling places the spaces beneath the hills and under the water, i.e. all the secretive, stony and hidden places of Ireland. These creatures were quixotic. They possessed magical powers, never aged and loved music and beauty. They could be humorous and mischievous, loving and beloved by humans or deadly dangerous and hideous. The term banshee derives from sidhe. Originally bain sidhe (woman of the sidhe), it later came to mean a creature who wails prior to the death of a family member.

Tara (*Tawr a*) Tara was the legendary seat of the High King of Tara. Located in County Meath, it once boasted a 700-foot banqueting hall, a school for poets, druids and warriors, a beautiful grianan or sun house for the women and many exquisitely decorated dwellings for the kings and chiefs of Ireland.

Tir Nan Og (*teer n'an awg*) Tir Nan Og has been variously called the Blessed Isle, the Western Isle, I Breasil and the Land of the Ever Young. It is a place in which there is no death, no aging, no illness and no sorrow. Feasting, song and dance form the entertainments of the place and time passes so swiftly there that hundreds of years seem to pass as a few brief days. The Celts had no fear of death, believing that the spirit went to Tir Nan Og after death and eventually reincarnated in an earthly form. Their art is representative of this belief, consisting of a series of unbroken spirals (often called knotwork) indicative of the continuous nature of life and death. Though the Celts believed in a panoply of Gods, many rather terrifying, they did not conceptualize a hell for the spirit after death.

PROLOGUE

Patrick the Briton

"Padraig!" I glanced up. Breogan, my scribe, ran toward me from across the field, his brown robe flapping, his red hair spiking in the wind. He waved his arms. I ignored him, bent deeper over the task of the monastery planting.

"Padraig!" he called again. He pronounced the name in his infernal Gaelic way. Paw drig. It was a language I spoke well enough—and one I had learned to loathe in the years of my captivity. I straightened, brushed my hands against each other, waited until he was standing before me.

"Brother," I began in my most patient teaching voice. "How will the others come to my name if you do not speak it? My name is not Padraig. It is Magonus Succatus Patricius. You may call me Abba or Brother or even Patricius, but not Padraig. You are my scribe, Breogan. You, of all others, should know this."

Breogan shook his head impatiently.

"Not now, Padraig," he said. In the usual fashion of these Hibernians, he had ignored all that I had said. He waved away my further remonstrances. "Look there!" He pointed off toward the woods line beyond the fields.

At the edge of the field, a man sat still as stone astride a white horse. His cloak of interwoven blue and green breacan moved like wings in the wind. He watched us, a sentinel, unmoving. From my distance, he looked young, his face unlined, his hair golden. I think about that even now, these many years gone, how young he seemed to me from that distance and I wonder. Does God send us those who change our lives? Does He intend them as miracles? And if we are too foolish, too blind, too much unbelievers to open our hearts, what becomes of us then?

I think these things now, but on that day, I thought only how angry I was with Breogan, angry at the way he spoke my name, angry at this foolish interruption of the planting for a stranger, angry at the other brothers gathering around me now, murmuring to themselves in their rough native tongue. I sighed, despairing.

"All right, Breogan. I will concede the moment to this foolish Hibernian need to know the life of every stranger. What must we do about this rider?"

The brothers regarded each other, murmuring in surprise. Breogan faced me.

"You do not know, Padraig?"

I regarded all of them. "Know what, man?" Breogan looked at the others, said nothing.

"Speak up, may the Devil take your soul!" I regretted my outburst immediately, crossed myself, placed my hands on Breogan's shoulders. I spoke in the simple way one must speak to these Hibernians. "Tell me, brother."

Breogan looked again at the stranger on the horse, who remained fixed at the edge of the forest, watching us, more a statue than a living being, but for the billowing of his cloak. Slowly, Breogan raised his arm, clenched his fist. The other brothers followed suit. The stranger returned the salute, his huge sinewy arm raised above the golden hair.

"He is a Fenian, Padraig. A Fenian is this rider."

Swiftly, I knocked Breogan's arm from the air.

"Brothers, don't be fools. Think, not as Hibernians, but as men of God. The Fenians are gone. If they ever lived at all. These are the years of our Lord, brothers! We are his servants here at Ard Macha and we will have none of this Fenian foolishness! Those days of Eire are gone."

But the brothers remained in salute, their eyes on the stranger. Breogan's arm crept back into the air. I knew that it would once again fall to me to bring these dreaming Hibernians back into the real world, the world of God.

I started across the field then, angry. The brothers followed, clustering around me.

The stranger swung his leg up over his horse. I saw the youthful strength in that gesture, saw that he was taller than his horse's back even with his feet on the ground. But as his foot touched the ground, he crumpled to the dirt.

It was then that I heard the Voice, the persistent one that forced me to return here to Eire, the place of my captivity, the place that I had resisted for so long. And the Voice was urgent.

"Run, Padraig!" it cried.

I ran, yanking up the cumbersome hem of my robe, my heart hammering against my ribs. When I reached the stranger, I saw that the distance or perhaps the cast of sunlight had fooled us. For the figure on the ground was older than any man I have ever seen. His long hair was white, not gold. His face was creased and folded in against itself. His hands were gnarled and twisted with the ropes of age. He stared at those hands, as if he too was surprised by their ancient timber. I knelt beside him, lifted him into my arms.

"Be still, old man," I admonished him in the guttural Hibernian tongue. "You sat too long astride in the sun. The brothers will fetch you water." He seemed confused by my words, shook his head.

"Old man," he repeated. "Old man."

I turned to Breogan.

"Tell him that we will bear him to the monastery. He seems not to comprehend my Gaelic."

But my scribe did not follow my instructions. He knelt beside the man for a long time, then spoke.

"You have been among the Other, have you not?"

The old man nodded. "I have. But now I am sent to one Padraig."

Breogan pointed at me. "This is Padraig."

The old man regarded me steadily with his ice-blue eyes.

"Where is Fionn Mac Cumhail? Where is Oscar? Where dwell the Fianna of Eire?"

"This Fenian foolishness again?" I shouted in my outrage. "Has the sun made all of you daft? Brothers, Fionn is dead! The Fianna no longer dwell in Eire! Who are you, old man?"

I looked back at the crumpled figure in my arms. Tears streamed down his face.

"Dead? All dead? How long was I among the Other? Too long, too long." He stared up at the blue sky, cried aloud. "And when I have told this one the tale, will you let me join them?"

I felt the brothers edge away. Only Breogan remained kneeling beside me, and he crossed himself fervently.

"Who are you, old man?" I asked again, insistent.

"I am Osian, poet of the Fianna, son of Fionn Mac Cumhail, father of Oscar, keeper of the Fenian tales." He regarded me steadily. "And you are Padraig, the one to whom I am sent."

My stomach clenched. Once more, once more, I was to be driven into the heart of Eire, country of my slavery. My heart refused the summons. I released my hold on the old man. Only Breogan's quick movements saved him from dropping head down into the dust, but I did not care. I stood and pointed at the brothers, at the stranger, now cradled so gently in Breogan's arms.

"I am not Padraig. I am Abba, Brother Magonus Succatus Patricius, a Briton of Roman descent and citizenship. I have come to Hibernia to bring the message of the true God to you who are heathen. When I have accomplished that task, I shall return to my own country. Please God that it be soon!" I took a deep calming breath, looked at the old man resting in Breogan's arms, gestured to the brothers.

"Convey this old one to the monastery. Feed him and give him drink, as is the way of good Christians. We will have no more of this foolishness, brothers. We have planting to complete."

But they would not leave him once he was refreshed. They lingered, acting like schoolboys, requesting tales of ancient heroes. I have learned to know these Hibernians well. I have been both slave and master in their country. They are simple and cruel, in both war and peace they are like children at a fireside, lost in their poems, their tales, their dreaming songs.

So it was I who made the decision. I called my scribe to me.

"Breogan, fetch your tools, your ink and your instruments. You will take down the stranger's story. I will read it to all of you after this evening's meal, brothers. That must satisfy. Now we must tend to the work of God."

They were reluctant to go, even when the scribe returned and settled himself beside the old man.

"Brothers," I threatened, "must I assign penance for idleness?"

They left then, returning to the fields. I made to follow when the old man called to me.

"Stay, Padraig." He seemed to read my thoughts for he spoke them. "There is more here than a fireside whim for the evening meal. There is in my story enough to make even you understand at last."

"What should I need to understand that my God has not already told me?"

"What do you know of the Fianna?"

"That they were warriors of the past. Or so the brothers say. And you, old man, were not of them. They have been gone nigh on two hundred years."

"You are wrong, Padraig. We will never be gone, for we were sustained as you are. By the truth that was in our hearts and the strength that was in our arms and the fulfillment that was in our tongues. We are Eire, Padraig. The light at the heart of Eire." He caressed the ancient word for his country, as though it were a thing of great price, instead of a boggy wasteland, filled with cruel heathens.

Breogan made so bold as to draw up a second stool. I shook my head, angry at him for presuming, angry at myself for hesitating. I retreated toward the door.

"I have little time, old man," I said.

"I am Osian." He pronounced it O sheen. He waited.

I shook my head at the impossibility of his claim. "Tell your tale to my scribe—Osian."

In the end, it was not Osian who made me sit, not Breogan with his eager pen. It was the voice, the capricious voice that set me on a ship bound for home, freed me from my captivity, then whispered, cajoled, forced me back to Hibernia when I wanted nothing of the place again. It was the voice that bade me run to the old man in the field. Despite all of my misgivings and my sorrows, it was the voice that directed the course of my life.

"Sit, Padraig," it said.

I sat, surprised.

Part One

"We beseech thee, boy,
come walk with us again."

—from the Confession of Patrick

1

What do you know of my father, Padraig? What do you know of Fionn Mac Cumhail?

"He was the leader of the Fenian warriors of ancient Eire. And he could not have been your father. Use your reason old man! Fionn Mac Cumhail has been dead for two hundred years."

"He was the leader of the Fianna, yes, but not at the start. His beginnings were none so glorious. He was born in the dead of winter, Padraig, born in the snow, with his mother hard on the run from the clans of Goll Mac Morna. Shall I tell you the tale?"

I closed my eyes, pressed my fingertips against the closed lids. Red and purple lights exploded behind the lids. I felt a huge sigh well up from me. Osian laughed.

"You sigh like a Fenian, Padraig."

"May that be the only thing I do like a Fenian. Tell your tale. It seems I am compelled to listen. But do not make it overlong."

"Over long." Osian paused and looked again in wonder at his gnarled, ancient hands. He smiled crookedly and I felt my heart wrench in pity. I shook my head to chase such weakness away. One should never pity these barbarians; they take advantage of such weakness. Osian began.

"My grandmother's name was Muirne, Padraig. She was young and beautiful with hair like the copper leaves of autumn. She was the daughter of a druidess, the wife of the great chief Cumhail Mac Trenmor. But none of that helped her in the winter of the clan wars. . . .

*   *   *

From her place on the pine boughs Muirne watched silently as the last stragglers of her people made their way into the forests. They moved in all directions, even back toward the oncoming army, creating many trails to confuse the warriors of Mac Morna, to lead them away from the boy child she had just birthed. Against her breasts, deep beneath the warm folds of her cloak the boy child was suckling. The woman lifted the folds and peered down at him, at the tiny hand curled leaflike against her breast and at the sweet puckered lips.

Around her the snow was still scattered with blood. So much blood. Muirne opened her palms to see if any flakes were filtering between the dense boughs, if the birthsigns would be covered by the time the armies of Goll Mac Morna arrived.

The captain of her husband's guard saw the gesture. He came with pine boughs, began to sweep over the blood to cover the traces. She gestured to him to stop. He knelt beside her, took her hand gently in his. His face mirrored the sorrow on her own.

"Let me stay," he whispered urgently. "It is what Cumhail would have wished. Or permit me to carry you."

"Nay," she hissed at him, her eyes still fixed on the suckling babe. "Cumhail would wish for his son to live, for his brother to live. You forget, Crimnall Mac Trenmor, that they will look for you as well." She patted his hand absently. "My husband would wish for clan na Bascna to rise again."

"Mac Morna will kill you, Muirne!"

"As long as Mac Morna wonders if my child lives, as long as he thinks that someone will come to me with news of my child, he will not harm me. He will let me go free, in the hope that I will lead him to the child. Now tell me of my other son, of Tulcha. Has he escaped to Alba?"

"He has, Muirne."

The woman nodded, rested her head wearily back against the trunk of the tree.

"Ask Bodhmall to come to me."

The old druidess came across the snow unbidden. Her gray hair twisted and lifted in the wind. She knelt beside Muirne, fixed her with her water-green stare.

"Give him to me now, lady. Goll Mac Morna comes." She held out her arms.

Gently, Muirne lifted the child from her breast. She watched dry-eyed as Bodhmall wrapped the infant in the blanket of clan plaid and handed him to the wet nurse to continue suckling. For a moment Muirne turned away, her copper hair spilling over her shoulder. She caught her hand in the spill of it, twisted it tight around her palm. She did not weep.

"You will take the warrior woman Liath with you. My son must learn the skills of warriors and druids."

"This is wise." Bodhmall stood.

"Bodhmall. Let me hold him just once more."

"You increase your pain, Muirne."

"It is my pain. I will carry it as I carry the pain of my husband's death at the hands of Goll Mac Morna. As I carry the pain of my firstborn son exiled to Alba."

"The pain of your lost babe will be worse," Bodhmall said, but she took the infant from the wet nurse and handed him into Muirne's arms. Muirne seemed to drink him in. She caressed the tufts of his hair, golden, even in the moonlit, snowy clearing. For a moment, the infant's eyes snapped open and fixed on his mother. They were huge, luminous orbs, blue and green, some combination of water and light and forest that Muirne had not seen in her other son. She started back at their intensity. The boy regarded her silently. He seemed aware of the moment.

"Demna," the woman said, glancing up at Bodhmall. "Call him Demna."

Bodhmall nodded, reached for the child. Quickly Muirne drew him to her. She pressed her nose against his neck and shoulder, smelled the sweet, out of the body smell of him. She touched a kiss against the downy cheek, against the curve of the little ear, rested her lips against the golden curls.

"I will not think of you as Demna," she whispered to the child, soft and close. "In my heart, you will be Fionn. Fionn, child of light."

Bodhmall stood, sniffed the air like a hound at hunt. "There is no more time, Muirne. Goll Mac Morna and his men are coming."

She took the child then, signalled to Liath, the warrior woman, to the wet nurse. The little group vanished swiftly and silently into the forest.

Still Muirne did not weep. She leaned against the pine boughs, watched as the flurries of snow sifted through the branches above her, covered the last traces of the birth.

Until Goll Mac Morna and his men entered the clearing, until Muirne saw their terrified faces and their hands making the signs against the evil, she did not realize that the high keening wails she heard were not those of a wolf. Even then she could not stop them, crying against the winter stars that she should be a mother without her child.

"Did she live then? Or did they kill her?" The old man had simply stopped talking. He looked at me squarely, smiled a crooked smile.

"I thought that you had no wish to hear my foolish tales."

I felt the hot blood of shame rush up into my face. I remembered this well—this Hibernian way of catching up the unsuspecting speaker, of pouncing like a smiling verbal cat upon the slightest word. But I had made my mind up long ago, when I was young and still a slave among them, that none so lowly as a Hibernian would ever best me. I stood and gathered the folds of my robe around me. Breogan was still scribbling; he did not look up from his paper.

"True enough," I answered him. "I do not wish to hear them; I can surely say that I do not believe them."

Osian said nothing; I grudged him the truth.

"However, you tell your story well. But I have found the telling of tales—especially untruthful ones—to be a skill of your people."

Osian took no offense at the barb; instead he nodded his head. I felt once again surprised by the lack of veracity these people could exhibit—and so blithely! The old man simply went on.

"I was the storyteller, Padraig, the poet. Telling tales was what I did. And my father loved them."

"What father you had may have indeed loved your stories, old man. But your father was not Fionn." I moved to the door. "Finish your scribbling Breogan and bring the tales to the refectory."

Breogan nodded and I moved to the door, but not before Osian could call out the last word.

"Padraig!" he said. "She lived."

I did not go to the old man's cell for all of the next week. I sent Brother Longan with a breakfast of stirabout and good brown bread; when his eyes lit up at the task, I put him under a vow of silence, so that he could not beseech the old man for stories. When he returned with his face shining, I took him off the task and rotated the brothers from then on, so that none of them would be with the old man for more than a few moments. Still, when I spoke the ChristMass in the mornings, I would notice their heads turning in the direction of his room, and it was that, more than anything, that convinced me that the old man must go.

On the first day of the second week, I went to the old man's room, filled with determination. He was not in his bed. He was standing at the window, fully dressed, wrapped in the blue and green cloak that I had seen him in that first day. From behind, I could almost forget that he was an old man. He was taller than all of the brothers and large; his head and shoulders filled the embrasure of the window. He stared out at the fields and the green treeline beyond. I had thought him unaware of my presence, but he spoke without turning.

"You are certain that all of them are gone?"

"All of the Fenians? I am certain."

He turned. I could see that the blue of his eyes shone with unshed water.

"You cannot imagine how I miss them, Padraig. My father was unlike any other. And my son. I should not have left them."

I wanted to say something biting, something to the effect that he could not have left them two hundred years ago and still be here. But the longing on his face was so naked and unprotected that my own heart remembered its sorrow.

"I know what it is to long for your family and not be able to go to them."

He stood in front of me then and fixed me with the intense blue of his gaze.

"Is that why you hate them so, Padraig?"

"Hate whom? There is no room for hate in the teachings of my God."

"But there is room in his druid." He spoke it low, threatening. "These boys you have gathered around you. All of them but Breogan a boy, warrior boys with no Fenians to join. But you punish them and render them to silence, and put them to digging in the fields like cumhals. They fear you, Padraig. Is that what you wish?"

I reached for the arm of a chair, sat down heavily. I fixed on his only statement that could be a spike for my anger.

"I am no druid."

He flung his arms at me.

"You fear to answer my question, Priest. That is what they call you, is it not? The Druid of Christ? Priest. Abba. Brother. Why do you hate them so?"

"What do you know of me, old man?"

"I know what Breogan has told me. And Lonan. And the others. I know that you have been here for less than one year. I know that you are called the Talkenn and the Adze-Head, for the tonsure of your hair. They say you teach of one called the White Christ. Breogan tells me that the druids predicted you long ago." He closed his eyes, recited.

"One will come from the Eastern Isle,
the Adze-Head, the Talkenn,
the Brown-Robed one.
Crooked his staff
and his table facing East
will prepare a new feast for
a god unheard of in our time.
Our gods he will overthrow,
our altars he will destroy.

> *From his altar he will sing;*
> *the people will answer So Be It*
> *forever."*

"This druidry is nonsense."

"It is why many of them are here. You were expected."

"I put them under a vow of silence." I said it weakly.

"Faugh!" The old man waved his hands. "Do you think they obey such fool-ishness? When they could hear the Fenian tales? When I am here with them? They are what they are, Padraig. They are Eireann; I told you before, the Feni-ans are the light at the heart of Eire. Your little vow cannot silence that."

Now the anger rose up in me white hot.

"Heart of Eire? I have been at the heart of Eire. There is nothing there of light, nothing but emptiness and cold."

"We come to it, then."

"Come to what? You speak in riddles and think yourself wise."

"I know that you were a slave in Eire."

"I was." I'm up now, shouting. I put my face close to the old man's. "A slave. But they could not keep me here. No, not my body nor my spirit. For both of them escaped this wretched place."

"And yet you returned."

"I returned. I returned because I had to. Because I had no choice. Because I was made to come."

"And now you make them slaves to pay for your enslavement and the anger of your return."

"That is not the way of it!"

"I say it is."

"What you say matters not at all! You will be gone on the morrow!"

I left the room and hurried along the hallway. I encountered Breogan in the hall, clutching his papers and boxes to his chest.

"Leave off with his tales. We will have no more Fenian foolishness. You are forbidden from his room."

Breogan said nothing, stood stock still in the hall. I could feel him turn and watch my retreating back, but I did not wait to see if he disobeyed my orders and went to the old man's chamber. I hurried out into the sunlight, raced for the old barn that served as our rude chapel and threw myself to my knees on the cold stones before the altar. I bent my body deep, doubling over my folded hands; when I still could not contain my fury I shouted it aloud to the one who had made me come here.

"WHY?"

It richocheted off the walls and thundered through the center of the chapel, then settled into silence. In that silence I waited, for I knew that the answer would come.

Morning passed into afternoon. The light changed windows, filtered through the dust motes. When darkness came on, Breogan came in and lighted the candles on the altar. I watched his back, the red of his hair. He wore a white robe, bordered in some gold embroidery; it was a druid's robe and I felt the anger flash high in me again. But when he turned to face me, it was not Breogan at all, but a brother whose face I did not know.

"Who are you?" I asked.

"I am sent," he answered.

Confusion moved darkly in me; I shook my head.

"Has the old man sent a druid to speak to me, then? What foolishness is this?"

The man laughed, a rich full laugh that filled the chapel. My heart grew lighter at the sound.

"Padraig, you wage war on everything around you, but moreso always on yourself."

I knew then that he was a messenger.

"Why does the One not speak to me himself? Always, he speaks to me here." I rested my fingertips on my forehead.

"Your mind is not still enough to hear the Voice. So I am sent instead."

He was laughing at me, his face a wide grin, but there was no malice in the laughter. The knot in my stomach unclenched and I felt my shoulders relax. I straightened my body.

"Sit, Padraig," he said. "You have been kneeling for many hours."

"Does the messenger of God mock me, that he also calls me Padraig? I am Magonus Succatus Patricius."

The messenger only smiled. He sat down across from me, ordinary. He crossed his legs and rested his hands on his knees. He spoke.

"I am the one called Victoricus."

"You! You!" I spat the words. "I know you then. I know you! Night after night, year after year, you came to me in dreams. You read to me a letter, from the people of the Foclut Wood, the village of my slavery. 'Come back to us boy,' the letter said. 'Come and walk among us.' I know you well; you are the agent of my misery. Why could you not leave me in Britain, at home with my parents and my beloved ones? Why have you tormented me these long years?"

"God told me to call you," the messenger said. He spread his hands, smiled.

Before I could say anything further, he spoke again.

"The old man has been sent to you."

I shook my head.

"This is not possible. He is contentious and full of lies. He speaks of druids and accosts me among my own brothers; he has ruined all the discipline I have built in this last year."

"But he brings stories, Padraig." He said it simply.

"Patricius," I responded. "And he brings pagan stories. Stories of ancient warriors and heathen practices. And the brothers eat these fancies with their stirabout spoons. Surely my Lord cannot intend for these things to happen."

Victoricus spoke sharply.

"You question the will of the Lord then?"

"I do not," I answered, still angry. "I am here, am I not? In the place where I wanted least to be. And you yourself had a hand in forcing me back here."

Now the messenger grinned. Something in the smile reminded me of the old man.

"You are here," he said. "But it took you eighteen years to return, Padraig."

I spread my hands and shrugged my shoulders. Victoricus continued.

"Listen to the old man, Padraig. He grows weaker in that body every day. His stories will be lost forever if you do not take them down. Stories are precious to the storyteller. And in the old man's tales there is a green love for this place that you so loathe."

"Faugh! This place. I tell you he will drag the brothers away from all the good that we have done here. He undoes discipline. These people are not like my own; they are too easily seduced by story and song."

The messenger actually laughed aloud again, throwing his head back. He held his hands up.

"You do choose the difficult ones," he said to the ceiling. To me he said nothing, but I knew that he spoke of me, so I continued my argument.

"Do you know that he claims to be Osian, son of Fionn Mac Cumhail of the Fenians? Will you have me take down the tales of a liar, an old man demented by the weight of his years?"

Victoricus said nothing; he looked at me directly and waited. I regarded him with incredulity.

"Will you tell me that he is Osian? Will you expect me to believe that? I do not think it possible."

"You among all others know that all things are possible to The Word."

When he spoke that name, I knew. My heart knew.

"He is Osian."

"He is," said the messenger.

"Then he shall stay."

"Of course he shall."

That night at supper, I lifted the vow of silence. Though they had been breaking it all along, the brothers showed no remorse. In fact, they favored me with a cheer.

Perhaps if I finish with these foolish stories, my God will allow me to go home. For I will never understand these Hibernians.

I rose early the next morning and rapped on the door of Breogan's cell. He was already awake, his writing tools set out before him. He began to gather them up as soon as he saw me.

"You knew?"

Breogan's face relaxed into a smile.

"I was your brother and your scribe long before we returned to Eire, Padraig. For five years now, I have traveled with you in your own country and on the Continent, at Auxerre. I have learned to understand you. Did you never think it strange that the bishops assigned you an Eireann scribe, albeit one who could write in the Roman tongue?"

"I never considered it at all, or if I did, I thought the match well-suited, for we both spoke the three tongues of our travels."

"I requested the position, Abba."

"Why?"

"Because I was told to request it in a dream."

"By one Victoricus I am supposing."

Breogan nodded his head, unsurprised.

"Yes, by just that one."

We progressed to the old man's room. He was fairly gleeful this morning, rubbing his hands together like dry leaves at our entry, booming out heartily.

"And what story shall I tell you this morning?"

"Does everyone know the future but me?" I asked glumly, settling into the cross-legged Roman chair.

But Osian only laughed.

"I have had breakfast. You have lifted the vow of silence. The brothers talk."

I expelled a long breath.

"Very well. As I recall, you left us with the tale of your father's birth. You had best begin at the beginning. Tell us of his childhood. But do not make the tale too long, old man. I have business of the monastery to attend to."

But Osian was staring at me in surprise.

"My father," he said. "You called him my father. So you know. I was not wrong when I called you a druid."

"If you can think of it no other way, you must think of me as the druid of Christ," I answered.

"Well," said Osian. "If it is this Christ who has told you of my father, he is one I would like to know."

I espied a kind of light then, and I smiled.

"Very well," I answered. "We will trade stories for stories. But for this morning you must begin."

Osian nodded.

"My father was raised in the mountains of Slieve Bloom. He was called Demna, as his mother had instructed. Bodhmall and Liath were the only mothers he ever knew. With the exception of wanderers and a few peddlars, they were the only other human beings he knew, at least until his fifteenth year. . . ."

Demna crouched low behind the rocks and watched in astonishment. Boys! Boys his own age! In all his life he had never seen anyone of his own age.

He watched as the boys raced down the field, laughing, their long hair whipping around their faces, their bodies glistening with sweat. Liath and Bodhmall would thrash him surely for this; they had warned him to have no contact with anyone, to hide if he saw strangers, but the excitement crawling in the pit of Demna's stomach was almost unbearable.

He had lived his entire fifteen years in the wild glens and valleys of the Slieve Bloom mountains. His companions had been Bodhmall, the ancient Druidess who had taught him magic and the tales of ancient Eire, and Liath, the warrior woman who had trained him to hunt and fish, to fight and throw a spear.

Besides the occasional wanderer or tradesman, Demna had known no other humans in his life. He watched the boys at their game with longing. They chased a ball with a curved stick. It seemed simple enough. Demna stood and stepped into the sunlight of the playing field.

"You, boy!" A tall fellow with long black hair swept down upon him. "You block the field!"

"I wish to join your game."

The boys of both teams swept up behind the black-haired runner, clustering around him, staring openly. At fifteen, Demna was already six feet tall. His body was muscular and taut, honed from years of hunting on foot in the silent forests of Slieve Bloom. In the sunlight of the playing field, his pale golden hair seemed haloed with white light, his blue-green eyes watery and strange.

"Do we know you?" asked the dark-haired one.

"I am called Demna. I am of these mountains. But I have not seen you before."

The dark-haired one gestured backwards toward the temporary dwellings at the far edge of the field.

"We travel with the army, the Fianna, for King Cormac."

Demna felt a strange sensation move within him. He tried to shake it off, but it persisted. What was it the Bodhmall was always saying? "You will know your destiny when it arrives, boy." Demna laughed aloud. Foolishness. The boys watched him expectantly.

"I would join your game," he said again.

"Are you good at hurling, then?" asked the dark-haired one.

"At what?"

The boys broke into wild laughter, clapping each other on the back. The dark-haired lad smiled.

"You may join my team. I will teach you what I can. I am called Caoilte. Caoilte Mac Ronan."

He tossed his stick. Demna caught it in midair.

The opposite team began to complain after Demna's seventh goal.

"The boy plays too well. We must divide the teams again. His team has the unfair advantage!"

"Take three away from us then," called Mac Ronan. He was amazed at the speed and strength of the light-haired boy. "We will play with fewer and keep Demna."

33

But even with its ranks swelled by three, the opposing team could not win. Demna was everywhere at once, running silent like the forest deer, tacking away and back like the wolves. The losing team grew angry.

"You knew him, Mac Ronan. You have sneaked him in on us!"

"By the Dagda, I swear that I did not. Ask the fionn one if he has ever met me before."

Demna, hurtling down the field with his stick at the ready, stopped dead in his tracks. He turned and stared at Mac Ronan.

"What have you called me?"

"The fionn one. The fair one. You are exceedingly fair with that white hair. Why do you stare so?"

Demna's skin crawled. He felt a cold clamminess begin beneath his breastbone. It spread up his chest and threatened to cut off his breathing. He threw down his stick, began edging toward the woods line.

"I must go."

"Nay, we have only begun the game."

"And you have not yet played for our team," shouted one red-headed fellow. "You put him up to this, Mac Ronan. Your team will win and we will have no chance to even the scores."

Demna saw the anger in their faces, felt it turning against him, but he felt powerless to deflect it. It was the word. Fionn. Fionn. It made him think of snow and something, someone warm. He closed his eyes, pictured a golden chariot, a woman in white pressing his six-year-old frame to her sobbing body. He did not fight back when the boys descended upon him, crushing him beneath their bodies, hammering at him with their sticks. He did not fight back until he thought of Bodhmall.

"She knows!" he cried aloud from the bottom of the pile. "She has always known! And now, by the gods, she will tell me!"

He came up from the pile in one swift movement, knocking the boys aside as if they were the straw dummies Liath had created for him to fight as a child. With the blood streaming from his nose and eye, he swung in on the more tenacious ones, fighting calmly, elbowing one here, catching one at the center of his nose there, pulling a third onto the heap from over his back.

Clear of the fighting, Demna turned to flee. Caoilte Mac Ronan stood facing him. Demna laughed.

"An interesting morning, Mac Ronan. But do not cross me."

Mac Ronan stepped back.

"We will meet again, Fionn," he answered.

Fionn loped away into the dappling forest before some of the boys had even realized his absence from the fight.

"You must tell me!"

Bodhmall moved one aged hand calmly along the yarn, twisting the spindle in the other, winding the wool into long skeins. Her gray braid snaked down the front of her gown.

"I will tell you, once you have allowed Liath to tend to your wounds."

Liath took his face firmly, turned it back toward her; she dabbed at the bloodied eye, pressed a cloth of cold river water against it.

"You were a fool to do this thing, Demna. Have we taught you nothing that you would leap into danger like a child?"

"You have taught me to fight, Liath. You see that I did that well enough. And Bodhmall has taught me that my destiny would come. I know now that it has. And you need no longer call me Demna. My name, I believe, is Fionn."

Liath sucked in her breath, turned toward Bodhmall.

"Nay boy, your name is Demna," she said quietly. "It is in the heart of your mother that you are known as Fionn."

"The woman in the chariot!"

Bodhmall smiled at him and nodded.

"You think well, boy, even in your agitation. She came when you were six years old. She could not bear her separation from you any longer. I had sent her word that you were well and she found us here. I told her never to come again."

"Why? Why did you do this cruel thing? Were you so jealous of me that you could not let me know my own mother!"

Liath cuffed him hard against the side of his head, but Bodhmall only watched him quietly.

"Is that what you think of me boy? Of our years together here?"

Fionn hung his head in shame.

"No, grandmother. I know that your love has always been for me. But still I do not understand."

"Your mother endangered you both by her coming. Even she knew this, boy. Your mother is Muirne, wife of Cumhail Mac Trenmor."

Fionn looked up startled.

"Mac Trenmor. You have told me many stories of Mac Trenmor."

"What do you remember?" asked Bodhmall in a deceptively quiet voice. "Tell me your lessons."

"Mac Trenmor was slain by Goll Mac Morna and his followers. Lia of Luachair, follower of Goll, stole from Mac Trenmor's body the craneskin bag which contains the symbols of leadership of the Fianna—the light spear of the sidhe, and the three sacred stones of Eire. But one day the Fianna will come back to its rightful leadership when Fionn, son of Cumhail Mac Trenmor . . . By the gods!"

He dropped to his knees before Bodhmall.

"Old woman, am I that Fionn?"

From the doorway of the hut, the two women watched his back as Fionn sat by the river.

"We must keep him with us!" Liath argued.

"We cannot! He has brought his destiny to him. How will we keep him when the wind is calling his name?"

"But he will not survive beyond Slieve Bloom. He knows nothing of the world outside Slieve Bloom. What does he know of kings, of warriors, of women?"

The old woman placed her hand on the younger one's shoulder.

"He knows to fight well, for you have taught him. He knows the ways of the forest as well as if he himself were a four-legged. Sometimes, I think the animals speak to him and he to them. He knows to fish, to hunt. He knows what I have taught him— the history of Eire, the poetry and the tales. He knows of the Other. Now he knows of his place in the destiny of Eire. There is no more we can teach him."

"There is one more thing. I can teach him one more thing, Bodhmall. And it will keep him safe with us." Liath began unbraiding her chestnut hair.

Bodhmall smiled sadly.

"I know what you think to teach him little warrior sister. You think to open your creamy thighs and let him enter. You think to suckle him on your breasts. You believe that your delights will hold him here. But I tell you they will not. You are a woman of forty years. You will not hold a boy of fifteen when the world is beckoning."

Liath swung the heavy hair loose with a determined motion.

"Do you deny me your permission to teach him this?"

Bodhmall sighed.

"No, no. It is best that he learn this power from one who loves him, one he respects."

"I tell you that it will keep him here with us," said Liath. She strode purposefully out the door and advanced on Fionn's back.

Bodhmall watched silently as Liath removed her tunic, knelt before the frowning boy, reached for the criss-cross lacing of his braichs. She sighed, turned from the doorway and returned to the fireside. She picked the wool up, but stopped for a moment to massage her fingers.

"I am grown old," she said. "Old, in the mountains of Slieve Bloom. But not too old to know that our frail bodies cannot keep destiny from our door."

"We have heard enough story for today."

Osian laughed aloud. "It does make the body hunger for the comfort of a woman."

"We do not take such comfort here," I answered. "We are celibate."

"Celibate?"

Breogan cleared his throat, bent deeper over his scribbling.

"We do not mate with women."

"By the gods! Why not?"

"We reserve our bodies for the service of our God."

"Does your God require this?"

"He does not."

"I am glad of it, for I would not wish to know more of him if he did."

"We choose this way, that we may dedicate ourselves more completely to our Lord."

"And does this 'celibate' make the dedication easier? Or more difficult?"

I shook my head, not knowing how to answer. In truth, my groin ached and my mind swirled with memory. I left the chamber, but all day long I thought of Fionn and the warrior woman until I was angry with myself, with Osian and his stories, with the One who had sent me the stories in the first place.

4

How many times may the mating be performed a day?"

Liath repressed a sigh, glanced down at Fionn's swollen braichs and smiled.

"At least three times each day by the evidence. You learn your lessons well as always."

Fionn smiled sheepishly, lowered the shoulder of her tunic. He gently kissed her nipple and watched it harden.

"It is a wondrous thing to see this happen," he said.

Liath smiled indulgently, lowered the other side of her tunic. She stroked her hand through Fionn's hair as he lowered himself to her breasts, talked above the white-gold hair.

"You are young and strong, Fionn, and there is no reason that you cannot do the mating as many times in any day as you wish. Only be sure that the woman you take is willing. Never take a woman when she is too tired or too heavy with child or when she tells you that she does not wish to bed with you."

Fionn drew back, eyed her with concern.

"Do I weary you with too much of this, Liath?"

"Come, boy!" Liath cuffed him playfully on the head. "In all our years together have you ever known me to weary on the hunt or when throwing the spears? I am a warrior."

It was not quite the truth. In her fifteen years of training Fionn, with the exception of one or two brief couplings with travellers through Slieve Bloom, Liath's life had been almost chaste. After three weeks of Fionn's explorations, she ached in places she had forgotten. But Liath would never tell Fionn of her weariness. She smiled and lowered his head again to her breasts.

"Which of the ways I have taught you would you like to practice this time?"

Fionn shrugged back and divested himself of his braichs. He stretched out on his back on the forest floor.

Liath smiled and moved down over him. She rocked gingerly at first, allowing her body to grow moist with the movement. Fionn drew an arm around her, gently cupped first one breast and then the other into his mouth. Liath moaned softly. Fionn smiled in delight.

"I do please you then."

Liath stroked her hand through the sides of his hair.

"As you have always been, you are an apt pupil." She began to rock a little faster. Fionn moved his hips up against hers and groaned.

Liath had curved her hands over his shoulders and was thrusting hard and deep against him when a rider on a horseback burst into the clearing.

"You taunt us with these recitations!" I stood from my chair and walked to the window. I faced out toward the garden.

Osian looked surprised to be interrupted in his storytelling.

"Nay, Padraig, I do no such thing. I simply tell the stories as my father told them to me."

"This is a story your father told you?"

"My father had a fondness for warrior women after Liath tutored him. He mated with many before he married with my mother. He called them strong and playful."

I placed both hands against the window embrasure and rested my head upon the cool stone. I let the cool of the rock pass through my body. Beyond the window, rain misted in the delicate undulating fog that only Eire can produce. Behind me there was a rustling sound. I turned around to see that Breogan had left the chamber.

"I asked him to leave." Osian spoke quietly.

"Ah," I said. "And for you they obey instantly."

"Breogan knows when you are troubled. Each time I speak of the mating you are angry. Is it that you have given up the company of women? Or have you known a woman who troubles your memory."

I sat in the window shelf, rested my hands in my lap.

"I was a slave in Eire, Osian. Six years a slave. Did you know that?"

"I knew."

"She was the foster daughter of the man who was my master. Miliuc was his name." I spat the word.

"I was a boy when I came into my slavery and she was younger still. We grew up together but we were as far apart as slave and master always are. Still, she smiled at me sometimes, spoke my name—softly, when her foster-father was out of earshot. She was beautiful. Her hair was the color of copper, long and thick and she had freckles here," I brushed at the bridge of my nose, "and skin as white and clear as dove's wings. I watched her. She knew that, I think. Women always know that."

"They do," he said. He was smiling.

I turned, looked out again at the rain. I told him the story looking away from him.

"It was in the third year of my captivity. I was almost broken then. Almost broken. I believed that I would never go home again. I rarely slept, ate less than even a slave's portion. I did not yet know how to pray; I was so lonely. I spent all day with the sheep in the fields; at night I slept with the wolfhounds. She came to me one night in the darkness when I lay in my sleeping hut. I was awake, staring into the darkness and I smelled her, sensed her before she was beside me. I felt such a lurch of joy then, as if I had been expecting her all along.

"She said nothing at all. She slipped her tunic from her shoulders and lay down beside me. She fed her breasts to me, cupping them in her own hands and holding them against my lips like succulent birds."

I curved my hand, stared at it in surprise.

"When I entered her, she did not cry out. She stroked back the sides of my hair and whispered, 'It will be better now, Padraig. Now it will be bearable.' "

I felt the hot flush of remembering her come up in my face, lowered my head and stared at the window sill.

Osian spoke from behind me. "And you did not see her again." It was not a question. I shook my head.

"Her foster-father must have discovered us. In the morning she was gone, sent from her fosterage back to her own family. But she relighted the fire that had been banked in me. I began to dream again of escape, of home. I fasted and prayed and in the prayers I was no longer lonely. I began to speak to the people of nearby Foclut Wood of my Lord and they listened. Then, in the sixth year of my captivity, the Voice told me how to find my ship for home.

"I journeyed the width of Eire and all through that journey I watched for her, prayed that I might see her. But I never found her. At last, I reached the coast and the ships were there. One captain after another I asked to take me home but all refused. I wore the collar of a slave boy; none were brave enough to risk a master's wrath. And then at last there was the ship with the cargo of unruly wolfhounds. Wolfhounds I could manage. After all, other than for her company they had been my only companions. I sailed home in a cargo hold full of barking wolfhounds, dreaming of her skin upon my own."

"Why should such a memory bring you shame or anger?"

I sighed. How could I explain the way of it to this heathen? I shook my head.

"When I went into my captivity I was a wild boy. I had no more notion of God or his ways than . . . than you do, old man. But I came to know my God in the fastness of my slavery, in the years of silence. That knowledge should have sufficed; I should not have dwelled in the body."

He made a sputtering sound, but I held up my hand.

"There is more. There is honor. I should have found her, should have told her what her gift was to me. I will still find her and when I do I will offer her the gift of the Christ in return."

"This Christ of yours. He is a god-being?"

"He is the Son of the Creator, the Light, the Word made flesh."

"He was a god of the body then?"

"He was."

"Did he mate with women? Many gods do."

"He did not. He dwelled in the body and he died in it."

"If he took no pleasure in the body, then why did he choose it?"

"But he did take pleasure in the body. He loved to walk in the hills. He loved to feast with his friends, eat and drink wine. He liked to fish and sail on the sea and tell stories. He loved to tell stories."

"Ah," said Osian.

I saw the trap then, but at the same time that my anger rose, I wanted to laugh at the clever old man.

"You argue like a sophist!" I spat at him.

"I do not know this term, but this god of yours is devious, Padraig. And subtle."

"Devious?"

"He must have greatly wanted you to return here to give you so sweet a

41

memory of Eire, a voice to whisper in your body, in its pleasures, in the memory of that woman, so that you cannot forget that you are human."

"I am ashamed of what I did. It was not God's gift, but my human weakness."

"Are you certain?" he asked me. "You are not so ashamed that you have forgotten." His voice was serious but his eyes were dancing.

I should have told him then that the body is a temporary dwelling place, that the needs of the flesh should be subjected to the needs of the spirit. I should have told him that I had returned to Eire to instill this sense of duty in the Hibernians, that they would dream less and work more, dedicate themselves to the work of God. But I could not tell him. I stared instead at my hand, at the long, slender fingers, at the work-hardened callouses in the palms, at the fine, almost feminine curve of the palm as I held it there.

"I mated with another once, when I had but fifteen summers. She was just a girl—a virgin of only thirteen years. I confessed this transgression to one I thought was my friend. He betrayed me to the bishops in Gaul."

"Yours is a good story, Padraig. But I will never tell it if you do not wish it told."

"I know that," I said and was surprised to find that I did. I felt suddenly buoyant. For two dozen years I had carried my transgression and had never felt lightened of it until I told it to an ancient heathen who was undoubtedly himself a gifted liar. I shook my head.

"I like this God of yours more than I thought I might, Padraig," Osian said.

"I am not Padraig," I said automatically. "And I am sure that my God is wonderfully gratified to have your approval." But something in me had lightened and I couldn't help smiling at him, even as I spoke.

I let the old man tell stories to the brothers that evening after supper, only making him promise that they would not be stories of mating. To judge by their excitement, one would think I had let the brothers sit at the Sermon on the Mount. They gathered around him, murmuring and laughing, shoving for places the closest by. We had given Osian a low Roman camp stool with arms, covered with wolfskins, and Breogan had brought him a huge mug of the abbey's finest ale. I could not help thinking as I watched him there, laughing down at the brothers around him, joking with one here, shaking a finger at another there, that it was like watching an ancient king, so sure in his powers that even his great age couldn't diminish him. And there was no one who could tell a story the way he could tell it—the held pauses, the sweeping gestures, the voice that seemed to memorize the sound of many tongues. I was glad that the messenger had told me to listen, for I would have been otherwise shamed to take so much pleasure in a heathen's tales.

"Where shall I begin?" he called aloud.

I answered him.

"Begin when Fionn must leave the forest and the care of Liath and Bodhmall."

"Ah yes," he said. "The day when Fionn was forced to leave the care of his beloved druidess—and of the warrior woman Liath." He looked right at me and he was laughing as he began.

The horseman swept into the clearing where Fionn was . . . with the warrior woman, Liath. He dismounted in a flurry and threw his cloak back over his shoulder.

"Caoilte Mac Ronan!" cried Fionn in delight. He donned his braichs and laced them up, clapped Mac Ronan on the shoulder. I remember you well. But how did you find me here?"

Liath came to stand beside Fionn, naked and glistening, her breath coming hard. She held a spear in her right hand. Fionn stayed her arm. Mac Ronan spoke.

"It was not I who found you. It was the warriors of Goll Mac Morna. After the game of hurley that day, you were all the boys could speak of—the fionn one who appeared from the forest. The one who played hurley as if he were his own team. The one who leaped like the deer, cut away like the wolf. Goll Mac Morna got word of you. He wondered at a warrior boy, so fair, living alone in the forest. He has had his Fenians searching the forest for you for days. Last night, they returned, reporting a boy who lived alone in the forest with two old women."

He eyed Liath for a moment.

"Their report was not entirely accurate."

Liath waved this away.

"Why have you come, boy?" she asked, her voice hard.

"Mac Morna knew immediately that the fionn one was Cumhail Mac Trenmor's

son. He cannot allow you to live; you have claim to the Fianna. He follows hard upon me. I learned of their plans and left before they could gather. But they bring an entire Fian—twelve men to cut you down, with Goll Mac Morna at their head.

Bodhmall walked into the clearing then, with a bundle in her hands. Calmly, she handed Liath a fresh tunic, calmly fastened the bundle to the saddle of Mac Ronan's horse.

"So it comes," she said simply. "There is food in the bundle, enough for several days journey, and fresh, dry clothes." She gave Liath a sardonic look. "Also the vanishing herb. You must go north, to the River Boanne, one hard day's ride. There is a wizard there named Finegas. You will be safe in his keeping, boy."

"Grandmother, I cannot leave you and Liath. How will you defend yourselves?"

Liath laughed aloud.

"What I cannot cut down, your Bodhmall will hide in a druidic fog." Her voice relished the possibilities. "We will be fine. And when they have departed, we will go south to . . ."

"Liath!" Bodhmall broke in quickly. "The boy must go now. Do you not feel the hoofbeats?"

Liath's whole body grew still. She nodded. Mac Ronan heaved himself up on the horse's back, stretched down his arm.

"Come, Fionn," he cried. "Our first adventure!" He laughed with exhilaration.

Fionn swung up onto the back of the black horse and they galloped from the clearing. The last sight Liath and Bodhmall had of Fionn was of his naked torso bending beneath the branches of the trees, the last sound his voice calling out,

"Mac Ronan! We must first find me a horse!"

By afternoon, the horse was spent, its withers heaving, its mouth flecked with foam. Mac Ronan led the beast to a stream, unsaddled him and let him drink his fill. He rubbed his sides with a blanket and lifted his hooves to check for stones.

In the distance, the sound of baying hounds drifted from the south.

"They are a fair way behind us," Fionn said softly. "But their hounds have caught our scent."

Mac Ronan nodded.

"But our double weight grows too much for the beast."

"You will have to turn him loose."

"Then we must hide until nightfall. We can find fresh mounts then."

"First you must teach me how to speak to him."

Mac Ronan looked at him in surprise.

"You do not ride?"

"I have lived all my life in the forests of Slieve Bloom. What need would I have of a horse? But now I see that I must learn to speak their tongue, so that we can ride together."

Mac Ronan shook his head.

"You do not speak to them. You calm them and guide their head. You learn how to control their movements."

"Show me how this is done."

Mac Ronan gathered the reins. He leaped onto the horse's back and pulled back on the reins. He backed the horse up, turned him from side to side, eased him through his paces. Fionn watched closely. But when Mac Ronan dismounted and handed Fionn the reins, Fionn walked to the horse's head; he pressed his forehead against the forehead of the beast and stood still. At last the horse lifted his head. Fionn cupped his hand beneath the chin of the animal. He blew softly into its nostrils and the animal made soft puffing breaths back. When Fionn mounted, he tied the reins over the horse's neck and rode with his hands free across the small meadow.

"So it is like the hurley game. You have done this before."

"Nay, brother, I have not. But I have learned from living in the forest that all the animals have a language. Once I have learned that language, they are my friends and I am theirs."

"They will say that you transform yourself as the beasts."

Fionn laughed and dismounted.

"You see me before you, just as I am. But my grandmother has taught me that all transformations are matters of the mind. And now to hiding!"

He leaned his forehead against the forehead of the horse again; in moments the animal galloped away. Fionn and Mac Ronan hid the saddle, then traveled down the stream bed to where it curved back into forest. Fionn reached into Bodhmall's bag and took out a small, curved, stone jar.

"Hold out your hands," he commanded Mac Ronan. He poured a thick black liquid into the boy's upturned palms.

"Faugh! It smells of death and rot!"

"It is the vanishing herb. You must rub it on your body and into your clothes. It will confuse the hounds and excite them too much to follow our trail."

"What is this compound?"

"The odor of many animals. Their offal and their rutting musk. And the juices of powerful plants."

"So now they will say that you vanish into the forest. But I will correct them Fionn. I will say that you vanish, but for your stink!"

At nightfall they crept from the small, brushy cave that indented the hillside. The sound of hounds had grown further away and shifted off to their west. Mac Ronan led them north and east until they came to a small rath at the forest edge.

Mac Ronan whispered to Fionn.

"It is but a poor village. Only the chief will have horses."

"We steal them?"

Mac Ronan nodded.

"Is this Mac Morna's way?"

"It is."

"It is not mine. When I am chief of the Fenians, we will not make the poor poorer."

He stood and strode to the gate of the rath. A sentry in a cloak of one color, the mark of the poor, barred their way.

"Speak your name."

"I am Fionn Mac Cumhail."

The sentry laughed.

"And I am the Dagda. State your name. We grieve here and have no heart for the foolishness of boys."

Fionn turned to Mac Ronan. "What is this fellow's illness that he refuses to believe a man who states his name?"

"You do not know?"

"Know what, man?"

"There are legends. Stories. They have come up from Kerry in the south for years and made their way to King Cormac's banqueting hall. Rumors that Cumhail Mac Trenmor had a son, tales that the son would rise and take the place that was stolen from his father. Mac Morna is no leader."

"Is that why you came for me today?"

"It is. I saw it in you at the hurley match. The gift to lead so that men would willingly follow." He turned to the sentry.

"Take this one into the light," he said.

"Bring a torch," the sentry cried. From within the rath, men stirred. A guttering

pine torch was brought to the causeway and Fionn stood in its circle, the light halo-
ing off his white hair. Soon the chief of the rath arrived. He was a man past middle
age, his face bloated and lined, his cloak askew. He stared at the boy in silence.

"I am Mac Earc. They say you claim to be Fionn Mac Cumhail."

"I do not claim it, father. It is who I am."

The chief looked silently at the boys for several moments, then motioned them
into his lodge. In the firelight, a woman was bent with weeping over the bier of a
young boy of some thirteen years.

"He was our only son, Glonda," the old chief said. "The child of our middle years.
He was slain this morning."

The woman's sobbing increased. Fionn moved behind her, placed his left palm flat
beneath her left shoulder bone. His right palm he wrapped across her forehead. He
stood that way, silent, his cloak rising and falling with his even breathing. Her sobbing
quieted to weak gasping, then stilled. In a moment she slept with her arms outstretched
across the body of the boy.

"What have you done?" asked the old chief.

"I have quieted her mind and slowed her heart. She will sleep for a while. But I
cannot take her grief away. Who did this thing, and why?"

"Lia of Luachair."

"One of Mac Morna's men," said Mac Ronan from behind Fionn.

"He did it for the horse my boy rode and the food he carried," said Mac Earc. "He
might as well have done for sport, for the horse was aged and the food a loaf of brown
bread and some cheese." The chief turned away and looked into the darkness.

"The honor price for this death should be his life; did he pay that, Mac Earc?"

The old chief turned and looked at Fionn.

"He is a Fenian boy. Do you think such a one as I could demand an honor price
from the warrior of King Cormac? He rode west toward Connaught and I think that
we shall not see him again."

"You shall," said Fionn, "for I shall bring you his head. His spirit will be required
to guard your household forever, Mac Earc. And I tell you that there will come a time
when the Fenians of Eire will prize honor above all other possessions."

When the villagers had saddled and provisioned the boys, they rode from the rath into
darkness. Fionn turned west. Mac Ronan held his bridle.

"This quest to avenge the boy must wait for another day, Fionn. Have you forgotten Goll Mac Morna? Or that we heard his hounds to the west?"

"I have not forgotten, but I have promised to do this thing. My word is my bond. You need not come, Mac Ronan."

But Mac Ronan wheeled up beside him and called aloud into the darkness,

"For the Fenians!"

"For Eire!" said Fionn.

The old man sagged back against the chair. He took a long draught from his mug of ale. I saw the slight trembling in the hands, the droop at the corner of his mouth. I felt a sudden urge to protect the old man, to not let the brothers see his weariness. I called aloud above their heads.

"Osian, strong to us is your voice! A blessing on the soul of Fionn!" I touched my own lips, so surprised was I at the words that had come from them. But they had the desired effect; the spell of the story was broken. The brothers began to murmur among themselves. They rose and filed to their cells, thanking Osian by patting him on the shoulder or touching his hands. One or two made the blessing in the air. They filed past me with their heads down, but one of the young brothers risked a smile as he passed and Longan made the blessing in the air.

"A blessing on you, Padraig," he whispered.

"I am not Padraig," I replied. Longan nodded and smiled.

And only Breogan and I knew how heavy the old man rested on us as we carried him to his cell.

We sat on a bench in the sunlight of the small garden. Osian rested his head against the monastery wall, opened his palms to the sun. Spring had gone to early summer in the time he had been with us. The leaves were green and full on the trees. The planting was finished. A few of the brothers weeded in the cool morning light, while others prepared to break the fast.

I felt surprised by the swift passage of time, wondered how much that speed had to do with the old man's stories. The years of my slavery in Hibernia had passed slowly, so slowly. Each day the sheep and the wolfhounds, each day my silence and my prayers. Every morning awakened to my fear that my parents thought me dead and would not remember their son. My sorrow reminded me of Osian's story of the slain boy.

I broke the early morning silence with my own curiosity.

"Did your father slay the one who murdered the boy?"

"He did. . . ."

It took two days for Fionn and Caoilte to pick up the trail of Lia of Luachair, but when they did it was the trail of a horse gone lame and a man so sure of himself that he was careless in his habits. His forest bothies were not torn down, his fires not shaken out and hidden in the streams. He left his refuse in plain sight. Clearly, he was a man who did not expect to be followed.

They came upon him on the afternoon of the fourth day. He was eating a haunch of rabbit before his bothy; he did not rise at their approach and even when he saw that they were boys and that one of them wore the cloak of the Fenians, he did not offer to share the meal he had prepared.

"What brings two boys to Connaught?" he growled from his seated place before the fire.

Fionn spoke first.

"We seek one Lia of Luachair."

"I am that one. Who searches for me?"

"I do, for you have taken the life of a boy and you must pay the honor price."

Now Luachair's curiosity was aroused; he looked up.

"Threats from a beardless boy. Was he your brother, now? At least let your companion here give me the challenge, for I see that he has two or three years upon you and by his cloak, I know he is a warrior."

Mac Ronan laughed.

"Do not underestimate this one, Luachair. It will be your last mistake."

He threw his sword at Fionn, who caught it in midair.

"I am Fionn Mac Cumhail, son of Cumhail Mac Trenmor. I will have none serve in the Fianna who cannot serve with honor."

Luachair came to his feet at the name.

"So. You are the one Mac Morna has been expecting. He has little to fear from such a youngling." He brought his own sword around two-handed and thrust at Fionn. But even as Luachair thrust, Fionn was not where he had been standing.

"He should fear me well. As should you, Luachair. For my fire will extinguish your dishonor."

Fionn's sword cut the air with a sound like wind. The head of Luachair toppled to the forest floor and rolled to a stop beside the trunk of a great tree.

Fionn unhobbled the horse of Glonda, watered it, rubbed it down and saw to its leg. He gathered the head of Lia of Luachair and tied it bloody and surprised to the neck of the horse. Then he turned the horse in the direction of the rath of Glonda.

"We will return the head to the boy's father. May it be some comfort to them . . ."

"Barbaric, this business of the head. Why should that be of comfort? It would only serve to remind them of their sorrow."

"The head is the seat of the soul, Padraig. Surely you would know this better than any other. My father was seeing to it that the soul of Luachair would be required to protect the parents of Glonda for as long as they lived."

"What do you mean when you speak of soul?"

"That part of us which continues. That part of us which goes into the next life and then returns again."

"You believe this? That the soul continues?" I came to my feet in a leap.

"Our druids have always taught this, priest. Did you not know this? You were six years among us."

"Not among you, but apart from you. But now I espy a truth that I can use. This is very like the teachings of my Christ."

"And this surprises you?"

"I am astonished, Osian. Astonished and delighted for a door has opened before me."

"So you will admit to me that you do not possess all answers?" His mouth quirked up.

"No such thing, Fenian. My God possesses all answers and gives me here another way to teach them."

Osian burst into laughter, shook with it until he wiped his eyes. His merriment irritated me.

"You dare laugh! You from a race of warriors who rode with heads bouncing against their saddles. And why? To keep the soul trapped against the withers of a horse! Such foolishness! The soul flies up and away, into the light. At least for those who are not heathens."

His laughter subsided; for a moment he regarded me in stony silence. When he spoke his voice was laced with sarcasm.

"Would that mine would fly up and away now, Padraig, Druid of Christ. Nor would I wish your head for my protection.

"Now may I continue my tale?"

Once the horse had departed, Fionn and Caoilte turned their attention to the camp-site. They drowned the fire, then placed the spoke logs of its frame into the nearby stream. They scattered the ashes and began to dismantle the bothy. At the rear of the bothy Fionn found the bag.

It was a long bag, longer than Fionn's arm, shaped like a curve and smooth as a bird's wing. Fionn stroked it. He could feel that it had been made from the skins of cranes, bird of Angus Og, god of the bird people, but the skin bag had been dyed and patterned in red and blue, with swirls and spirals over its surface. Fionn lifted it free from the bothy, held it out toward Mac Ronan.

"Look what odd thing I have found."

Mac Ronan went still and pale.

"If I did not believe in prophecy before now, I can no longer deny it."

"What is it?"

"It is the bag which belonged to your father. I have heard for years that Luachair took it from your father upon his death, but I did not believe it until now."

Fionn stared at the bag and his hands trembled.

"I know the contents of this bag, Mac Ronan. Bodhmall told me from the time I was a child."

He recited,

"There was a bag that belonged to Cumhail Mac Trenmor, and in it was the sovereignty of Eire, the sacred stones and the sword forged in the smithies of the sidhe."

Mac Ronan lifted off his cloak of blue and green and spread it on the ground. Gently, Fionn spread the treasures of the bag on the cloak. There were indeed three stones, one a ruby, glittering like firelight, one an emerald that seemed to give off fire of its own, one a flat green stone, shaped like a table, speckled like the back of a fish. Fionn lifted the stones in his hands and recited what Bodhmall had taught him.

"This ruby is the blood of Eire, that we who live and die for her remain always at her heart. The emerald is the green fields and forests of Eire, that we take joy in her beauty and protect her from harm. This last stone is the sea which surrounds her, rich with the creatures who dwell there, our great provider and protection."

Together Fionn and Caoilte lifted free the sword. Its hilt was set with three smaller versions of the stones, chased with spirals and braids. The blade of the sword gleamed and flashed; the letters of ogham, the ancient stick language of the druids, were incised down its length.

"What does it say?"

"I do not know. This is not a language Bodhmall taught me. This sword was made by the Others, the dwellers in hill and sea. The language must be theirs."

"I know one who would know." Mac Ronan ran his hands along the hilt. "But I do not know if he lives. Your father had a brother. . . ."

"I know of this brother! He was Crimnall Mac Trenmor. Bodhmall has told me. He wished to sacrifice himself to save Muirne, mother of . . . my mother. But she would not let him. She bade him keep the core of the Fenians alive. Does he live still?"

"There have been rumors for years that a band of Fenians dwells in Connaught, *in the wilds of the stone forests. I did not believe them until now, but I think it possible. Why else would Mac Morna's hounds have turned west when he could not find you? Why else would we find Luachair here at the Connaught borders, carrying the craneskin bag of power? They must believe that your uncle lives!"*

"Then we must find him!"

Fionn replaced the items in the bag and slung it over his shoulder. When he mounted, the bag curved across his back and along the flank of the horse, shaped perfectly for riding. Together, the boys headed west, deeper into the wild country, in search of the remnants of the once great Fianna.

"It is a good tale, but your father wandered much when Bodhmall had instructed him to find Finegas the wizard."

"My father wandered over all of Eire in his lifetime. The length and breadth. He knew all of the forests and streams, all of the raths and chieftains. And all men knew him and respected him. A journey has its own wisdom and my father taught me always to listen to that wisdom."

Osian looked around him.

"What is it that you wish to do here, priest?"

"I wish to spread the truth of my God."

"Do you think to do that in this poor rath?"

I looked around me. The monastery building was small. It was a rectangular hall composed of mud and straw and stone, much like the halls of the local chiefs, only that I had taught the brothers to build partitions of wood and rooms with doors in the interior of the building. There were twelve such cells and a dining hall, for that was all of our number. Our rude little barn of a chapel stood at the other side of the garden so that our monastery formed one long side and one half side of a square.

"This poor rath was hard won, old man."

"Who did you fight for it?"

I laughed aloud.

"I fought the dogs of Dichu, the local chief. I came to him preaching of the Christ and he wanted none of it. He set his dogs upon me. There must have been a dozen of them, huge wolfhounds. They came roaring at me and I knelt among them and made the sounds and gestures I had learned to make as a sheepherder. I lived among the wolfhounds then; they were my only companions. I guess your father would say I had learned to speak their language. At any rate, they knocked me flat to the ground, but it wasn't long before I was kneeling up among them and they frolicking around me like puppies, licking my face and hands."

I began to laugh at the memory.

"So I thought for good measure that I should make the sign of blessing upon them. I crossed their foreheads, each one. You should have seen old Dichu's face. He thought that they would take me apart. He converted on the spot, kneeling down and taking the blessing, then sending me these boys to build what we have here. He gave us the barn that serves as our chapel. He wanted to send women too, as seamstresses and cooks, but I would have none of it."

Osian began to laugh now too.

"This is a good story, one that I would like to tell."

"You may add it to your bag of tales, old man, only leave out that it was not magic but the knowledge of a slave boy that saved me."

"But that is a kind of magic, priest. Think if your god had not sent you here. You escaped to home on a ship of wolfhounds and gathered your first followers with the help of wolfhounds. Perhaps your god did you a favor with your slavery."

I looked at him sharply.

"You are too clever for both of us, old man."

Osian laughed.

"But tell me again what you hope to do here."

"Why, just what I have done. I hope to introduce my God to these people, to get them started on the proper way. When I have achieved that, I will leave someone like Breogan in charge and I will return home."

"I think that you will not return home. You will remain here among the Eireann."

"I will not. They are a barbaric people. They take slaves and cut off the heads of their enemies. They dwell in squalid huts and think them palaces. They think the green land around them lives and breathes and has a spirit. They believe in these creatures they call the Other. They live in their stories and songs and poems as if such frivolity had life itself. They are foolish dreamers. Where I come from, the people knew how to organize. My father was Calpornius. He was a Christian and a decurion, an official of the Roman government, or rather of what is left of it there in Britain. He was a responsible man of high office. My mother was Conchessa. She was beautiful and quiet; she deferred in all things to my father. There would have been no talk in our house of warrior women or druidesses.

"We lived in a beautiful villa, Osian, white with red-tiled roofs. It was shaped in a square and in the center were gardens and fountains. I remember that house every day. Its floors were of inlaid tile and mosaics of fish and birds. We had heat piped from below the floor and hot baths every day. The rooms were strewn with lighted braziers and soft couches and statues of alabaster. We were civilized people.

"All of that was taken away from me when I was taken into slavery. All. I was a boy of sixteen. I did not see my parents or my home again for six years. I left a youthful boy, full of hopes and dreams and high spirits. I came home a man, beaten, half-starved, companion of animals, almost forgetful of language.

"Faugh! These Hibernians! I would no more stay with them than with the devil."

"And yet you came back."

"I came back. But I did everything to avoid it. I studied for the priesthood. I lived at my uncle's monastery in Auxerre. Now there was a monastery, stone, all stone. . . ."

"Why did you come back?"

"Because I had to." I was on my feet, shouting at him now, but I couldn't calm myself.

"Because he sent visions and dreams and voices. For eighteen years, Victoricus, the messenger, read me a letter, the same letter, every night. 'Boy, oh come ye back to Eire and walk among us.' For eighteen years he would not leave me alone! Never a minute of peace. So I returned. I returned." I sat down heavily, dropped my head into my hands.

"And I will do the duty he requires of me. Then perhaps he will leave me alone to return to my own people."

"I think he will not, Padraig. I think you are of these people now. I think that you will be of them forever."

"You are wrong! I have tried to tell you. I am not Padraig and never will be. I am Magonus Succatus Patricius, of Bannaevum near Tiburnae. I have no wish to be Padraig! Never!"

"You are already Padraig to them." He gestured toward the boys weeding in the garden. "I think your god wishes it for you."

There were no words for the anger I felt for him in that moment.

"Damn your soul, old man," I said.

And I left him alone in the garden.

B y afternoon I was ashamed of myself for being so nettled by the old man and more ashamed still that I had cursed him. I arrived at his chamber to find Breogan taking down the same story Osian had told me in the morning. I waved him away from the chamber, but his look at me told me that he knew, as did the other brothers, that I had cursed the old man and left him in the garden.

I knelt by his bed filled with my shame.

"I am sorry, old man."

"Sorry? What have we to be sorry for?"

"I should not have cursed you and I should not have stormed away. I was angry and I ask your forgiveness."

Osian laughed.

"Strong men should speak strongly."

"I should not have cursed you."

"But I do not know what this means."

"It means that I have wished your spirit into eternal darkness."

"I do not believe in darkness. My spirit will go to Tir Nan Og when this body dies. I await the day."

"I pray that it will, but I ask your permission to make the sign of blessing upon you to remove what I have spoken."

"But since I do not believe in your signs and curses, no such thing is necessary."

I felt my ire rise again and I stood.

"Just let me do it! You need not believe, but let me make the sign."

"If it will ease your mind you may make what sign you wish, Padraig."

I expelled my frustration in a rush of breath, then made the sign upon his forehead, whispering the holy names in Latin, asking God to bring blessings upon his storyteller. I could not help but notice, as my fingers traced the pattern on his forehead, that there was a soft patch of something beneath his hair that felt like fur. But I brought my mind back to the business of God and completed the blessing, then prayed for forgiveness for my own reluctant soul as well. When I was finished, he smiled up at me.

"Did that give you easement, Padraig?"

"It has helped."

"Then I am glad of it. And now what story can I tell you?"

But I was not in the mood for stories.

"You asked me what I wished to do here and I told you. You said that my God has wished this place upon me. What did you mean by these things?"

Osian's eyes twinkled up at me.

"I will tell you only if you promise not to curse me to darkness again."

The laughter exploded from me, then and I leaned against the wall and wiped the water from my eyes.

"You have my word," I said in my most somber voice.

Osian began.

"My father had a light in him, Padraig. It was a light that all around him could see. Only once in his long life did I ever see him betray that light and that betrayal cost him dearly. There is a light that moves in you as well. I see it. Breogan and the brothers see it. Dichu saw it despite the slobbering dogs, not because of them. But you yourself refuse to see it. You have built this little monastery at the edge of the Eire and you hope that if you gather your few brothers here and hide, your God will count that well enough and let you go. But you yourself will not count that well enough."

"Then what would you suggest I do?"

"Teach your God as a Fenian would do. Gather your people around you and travel from town to town. Go the way the Fenians went, with horses and dogs and women and children. Go with joy and song. Bring gifts to the chieftains. Let the people see you and come to you. Then when you speak to them of your God, they will see your light and hear your voice of joy. And they will come to you, but not from fear."

I tell you now that there are moments in this life when a truth comes that the heart has known all along. At those moments there is a deep silence, a sound at the center of the world like drumming. I knew what he said was true. The Voice had spoken it to me, but I had shut it in a chamber of my heart. I was speechless before the old man. I left the chamber and the monastery. I went to the chapel and knelt before the altar, but the place was too small to contain my feelings.

At last I went to the estuary that led to the sea and I sat there all of that afternoon and through the long night. Moonlight shone down upon the waters and the tiny froths of the waves curled white in the distance. Now and then the gleaming creatures that hold their light in darkness skimmed along the surface of the sea. I waited for the Voice that I knew would come.

Hours passed and I made my center still and quiet. And then at last I spoke the words.

"If this is what you wish from me, this is what I will give."

The Voice came then. Just as it had when I was a slave and it had directed me home. Just as it had come in visions and letters calling me back. Just as it had haunted me on the continent, whispering the Eireann words in dreams, singing to me of the green hills and the blue sea. It came. And this time it was laughing.

I gathered the brothers in the dining hall and I gave Osian the seat at the front. Once I had told him what I wanted to do, he'd dressed in his finest and braided his hair at the back of his head. He'd clapped me on the shoulder when I was leaving his chamber and boomed out,

"It is well, Padraig! I have a story to fit this plan. You will not be sorry."

I did not answer him, but I felt the exuberance of it too.

I stood beside him on the dais when the brothers clustered around him.

"Brothers," I said. "Tonight our storyteller tells us a special tale of the rebirth of the Fianna."

They murmured to each other at first, wondered why I was introducing this tale to them, but they were lost in the story as soon as Osian began. . . .

Fionn and Caoilte Mac Ronan wandered for many days in the western country. It was a desolate landscape, rocky and blasted with stretches of emptiness alternating with dense forests in which huge stones rose from between the trees like ancient sentinels. Always Fionn and Caoilte were alert for the sound of Mac Morna's hounds, but after several days they decided that Mac Morna must have abandoned chase and they began to enjoy the free life of the open air.

By night they built bothies, three-sided dwellings roofed and walled with the boughs of pines. In the stony country they slept in the clefts of rocks or in caves hollowed like rooms beneath two upright stones and a capstone. They hunted rabbits and birds, fished from the plentiful streams. Fionn showed Caoilte how to dig a pit and line it with stone, then wrap the fish in grasses and let them steam. When the fresh white meat flaked off the bone, Mac Ronan vowed he would never eat fish by any other way.

By starlight Fionn told Caoilte of his life in the forests with Bodhmall and Liath and Mac Ronan told Fionn of the life in the court of Cormac Mac Art, of the huge festivals held at the Hill of Tara, of poets and chariot races and women so beautiful and fair that their skin was like snow on the ground.

"One day I will return to the Hill of Tara. There I will claim captaincy of the Fianna and I will return it to the glory it held in my father's day."

Mac Ronan nodded.

"Mac Morna is not an evil man, but dogged and stupid. He has not served the Fianna well. Under his captaincy the numbers have shrunk; Cormac Mac Art has had to swell our ranks with mercenaries from the northern countries. They fight only for money and will turn against us for the least imagined wrong. There was a day when it was an honor for a man to be a Fenian and so many of the young men of Eire were ready to swear fealty that your father instituted tests of skill and intellect to choose the best among them."

"Why did you join them?"

"I was born to be a warrior. This life," he gestured around him. "The life of open air, of new excitements. It suits me. I would be stifled as a cattleman, worthless as a chieftain responsible for the welfare of my people. I think that I will never marry or breed. But what of you?"

Fionn smiled.

"I like the mating well."

"I saw that, brother."

The two laughed.

"A woman who is strong and bright and magical. For her, I could cease all warring."

"Is there such a one?"

"I would know her if I found her."

Mac Ronan laughed.

"You are a dreamer then."

"Perhaps so. But for this journey I dream a different dream."

*   *   *

Late in an evening of the third week of their wandering, the boys made camp in a dense forest. While Mac Ronan built the bothy, Fionn loped away with his spear in hand. He returned less than an hour later with a deer slung across his shoulders.

"Well done, brother!" said Mac Ronan. "We will feast for many days."

The two set up a spit and began roasting the haunch and several other fine pieces while Fionn began to strip off thin slices of venison to dry. Suddenly, his knife went still; his body came up from its seated position into a crouch.

"What is it?" Mac Ronan whispered.

"Do you not sense them?"

Mac Ronan stood still, sniffed the air around him, listened closely.

"I do now. They surround us on three sides. But I cannot fathom what beast they are."

"Beasts of the two-legged kind. I can tell by their movements."

Fionn stood from the campfire, stretched casually.

"One moment, brother," he said aloud. "I go to make water."

He disappeared into the forest in one swift movement. Mac Ronan picked up where Fionn had left off, flaying thin pieces of deer meat, his back to the bothy. He remained in a crouched position.

Time passed.

Suddenly Fionn appeared from the forest pushing before him two ancient, scraggly, skinny old men.

Mac Ronan stood beside the bothy, lifted a second knife so that he now held two knives, one in each fist. Their metal gleamed in the firelight.

Fionn called aloud.

"Come out now, the rest of you. Or I will kill the comrades I hold here and carry their heads to guard my journey."

The leaves around the boys began to rustle and one by one fifteen bent and aged men crept into the clearing. Their hair was wild; some of them had beards that reached below their heart. All of them were skinny, with legs like knotted ropes and arms too thin to heft a weapon. They wore clothing of skins, motley at best, deerhide intermixed with wolf pelts and here or there a sealskin. On their feet were rough boots of gathered hide.

They clustered silently in the clearing, one or two eyeing the roasting haunch of deer.

Mac Ronan spoke first.

61

"We are Fenians, old men. We share what we have. Will you partake with us of our evening's repast?"

Over the heads of the old men, Fionn grinned at the formal nature of his invitation.

"My brother Caoilte speaks well, grandfathers. Gather yourselves and we will feast."

They were silent in the circle, silent as they ate their portions of haunch and hind. Some of them ate as hounds eat, tearing at the meat until their faces dripped with juice, then crunching the bone to get at the marrow. But one among them ate his meal slowly, savoring the taste. Though he was thin and ragged as the rest, his beard was trimmed and he sat with a kind of dignity. When they had eaten their fill, Fionn addressed his questions to him.

"We come to this forest to search for one Crimnall Mac Trenmor. Have you knowledge of such a one?"

There was a stirring at the fire, an edginess.

The old one spoke.

"I am old and I remember the ancient days of Eire. There was such a one, once. He was brother to Cumhail Mac Trenmor. But he died with his brother at the hand of Goll Mac Morna."

Fionn stood now. The firelight played off his face and cast light on the white hair that framed it.

"He did not die, for it was he who offered his life for my mother."

"Your mother?"

The old man stood awkwardly. Bent and stiff, he moved toward the boy. He had to bend his head up and tilt back to gaze into the face of the youth, but as he did, his wizened companions circled about him, murmuring.

"Demna," he breathed. "Though your mother called you . . ."

"Fionn. I am Fionn, son of Cumhail. And you are my uncle, father to my brother."

Fionn went to the bothy and brought out the craneskin bag. He knelt before his uncle and held it forward.

"The bag of power of the Fenians of Eire. For the brother of my father."

The old man began to weep then, in the cracked and brittle voice of the very old. His head bowed and his shoulders shook. He placed his hand on the head of the boy.

"Fionn," he whispered. "Child of light. You have come to lead us home."

From the craneskin bag, Fionn drew forth the sword. Its jeweled hilt flashed in the light, but Fionn ran his thumb across the ancient ogham words.

"What do they say, uncle?"

"I do not know, boy. I do not think even your father knew. But I believe that you will learn their meaning."

By morning the strange and decrepit group of old men had transformed. They had shaved their beards and braided their hair in the old way. They had bathed in the stream. Together they showed Fionn the caves and rude mud dwellings they had occupied for fifteen years. Crimnall spoke.

"At first, the armies of Goll hounded us by day and night. We broke apart, but with the promise that we would meet in the west country, those of us who survived. We were four of your father's fians who survived the battle with Mac Morna. Forty-eight men. You see here all that remain from these long years.

"When we came here, we lived like the wolves and foxes, hiding in the earth, eating what we could catch. Then we built these dwellings and waited for our return. We kept our weapons polished and honed. We trained in the forests. For years we ventured by twos and threes into the world of humans, searching for word of Goll Mac Morna, searching for those who would support us in our overthrow. But every time that Goll got word of us, he hunted us down and slaughtered those he could find. At last we gave up hope."

He held up his rusted sword.

"We have lived this way now for longer than I can name. We had almost forgotten that Cumhail had a son; we ceased to mention it for fear that Mac Morna would hunt you down and slaughter you as well."

Fionn nodded.

"He hunts me now."

Mac Ronan chimed in.

"But he stands no chance against the Fionn one. He can disappear into the forest, leaving only the scent of death behind."

The two laughed.

One or two of the men chimed in with laughter.

"You make us young again," said Crimnall.

"We will follow you, Fionn," cried one of the other ancients.

But Crimnall held up his hand.

"Nay. What we have learned to do in these years will best help our nephew. We will go by twos and twos among the society of men. By rumor and story and song we will spread the word that Fionn Mac Cumhail comes to take his rightful place at the head of the Fianna. By the time you are ready, boy, Eire will be ready for you."

He raised his fist in the Fenian salute and the old men followed suit.

Fionn and Caoilte saluted them back. Then Fionn gathered the old man into his huge embrace.

"It is good to know that one of my blood survives, Uncle."

"Do not forget your lady mother, boy."

Fionn drew back and stared at Crimnall. His throat closed and he could not speak. Mac Ronan spoke for him.

"His mother lives?"

"She is a married woman, well-protected. She dwells in Kerry to the south. Boy, you did not know?"

Fionn shook his head. He turned to Mac Ronan.

"Liath. On the day we departed. Remember? She said that they would go south. But Bodhmall interrupted her. They go to my mother, to tell her."

Mac Ronan was already saddling the horses.

Fionn clutched his uncle by the arms.

"You will keep the craneskin bag for me?"

"Safe, for the day of your return."

He saluted the Fenians.

"We will meet again, brothers," he shouted.

Then he mounted and they turned the horses south, toward the Kerry coast.

I stood beside him when he had finished, while the brothers were still in the spell of the story. I raised my hands in the gesture of blessing. They looked up at me expectantly. I drew in my breath, closed my eyes at what I was about to begin.

"My brothers," I said. "The time has come for us to leave the safety of our monastery. We too must venture into Eire to spread the word of the Christ. We must go first to Dichu. We will accept his offer of seamstresses and cooks. We will make ourselves here the people of Christ, his body. And when we have established our city here, we will choose those who will venture forth with me to spread the good news.

"Brothers, are you willing to accompany me on this journey? It will be dangerous and hard. We will sleep in the cold of night and walk in the light of day. We will encounter those who will not believe and who will wish us dead and set all manner of trouble upon us. But we will go in the joy of the White Christ, sure in the sweetness of his song.

"What say you, my brothers?"

They regarded me in silence, their young faces white with surprise—or perhaps fear. A few of them looked toward Osian and back at me. I glanced at him as well, saw him smile broadly in my direction. I had set the journey in motion; I prayed that I would have the wisdom—and the willing brothers—to see it through.

It was Breogan who did it first. He raised his arm in the Fenian salute. He held it high. The brothers followed suit, all of them boys, standing and lifting their arms in silence. I blessed them that way, just that way, standing so. And I did it through the water of my tears.

Dichu and his people came at our first invitation. He brought his best builders and they raised an entire rath in one month's time. They left the main building of the monastery with its garden for the first of the brothers, but they added a rectangular hall for meetings, numerous small dwellings for families, a bakehouse, a smithy and storage houses on tall roofed platforms to keep grain dry and above the ground, where animals could not reach it.

To watch them work was a wonder. By the start of the second week I had learned enough to roll up the sleeves of my robe and join them. We drove the uprights of the houses into the ground in circles, then wove the walls of wickerwork, using reeds and young saplings. Within that framework, we put a kind of plaster made of mud and cow dung and lime. Over it all we thatched a roof on a conical frame, leaving a central hole for the smoke to exit the dwelling. The work was hard, but fulfilling and the camaraderie and calling back and forth of the workers was a joy to me, who had known so much solitude.

When the main buildings of our little village were finished, Dichu called all of his people together. There were perhaps two hundred of the villagers. Dichu gave them his permission.

"Some of you will wish to live here with Padraig and our young men as brothers and sisters of the new Christ. We have built here a village to sustain some thirty people. We will be the sister rath of this new dwelling place. We will call this place Sabhal Padraig."

I stood to protest the name, but Osian stilled my hand.

"What would you have them call it, priest? Sabhal Succatus?"

The name did have a strange sound, but I whispered to him,

"Why must they name it after me at all?"

He simply made an exasperated sound, so I stood and made the sign of blessing.

Dichu continued.

"Which of you will be residents of Sabhal Padraig?"

A few young men stood, ready to join the ranks of the brothers. Then the daughter of Dichu came forward. She stood before me and looked me directly in the eye.

"Does the White Christ of Padraig accept women as his warriors?"

She called it loud, and I heard other women murmuring in the background.

I thought of Martha and Mary, the friends of my Lord and I called back in my loudest voice.

"He accepts them and loves them as his sisters."

"Then we will join this rath."

Four women moved up beside her.

A blacksmith came next and then a sheepherder with a good herd of sheep. A honeymaker offered his bees and then a brewer stepped forward.

"Our Lord relished the fruit of the vine," I called to him. "Your brews will be welcome here."

Two families came forward with their children.

Last, a small boy of about ten stepped forward.

"I am Benin," he said simply.

"Where are your parents, Benin?" I looked around, for I thought it a poor idea to separate a child from his parents, but he shook his head.

"They are dead, Padraig, but if you will take me, I have a gift to offer the White Christ."

I smiled at the child.

"Our Lord loved the gifts of children above all others."

At that the child began to sing, in a high, sweet voice. My heart swelled at the sound, and when he finished I made the sign of blessing over his head.

"Truly the Lord has given us many gifts today," I cried aloud. "Those of you who wish to be baptized, step forward."

They came then, those who had chosen Sabhal Padraig, and I sprinkled water over them and spoke the names of the Three-in-One. When I had finished Dichu called aloud,

"There is one thing more, Padraig. Many will wish to attend the Christ Mass and your barn will not suffice. We will build you a place of worship here at Sabhal Padraig. We will build it of stone that it will last beyond our lifetimes."

My heart was full and I turned to Osian and held my palms up for I felt helpless before such an outpouring.

"A feast," he hissed. "Declare a feast for three days from this time."

I have been to feasts before. My parents gave a feast for my return, and at our monastery in Auxerre we feasted visiting dignitaries. But I should have known that with these Hibernians a feast would mean that and more than that. Much more.

Oh it began with food well enough. There was fresh venison and roasted boar and four kinds of fish, each done differently. There were more than three hundred whole loaves of bread with pots of golden honey. One table was stacked with whole rounds of cheese and foaming pitchers of milk.

There were tankards of ale and mead, passed in a common cup from hand to hand. I confess that it passed me too many times. By the time the feasting was over I had to steady myself on the back of my chair. By then, someone had begun to drum on a bodhran and the deep tones of the drum brought out the dancers. They moved in and out, weaving patterns, their cloaks swirling with so many colors that after a time they seemed to me like a moving sunset or a rainbow. The women called for me to dance with them and I protested, but the women of Eire do not take no as answer. They dragged me down among them and though at first I stumbled like a fool, soon the steps made sense to me. I moved through the rhythms, feeling lighter and lighter.

"Par-rig. Par-rig," they called and I felt no anger at the misnomer, only a kind of dizzy lightness. On and on I went until at last my mead-filled head could steady itself no more and I fell hard down in the dust on my backside.

They roared with laughter and picked me up, but rather than being shamed by my foolishness, they dusted me off and clapped me on the shoulder.

"Good man!" the men called out and the women vied for my partnership.

"I dance with Par-rig next."

"No, I."

For the first time I knew that there was at the heart of Eire a greater generosity than I had realized. My heart began to laugh the way it had laughed when I was a boy of sixteen. I, who had never expected to laugh among my captors, felt giddy as a lad.

When I pulled myself from the dancers, I dropped hard before the chair of Osian. I rested my hand on his knee and smiled up at him.

"Tis you who have done this thing," I said.

But he only smiled.

"I think not, Parrig," he said "Tis neither of us who are doing this thing."

The dancing went on till well past the turn of the night and then the singing began. And oh the songs, sad and longing songs of love, rousing songs of war and then the ones to make my face feel warm, the mating songs. The married couples eyed each other and sometimes the wife slapped her husband on the arm. I watched as some of the young men and women slipped away, hand in hand, and I had not the heart to call them back.

It was almost dawn when the people called for stories. Osian had been dozing in his chair, but roused to the sound of his name.

The hour was hushed. The children were asleep on the laps of their mothers and the old folks sat huddled beneath their robes in the summer night breeze.

Osian stood and threw his cloak over his shoulders.

"I will tell the story of Fionn's reunion with his mother," he said softly and a murmur of assent went through the crowd.

The woman stood in the wooden tower and looked off to the north as she had done every day since Bodhmall and Liath had come.

"Why have we not heard?" she asked.

Bodhmall answered her softly.

"I do not know, Muirne. I told him to go to Finegas. I sent him with the boy Mac Ronan. Finegas would have sent me word by now."

"He is hurt or worse."

"I think not, Muirne. He is a headstrong boy. He has gone his own way, has not

done what I told him to do. He spent much of his childhood doing just that. Why, I remember once . . ."

Muirne waved her hand at the old woman.

"Do not tell me. It pierces my heart to hear him told of as a little boy when I could not be with him. If only I could see him one more time, tell him how much I have loved him all this time."

"His heart knows, for he remembered well when you came to see him in your chariot."

"He remembers a woman. He knows not who she was."

"He knows."

"You told him."

"I did."

"And what was his reaction?"

"He blamed me for keeping him from you."

Muirne turned then and her face twisted with sorrow for the old woman.

"I would not wish such a thing."

"It is well," said Bodhmall. "His heart knows my love for him as well."

Muirne looked out to the north.

"He will come," said Bodhmall. "You will see, Muirne. The boy is like the wind, or like the swift and silent ones who move beneath the water."

Fionn and Caoilte rode up to the gates of the great dun side by side.

"This Gleor must be powerful indeed."

"They did not overspeak of him," Caoilte agreed. For days now, as they came closer and closer to the coast, they had asked the people for the name of the most powerful chief of the region. Now the great rath of Gleor gave proof of that power. It was ringed around by three deep ditches lined with sharpened sticks and stones. Two causeways led to great gates, one opening toward the sea, the other toward the north. Both were guarded by soldiers bristling with weaponry. Towers posted at intervals along the inner wall gave evidence of sentries.

"What shall we say to gain entrance?" Fionn asked.

"We shall say that we are Fenians, come to take service with Gleor," said Caoilte.

Once inside, their horses were stabled and they were led to the great hall. Gleor sat at a raised dais. He was a man in his middle-fifties, short and stocky with graying hair, but he exuded contained power, like a bear.

"I am told that you are Fenians seeking service," he addressed them, looking up from the game of fidchell he was playing.

"We are," said Caoilte.

He stared at them for some time.

"What trouble have you found that brings you so far south?"

"We are out of favor with Goll Mac Morna."

"Ah. So are many."

Gleor stared intensely at Fionn.

"You, fionn one. Do you play fidchell?" Laughter played at the corner of his mouth.

Fionn nodded.

"I do, sir."

Gleor waved his partner away.

"Come then. And may you be more of a challenge than this one."

Fionn bested the old chief at seven games, moving his pieces with delicacy and skill, outmaneuvering the chief at the last minute in every game. At last, Gleor swept the pieces to the ground and laughed aloud.

"You are better even than your mother would have had me believe. But I wonder if you will ever ask to see her."

"You knew?" said Fionn, as they threaded their way across the yard toward the grianan, the sun hall of the women.

"I have not protected your mother's life for twelve of your fifteen years without knowing all of her secrets, boy."

"Then I owe you a great debt," said Fionn.

"Muirne is payment of all debts ever owed me in my life," said Gleor and his voice softened at the mention of her name. He gestured toward a bench in the center of the room.

Fionn's heart beat in his chest like a trapped bird.

The woman seated in the garden was at the end of her forty years, but she was the same woman Fionn remembered from the chariot. Her hair was copper, laced through with only a few strands of gray. The light haloed from it and from the white of her gown. Fionn stood as still as a deer and watched her, but her eyes came open, as if she sensed his presence. She made no sound, pressed her hand against her mouth. Only her eyes widened at the sight of him.

He strode to where she was sitting, dropped to his knees before her.

"Fionn," she whispered. "Oh my beloved child."

She wrapped her arms around him and pressed her lips against the crown of his head.

For the first time in his life, Fionn Mac Cumhail wept.

His arm went around me at the end of the story and I knew that it was not just amity that put it there. I could feel his weight resting on my shoulders and I helped him into his chair as swiftly as I could without letting the crowd know his weariness.

"Tell another," some urged softly from the crowd.

"Yes, Osian, another," a woman's voice pleaded.

"My brother Padraig will tell you one," he said.

I turned to him and hissed.

"Have you taken leave of your senses, man? I am no storyteller."

"I can tell no more, brother. I am too weary."

I stood before the assembly and smiled. I thought of the stories of my childhood and the stories I had told myself to keep amused in my long captivity. None would serve. The silence grew long.

"Come, Padraig," someone cried.

Osian spoke from behind me.

"You said that your Christ loved to tell stories, Padraig."

And then I knew what story to tell.

There was a man who had two sons, and he loved both of them dearly. One was all a father could desire; he managed his father's cattle and his fields, married well and fathered many children. But the other boy was a wild youth.

Here I paused and thought for a moment.

He became a Fenian, but he did not serve with honor. Nay, he stole horses from the poor and disgraced his father's name by consorting with mercenaries.

Behind me Osian cleared his throat, but the people nodded in understanding.

At last, the Fenians turned the boy away and he took up with thieves, living wild and ragged in the forests of Eire and stealing for his meals. This went on for more than a year and then one day the boy could bear his shame no more.

"I was the beloved of my father once," the boy said to himself one day. "I will go home and see if he will welcome me again."

The sureness of the story grew in me, and the way of telling it as though it was of these people themselves.

Now the boy approached his father's rath and the sentries at the gate espied him coming. The message passed quickly to his father. The father ran to gather raiment for his son. He chose a cloak of many colors, swirled with spirals and decorated with leaping birds. He brought the finest silk tunic and a golden torque for his son's throat.

He called to his servants and his family.

"Our son returns. Prepare a feast of venison and boar. Bake loaves of bread and bring the finest ale."

When the son saw his father standing at the causeway, holding all the fine raiment, he fell to his knees with weeping and cried aloud his sorrow at what he had done.

But his father lifted him to his feet and folded him into his arms saying only, "You are returned. All is forgiven"

"But what of the other son?" asked a man's voice from the crowd.

"A wise question," I answered.

Now when the other son returned from herding the cattle, he was furious. He accosted his father.

"I have brought our name only honor. I have herded the cattle and tended your fields. I have sired many fine sons and daughters for the joy of your old age. Never once have I left you."

And the father drew his son into his arms and pressed his forehead against him and whispered,

"You are my beloved one who has never left me and who dwells at the core of my heart. But rejoice with me. For your brother was lost and he is found. His spirit was dead, but now it is alive again."

"What father of Eire do you speak of, Padraig?" someone called from the crowd.

"That father is our Lord," I called back. "He will welcome you as you have welcomed me. Whenever you come, your arrival will bring joy to his household."

"Well told, Padraig," said a voice from behind me.

"I had a good teacher," I answered.

I confess that I felt just like that prodigal boy, returned—and welcomed—to the country of his childhood.

8

We almost lost the old man in the morning. I had slept after Matins, slept almost until lauds, but I rose for the morning prayers and went to his room after. My head was still thundering like the bodhran we had danced to the night before, and my legs felt wobbly, the way I remembered them feeling at sea, but I was buoyed by a giddy happiness and I wished to share it with the old man. I knew as soon as I entered the room that he was dying.

His face was the color and texture of poor candlewax, cold to the touch. He slept under his Fenian cloak and his gnarled hands were white where they held the cloak to his chest. I placed my hand just above his lips and nose and waited for the warm moisture of breath; none came. When I placed my hand against the side of the neck where the heart rhythm beats, my hands were shaking so that I couldn't hold them still. There was a roaring in my ears that would not let me hear any sound. I moved my hand against his neck until I felt a slight flutter, tentative, wounded, but there.

I raced to the doorway and called Breogan in my loudest voice. He must have sensed my panic, because he came in only his loincloth, all pale Eireann skin and skinny ribs and arms. He stared down at Osian.

"Go out among the people," I shouted. "See if there is a healer at Dichu's village. Anywhere. Find a horse. We must bring him a healer."

At that moment, little Benin the singer came into the doorway, a bunch of wildflowers clutched in his hand. He took in the unclothed Breogan, the pale and silent Osian. He handed the flowers to me.

"I brought these for you, Padraig," he said, but before I could shout not now, he turned back.

"I know who to bring for the storyteller."

He returned with a woman of some years near my own. She entered the room with a sweep of cloaks and the scent of pine forest. Her glance swept past me with disdain, past Breogan, who had donned his habit. She walked to the bed and looked down at Osian. She closed her hands over his and lifted his arms a little way into the air.

"Come back, traveler," she said.

She dropped the arms.

A strange popping sound issued from Osian's mouth, like the sound someone makes when their lips grow dry and need water. Then he let out a long, weary sigh. He opened his eyes. He looked up in silence at the woman for a long time. Then the tears began to seep from the corners of his eyes, back into his hairline.

She turned to me then; I took her appearance.

She was near my age, I having just passed four decades then. Her hair was dark red, the color of spilled wine, her eyes the clearest gray I have ever seen. Or they appeared gray at first. By the time she stepped closer to me I could see that they were green. She wore a brown cloak, put on in haste and not fastened with a brooch. Beneath the cloak was a white gown, bordered in gold. I knew that design.

It was the dress of a druid.

She spoke before I could gather my confused thoughts.

"The boy feared he was dead."

I made no reply. She shook her head in disgust.

"Faugh! I have heard of your brotherhood. Now I see what knowledge you lack. The simplest three year apprentice could have seen that he was traveling."

She turned back to Osian.

"Where did you journey that it brings you sorrow?"

"My wife." He choked out the words.

I tried to sort through my shock and confusion. I had thought him dead. I had not known he had a wife. I stood holding the drooping bouquet of Benin's wildflowers, feeling like a mute simpleton.

She must have thought the same thing, for she snapped her next question at me.

"Do you speak?"

My voice came back.

"Of course I speak. I am Abba Magonus Succatus Patricius of Sabhal Padraig."

I sounded like a bombastic fool.

"Well, Succatus," she said. It seemed to me that she deliberately chose my baptismal name. "Your friend was not dead. He traveled. As you see, he has returned."

I shook my head, regretting my consumption of mead at last night's feast. The words came to me slowly, as if from underwater, and I kept trying to translate them to Gaelic or Latin, to find some other meaning for her word, traveled. Finally, I gave up; she waited for me to do so, I swear.

"I do not understand this 'traveled,'" I said.

"Your friend's spirit left his body and went on a journey. The body stayed here while the spirit went elsewhere. When the spirit is traveling, the body does not need to eat or breathe deeply. It maintains itself in waiting."

I allowed myself the relief of a good laugh. I turned to Benin.

"Where did you find her, boy?"

Benin looked confused and a little afraid. I put my hand on his head.

"Nay, you did well, for look how Osian's color returns."

I did not want to tell him that it was not because of any ministrations of this crazy woman.

"But she is Ainfean, the healer," he said, perplexed.

"And I thank you for finding her," I said. "Now you must go so that I may talk to this healer."

He left and I turned on her.

"Lunacy and nonsense. Will you frighten the boy with talk of spirits leaving the body and wandering? You are a druid; it will do no good to hide it, though I see that you have not taken particular pains with that." I gestured at her dress.

"Now go from here and do not return with any of your druidic foolery."

I made a motion of disgust.

Osian spoke softly from the bed.

"She speaks truth, Padraig. I was with my wife. I was with Niamh of the Golden Hair. Had Ainfean not called me back, I would have stayed there until this body ceased its beating altogether. Would that you had let me stay, wise one."

She stepped up beside the bed.

"It was not your time, old man. I could hear it in your dreaming. There is something you must do for this one," here she looked at me. I saw with a start that her eyes were now deep blue. "Though I must say the temptation was strong to let you go." She shook her head. "But all things must be done in their time."

She motioned to Breogan.

"Bring water," she said.

He returned with a wooden goblet filled with cold water. She lifted it to Osian's lips and he drank in small sips. Then she set the goblet beside the sleeping platform, reached over, took the wilting flowers from my hand and plunked them into the remaining water.

My anger and confusion exploded.

"Who are you to come here and spout these lies and order us to bring water as if we were idiot boys? The soul does not leave the body until death and even then it does not know if it travels to light or darkness."

"We agree on one thing, Succatus," she said deliberately. "There is indeed light and again darkness. Your mistake is in believing that I am the darkness."

She walked to the door, turned at the entranceway.

"We will meet again, priest," she said, quietly.

I did not doubt it and I was filled with dread at the thought. I turned toward Breogan.

"It means something, this name, Ainfean," I said. "But I cannot clear my mind enough to capture the meaning."

Osian spoke quietly from the bed.

"It means storm of fury," he said. I could have sworn he was laughing.

I set the brothers on him in rotation for all of that day, for I feared that he would slip again into the death trance. I came to him after vespers, in the evening. I carried a torch and placed it high in the wall sconce of his chamber, then sat beside his bed.

What I saw frightened me. He seemed too pale, his shoulders shrunken and thin, his hands laying useless on the coverlet. I blurted out what I saw.

"You are old and withered."

"I am older than I was when I came here." He said it agreeably, with a nod, as though the idea suited him.

"That was only three months ago," I said. "You cannot have aged so much in so short a time."

"I do not know how long I am required to stay," he said.

"What do you mean, required? And where will you go?"

"I would go back to her, to Niamh."

"Your wife. I am sorry that I never asked you. When did she die, Osian?"

"She is not dead."

I nodded.

"It is good that you believe so. Our Lord gave us that gift. The spirit does not die. It continues in the kingdom . . ." He broke in.

"Your Lord teaches you of Tir Nan Og?"

"What is this?"

"It is the land of eternal youth, the place of laughter and feasting."

I regarded him silently.

"We call this Heaven. Is this where your wife dwells?"

"It is." He seemed happy to have me know it.

"She begged me not to leave her. She said that my body would wither and die, just as it is doing. But I had to come. There was my father and my brother and you, Padraig."

Now I felt confused again.

"Are you saying that you were with her? That you were in Heaven?"

"We were in Tir Nan Og."

"Are you an angel, then?"

"What is this angel?"

"They are the heavenly messengers, the beings of light, the ones who bring the word of the Creator."

Osian laughed aloud.

"No angel, Padraig. A man like you. A warrior and a husband."

"This day has been too confusing, Osian. I will not partake of the drink again."

"You should let the woman teach you."

"What woman?"

"Ainfean the druidess."

"Teach me? I should be taught by a druidess? I know of the druids. In my country, their kind were destroyed long ago by the Romans. They are dark and evil; their ways are the ways of heathens. I will destroy the druids of Eire; I will cast them out and bring in the light of the Lord."

Osian sighed.

"Padraig, your God is the One Who Comes. I know this; I see it here at Sabhal Padraig. But before you seek to destroy a thing, first understand it. You must know what it is you destroy. You must know if there is aught of it that you can save. Think, Padraig! The people have lived by their ways since before you were born. Since before I was born. If you run over them with your Christ, will they love him or will they hate him? Will they fear you and wish you ill? Is this how your Christ taught you to know him?"

I was silent for a very long time. I thought of the gentle, quiet ways of my Lord. I thought of how much I was unlike him for all my striving.

"Sometimes you are wiser than you know, old man." I sighed, pressed my hands against my temples. "I am very unlike my Lord, who gathered all to him, heathens and Jews and Gentiles. I must think that he would have gathered even you Hibernians to him, or why else would he have sent me here?" I paused.

"I do not wish to learn from a druidess; I am learning much from you. And that woman is overbearing and far too sure of herself."

Osian laughed. "She is a woman of Eire, Padraig. They take their power from themselves; they fear little. And she is much more. Ainfean is the daughter of a great chief of Eire. Her mother was a druidess and healer of repute. Ainfean herself has apprenticed for twenty years to learn the ways of the wise ones. She can speak the ancient tongues and knows the ways of the plants and animals. She herself has traveled widely in the spirit world."

My breath exploded from me.

"How do you believe this folderol? Traveling in the spirit world! Knowing the ways of the animals! This is superstition, old man; these are like the stories of Fionn Mac Cumhail."

"Yes, they are. They are also very like the stories you have told me of the messenger, the one who haunted your dreams for eighteen years. Or like the story of the Voice who prepared a ship for you in the middle of a sheep pasture."

His eyes regarded me steadily while I pondered this truth. At last I nodded.

"I will concede their similarity, though they come from a different source. Still, I do not wish any further contact with that woman. I will learn from you. For that reason, you must promise me that you will not leave your body yet."

"You think that you cannot do this without me. But you are wrong, Padraig. You are your Christ's druid. You told me that yourself. Will not his voice tell you all you need to know?"

"Promise me."

"Not for a while then," he said softly.

I leaned my head back against the wall of his chamber, dozed for a while. I dreamed of a river. I dreamed that I was swimming naked up the river against the current, but that no matter how hard I stroked I could go nowhere against the rushing of that stream. Beside me salmon leaped like rainbows up the waterfalls, disappearing into the mist above me, seeming effortless against the stream. I grew weary with trying to follow them and my arms ached. I stopped my paddling and I began to drift backward down the current. From downstream a huge salmon, with gleaming scales of light, arced toward me and swam for a moment by my side.

"How is it done?" I asked him.

He turned toward me and his eyes were gentle. His voice was the Voice that comes in my dreams.

"It is the joy of the leap," he said. "The joy of the leap will sustain you."

I awoke with a start.

Beside me Osian was still wide awake, staring into the darkness.

"Shall I tell you what Fionn learned from the druid Finegas?" he asked.

I nodded in the darkness.

"Good," he said, though he could not have seen my nod. "Then we will speak of the salmon of knowledge."

The woman hurried across the hillside of Dun Gleor. She wore no cloak. She had pulled her dark green tunic forward so that the tops of her breasts showed above the fabric and she had oiled her breasts so that the silk would cling to the hardened nipples. . . .

"This is to be another mating story? I thought we spoke of salmon."

"It begins with a mating story."

I groaned.

"Should I not tell it then?"

"Nay, tell it, old man. I will bathe in the lake before dawnlight."

"Will that suffice?"

"Nay."

He chuckled in the darkness. "Nor for me, Padraig."

I sighed. Osian continued.

She paused for a moment outside the lodge where Fionn Mac Cumhail slept, pressed the flat of her hand against the knife which was strapped to the top of her thigh. It would be tricky, this. They said he was an uncommon warrior. Still, he was only a stripling boy. And she knew her own powers. She had used them often enough in the service of Mac Morna. This thing could be done.

She braced herself, stepped into the conical dwelling. The fire had burned low, but by its light she could see that he was already sitting up, his eyes fixed on the doorway.

A part of her wanted to laugh. They had said he was a boy of fifteen years. She had expected a thin stripling with bad skin, someone easy to overwhelm. This boy was huge, his shoulder span wider than a sword from hilt to tip, his eyes calm and steady, a strange blue-green. He watched her and said nothing.

Her mind raced. She cursed Mac Morna for his bad information, but it was not the first time he had sent her into danger. She had been gathering information for the last three of her eighteen years, sometimes by only listening, sometimes by using her feminine wiles. She had found that with most men a little kissing, some pressing of soft flesh, they melted, told her what she needed to know even while she praised them for it. And the little knife at her thigh kept her from having to mate with them. If she didn't wish to. Something told her that such wiles would not work with this boy.

He appraised her frankly, his hands easy on his lap robe. He took in every detail of her black hair, her clinging tunic, and when he had finished looking at her, he smiled gently, sweetly.

Her heart lurched.

She took a step toward him. He spoke one word.

"Caoilte."

From the other side of the hut in the folded shadows of the wall, another sat up. He shook out his long black hair, as a dog would shake itself from sleep. He looked over at the fionn one, then followed the direction of his gaze. When he looked at her his eyes widened.

"By the gods!"

The woman felt her hands go clammy. Cursed Mac Morna. Cursed fool Mac Morna. She was told that the boy would be alone. She had no intention of taking on both of them. She had been in that situation once, had vowed never to be trapped that way again. There were two many dangers that she couldn't control when there were two.

She cleared her throat, pressed her palms together.

The dark-haired one spoke.

"Should I trouble myself to ask what you want?"

"I am a Fenian," she answered. That much was true. That had been her reward for passing information to Mac Morna. The only thing she wanted. Membership in the Fianna. For all the good it had done her. She thought some more. She had learned that it was best to tell as much of the truth as possible. Then the victim was less likely to see the thin silver threads of the lies until they trapped him.

"My name is Aindir." That much also was true.

The two men waited, said nothing further.

"I wish to ride with you when you depart."

She wondered if either of them would accept that when she stood here in her thin tunic with her oiled breasts. She felt foolish and desperate.

The dark-haired one spoke again.

"We are departing?"

Now an inspiration came to her. She spoke fast.

"The spies of Goll Mac Morna are everywhere at Dun Gleor. He watches the fionn one and his mother."

She wondered why Mac Morna had not informed her about the dark-haired one. He seemed to be spokesman for the two, so she spoke in his direction.

"I know Mac Morna's ways. When he has gathered enough information, he will send assassins. They will not stop with the fionn one. They will take all who are close to him, including his mother. I tell you this because the lady Muirne has been good to me and kind. I would not wish her hurt. I came to you from my bedchamber like a thief in the dark, so that none would see me. You see how disrobed I am." She gestured at her gown.

The dark-haired one smiled.

Aindir stopped. She watched their faces. Every word of it had been true, excepting the part that she was disrobed for haste and secrecy. And leaving out the part that she was one of Mac Morna's best informers. She hoped that they would believe her story. She waited.

The fionn one spoke now.

"I thank you," he said. Not a word of whether they would go or not. A part of her was relieved. She would have no information to give Mac Morna, but she had no intention of riding with them.

The fionn one lifted his dark cloak from the ground beside him. He threw it to her and she caught it in the air.

"You had best take my cloak," he said. "The night air is chill."

He was not smiling.

She wrapped the cloak around her. It was far too long for her. She backed toward the door, nearly tripping on the hem in her haste to leave the dwelling. Once outside, she turned and ran for the grianan, cursing Mac Morna with every step.

When her light footsteps had faded, Caoilte turned to Fionn.

"What of that?"

"What she said of Mac Morna was true. We have been here almost four turnings of the moon. He has had plenty of time to locate us, to watch. He has not acted only because Dun Gleor is so strong."

He paused for a moment and thought. Caoilte watched an old sorrow shift across his face.

"I cannot put my mother in danger. I must leave here."

Caoilte spoke softly.

"Strange how the tide turns back on itself, Fionn."

"Strange indeed, brother," he said, and his voice was strangled.

They were silent for a while and then Caoilte spoke again.

"If she is a Fenian, she would know that we would know these things. We would be fools otherwise."

"She is Mac Morna's then."

"She asked to ride with us. I think we should accept her offer."

Fionn laughed ruefully.

"It becomes like a game of seek-and-find. No one knows who seeks, who finds."

"I will find her in the morning while you say farewell to your mother."

He found his mother in the high tower, looking north, away from the sea. She spoke simply.

"You will leave us now."

"How did you know?"

"I was the wife of a Fenian. I learned to read the wind as well as he."

She smiled and placed her hand on Fionn's forearm.

"We have been given a gift that I never thought to receive. These days that we have spent together were more than I ever thought to have when I watched you disappear with Liath and Bodhmall that long-ago winter."

"When I am chief of the Fenians again I will bring you to the hill of Tara. I will build you a fine lodge and you need never fear again."

"My place is here with Gleor, Fionn."

"Gleor will be welcome! He is a good man and I like him well."

But Muirne shook her head.

"I have been at the center of Eire. I have been privy to the counsel of warriors and kings. But I was a younger woman then. Now it is enough for me to ride my horse beside the sea, to play fidchell with my husband. Your destiny calls you and you must go. I am always here and you can return to me whenever you are weary or fearful."

Fionn took both of her hands in his. He lowered his head.

Muirne spoke again.

"I know that you protect me with your leavetaking. I know how difficult a thing it is to do."

Fionn wrapped her in his arms then and held her close to him.

"You came to me when I was six," he said. "And you held me just so. Now I know how it tore your heart to leave me."

When he had descended the platform, she watched his figure threading through the warriors and horses, watched the light casting from his hair.

"Goodbye, my little fionn one," she whispered.

She did not allow herself to weep until she could no longer see him.

"It is sad, this."

I spoke softly. Out beyond the window dawnlight began to shape shadows and forms from the black of the night.

"They saw each other many times over the course of a long life, Padraig. I remember my grandmother well, for she remained vigorous for thirty more years."

"My parents are dead. My mother died many years ago, my father two years before I returned to Eire."

"That explains much."

"Do you know how I came here?" I asked. I felt the guilt of it, but I spoke it anyway. "I sold my father's lands, his villa, his title, his position. I sold it all to return to Eire."

"That was most wise."

"Wise? I sold my paternity, my citizenship in my own land."

"A man who sells all he owns in pursuit of a great thing is a wise man, Padraig. He cannot turn back; he cannot go home. He can only go forward."

"I cannot go home," I said softly. Saying it made me think of the fish. "The joy of the leap." I said it tentatively, out loud.

"What is that?" asked Osian.

"You said that we would speak of salmon. You called it the salmon of knowledge."

The woman Ainfean returned so suddenly that I did not hear her coming.

"Salmon?" She stood in the doorway, her hands on her hips.

"Dear God, she's back," I hissed at Osian.

"Did you not let him sleep at all? Are you daft, priest? A traveller must rest when he returns. Now get out. Get out! I must minister to Osian."

From behind her, Benin peeked his head around the doorway. His little face looked terrified.

"I'm sorry, Abba," he said, bobbing up and down. "She woke me at first dawn and said we would return. I told her that I thought you would not like it much, but by then she was already halfway here. Have I done wrong?"

"Leave me, Padraig," Osian said, laughing. "I will be safe with the wise woman."

I grabbed Benin and rushed from the room. I feel no shame in saying that I was glad to go.

9

He did look better by the evening meal, his color higher and his step
more firm upon the ground. He came into the dining hall on her arm
and took his place at the table, in the spot next to mine. He offered her the
chair to his right, but I stood before she could sit. We had taken to dining
with the people of Sabhal Padraig three evenings a week; it was customary
that the benches of the hall would be crowded with parents and children,
with the sisters, as I had come to call the women of Dichu's tribe who had
joined us.

But I would not have a druidess sitting at the table that ran across the
head of the long refectory benches. I stepped to one of the long tables, indicated a spot for her on the bench.

"You are welcome to share our meal with us," I said. "You may sit here."

I could see Osian couching his laughter behind his hand as he sat in his
chair, but she did not laugh.

She put her hands on her hips and spoke in a voice that was overly loud.

"Ah, so the great Succatus will not share his table with a druid."

I wanted to slap the woman's silly face. But I maintained my composure.

"I will sit here with you, if you like," I said calmly, through gritted teeth.
"I reserve that table for my brothers and our storyteller."

The room had grown silent, of course, with all of them listening to us.
Even the servers of the evening had stopped moving about with their
wooden boards of bread and milk. I could see the four sisters of Dichu's
people watching me intently.

I wanted to throw her out. I wanted to tell her to go away and never come back. But I remembered what Osian had said about not destroying the old ways. And I remembered our Lord, how he had dined happily with tax-gatherers and comfort-women and sinners of all manner.

Benin came to my rescue. He sidled up to me and took my hand.

"Thank you for remembering, Abba," he said, sweetly.

I smiled down at him. I had no idea what I was to remember. He turned to Ainfean, all sweetness.

"Padraig promised me that I could sit with him at the evening meal. He only protects my place at the table, so there will be room."

Above his head, the woman and I glared at each other. Then I spied a way to gain the upper hand.

"The three of us shall sit here together at the lower table," I said sweetly. "That way no one shall regret the loss of a place."

The people smiled and nodded. I looked magnanimous and one or two called out their praise of my decision.

The woman fumed.

We sat with Benin between us.

"You were lucky, priest," she hissed above his head.

"You are rude, druidess," I replied in turn. "You intrude where you are not wanted."

I put my arm around Benin.

"Bless you, child," I said.

"Would you like some bread, Abba?" he asked, handing me a loaf.

The meal went forward with two empty spaces at the table of brothers, one on either side of Osian, who did not seem bothered at all by the fracas, eating with relish and smiling down upon us.

The woman ate like a starving person, wolfing down a loaf of bread, two helpings of fish and three berry cakes and drinking great quantities of milk.

"You eat like a wolf," I commented, bending above my plate.

"You like a starveling bird," she countered. "Food is a gift to be enjoyed."

"In my country, a woman serves the men of her family first and eats in silence, enjoying their conversation."

"Perhaps she eats in silence because their conversation is not worthy of her comment."

"As your conversation is unworthy of our comment," I answered, rankled.

She smiled up at me all sweetness. "And yet you seem to be unable to stop yourself from commenting."

I started to rise to my feet, to do what I did not know.

From above us Osian cleared his throat.

"I have been telling Padraig the story of how Fionn traveled to study with Finegas the wizard in the company of Caoilte and Ainder. Shall I continue the tale?"

I braced my hands against the table and sat back down.

I thanked God fervently for having sent us the storyteller.

Ainder had been forced to ride with Fionn and Caoilte for three days. Her hair was a tangle of branches and briars, her gown soiled and torn at the hem. Only her blue plaid Fenian cloak looked the way it had looked when she left the Dun of Gleor, riding out beside Caoilte, cursing Mac Morna with every beat of the horses' hooves.

Her hips and legs and buttocks ached. Something was blistered, but she did not dare to check what it was. She could not let them know what a poor rider she was. A Fenian should be able to ride; a gatherer of information rode seldom and then not horses.

She moved stiffly to help set up the camp, hobbling the horses while Caoilte made the bothy and built the fire. Fionn was off hunting, as he did each night when they stopped their ride.

For two nights she had eaten with them at the campfire, slept between them in the bothy, yet they rarely spoke and not at all to her.

So she was startled when Caoilte spoke to her.

"We have ridden too hard for you, Fenian sister. I can tell that your limbs are stiff and sore. Come and I will rub them with soothing ointment that they will not stiffen on the morrow."

The hair at the back of her neck prickled and she looked toward the woods line for Fionn.

"He will be back soon," said Caoilte. "Do you fear me? You are a Fenian. You know our code. No man among us would do you harm."

She wanted to say that it was not a code Mac Morna followed, but she bit her tongue.

She put her hand in his palm, stepped toward him. He smiled at her. He held a pouch in his free hand. He lifted it to her nose and she inhaled. It smelled of mint and sweet berries.

"It is good liniment. I use it myself when my body tires."

She nodded.

"Come then. Sit before the fire and lower your tunic. I will begin with your back."

She felt like a cat being baited. The fionn one had been gone uncommonly long. Usually he was back in a trice, game in his hand. She looked directly into Caoilte's eyes. It crossed her mind that two could play his game. She reached up and unfastened her tunic shoulders; she let it drop to the forest floor. She stood naked but for the dagger tied around her right thigh.

She watched Caoilte's eyes widen, hid her smile of triumph behind a yawn. He did not ask her to remove the dagger.

"You are right that I am most tired. At Dun Gleor I did not ride except for sport. Come then, Fenian brother. And when you have finished, I will return the favor."

She sat before the fire, using her abandoned tunic as a rug. He began to rub the liniment on her back. The minty smell and his strong hands made her feel warm and comfortable. In all of her three years with Mac Morna's fian bands, not one of them had ever called her sister, not one had seen to her welfare the way they saw to each other's. She was the butt of their jokes and the target of their foolish advances, but she was not their comrade. And it had been all she wanted. All she wanted from the time she was a child. To be a warrior of the Fenians.

She sighed.

"It eases you?"

His voice sounded thick, choky. Her senses came alert again. She stood in a single fluid motion and lifted her tunic over her head.

"It was most comforting, brother. Now I will ease your back."

"Nay we have not ridden hard enough yet for me to be sore. But when I am I will tell you."

He smiled at her, a lazy flicker of his white teeth.

He brought his blanket from his saddlebag and laid it before the fire.

"Lay down and I will rub your legs."

She stretched out on her stomach, her heart beating hard against the forest floor.

He kneaded the muscles between his fingers, pressed them at the aching points. She sighed. He lifted the tunic higher. Ainder lay perfectly still. Suddenly he made a small explosive sound.

"There is blood on your tunic."

He lifted it all the way up.

"You have a blister," he said.

Something in his voice had changed.

"I told you that I did not ride at Dun Gleor. Perhaps only once a week. Never for hunt. Only for sport."

She could hear herself babbling in her panic. She tried to scramble to her feet, but he held her down hard with his palm.

"Lie still, lie still. We must clean and bandage the wound so it will not become infected."

Surprise ran through Ainder. He was no longer playing with her. She lay quite still, clenching her fists as he cleaned the wound, applied another salve to the area.

Fionn returned, carrying a deer slung over his shoulders.

"What is it?"

He placed his catch by the fire, knelt by where she lay. He whistled softly.

Caoilte lifted his tunic over his head, tore a long strip from the hem. He wrapped it around her leg and tied it. Fionn spoke.

"We have been playing with you, sister. That was unfair."

"Playing with me?"

"We have been riding you too hard. This is our fault. Tomorrow we will not ride. Now lie still while we prepare the venison. Sleep if you will. We will wake you when it is ready."

Ainder pressed her face hard into the blankets. She felt hot waves of shame rush over her. How could she tell Mac Morna what she knew of them now? To do so would betray their kindness. She held perfectly still until the heat from the fire relaxed her and she drifted into sleep.

By the fire, Fionn looked hard at Caoilte.

"Did you think to soften her toward us?" He whispered the words.

"I did until I saw the wound. And then I felt ashamed. No, not ashamed." He shook his head in confusion. "I felt angry. At myself. At Mac Morna." He looked at the sleeping form. "At her."

"Be careful, brother," Fionn said, laughing. "You were the one who said you would never marry. Do not forget that she is Mac Morna's spy."

"Not by choice, I think."

Fionn smiled.

"I think you are right."

They fed her tenderly, like a little child, as she lay on her side by the fire. When the time came for sleep, they placed her carefully between them, all three of them stretched out on their sides. They wrapped her in a robe, making certain that she did not lay on the wounded spot. She fought back panic. She alternated between an urge to weep and an urge to tell them everything. But then these ministrations would cease. Then they would probably kill her for a spy. She sighed long and deep.

Fionn spoke from the darkness behind her.

"Mac Morna has not treated you well, sister Fenian."

Her whole body went still and tense.

"You knew."

Caoilte spoke from before her.

"We suspected."

It all poured out from her, then, all of the information she had gathered for him, the places she had lived, lonely and friendless, while she searched out answers for Mac Morna.

"And all that time," she said. "All that time, he never once asked me to ride with the Fenians. To hunt with them. To feast with them at Tara. In the time of Cumhail Mac Trenmor there were women among the Fenians. They were runners and lookouts. They lived on the cliffs and the hilltops. They rode hard when invaders came. Some of them fought with their brothers."

"Cumhail was my father," said Fionn.

"Yes," said Ainder.

"You ride with us now."

"Yes," said Ainder. Was it really so simple? She let the hot tears come.

Fionn patted her shoulder awkwardly. She lifted her arm over Caoilte's shoulder. He took her hand and kissed the open palm.

For the next three days as she rode between them she told them everything she knew of Mac Morna, the strength of his fians, his edgy relationship with King Cormac.

"He is not a good ruler and Cormac knows that. But there is no challenger, so Cormac works with what he has. Mac Morna is like a bear. He eats, he sleeps, but he can be made dangerous if he is angry."

At night, Caoilte would dress her wound and rub her back. She braided his hair. During the day she would lay her hand on his forearm again and again, as if she thought he might vanish without her touch. Fionn watched them and said nothing.

On the morning of the seventh day, they came to the River Boanne. Fionn walked upriver. He bathed in the cold autumn waters and scooped some fish to the banks for their breakfast. He was at the edge of the camp when he saw them. Ainder stood with her back to a tree, her hands over Caoilte's shoulders. As Fionn watched they kissed over and over again, their mouths quick and hungry, their bodies melding with each *other, pressing as though they would vanish into the tree. He felt a mixed joy and sadness. He hung the fish in a tree by the edge of the camp and wandered away. He had walked upriver until the sun was almost at the middle of the sky when he saw an old man standing by the river with a fish spear in his hand.*

The man turned and looked at him, shielding his eyes.

"Come, boy," he called. "Do you fish?"

Fionn felt surprised to be addressed so by a stranger, but he answered politely.

"I do. May I be of service to you?"

"I tremble too much to spear him. Old man's palsy. Faugh! But there is a fish I must have. I have seen him today. A salmon. Big."

He spread his hands apart, the spear in one hand.

"I will help you then."

The old man handed him the spear.

"Good. And boy——"

Fionn looked at him.

"Do not touch him when you spear him. Bring him straightaway to me."

Fionn stood for hours watching the water. He thought of Caoilte and Ainder there by the tree. He thought of his father and the Fianna. He thought of his mother. He remembered Bodhmall's sharp words to him when he departed Dun Gleor.

"This time, go where I told you to go boy." She had smacked him hard on the side of the head. Fionn laughed aloud.

He remembered pressing Liath to him, feeling her breasts against his chest beneath the thin tunic. She had smiled up at him.

"Now go find a girl your own age to mate with, boy," she had said, smiling.

He had never felt more alone in his life than he felt that day by the water.

The afternoon moved into the shank of the day. The light began to sink toward the west. It cast low and red on the surface of the water. Just then, Fionn saw a quick movement below the surface. A flash! Again!

He moved his body forward, careful that his shadow did not cross the surface. Beneath him, the largest salmon he had ever seen moved in a wide circle. The old man had not been lying.

Fionn closed his fingers around the spear. He rested the haft in the curve of his thumb. He drew back, thrust with all his might.

The huge salmon came out of the water, squirming and splashing water like droplets of the rainbow.

Careful not to touch the fish, Fionn took it to the old man.

The ancient was delighted. He took the fish and carefully skewered it. He placed it between two upright sticks over the fire. He clapped Fionn on the shoulder.

"This is good work, boy. For ten years I have tried to catch him. Ten years! You came along just at the right time."

This seemed to worry the old man and he shook his head.

"Too right. Boy! You did not touch the fish, did you?"

"Nay, I did not," said Fionn.

"Good, good. Sit over there." He gestured to a bench along the wall of his dwelling. Fionn sat down and studied the old man. He was older than Bodhmall, older than any man Fionn had ever seen. His hair was all white; no gray remained in it. His face was like a dried apple, curved and curled upon itself. His white beard cascaded down his chest. He wore a white tunic embroidered in gold.

"You are a druid!"

The old man looked up from where he was muttering over the fish.

"What of it?"

"My tutor was a druid."

The old man looked up, surprised.

"Was he? What did he teach you?"

"She. She taught me the legends of Eire and some of the forms of poetry. I know of herbs and plants for eating and healing and hiding. I know the turnings of the moon and the great turnings of the year. I know the festivals. I have learned of the people of the Other."

The old man snorted.

"Apprentice learning."

Fionn had a sudden suspicion about the old man. He started to ask him his name when the druid looked up.

"Boy! I need you to turn this fish. It requires leeks and some good mead."

Fionn came to stand beside the old man. The ancient put his hand around Fionn's wrist. The grasp had power, like the claws of a skybird. Fionn looked down at the hand, surprised. The old man chortled, but he did not release the hand.

"Hear me good, boy. This fish cannot burn. There can be no burns or blisters on it. Do you hear me?"

Fionn nodded. He thought the man a little mad.

"If you can do that for me, cook it without burning it, I will let you share this feast with me. Yes, yes. I am a fair and judicious man, not greedy, not greedy. I can share some of this fish with you. Not the first portion."

He shook his finger in the air.

"The first portion is mine. But I can share."

Fionn sighed in exasperation.

"I have cooked many fish and caught many as well. I can do this."

The old man nodded. He left the hut.

Fionn turned the fish carefully. He watched the skin, listened to the fire below the fish sizzle as the juices dropped into the flame. He smelled the rich texture of the meat.

"A fish is a fish," he said aloud. "This is a great, large salmon and will make good eating, but after all it is only a fish."

He shook his head over the old man's silliness.

A blister began to rise up on the skin of the fish and Fionn sighed. The old man had specifically said no burns or blisters, so Fionn wet his thumb and pressed it hard against the side of the fish. The blister went down, but the thumb grew red and throbbed with the heat.

"I hope he is satisfied that I have burned my thumb for his fish," Fionn muttered.

He heard the old man coming toward the door.

"Take your fish for a moment," he called to him. "I have burned my thumb."

"No!" the old man shouted. He raced into the hut, waving his arms at Fionn. Fionn shook his head at the crazy behavior, lifted the burned thumb to his mouth and began to suck on it.

What he felt at first surprised him.

The air breathed. The light breathed. He felt dizzy and light and strange.

He stumbled outside and sank to his knees in the grass beside the river.

The river breathed. The trees. The wind. The world turned inside out; he saw it as if from the surface of a lake, as if from the bottom of a golden chalice. He saw his mother; there was a child at her breast. Himself. The snow fell all around them. He saw his father's face. His father's face. He knew it as he knew his own, yet he had never seen it before. He felt Bodhmall rocking him, felt Liath's hand as she guided his spear for the first time. He saw Caoilte and Ainder, entwined in the forest, speaking of his absence. He wept for their love of each other. He heard the deer breathing to their children in the forest. Fionn. Our brother Fionn. One of them became the face of a woman more beautiful than any. My love, she whispered. He heard whales singing in the sea at the coast of Eire. He knew them. Brother whales, he thought. We sing. An eagle picked him up and carried him; he was the eagle. He hurtled past Eire across the the ocean. He saw a great green continent beyond the sea, vast beyond all lands he had known. He lifted toward the stars, floated among them. Voices drifted from some of them in tongues he had not yet named. He heard the great heart beating at the center of everything. A light surrounded him. All warm. All kind. All laughter. All joy.

He came back to himself kneeling on the ground by the River Boanne. He shook with sobs and laughter.

He looked up to see the old man beating his fist against his palm in frustration.

"Father Finegas," he said. "I am Fionn, come to learn the knowledge you are keeping for me."

10

Those few who had gathered before me for the Christ Mass in the early dawn looked up expectantly. I had taken to letting Benin be my acolyte and he moved about in his cloak, making swishing sounds against the stone as he lighted candles and prepared the table of the Lord.

I turned my back to the people and knelt in prayer. I knew what he wanted of me now. He had sent me Osian that I might become a storyteller, that I might woo these dreaming Hibernians to Him with his own tales.

But I did not have the words.

My people were not storytellers; they were functionaries, organized and civilized, but they were not tellers of tales. And my captivity had been so long and silent that it was here I felt most comfortable, here in the silent cradle of my prayers. For the first time in my life I envied these Hibernians, who saw all of life as a necklace beaded with tales.

I knew the truth of Osian's story. What Fionn saw when he ate of the salmon. That knowledge was the knowledge I carried in my heart. Each time I ate and drank at the table of my Christ I knew the world again as Fionn had known it, whole, too beautiful, too sorrowful, for my dusty human heart to bear.

But I had no words to say it.

They must have thought my prayer would go on forever.

At last I stood and faced them. I spoke the truth.

"People of Sabhal Padraig," I said. "I know you think me a man of miracles, a learned one from across the sea, who brings new signs, new wonders from the White Christ. For me, you believe, the dogs of Dichu were calmed, to me the great Osian has come as storyteller.

"But I tell you now that I am a rustic, an unlearned man, weak in the tongue of the church I serve, so unlearned in letters that my scribe must write for me." I gestured to Breogan, who looked at the floor.

"I know only that my God has sent me here. I tried not to come, but he wished me to be with you. I was wrong. I see now that you are the people ready for the Light, that you are the people to tell the stories of my Lord. He is the One, the Three-in-One. He is Father-Son-Spirit. He is the Light at the heart of everything, the Word who breathes into being. He is the salmon of knowledge, who feeds us when we are hungry, who feeds us even when it seems there is no food."

I pressed my hand to my lips, thought hard.

"I will tell you a story, though it be rudely told."

The Lord crossed the sea with his followers and went into the hills to rest and be quiet.

By this time there was nowhere for him to be at peace anymore. He healed the sick, made the blind see and the lame walk. The people followed him everywhere, the crowds growing larger and larger.

On this day, though he was going far from the city, so many followed him that the hillsides were crowded with their numbers.

Our Lord was tired and dusty. His back was sore and his throat ached with thirst. But when he saw their faces lifted to him like expectant children, his heart took pity on them, and he knew they needed stories or they would die.

So he told them stories until the light began to decline in the west. The people listened and the stories nourished their souls.

At last it grew toward suppertime. Our Lord was hungry and he knew that the people would be hungry as well.

He called his followers to him—he called them the Twelve, like the fian bands of old. He told them to feed the crowd, but his fian protested.

"We are not wealthy men and even if we were, we are far from town. Send them home, Lord, for we cannot feed them all. Look at them; they number more than all the Fenians of Eire."

*   *   *

My little congregation gasped.

I nodded.

"That many. So many who followed him."

I closed my eyes, pictured the heat and dust of the day. I continued.

But there was a small boy in the crowd selling barley loaves and dried fish. Christ called to him and he came and gave his baskets willingly. The fian of our Lord peered into the baskets and laughed,. They contained only five barley loaves and two dried fish! So little would never feed so many.

Our Lord raised the baskets above his head. He turned his gaze skyward. He spoke thanks to the Creator for his bounty. Then he handed the baskets to his fian and told them to pass them among the crowd.

The Fenians of Christ were worried; they knew that the food would run out; not all of the people would be fed. They would turn against the Christ and his fian feared they would do him harm.

"Do not do this, Lord," they whispered.

But he spoke one word to them.

"Believe."

They passed the baskets of dried fish and barley loaves and each time they thought the baskets empty, they were replenished. They fed all of the people who had gathered there and more, for when the feast was finished, the fian of Christ gathered twelve baskets more of bread and fish.

"People of Sabhal Padraig, this is the way of our Lord. Those who are hungry, he feeds. More than they need, he feeds them.

"This is how he will feed us here at Sabhal Padraig and over all the length and breadth of Eire. We will feast on the stories of the Lord; we will feast on the bread and wine of his table."

That afternoon I saw the men of the village begin work on another rath. I hurried to join them, my heart grateful that more had come to be baptized.

I was up to my elbows in mud when the druid woman accosted me.

"I heard your story this morning, Succatus. There may be hope for you."

I was surprised; I had not seen her at the Christ Mass.

"There is no hope for the druids. My stories will be their destruction."

"You should not think to destroy, but to absorb."

"I have no desire to absorb the priests of the heathen religion. Their ways are devious. They will try to defeat my Lord from within our ranks."

"If your Lord is the true Lord as you say, Succatus, I think that he will not be defeated."

I expelled a long breath.

"You see before you the proof that he is the true Lord. More come to live with us every day. More come to be baptized."

Ainfean laughed aloud.

"This is my house you are building, Succatus."

Part Two

"Where now my littleness is placed among strangers."

—from the Confession of Patrick

11

I do not want her here!"

"You did not want me here when I came either."

"That was different."

"How so?"

"You are a storyteller. She is a druid."

"She is a healer and a wise woman. She comes from a noble family—a family of honorable men and women. The people respect her. You should wish her among your number, Padraig. She brings the respect of a highborn family to your rath. You should seek more of her kind." Osian stood by the window of his chamber, watched the hut being built in the village.

"I want no more of her kind; she is a druid!"

"What of that? I have known druids more wise than you can imagine. My grandmother Muirne was the daughter of a druid and my father's teachers Bodhmall and Finegas were both druids."

"They are dead. Stories from the past. I know of these druids; they think to cast spells and practice magic. They are heathen idolators."

"My father lived with Finegas for seven years. In that time he taught Fionn much. He taught him the twelve forms of poetry and the history of Eire and the known world. He taught him of the moon and the stars and the stories the stars tell. He taught him to heal illnesses and stitch wounds, the medical simples that a warrior would need. He taught him the ogham, the stick language of the druids. They practiced the imbas forosna, how to speak that language with the fingers, how to read it from the rowan sticks of the druids. Finegas taught him the teinm laida, the poetry which comes by inspiration. They spoke of the Other and the land of Tir Nan Og. Finegas taught my father the names of the gods and their functions, certainly, but he did not teach my father the practice of magic or the worship of idols, as you call them."

"He sounds like a good teacher," I said, sulkily.

"Many druids are, Padraig. There are some who choose the black practice, the dark gods, but there are those in any place and time. Most are the keepers of the great wisdom and learning."

"She is too young to be the keeper of great wisdom."

"I think her of your age, Padraig. Some forty years. And she has studied for more than half of those years to gain wisdom. From what you have told me of your years in Britain, she has studied longer than you have done."

The thought made me angry. "She has studied false idols and superstition. What kind of study is that?"

"The kind that has brought wisdom to Eire for thousands of years, Padraig. But perhaps you are too young to possess any wisdom. A wise man would go and learn from her."

"I should learn from a druid? I will destroy those who believe in false gods."

"My father had a saying, Padraig. He said that you should know your enemy well. Thus, by knowing him, you would be able to defeat him or to win him to your cause."

"I have no wish to win her to my cause."

"She would be a good ally. She is a woman of strong mind. I have told you that she is the daughter of a great chief."

"Why is she putting her dwelling in the village?"

"I do not know. Why do you not ask her?"

"I will not."

Osian laughed aloud.

"I see now! You find the woman attractive."

"Of course not. We are celibate here."

"Does that also make you blind?"

Breogan stifled a choking sound, bent to rearranging his writing tools on his little table.

"I am not blind. She is the most thoroughly dislikeable female I have ever known, insufferable, opinionated, headstrong, intrusive."

"Perhaps that is why you dislike her. She is so like you."

"I am in no way like those attributes."

I watched Breogan's shoulders shaking as he bent above his table.

"All right, perhaps I am somewhat headstrong, but I am a meek lamb compared to the gall of that woman."

Osian spoke quietly.

"This is her land, Padraig. You are the intruder here. Perhaps she moves into your rath to watch what you will do with her people. She follows my father's dictum well."

"And did that rule always work so well for your father? Was Fionn always able to defeat his enemies or win them to him?"

"Not always. But he won Goll Mac Morna to his side."

I forgot the woman in my amazement.

"The same Goll Mac Morna who slew his father?"

"The same."

"How was this done? This is the story you must tell."

Osian smiled.

"I will tell it if you promise to speak to this druidess."

"I promise nothing to heathens," I answered.

And he told the story anyway.

Fionn stayed with Finegas for seven years. When he had learned all that Finegas could teach him, the old man called him one day to the river. They sat side by side in the late autumn sunlight and Finegas spoke.

"When you came to me a gangling boy of fifteen, and caught the salmon of knowledge, I railed at the gods that they had sent a foolish boy to learn what should have been mine.

"Ah, but boy, I was wrong.

"You are a man now, but you have learned each task from me with patience and persistence. You have sat with me silent beneath the stars and swum for overlong beneath the river when I told you to do so. You have put to memory each lesson I have given you. And then you have done what each teacher wishes for just one student to do. You have added more to what I have taught you. You have become the master, Fionn."

Fionn protested, but Finegas held up his hand.

"I know now that the gods intended you to come to me. I know now that this was my gift. For what I would have learned from the salmon would have died with me in this lonely old body.

"But your name will live forever, Fionn. What you learned and the honor with which you lived will live forever. Even when twelve generations have passed beneath the stones, they will speak of Fionn. And my name will live with yours as well. I am well satisfied with the gift I have been given, boy."

He rested his hand on Fionn's arm.

"The time has come for you to reclaim what you have lost. The time has come for the Fenians of Eire to reclaim their honor.

"You must leave me now and go to the hill of Tara."

Fionn embraced the old man, for he had come to love him well.

"Will we meet again, wise one?"

"We will meet again at the feast in Tir Nan Og."

Now it was the custom in those days that the Ard-Ri, the high king of Eire, would hold a great feast at samhain, the turning of the year. This feis would last for seven days, for it was the most important time of the year, when the fires of the old year were extinguished and those of the new year lighted on the great Hill of Tara. There would be much feasting and merrymaking, but the entire feast was under an edict of peace. No weapons could be lifted against another for any reason for the duration of the samhain feis.

Fionn chose this feis to return to Tara.

He did not enter the rath of the Hill of Tara unnoticed, for by now he was taller and broader of shoulder than any of the Fenians, and his hair was more white than gold. He slipped into the banqueting hall and took his place among the Fenians, sitting down as though he had belonged there all his life.

All the Fenians around him whispered among themselves and stared, but before one could ask him his name, Cormac Mac Art, the high king of Eire, entered the hall.

He was flanked by the wolves who were his companions and he shone in the seven colors of kingship. He strode to the high dais and seated himself at the head of the company.

The first thing he noticed was the striking stranger seated among the warriors of Eire.

He nodded a welcome and gestured with his right arm.

"Boy, stand up and state your name, for we have not seen you in our company before."

Fionn stood. He took a long steadying breath, then spoke in his clearest voice.

"I am Fionn Mac Cumhail, son of Cumhail Mac Trenmor of Clan na Bascna.

I have come to pledge my oath as a Fionn of Eire of Cormac Mac Art, Ard-Ri of Eire!"

The room exploded.

Goll Mac Morna strode to the dais and Fionn had the first sight of his father's murderer. A shock ran through him for Goll Mac Morna had only one eye. He was short and stocky. Most of what had once been muscle had gone loose and unattended and he was well past middle years.

But his voice was still strong when he issued the challenge.

"This boy is a liar. He has heard the legends of the fionn one and stakes his claim among us as a stranger."

Cormac Mac Art's face had grown serious and thoughtful. He rested his chin on his palm for a moment, then spoke.

"It is true that we know nothing of this fionn one. Yet it is also true that for seven years we have heard the whispered stories of Fionn, the son of Cumhail. Is there one among us who can speak to the truth of his claim?"

There was a rustle among the Fenians and a young man with dark hair stood.

"I speak the truth of his claim!"

Fionn whirled around and shouted aloud.

"Caoilte Mac Ronan! My Fenian brother."

Caoilte raised his arm in salute to Fionn.

"This is the one of whom you have heard, brothers, for it was I who found him living alone in the forest with the druidess and the warrior woman. It was I who accompanied him when we found the remnants of Clan na Bascna, living in the wilds of Connaught, I who journeyed with him to see his mother, the lady Muirne, wife of Cumhail Mac Trenmor.

"Fionn speaks truth. I hail him as the rightful leader of the Fianna!"

"Nay!" roared Goll Mac Morna. "He will battle me first for that honor!"

Fionn strode toward the dais and stood towering over Mac Morna.

"It is well! Your life for the life of my father!"

But Cormac Mac Art stood and raised his arms.

"This is the time of samhain feis. No one shall raise arms against another, for he who breaks the peace will forfeit his life."

Fionn looked at the king. He drew his sword from its scabbard and placed it gently at the feet of Cormac Mac Art.

"I am Fionn," he cried, "protector of Eire. I keep her laws with honor."

Cormac nodded.

"Mac Morna," he said, coldly.

Mac Morna let his weapon clatter to the wood of the dais.

"You have my pledge," he said, coldly. "But I say also that this matter must be resolved."

Pandemonium ruled the room. Fenians shouted. Old men from the back of the hall cried out for Fionn. When he looked to where the voices called his name, he saw the face of his uncle Crimnall in the crowd. The men of Mac Morna called his name and cried for justice.

Cormac allowed the noise to build to a crescendo, then raised his arms.

Silence fell like a curtain.

"I do espy a way that justice may be met. Each year, on the central night of samhain feis, the creature known as Aillen of the Sidhe comes among us. Each year, he burns something of our great rath to the ground. I propose that the one who can stop him will be chief of the Fianna."

Mac Morna said nothing. He shifted his weight from foot to foot and looked at the golden-haired man.

Fionn had no idea of what had been proposed, but he lifted the edge of his thumb to his teeth and bit upon it briefly. There in his mind a picture formed of fire and of the creature who created it. Fionn nodded.

"I will destroy this creature," he cried. "I will make the Hill of Tara safe again. And when I have done so, I will lead the armies of Eire. We will make the coasts and forests safe, so that, in all of Eire, none will sleep again in fear."

Then he drew his cloak around him and swept from the great hall with Caoilte and some of the old men of his father's company close upon his heels.

Outside by the flickering light of one of the hillside campfires, Fionn hugged old Crimnall to his chest, then clasped Mac Ronan by the forearms.

"Brother! My heart lifted when I heard your voice in the crowd! But where is the Fenian woman spy we won to our company?"

Mac Ronan clapped him on his arms.

"She is heavy with our second child, else she would have been beside me shouting your name. But brother, when you were so long with Finegas, we," he gestured at the old men, "all of us, began to give up hope."

Fionn smiled at him.

"I have learned that all things weave themselves in their own time. I was a boy. Now I am a man. I am ready."

Old Crimnall spoke.

"It will not be as easy as you think. This one who burns the Hill of Tara is a demon of darkness. Many of them have tried. He soothes them to sleep with the music of his harp and when they are deep in the spell, he burns another dwelling to the ground. Many have died in his dark fire."

"Guide me in the ways of wisdom, uncle," Fionn said quietly.

Crimnall nodded.

"It is time."

He stood and left the little circle, moving awkwardly down the hill. The moon passed behind a cloud and returned again before he came back among them, carrying the craneskin bag. He brought the sword of the Fenians into the firelight.

"This sword has belonged to the one who leads the Fenians for as long as we have been the warriors of Eire. Its hilt bears all the sweat and strength of the men who carried it in her defense. Its blade sings their courage songs. We call this sword Good Striker. You will take it with you when you fight against Aillen of the Sidhe. With the power of the leaders of Eire, the evil one will be defeated."

Fionn held the sword aloft.

"My Fenian brothers, Finegas the wise has taught me to read the ancient language."

He traced his fingers along the ogham sticks incised below the hilt and when he had finished he spoke softly.

"Dwell in the light," he said. "So the ancient words speak. Dwell in the light. Generations from now may it be said of us that we did so."

Samhain night came cold and cloudless. A three-quarters moon hung like a light in the sky.

From the branches of the trees, the druids had hung skulls, in the hope that so many guardian spirits would frighten Aillen of the Sidhe away. Many glowed in the darkness, lit from within by candles.

Fionn paced at the edge of the hill. His heart hammered at his ribs and he could hear the ragged, shallow rhythm of his own breathing, but he made no noise as he waited, for he had sheathed his winter boots with heavy wool to muffle the sound.

He held Good Striker firm in his hands.

From far off in the distance, he thought that he heard a sweet music. He leaned toward it, listening.

It grew closer.

It was the most compelling music he had ever heard, the trembling of harpstrings, the rhythmic thrum. He felt a lovely drowsiness steal over his limbs.

Slowly, as if from underwater, he lifted Good Striker. He place the hilt against his forehead, pressed the ruby of the blood of Eire into his flesh. In that blood, in the trickle of his own blood, he remained awake, even as the sound grew louder and closer.

At last he could see the evil one moving toward him across the hillside.

He was short and he seemed to move on the legs of a goat. His hair was twisted up into shapes like spiral cones and the tips burned blue in the darkness. He strummed on his harp, looking neither right nor left.

So it was that when Fionn called his name, he dropped the harp on the ground and stood rooted with surprise that any had been able to resist his music.

"What are you called, boy?" the goblin asked. The voice was melodic, kind.

"I am Fionn, son of Cumhail, sent that you will cease all burning."

The goblin shook his head.

"So they grow desperate. They send a boy sacrifice to appease me."

"No sacrifice, Aillen of the Sidhe. None but the forfeit of your life."

The goblin sighed and bent towards his harp. Fionn placed his foot over it.

"We will have no more music."

Suddenly the goblin's head snapped up. He opened his mouth and breathed toward Fionn. Blue flames shot from his tongue. Before Fionn could move, the flames licked across the backs of his hands. The heat was searing, intense. Fionn could smell the charring scent of his own flesh; blisters rose tender and angry from his skin.

Fionn let out a scream of surprise and pain.

He hefted Good Striker high into the air and swung, but the pain had slowed him. The goblin moved and as Fionn swung to follow the motion, the goblin bent and scooped the harp into his hands, strumming as he arose.

Fionn felt the slow drowsiness steal across his limbs and he sank to his knees.

Again the goblin breathed. Fire licked around Fionn's face and singed the ends of his hair. He lowered his face to the ground to escape the intense heat.

From above his kneeling form, the goblin strummed gently and spoke in his soft voice.

"You are quite beautiful, boy sacrifice Fionn. I shall remember your burning with pleasure."

The harp song ceased and Fionn felt the flames lick hot against the leather of his battle vest and creep up his back toward his hair. But the drowsiness left him! With a roar, Fionn rolled to his back and thrust upward, impaling the goblin below the throat. Using the dangling sword to rise, Fionn heaved himself to his feet.

The goblin regarded Fionn with astonishment, as blue-green blood oozed from the wound.

Fionn withdrew the sword with a mighty yank and turned around in a circle, holding it before him with both hands, his arms outstretched. The wind-splitting arc of the sword made its own music; the surprised face of Aillen of the Sidhe toppled to the ground.

Fionn used the last of his strength to smash the harp to smithereens.

Then he gathered the head, placed it on a pike and set it before the Great Hall of Cormac Mac Art.

In the morning, Fionn appeared before the assembly at the Hill of Tara with his hands swathed in white bandages and much of the length of his golden hair shorn. Too, his face had a ruddy cast and one of his eyebrows was singed almost to nothing.

But he was named leader of the Fenian warriors of Eire before a cheering crowd.

With the help of Crimnall and Caoilte, Fionn was dressed in full Fenian raiment, a green silk tunic and a cloak of blue and green plaid fastened with a brooch of golden filagree. His hair was braided and threaded with ribbon of Fenian green and he carried Good Striker before him. Only a few people saw him wince with pain as he lifted the sword into the air, for the moment he spoke, the people knew that Eire would never be the same.

"I am Fionn, son of Cumhail," he cried aloud.

"I pledge to Eire my honor and my life. For as long as I am leader of the Fenians of Eire we of the Fenians will always stand to care for the people of Eire. Never will we take cattle or horses by force; the common people will speak of us by our gentle hands. Two-thirds of all our kindness we will dispense to women and children and to the poets of Eire, for in their wisdoms we are made human and strong. No dog of Eire will be beaten by a Fenian hand. We will be ecland and dithir, landless and clanless, that none of us claim honor price from his Fenian sisters and brothers. We will live and die in the defense of this green land and our great king Cormac Mac Art.

"Those who serve will pass four tests of strength and honor and our brotherhood will not require mercenaries among us.

"When we are gone, they will say of us:

"Those were the days of Eire, when every Fenian was honorable, when the land was green and growing, when the people lived free of fear.

"So saying, I ask you to join me."

There was a mighty roar and men and women began to cluster around Fionn, to drop to their knees before him and hold their sword hilts to his hands.

But in the middle of the melee, Mac Morna roared out,

"King Cormac, what of Clan Mac Morna, who has served you well for all these years?"

An uneasy silence fell over the crowd. People who had been standing near Mac Morna moved away from him until he stood alone.

Cormac, who had been standing with his arm across Fionn's shoulders, moved forward.

"I leave the decision of the soldiers of Mac Morna to Fionn Mac Cumhail. As for you, Goll Mac Morna, you are banished to Alba, never to return to Eire in your lifetime."

Fionn turned then and said something softly into Cormac's ear. Cormac looked surprised, but nodded. Fionn called aloud to Mac Morna.

"If the soldiers of Mac Morna wish to serve with me, they are welcome, if they can pass the Fenian trial."

A cheer went up from some of Mac Morna's clansmen. Mac Morna glared at them from across the hall.

"But I say this to you, Mac Morna. From this day on, the Fenians will be known for justice. If you can swear fealty to me and keep it, if you can serve with me loyally and without question, I will lift from you your sentence of banishment!"

Mac Morna stood still and quiet. He looked around the room. Finally, he looked at the warrior who dominated the dais.

"I would not have done as much for you, boy," he growled.

Fionn said nothing.

Mac Morna lumbered to the front of the room and dropped to one knee. He spoke aloud and looked up into the face of his new leader.

"For as long as I shall dwell in this body, I pledge my loyalty to Fionn Mac Cumhail, leader of the Fenian warriors of Eire. I will serve with what strength and what honor I have!"

From the back of the hall, Caoilte Mac Ronan raised a goblet high.

"To Fionn!" he cried.

But from the dais, Fionn raised Good Striker until the light flashed from its stones and cascaded like lightning from its blade.

"For Eire!" he cried.

And the echo of it lifted from the hillside and reached up into the night stars. It reached the listening heart of an old druid and the linked hands of the mother of Fionn and his teachers.

"For Eire," they echoed.

"And that was how my father came to lead the Fenians." Osian leaned back against his cushions, exhausted by the telling. "And for the rest of his life, Goll Mac Morna served my father well."

"Do you believe that Fionn slew this Aillen of the Sidhe?"

"I do believe that evil exists. Do you not, Padraig?"

"Nay, I believe it well."

I stood and looked out the window of his room where the men were beginning to thatch the roof of the druidess's dwelling.

"Only that you do not mistake it," said Osian quietly.

But I waved that away, for an idea had been forming in my mind.

"Breogan," I said. He stopped his writing.

"Bring Benin to us."

The boy returned swiftly, dashing like a puppy into the room, hugging me around the knees, then leaping into Osian's lap.

"He was listening outside the window," Breogan said, grinning.

I laughed at the cherubic face of the boy.

"Then you will know sooner what I wish to ask you. This feis at Tara Hill that Osian spoke of . . ."

"The samhain feis."

"That is the one. Is it still held in these times?"

"It is."

Osian sat bolt upright, his face transformed.

"You think to go, Padraig. By the gods! You think to go!"

"By the grace of God," I corrected him. "The One True God. Darkness was defeated once at the Hill of Tara, Osian. And it was your father who defeated it. Now it will be the Father of All who defeats the darkness yet again at the Hill of Tara. And yes, you must all come with me."

It was September when I made the decision to go and in a little month there was much to be done. I decided to listen to the wisdom of Osian and go in the way the old poets and chieftains traveled, with chariots and horsemen, wrapped in colorful cloaks, accompanied by musicians and bell-ringers and bearing gifts to the king of Eire.

If I was to take my Lord to the Great Hill of Tara, I would bear him before me in the way these people would understand.

Dichu donated his chariot for me to ride in; our smith began immediately refurbishing the leather and the ironwork. We cast a little bell for Benin, who would ring it to announce the presence of the Lord as we approached the great feis. The sisters began work on ornamental embroidery of crosses, which I showed them how to make. They added their own Eireann flourish and the result was a cross embellished with rings and spirals, most beautiful to behold.

For the brothers and myself, I had determined that we would go in our homespun robes, as we should carry within us the simplicity of Christ. Thus it was that I was sitting with the sisters, mending a tear in my own robe, when the druid woman accosted me.

"It is good that you work with your hands, Succatus," she said, standing at the opposite side of the table.

I felt heat rise up my neck and I glared up at her.

"Followers of the Christ feel no shame in any work that is honest."

"Shame? Nay I spoke honestly. I did not mean to offend, Succatus." She held up her hands.

"Stop calling me Succatus! Your purpose is to irritate."

A little smile played at the edges of her lips, but she denied it.

"But I am told that you dislike the name Padraig. You rail against the brothers for its use. You are not my father, so I cannot call you Abba. Nor are you brother to me. Succatus seemed the least offensive choice. And its meaning so suits you."

"What do you know of its meaning?"

"I speak the language of your church, Succatus. I know that your name means 'clever in war.' "

She watched as I closed the last stitch on my garment.

I have never disliked a woman as I loathed Ainfean at that moment. I folded my garment with care and spoke kindly to the sisters, all the while seething with anger. I stood and walked calmly from the table, but she followed me.

Halfway across the yard I turned back and faced her.

"You lie if you say you speak the language of Rome."

"You wish for it to be a lie because you do not speak it well."

I was on her in a flash, gripped her upper arms hard with my hands, bent my head close to hers, bared my teeth. She did not flinch back, remained with her face close to mine, her eyes a strange blue. There was a perfume to her hair like late summer flowers and the light cast red glints from its depths. The impulse to shake her passed and another impulse took its place. I dropped her arms, rubbed my palms against my robe. I turned to walk away.

"Your God is the One Who Comes." She said it softly.

I turned back, but kept my distance from her. She continued, chanting something that sounded like a poem.

"There is a god above the gods, a god whose name is known to none. You will know him on his day. This god is the One Who Comes."

We looked at each other from our wary distance.

"What do you speak?"

"It is a druid teaching. Very old. Many generations of us have passed it down. We knew that one would come; I believe that one is your God. I do speak the language of your church. I traveled when I was young on the continent of Gaul and there I heard of the Three-in-One. And I knew that it was the god of our predicting. It is why I am here. I wished to learn more of this god, to learn if he will enlighten or destroy. I thought that I could learn from you and you from me, but I think now that will not be possible."

She turned away from me and started across the village.

A pulse beat at my throat and would not stop. It felt like a trapped bird. I clenched my fists hard and told myself to let her go. My own voice surprised me.

"Ainfean."

It came out like a groan.

She faced me immediately. I could see the same bird beating in her throat. She brought her hands together and clenched them beneath her breasts. She said nothing.

"You may stay," I said.

A silence spun itself between us like a cloak.

Finally she broke it.

"You will need to know of our gods and of the druids if you plan to travel to Tara Hill. And I will need to know more of your God if I am to speak of him to my fellow priests."

"You will not accompany us to Tara Hill." I felt an edgy panic.

"I will most certainly accompany you."

"I have not asked you to come, nor do I wish your company."

"I do not live and die by your wishes, Succat. I am a druid priestess of Eire. I come and go as I please."

She stalked away and the strangeness of the moment that had passed between us was replaced by my anger.

I was glad of it.

That evening after the dinner meal, when the people of Sabhal Padraig were gathered in the great hall, Dichu arrived from his village accompanied by two of his great wolfhounds. They clambered and frolicked about and took an especial liking to Osian, licking him like puppies, rubbing their noses up under his hair, to sniff at the spot I had felt when I had blessed him.

"They remind me of my father's hounds, Bran and Sgeolan," Osian cried out between wrestling the wolfhounds away from his face and laughing at their return. "They have not the size, but they have the spirit."

"Your father's hounds were larger that this?"

I moved between the hounds and made calming sounds and motions. They listened to me, lying down on either side of Osian like flanking lions. I saw Dichu cross himself and I laughed aloud.

"Old man, surely you know me well enough now to know this is no miracle but only that I am good with dogs."

But Dichu shook his head.

"My dogs calm for no one but you, Padraig. That is why I have brought them here, that they may accompany you to Tara Hill where all will see that even the beasts of the forests of Eire heed the priest of the One Who Comes. They are my gift to you and will henceforward be called by your name."

Osian nodded.

"This is how it was for my father. His wolfhounds, Bran and Sgeolan, were bigger than ponies, but they behaved for him as obedient children." He stroked the heads of the dogs beside him.

I saw that his eyes had grown watery and I bent to him.

"What is it, old man?" I asked, concerned.

But he shook his head and looked up smiling.

"Shall I tell you the stories of how my father came by his hounds? They are fanciful tales indeed."

The people shouted their approval. Dichu and his men straddled the benches of our hall, ready to stay for the storytelling. I felt a great contentment settle over me and I called my blessing aloud.

"Sweet is your voice to us, Osian. A blessing on the soul of Fionn your father. Now tell us the tale of the hounds of Fionn Mac Cumhail."

After Fionn was once again chief of the Fianna of Eire, his reputation spread far and wide, even across the waters to Alba.

Thus it was that a chief of Alba sailed across the water and sought Fionn for his help. Now this chief of Alba had been blessed by the birth of a fine son, but the child had been stolen at birth, by a great black claw descending down the chimney of the chamber where his wife was lying in. The man's wife was once again heavy with child. She could not bear to lose another babe, nor could the chief of Alba bear the loss of another son.

He beseeched Fionn for help.

"I have stationed guards around her room and hired only the best midwives to assist her. I myself will watch with her in the chamber, but I fear the power of this darkness. My beloved wife will not survive the loss of another child. She weeps day and night and cries that it would be better for the babe to be born dead, then to have it stolen from her again.

"Fionn, we have heard of you in Alba. They say there is no creature of the forest who is swifter, no trail you cannot follow, no scent you cannot name. Please come back with me to Alba. Give my wife heartsease, that if I cannot defeat this darkness, you can follow it and find my son for me."

But Fionn feared a trap and said that he would not go.

Now the chief of Alba grew desperate. He placed a geis on Fionn to follow him and then he sailed for Alba.

A little gasp went up from our seated crowd. I shook my head in confusion.

"What is this geis?"

"It is a sacred promise, a promise that a warrior cannot break even under pain of death. It was a geis that later caused my father the greatest sorrow of his life."

Osian shook his head.

"But that is a story for another time."

I motioned at him to continue.

Under pain of the geis, Fionn sailed for Alba, but he would allow only Caoilte Mac Ronan and Goll Mac Morna to accompany him as he still feared a trap.

They arrived in Alba on the day that the woman was to give birth.

Fionn agreed to watch with the man in the chamber of his wife, but he set Caoilte and Goll to find among the common men and warriors of Alba the men he might need, if a problem arose.

And trouble did indeed begin that very night.

The woman gave birth well enough, to a fine healthy son.

Fionn knew that no trap had been set when he saw the joy of the chief of Alba and the fearful joy of his wife.

Together Fionn and the chief set soldiers to watch outside the new mother's door and at the entrances to the village. They guarded the walls and outside the dwelling.

Fionn and the chief himself guarded the inside of the chamber.

The midwife who had assisted the woman in giving birth was the same one who had helped her before. She tried to soothe her agitated mistress, but the woman would not be calmed, weeping and holding the child to her breast and crying aloud her fear that he would be stolen from her.

At last, the midwife begged permission of the chief of Alba to give his wife a posset to comfort her.

The chief gave his permission and together they persuaded the poor, distracted mother to drink, after which she fell into a deep sleep, punctuated occasionally by her dreaming cries of alarm. The child slept too, and the chamber settled into quiet.

The old midwife cleaned up the chamber and set to burning a small bowl of sweet-smelling herbs. Then she smiled at Fionn and the chief of Alba, lay down on a mat at the foot of the bed and went to sleep.

The night moved along slowly. Fionn and the chief of Alba did not speak nor did they sleep, but the longer the pot of herbs simmered on the fire, the heavier their limbs felt, until at last Fionn could barely lift his arm to check his dagger at his side.

Just then the old woman leapt to her feet, spry as a young girl. She dashed to the crib and lifted the sleeping infant and ran to the chimney.

"Coille," she called.

A small dwarf dressed all in black appeared from the chimney, dangling from a rope and holding out his arm. He was all covered with soot and he seemed angry.

"'Twas evil hot in that chimney, woman! Why have you been so long about it?"

The midwife gestured toward Fionn and the chief of Alba, who were trying to rise, but who could not move, their limbs flailing out strangely, like swimmers under water.

"They are big men. Not like the last time when it was only she and me. I had to wait for the potion to take effect."

She handed the babe into the waiting arms of the dwarf, who disappeared up the chimney. Then she looked at Fionn and the chief of Alba.

"I cannot get away with saying a great claw took him this time. But I can still get away."

She flung open the door and cried to the guards.

"Help! Help! The babe has been stolen even as Fionn and the great chief of Alba sleep in a drunken stupor!"

As the guards rushed into the room, the old woman slipped past them into the night.

Fionn and the chief of Alba could speak only as drowsy drunkards, but at last they made known their wish that the burning pot of herbs be removed. It took some time, but as the effects of the drug wore off, they were able to speak more clearly. And oh what a railing cry the poor mother let out when she awoke and found her newborn gone.

But Fionn spoke above the din.

"I have brought with me two of my warriors from Eire and even as we watched here they have gathered to them all the men we need. For I suspected the story of the claw and thought we might have someone to follow."

Then Mac Ronan and Mac Morna came into the chamber, bringing the men Fionn had requested. There were a woodsman of Alba and a boatbuilder, a climber, a listener, a marksman and a thief. Together, Fionn and the chief of Alba set out with this company to find the stolen child.

The woodsman led them through the stony forests of Alba for many days until they came to the shores of a clear, cold lake. There, the signs that they had been following ceased. They huddled in silence on the shores of the lake until at last the listener nodded.

"I hear the cries of a child. There, from the island at the center of the lake."

Now the boatbuilder took over, building a small skin boat from the trees of the forest and the skins in his pack. In this little vessel, he ferried them in darkness to the island—Fionn, the chief of Alba, the climber and the thief. The rest waited without fire or food on the shore.

At the great stone tower at the center of the island, the climber scaled the walls and then reported back to Fionn and the chief of Alba.

"The newborn child is there but there is another child as well, a boy of some three years."

Now the king of Alba grasped Fionn by the upper arms, for he knew the other child was his missing son.

The climber continued.

"They are not guarded by the dwarf and the woman alone, my chief. They are guarded by two soldiers in the plaid of Mac an Bheatha."

Now the chief of Alba knew who had stolen his sons, for these were the soldiers of his great enemy, whom he had defeated in war.

"There is more," said the climber. "Close beside the boys sleeps a huge wolfhound with a new puppy by her side."

Now the little group made their plans. They tied the skin boat by the water door of the tower and waited until the middle of the night. Then Fionn whispered to the climber.

"You must scale the walls and open this little door that leads to the water."

He gestured to the thief.

"You must slip into the castle so silently that none will hear you and be awak-

ened. There you must steal the boys, careful not to awaken them, and bring them here to the water door."

"I can do this," said the thief, "for I have slipped horses and cattle from their masters' doors with no sound of hoofbeats."

Fionn nodded.

"Seaman," he said, "you will ferry the chief of Alba with his children to the shore, then you will return for each of us."

The chief of Alba spoke.

"I fear that this is too many trips. Someone will awaken."

Fionn nodded.

"I have thought of this. But I have a distraction in mind."

So the thief slipped into the castle and returned with the sleeping boys, who were ferried to the further shore without incident. He returned for the climber and while they moved through the water Fionn whispered to the thief.

"I issue you a challenge. Do you think you can steal the puppy without awakening his dam?"

The thief grinned and nodded. He returned with the brindled pup beneath his arm just as the boatmen arrived to ferry them back. But the boatman, easing up to the shore, accidently brushed his paddle against a stone and the huge wolfhound awoke.

"Paddle!" cried Fionn.

"What of you?" cried the boatman and the thief, who held the squirming puppy tight in his arms.

"I will swim for it," Fionn called. "But when I call to you, you must throw the puppy into the water."

So Fionn leapt into the water and the boat headed for the farther shore, just as the dog leaped from the water door and swam after the boat.

By now the racket had awakened the soldiers who guarded the children and they came running, all unbraced, unable to see in the darkness. By the time they gathered torches, the little skin boat was halfway across the lake, with the huge wolfhound so hard upon it that she would tip it any moment.

"Now!" cried Fionn and the thief heaved the puppy into the water.

But he heaved it in Fionn's direction!

Of course the mother did just what Fionn had hoped she would do. She turned from the little boat and swam toward her pup, but she was swimming directly toward Fionn, her great jaws gaping. Beside him in the water, the little puppy struggled, making mewling sounds. Fionn took pity on the poor little animal. He gathered it onto his shoulders, where the frightened pup stood whimpering, then swam for the shore with all of his power. He arrived with the great wolfhound tearing at his heels, but when he set the puppy on the ground at the mother's feet, she quieted and licked the little ball of fur dry and fed him.

By now, the soldiers of Mac an Bheatha had gathered their weapons and their strong boats and were cresting the water toward the shore, their torches casting eerie lights upon the surface of the lake.

Now the marksman Fionn had hired fired stones from his sling across the water, Caoilte Mac Ronan by his side with his spear. Together they picked off the soldiers one by one, until all three had tumbled into the water and the dwarf and the evil midwife were left alone on the island, boatless and sure to be in trouble with Mac an Bheatha.

Imagine the joy when the wife of the chief of Alba was reunited with not one, but both of her children. And when Fionn left Alba, he left with the friendship of the chief, who gave him the little brindled pup as a gift. Fionn named him Bran and that pup grew larger than an island pony and never left Fionn's side for all of his life.

Osian finished and took a long draught of his ale.

"What of Sgeolan?" cried Dichu. "You have told us only of Bran."

"Will you drain me dry of all my tales in just one night?" asked Osian.

But Dichu only laughed.

"As if the poet of the Fenians could run out of things to say!"

Osian laughed too then and acquiesced.

"But I will make the tale of Sgeolan short in the telling. There was another time that my father agreed to help one from another country, but this time it was a trap. Still, the trap brought him Sgeolan and more, so my father did not count it as a loss."

Fionn took into service a son of the king of Lochlan, those who are sometimes called the Norsemen, raiders of the far north.

This boy, Fionn came to love as a brother, and when the boy's year of service was up and he asked Fionn to return with him to meet his father, Fionn was only too glad to travel to the north.

But the journey was a trap.

Fionn had no sooner set foot on the shore, than the thanks he received for his care of the boy was to be set upon and beaten by the king of Lochlan and his men, who feared the great strength of Fionn's armies.

They left him for dead, dragging him into a high valley surrounded by impassible mountains. In that valley lived a ravenous wolfhound who fed upon any unwary sheep who chanced to stray into its domain.

Here the men of Lochlan left the body of Fionn, bloody and broken, believing that the wolfhound would tear off the limbs and digest the bones.

But they did not know Fionn's way with the four-legged creatures.

For when the dog came sniffing at the wounds of Fionn, Fionn spoke to the dog in its language and asked it for healing. And so the dog licked the wounds clean and slept beside Fionn as a blanket, night after night in the cold north air.

At last Fionn healed enough to stumble down from the mountains, with the great dog at his side.

At the entrance to the valley Fionn found the cabin of an old sheepherder and his wife. Imagine their fear when they saw a huge stranger, wild and scraggly, accompanied by the beast who ate their sheep.

But once Fionn had told them his tale, they took him in, fed and bathed him.

No lovers of the king of Lochlan, who treated his subjects with a greedy meanness, the old couple took it upon themselves to send their son to Eire with a message for the warriors of Fionn.

Their daughter brought other messages to Fionn in the darkness and he was attentive to her for the year that he dwelled in Lochlan. Some say that the grandsons and granddaughters of Fionn Mac Cumhail dwell even today in the Norse country.

At last, however, the warriors of Fionn returned and defeated the armies of Lochlan in battle.

Though Fionn beseeched the old couple and their daughter to return with him to Eire, they preferred to remain in their beloved mountains. So Fionn returned with the huge wolfhound, whom he called Sgeolan.

Bran and Sgeolan became the hunting brothers of Fionn and were the two creatures on earth who understood him best and never deserted him.

I looked over to see tears running down the face of the old man.

"What is it?" I asked gently, kneeling before him.

But he was overcome by some emotion and could not speak.

I knew then how much I had come to love the old man, for his sorrow moved in me as well and I wished to ease it.

So I stood before our little community and called aloud,

"These hounds that Dichu has brought to us have given us the gift of two fine stories. Therefore, we shall call these hounds Bran and Sgeolan, after the hounds of Fionn Mac Cumhail. They will be the hounds of our beloved storyteller, fitting companions to a Fenian. Together they will accompany us to the Great Hill of Tara!"

My people applauded and shouted their approbation and I realized, of a sudden and with a lurch of joy, that I had thought of them as my people. My people. The people of Eire. The people of God.

I looked back to see Osian nodding his head, smiling through the tears.

The hounds, as if sensing their new kinship to the storyteller, were nudging at his hands and licking the tears from his ancient cheeks.

13

I stooped through the lintel and entered her hut. The fire burned brightly at the center of the circle, but she was nowhere to be seen. I looked around me.

The dwelling was tidy, two sleeping platforms against one wall, spread with furs and woven blankets. From the ceiling hung bunches of herbs and flowers, and the whole dwelling smelled of their profusion. Along the wall opposite the bed, the woman had created a kind of table. Spread upon it were roots, powders in little bowls, one or two bowls of pungent liquid. Resting above the table in two indentations of the wall were two grinning skulls.

I grimaced at them, stepped backward.

Benin spoke from behind me and he startled me.

"Do you seek the druidess, Abba?"

I turned to face him.

"I do. Who shares this dwelling with her?"

"I do," said Benin simply.

I stared at him, speechless. He was a child of ten with no parents and I had not thought to ask him where he slept. I, who had slept alone in a stone hut, far from my home and my parents. Shame washed over me.

"You may sleep with the brothers in the monastery. I will have a room made for you today."

Benin smiled brightly, but shook his head.

"I am obliged to you Abba, but I will stay with the druidess. She is lonely and she teaches me many things."

"How is she lonely? Osian tells me that she is of a highborn family."

"That is so, Padraig, but they live far to the south and you do not include her in the festivities of the brothers or sisters at Sabhal Padraig as you do me. Do you dislike the druidess, Abba?"

"Nay, not at all, child. But we are busy here and I think not on her." This was a lie; I thought of her often and my face grew warm. "It is good that she has your companionship, Benin; you must bring her joy." This was true and his face lit up at the hearing of it.

"So she has said. I sing for her and bring her wildflowers."

The simple grace of it, the sweetness, filled me with shame; my face grew warm. My own selfishness came plain to me as I regarded Benin.

"What does the druidess teach you, Benin?"

"The ways of healing and the poetry of the old ones."

"Does she teach you of her gods and goddesses?"

"She does, but she also speaks of the Three-in-One, the One Who Comes."

My sympathy for her loneliness vanished in a wash of anger that she should teach this boy of the old gods. I determined that I would have to remove the boy from her care, but the thought of her reaction left me speechless. I fell back on the purpose of my errand.

"Where is she, Benin?"

"She is in the fidnemid."

I shook my head, uncomprehending.

"In the sacred grove. I will take you there."

"Benin," I said, calling him back. "Why does she keep such grisly reminders here in her hut?" I gestured at the skulls.

Benin smiled at me.

"Those are the skulls of her grandmother and her teacher. She keeps them that their spirits might be with her always. They make me feel safe when I am here."

"They would not do so for me."

"Do they frighten you, Abba?"

He looked up at me trustingly. I thought about his question for a few moments, turned back and looked at the skulls.

"No," I answered. "We are safe in the care of the Lord. We need not be frightened of anything."

"But what of the spirits of the old ones?"

"They are in Heaven, those that were baptized."

A terrified look crossed his face.

"My mother and father? They cannot be with me? They cannot be in Heaven? They were not baptized, Abba."

I looked at his little face for a long time. Then I knelt and folded him in my arms.

"The spirits of your mother and father are with you always," I said. I did not have the heart to discuss the fate of the unbaptized with him. I realized suddenly that all of the people of Eire might feel just so, sundered from their ancestors.

"You have given me much to think on, Benin."

"I have?"

"I see now that I do not understand things in the way the people of Eire understand them. Osian was right. I cannot replace what I cannot understand. I will tear out the hearts of the people."

"Take me to the druidess."

He left me at the fidnemid, scampering away like a squirrel.

There was a weight to the place, I must admit. To say I did not sense it would be a lie. Perhaps it was the weight of centuries of prayer or sacrifice. Perhaps it was just the green silence of the forest. The place that Benin had called the fidnemid was an oak grove. The tree at its center was ancient and gnarled, with twisted arms reaching toward the little patches of light above it. The entire grove was circled by blackthorn bushes. It was silent in that circle, mossy and green. A little stone altar stood at the edge of the circle and she stood there, her hands on the stone, her eyes closed.

She had certainly heard us coming, but she continued to pray while I watched her.

And it was prayer; I could see that well enough.

At last she opened her eyes.

Neither of us said anything for a moment, wary of the anger our exchanges always provoked. At last I spoke first.

"To whom do you pray?"

"I pray to the three . . ."

"But this is well!"

"To the three-part goddess."

"I do not know of this goddess."

"There is much you do not know."

I held back my sharp retort, breathed evenly.

"Tell me then, that I may learn."

Ainfean looked surprised.

"She is the three-part goddess, Brighid-Anu-Dana. She is the protector of women and children, of poets and songs and lambs."

"Are there many of these three-part gods?"

"Enough that I knew that your God was real, the Three-in-One Who Comes. There is the Morrigna-Badb-Macha, the Morrigu, dark goddesses of panic, fear and war; they delight in battlefields. There are the hooded gods, the nameless three. Some of the druids say that they are nameless because they are the Three-in-One."

"I see how well my Lord has prepared the land of Eire for his reception."

She was warming to her subject now.

"Better than you know, priest, for there is the Dagda, the good god who bestows all bounty and Lugh, the Son of the Light, who does all things well."

I held up my hand.

"It matters not how many there are, for the Christ will replace them with his presence and the people of Eire will worship the one, true God."

"Replace them?"

"Yes, the false gods that you of the druids teach."

She laughed in astonishment.

"You think to replace them?"

"Of course. Did you not know that to be true? I thought that you believed that my God is the One Who Comes."

"I do. He will be welcomed here. He has been already. Do you think that you are the first one to spread his message on this soil? Before you there was Palladius. And even now there are others throughout the land, men of Eire who have studied the Christ from afar and brought him home. I know of Ciaran, Ailbe, Ibar, Declan . . ."

I raised my hand, palm up.

"How do they teach my Lord if they do not teach the destruction of other gods?"

"I do not think they speak of destruction, Succatus. They teach of the gentleness of your Christ. They teach his stories. They teach of his promises of Tir Nan Og and of beginning again in his water. Why must you teach destruction?"

"There is only one God!" I thundered it at her.

"You will win many converts that way, Succat. Perhaps you can terrify them into belief. Fool! You must teach your truth and allow the people to hear it. Allow them to come to it because it speaks to them. Threaten destruction and you will frighten them. You will threaten the druids. You threaten me!"

She stopped for a moment and thought about this.

"Are there priests of my sex in your new religion?"

"Some few. Not many. Most women serve as holy sisters."

In truth, I had heard talk of women Christianizers, but the Church ordained few women. And no woman apostle had accompanied our Lord. The wisdom of that choice seemed to me obvious in the company of this woman.

"That is a great mistake, priest. Women are the givers of life and the sustainers. We understand the sacred far more readily than you do."

"The role of women is to give life and sustain it. That is the role the mother of Christ fulfilled."

"Then do the holy sisters give life and sustain it?"

I shook my head in frustration.

"The priests and sisters of the Lord are celibate."

"What is this?"

"We have no . . . relations."

A red flush stained her chest and she looked surprised.

"This is not true. On the continent, I heard of priests who married and fathered children."

I nodded.

"Some do. My grandfather was a priest and he was father of many. Some of us choose to dedicate ourselves completely."

"Is that what you have chosen?"

"I have."

She walked to me then and stood just inches from me. She lifted her face and looked directly into my eyes. The forest seemed weighted with green, so silent and still. A bird whisked from the tree above me. His flight startled me so that I stepped back, but she did not move.

"Why did you come here today?" She asked it low, angry.

"I . . . Osian . . . He is not well."

"Why do you come to me?"

"He weeps and will not eat. I cannot make him say what troubles him."

"Why do you come to me?"

"I thought perhaps he would speak to you."

"Why?"

"You are a druid. He understands your ways. And you his. I am . . . Sometimes I am . . ."

"Stupid," she finished for me.

"That is not what I would say."

"I am happy to say it for you."

I waved my hand at her.

"Enough of this. Can you do nothing to heal him?"

"Can you?"

"I am not a physician."

"His is not a sickness of the body. It is his spirit which sickens; he is overwhelmed by sorrow. You must speak to him of that."

"I have asked him since the night of the dogs; he says nothing, only turns away in sorrow. Damn Dichu for those wolfhounds."

I regretted the outburst as I always did, crossed myself.

She put her hand on my wrist.

The place burned and I stared at it silently. My tongue felt thick when I looked at her. She removed the hand.

"You love him."

She said it simply.

"He has become indispensible here. The people love his stories. I learn from him. He will be a great asset on the journey to Tara."

She looked at me, said nothing.

I spread my hands in surrender.

"I love him," I said.

Amazingly, she smiled at me.

"Does your choice give you happiness, Succat?"

I closed my eyes. I knew what choice she spoke of. The bird in the tree above me began to trill. I sighed heavily.

"My Lord gives me happiness. In my Lord I have found great joy."

I opened my eyes.

She was still smiling. Gently, sweetly. She nodded at me.

"You are a man of some courage."

"No courage but what I have been given. And not enough of that for Eire, I think."

I allowed myself to smile back at her.

"How handsome you are when you smile, Padraig," she said.

"You have called me Padraig."

We both began to laugh then, letting it shake us, filling the oak grove.

"Come then," she said and she held out her hand. "We will see to Osian."

"What is it that makes you sorrow so, old man?"

Osian shook his head.

She rested her palm on his head, bent above his breathing and inhaled. She pressed against his chest and his stomach. He submitted to her ministrations, but turned his head away toward the window, saying nothing.

"Old man," I said softly. "The month is November."

"I do not understand."

"Samhain comes. Soon we must depart for the Hill of Tara."

"You must go without me."

"I cannot!"

He must have heard the real panic in my voice for he turned toward me.

"You came here without me."

"I have learned much from you. More than stories. You were correct when you said that on the first day. I do not understand these people. Not their gods, not their ways. You speak for them to me, Osian. Without you I will be all noise and no understanding."

On any other day my revelation would have made him throw back his head and howl with victory. But now he regarded me seriously, with great sadness.

"I will not always be with you, Padraig. Look at this body. See how old and frail it grows."

I looked, really looked then. His face was folded in on itself and the thick gray hair that he had tied back when he first came to us had grown wispy and thin around his face. His fingers had begun to gnarl and his bones stood out from his shoulders like two escarpments.

I nodded, spoke honestly.

"I see how old the body grows. But must you depart it today?"

This brought a little chuckle from him.

"Sometimes your blunt tongue reminds me of my father."

"Then I am honored."

"Think you that I shall see them again, my father and my son?"

I did not know what to say. The woman spoke.

"You will see them again in Tir Nan Og. They await you at the feasting there."

"I think that Padraig does not believe such a thing."

"Padraig does not yet understand our ways."

"I do know of Tir Nan Og. It is like what we call Heaven."

I smiled at the old man.

"Let me baptize you and give you heartsease. Then your spirit will be in Heaven when it departs your body."

"Will I see my father there or my son?"

I said nothing.

Osian shook his head.

"I cannot let you baptize me, Padraig. For I would see them once again. I would see my father. And Oscar my son. And Caoilte Mac Ronan, and all of them. All of the Fenians of Eire."

He looked away again to the window.

"I tell you that if there is no room for them in your Heaven, Padraig, it is not a place I would wish to go. For no man was better than my father. No man. If the leaves of the trees were gold and the waves of the ocean silver, my father would give them all away, so generous was his heart. He loved everything of the great creation, the glen ringing with laughter and the song of the blackbird, the curl of the wave upon the shore and the whistling of the dawn wind, the magic songs of the minstrels, the great feasts with his Fenians, the baying of his hounds on the hunt."

This thought seemed to trouble him again and fresh tears rolled down his cheeks.

"I believe that your father was a man of great heart, vast courage."

I took his hand in mine.

"Something about these hounds has troubled you. I am sorry that they ever came." I motioned to Dichu's hounds, about to send them from the room, but he stayed me.

"Not the hounds, Padraig. I must ask you this. Do you believe that there is a place where those who loved on earth are reunited?"

"I believe it most fervently."

"Then perhaps Fionn is with her even now."

"With whom?"

"With Sabh."

When Fionn had been chief of the Fenians for several years, he looked to find a wife. Many women offered to bed with him and some of these he happily accepted. But no woman possessed what he looked for, a spirit strong and bright and magical. So Fionn remained unmarried and childless and the Fenians began to worry for him as he passed his thirtieth year.

By this time, Fionn had established a stronghold at Almhuin in Kildare. It was called the Dun of the White Walls and it was there that Fionn retreated when he was not needed for the business of Eire.

There he loved nothing more than to hunt the forests with his beloved dogs Bran and Sgeolan.

One day Fionn was hunting with his closest Fenians. Caoilte Mac Ronan was beside him, of course, as was the young man called Dhiarmuid Ui Duibhne, the beautiful one beloved of all the young women. There was Goll Mac Morna, who had grown fiercely loyal to Fionn over the years and Conan Maor of the evil tongue. They were chasing deer with the hounds hard at their heels when a beautiful white doe slipped from the forest and into a glen of sunlight,

Fionn was immediately taken with the creature and called to his Fenians to follow her.

"Did you see her, Caoilte? She is whiter than the snows of winter."

"I did, but she is most fleet of foot."

"All the better for our chase."

"Go, then. We follow."

With Bran and Sgeolan at his side, Fionn wheeled his horse after the deer and sped into the green forest.

For a while, his fian kept pace, but at last they all fell behind but Caoilte.

"Fionn, I think we should abandon this hunt."

"Abandon her? But the chase grows lively."

"Already we have ridden hard behind her for most of the day. The light is going in the west."

"Mac Ronan, you are hungry for your Fenian woman."

"I am that. I admit it still."

"Go home to her. The hounds and I will follow the white hind a little longer, for I have not the heart to slay her. I will see you at Almhuin."

No sooner had Caoilte turned about and ridden back toward Almhuin than the white doe began to double back on her tracks, turning in a wide circle toward the Dun of the White Walls. Fionn noticed the shift in direction and puzzled at what this might mean, but he gave the hounds their head and followed behind.

By now the light was nearly gone and Fionn was riding in the gathering twilight, following the baying of his hounds, when suddenly that sound stopped.

Fionn reined his horse in a clearing and saw the strangest thing he had ever seen hunting.

The beautiful doe was lying on her side in the clearing and Bran and Sgeolan, who would usually trap a prey and keep it at bay, were whining softly and nuzzling the face of the deer.

Fionn did not know what it meant, but he knew enough not to question things that cannot be explained.

He lifted the deer across his saddle and rode home to Almhuin.

"What?" cried Goll Mac Morna when he saw Fionn cradling the doe. "Will you make pets of our supper now?"

But Fionn only smiled and carried the doe to his own chamber, where he made it a bed of straw and lined it with his own cloak and fed it warm mash and good milk.

That night he settled down to sleep and saw the great dark eyes of the doe watching him from the darkness.

"Hush, now," he whispered. "All will be well."

Fionn awoke with a start. It was deep into the night and the light of the full moon shone into his window.

Standing beside his bed was a woman of such beauty and grace that he could not speak.

She was naked, long of limb and her skin was milky white. Her hair too was almost white and the moonlight cast little lights from it as iridescence casts from snow.

Fionn reached out his hand to her and she came to him without speaking and lay by his side. Gently he stroked her hair and the pure whiteness of her limbs.

"Who are you?" he whispered, though his heart knew.

"I am the white doe of the forests, though this that you see before you is my real form. I am Sabh. I have been hidden in the form of the deer by a dark druid who wished my hand in marriage and who took this vengeance on me when I declined.

"For many months now, I have watched you hunt in the forest with your warriors. I came to know you, Fionn Mac Cumhail. You are of the forest and the wild things more than you are of these walls. I knew that with you I would be protected. That is why today I led you away from your men. Though I feared your hounds, I spoke to them and they heard my language and knew it as the tongue you speak with them."

"He cannot come for you here. You are safe within these walls."

"I am safe with you," she whispered.

She slept that night in the circle of his arms and every night from then on. On the twelfth night that Sabh was with him, Fionn asked her to be his wife.

"Only that you do not ask me out of pity or duty."

"I ask you from the fullness of my heart, for I have known the joys of the flesh before now, but I have not known that my soul could be one with any other soul until you came. And I will never be whole without you again."

So it was that the Fenian warriors of Eire celebrated the wedding feast of their leader Fionn Mac Cumhail. The men of Eire said that there had never been a woman as beautiful as Sabh. The women of Eire said that there had never been a woman more kind or gentle, so beloved was she of everyone.

Fionn loved her with more than his body, more than his heart. He loved her with his soul. He gave up the hunt and he gave up all warring and he stayed by her side day and night.

The Fenians would see them walking hand in hand in the moonlight, pressed together in a passionate embrace, or laughing together in daylight as they played in the fields of Almhuin. In their years together, there was no sorrow at the Dun of the White Walls.

They had three years. Three short years.

The call came from Cormac Mac Art on a warm summer morning. Fionn and Sabh lay entwined in their bed. The sunshine streamed through the window and lit their white hair; Fionn lifted hers in his hand and let it stream down his arms.

"You grow more beautiful with each year that passes."

She laughed and twined her hand in his hair.

"Only that you grow more besotted, Fenian."

"That is so. I admit it with no shame."

Sabh moved her hand against the soft mound of her belly. She lifted Fionn's hand and pressed it there. The time had come to tell him. She kissed him gently.

The knock came on the door.

"Fionn!" Caoilte burst in. He was dressed in his war gear, his cloak still damp from riding.

Fionn stood naked from the bed and handed his cloak to Sabh. He smiled at Caoilte.

"This must be important, brother."

"I have ridden hard from Tara. The king of Lochlan attacks. The Norse ships have been sighted."

Fionn threw on his braichs and tunic. He sat on the bed to lace his boots. Sabh gazed at him white-faced.

"Husband, do not leave me."

He lifted her hand to his lips.

"I must. A man lives after his life, but not after his honor."

Goll Mac Morna stood in the doorway.

"I will keep watch on her for you."

"Only do not leave the walls of Almhuin. Sabh, do you hear me? Stay within these walls where Goll will keep you safe."

"I will, husband. Only return to me. Come back safe to me."

"I will return. And I will carry you here." He smote his heart. He gathered her into his arms. The cloak fell backwards and she clung to him, heedless of the watching men.

When he was gone, she watched his horse ride away and she whispered to the retreating form.

"Husband, I carry your child."

From that day on Sabh watched from the walls of Almhuin. She paced them night and day, watching by sunlight and moonlight, taking little food and only water to drink.

On the seventh day, the people heard her glad cry.

"Look where he comes! Fionn comes!"

She rushed for the gates of Almhuin. Goll Mac Morna climbed quickly to the tower and looked out. It did indeed look to be Fionn, riding his white horse, his hair gleaming in the sunlight, two hounds cavorting beside him. But where was Caoilte Mac Ronan? Dhiarmuid Ui Duibhne? Where were the rest of the Fenians? And the strange way Fionn rode his horse . . .

"No!" Goll Mac Morna roared. "No, lady. It is not Fionn!"

But it was too late. Sabh had flung open the doors and rushed toward the man she thought was her beloved. Before Goll Mac Morna had reached the gate, the figure had disappeared and in the field stood a white doe. She looked back longingly at the gates of Almhuin, then disappeared into the forest.

*   *   *

Fionn returned on the eighth day.

He heard the tale from Goll Mac Morna, who wept openly as he told it.

"We searched all through the night, but we could not find her."

Mac Morna took out his dagger and handed it to Fionn.

"I offer you my life, boy. For I have failed you. Failed you when you had the grace to forgive me the death of your father. Cut out my heart. For I lost it when I lost Sabh."

But Fionn only stared at the dagger in his hand and shook his head.

The dagger clattered to the floor. Fionn smote his heart with his hand.

"Nay, Mac Morna. It was the dark one. You could not have known. She did not know. But I will go and search for her."

"Then I will be by your side."

"And I," said Caoilte Mac Ronan.

"And we," echoed the Fenian brothers.

Days stretched into weeks. They searched the forests and glens around Almhuin and when those yielded no sign of the white deer, Fionn searched the mountains of Wicklow and the Slieve Bloom mountains of his childhood.

When the weeks became months, Fionn sent the Fenians out to tend to the business of Eire and he rode south to his mother, who was then a woman near her seventieth year. She sent the warriors of her husband to search, for she saw the pain in her son's eyes, but in her heart she knew that Fionn would never see Sabh again.

At last, Fionn's heart knew this truth as well and he simply disappeared into the forests of Eire, taking Bran and Sgeolan with him.

No one knows, even now, where he went or how he lived. He returned many months later and he was not the man they remembered. He had grown thin and gaunt and the light had gone out in his eyes. His dogs moved beside him like old men.

He came through the gates of Almhuin and the Fenians clustered around him. He looked at them quietly and spoke like a man who has forgotten fire.

"We must tend to the business of Eire," he said.

And so he did.

By winter, Fionn rode from village to village, checking on the Fenians billeted there, listening to the people, making certain that all of the warriors abided by the Fenian code.

By summer, he went with Goll and Caoilte and Dhiarmuid Ui Duibhne into the forests of Eire. They built bothies and hunted in the old way, but Fionn's heart was not in the hunting; often he would leave the Fenians and wander the forests with Bran and Sgeolan, hoping to catch just a glimpse of the white doe.

And then one day when seven years had passed, Fionn and the Fenians were hunting near a wolf den when Bran and Sgeolan treed a quarry and circled the tree, howling and barking more furiously then usual. Fionn and Caoilte rode up together and there in the tree they saw a boy of seven years.

He was naked and scraggly, his body dirty, his hair matted and unkempt. He made the sounds of wild animals at the men and his eyes were frightened and uncomprehending. But Fionn climbed the tree next to the boy. He pressed his forehead against the forehead of the boy and the poor wild thing calmed. He let Fionn coax him from the tree and he wrapped the little child in his cloak and set him before him on his saddle and took him back to Almhuin.

There the women wanted to fuss over the boy, to bathe him and cut his hair, but when they made to reach for him, the boy clung to Fionn's neck and would not let go.

So Fionn bathed him gently and washed his hair. And there on the forehead of the boy was the strangest birthmark he had ever seen, for it was a small triangle of white, like the soft hide of a white doe.

Fionn placed the tip of his thumb in his mouth then, and bit down. He closed his eyes. In a moment, he nodded, and kissed the birthmark gently and wept above the head of the boy.

Then he cut the child's hair with his own dagger and braided it clean and shining. He dressed the boy in the softest silk tunic and fed him from his own hand, for the boy had no use for bowls or trenchers and ate as the animals eat.

At first, the boy moved on all fours. He had no tongue and when Fionn would speak to him he could answer only with yips and howls and mewling sounds. But slowly he learned the words that Fionn spoke to him and then one day he spoke his first word.

"Fionn!" It came out awkward and strange. Fahn. But the boy was taken with the excitement of it and circled around, dropping to all fours as he did whenever he was overcome with emotion.

Fionn lifted the boy gently to his feet and drew his arms around him.

The little fellow rested his head on the great shoulder.

"Fionn," he said again.

From that day he learned the names of things rapidly. He would point to an item and Fionn would say its name. The boy would repeat the word and the two of them would applaud each other thunderously.

Fionn had a sleeping platform built in his own chamber and there the boy slept. He became Fionn's shadow and followed him everywhere.

Then one day Goll Mac Morna returned from the hunt with a brown doe slung *across his shoulders and the language that the boy had been gathering burst from him in a torrent of words.*

"Mother. Mother."

He ran to Fionn.

"Mother. Doe. White doe."

Fionn looked at the boy strangely, calmly. He put his hands on the little shoulders and braced the child between his arms. The child spoke.

"She kept me. Forest. She deer more. I see more. Her eyes mine. Like mine. Alone. We two. Always. But dark one, sometime. Dark One came. Fear. My mother. Fear. Until he gone. Strong. Her love. For me. Strong. Her body . . . between . . . my body and dark one. Then one day. Dark One came. Struck her. Stick. Struck her. I ran. Teeth. Tore arm. He pulled her. Away. She turned back. Weeping. My mother. Tears. He said, 'No touch. No kiss.' But I ran. She kiss. Here. Forehead. Then gone. Gone. So empty. My . . . heart. Brothers took me. Wolf brothers. I live. Until Fionn. Until Fionn."

"Oh Sabh," cried Fionn. "Oh Sabh, my love. He has spoken what my heart knew. Something of us lives. He is our son. Our son. I will call him Little Deer."

He lifted back the hair over the forehead of the boy and kissed the strange marking there. Then he called aloud.

"Sabh, if we never meet again until Tir Nan Og I will love him and protect him with all my strength and all my heart."

From that day forward the Fenians said that Fionn regained his joy.

"It is a strange and sad tale."

"More strange than you know, Padraig. But I do not think that you believe it."

"I have trouble believing in shapeshifters. But I do believe in evil. I have told you before."

"She was not evil." He spoke it low, ominous.

"Not her. The Dark One. He was a druid?"

"He was."

Ainfean made an exasperated sound.

I waved my hand at her.

"I begin to understand. Some of you turn toward the light, others toward the dark. Is that the way?"

"It is."

"Then he was dark. And his darkness must have hidden her from Fionn all those years. But even his evil could not disguise her goodness, for even trapped in his evil, she was as white as the light."

I nodded, having explained it to myself.

"Yes," said Osian, softly, "that is what I have always thought. Her goodness was a light that shined through even his evil curse."

"And Fionn never saw her again."

"We never did."

I looked at him askance.

"Sabh was my mother." He said it softly.

It came on me then in a rush.

"Little Deer," I said. "Osian. Little Deer. She was your mother? You were that wild boy of the forests?"

"It is why I became a storyteller, Padraig. That I might never be without language again."

I shook my head as if to clear it.

"But then this is not just a tale, a parable of darkness and light?"

"What is this parable?"

"The stories he tells," said Ainfean. She watched me intensely. "The little fables. Like the one about the loaves and the fishes."

"That was no fable. That happened. That was real."

"Ah."

It was all she said.

Osian lifted back the gray hair from his forehead and there on the aged skin I saw it, a triangular patch, white and soft like the skin of a deer.

"I remember this," I said. "I touched it once."

He said nothing.

And then because I was moved by his story and taken in by its strangeness, I did a thing I did not expect to do.

I made the sign on his forehead, blessed the little birthmark, that my Lord might keep this unbaptized heathen beneath his arm.

Osian caught the hand in his own. He lifted it to his lips and kissed it.

"Thank you, Padraig," he whispered.

And I knew that he thanked me not for blessing, but for belief.

What a strange and motley retinue we made as we departed for the samhain feis at Tara. We had made a litter for Osian, but he refused it, insisting that he ride astride. Dichu had provided him with his finest horse, for Osian's horse had vanished on the day he came to us and had not been seen since. Even in his aged frame, Osian was a head taller than most of the brothers. Atop the great horse, he was an impressive figure in his Fenian cloak, the two wolfhounds cavorting beside him.

The druid woman had insisted on coming as well; she was dressed in a white silk gown and cloak, riding a white horse, all of which so angered me that I refused to acknowledge her presence.

Most of the brothers had been raised in Dichu's village and came to horse naturally, except for Breogan, who had been raised in my country and on the continent. In consequence, he sat his horse like an unfastened cloak, slipping and sliding on his leather saddle, his horse starting and blowing beneath him. He was the occasion of much mirth for Osian and some of the brothers.

For me, I rode standing in a chariot, with one of Dichu's warriors as my driver. I braced little Benin with his bell before me and straddled the contraption like the deck of a boat at sea. The riding was just as uneven and unpleasant; I found every excuse to stop a relief, though Benin seemed to think the trip a lark and laughed aloud at any rut or hole.

By the third day of the trip, our high good humor of departure had settled into murmured complaints and vague questions about the distance left to travel. I cursed the Hibernians hourly and wished for the convenience of good Roman roads, while Breogan was reduced to wordlessness, leaning over his saddle and moaning whenever his horse bounced his beleaguered backside.

One of these moans caused Osian to laugh aloud. While Breogan was usually the mildest of all the brothers, Osian's laughter was more pain than he could bear.

"Damn your eyes for your laughter, Fenian. I was not bred to a horse!"

"I did not laugh at you, brother," said Osian. He held up his hand, still convulsing over his saddle.

Some of the brothers hid their faces behind their hands.

"Nay, I laughed at something that happened to my father and his Fenians."

"If the occasion had to do with one of these beasts," said Breogan, "then there could be nothing funny in it."

"Oh but there was. Shall I tell the story and make the time of the journey pass faster?"

Breogan's horse hit a rut in the road and Breogan moaned aloud.

"Nothing could make this journey pass faster," he said.

But Osian began the tale in spite of him.

Often warriors from other lands would come to offer their services to Fionn and the Fenians and such a one was the Gilly Dachar. He arrived one day at the Dun of the White Walls on a horse so large that it dwarfed the war horses of the Fenians.

Now the Gilly Dachar himself was a large man, being more than a head taller than great Fionn himself and the Fenians took to calling him the giant and his horse, the giant's horse.

Gilly Dachar was a rough, crude man. He lacked the manners of a Fenian, burping and slurping, eating his meals like a hound, breaking wind in company and laughing aloud.

But his horse was worse by far, for it would not behave in the company of other horses, biting and kicking out until it broke the leg of a Fenian mount, put out the eye of another and snapped off the ear of a third.

Now among the Fenians was one named Conan Maor. Maor was known for his quick temper and the evil tongue which matched it, and when it was his own horse who lost an eye Conan Maor let loose on the rough Gilly.

"Ye're a bloody brute and no warrior of Eire. We of the Fenians don't want ye

here," he screamed. "But what makes it worse is that ye can't even handle a horse, a thing a Fenian can do from a boy. That great galloping beast of yours is a danger and should be shot or tamed and I'm the man to do it!"

With that Conan Maor drew back his spear, but the Gilly whistled and his horse came charging straight for Conan Maor.

Well, there was nothing for it but to grab the beast by the neck and swing astride. Conan Maor ended up on the back of the huge horse, who swung from side to side with such a wild gait that Maor slipped first to the right and then to the left, clinging to the mane of the beast and cursing for all he was worth.

The sight was so funny that Fionn convulsed with laughter as the horse circled the yard, but at last he saw that Conan Maor was weakening and could not hold on much longer. He called to Goll Mac Morna and Dhiarmuid Ui Duibhne to ride flank on the the great horse and stop him, but the horse jumped the gate and took off across the field, with Mac Morna and Ui Duibhne splitting the wind to catch him.

At last they came astride, but the horse would not slow. Both Mac Morna and Ui Duibhne leapt upon the horse's back; now all three of them slipped and slid, pulling each other left and right. Fionn and the Fenians laughed so hard they could barely see them through their tears.

And that was how the Gilly Dachar managed to get astride Fionn's best war horse and ride out across the field.

The minute the huge horse saw the Gilly Dachar coming, he bolted for the east, the Gilly Dachar hard behind him and shouting something that sounded suspiciously like "Go!"

Now Fionn called to the rest of his fian. They saddled horses and rode out after the retreating group. Before them, they could see Maor, Mac Morna and Ui Duibhne bouncing up and down and side to side like children's dolls.

Eventually Fionn came to see that the Gilly Dachar was urging the horse on; the chase went on for two days until at last the whole group came to the sea.

There Fionn was surprised to see two great warships drawn up in the lea.

The horse of the Gilly Dachar plunged right into the sea and swam hard for the ships, with the now wet Fenian threesome clinging, exhausted, to his back.

The Gilly Dachar would likewise have plunged into the sea, but Fionn's great horse refused. Fionn caught up to them then, and he and his fian surrounded the Gilly Dachar and held him at swordpoint.

The Gilly called aloud to the ships. Boats put out for shore and when they *reached the Gilly Dachar, the men made obeisance before him and brought him a fine robe and a golden brooch and a circlet of gold for his head.*

Then, in the tones of a cultured man, the Gilly Dachar turned to Fionn.

"You see before you a chief of Britain who has heard of your repute in war. We are harassed on our shore by the Norsemen, and I wished to ask your aid, but first to take your measure.

"I apologize for this trick to bring you to the shore, but if you will accompany us to my country, we will reward you richly for your aid in battle."

By now, Dhiarmuid Ui Duibhne and Goll Mac Morna had slid from the back of the Gilly's horse. They were swimming toward shore in their sodden cloaks and braichs, dragging behind them a coughing, sputtering Conan Maor, who could not swim, but who had not forgotten how to curse.

Above the waves, he shouted every curse he remembered, and colored them in with what he would do to the Gilly Dachar when he had him in his hands.

On the shore, Fionn convulsed again in laughter and held out his hand to the Gilly.

"You needed no trick to bring me here," he said, "for my laughter alone would have drawn me. And I will be glad to assist in battle one who has given me this story to tell at the Fenian fires."

The soaking threesome emerged from the sea and Conan Maor crawled up the beach toward the Gilly, his wet cloak dragging, his unceasing curses filling the air.

Though he went with them too, to fight the Norsemen in Britain, Conan Maor's cursing punctuated every telling of the tale for many years to come.

Even Breogan had to laugh at the ridiculous tale. Thus, borne on a wind of laughter, we came to the River Boanne and saw spread before us the Great Feis of Tara.

I have traveled on the continent and in my own country, but even so, the great panorama of that festival left me speechless. Hundreds of dwellings and thousands of people cluttered the plain around the hill.

There were bothies and tents and more permanent houses. There were booths selling every type of ware imagineable, ornaments of gold and silver, beautiful embroidered cloaks and gowns, ribbons for the ladies' hair and mirrors to see them, loaves of bread and pots of honey, steamed fish and sweetcakes.

Thanks to Dichu's generosity, I fed all of our company but Ainfean, who disappeared the moment we crossed the river, riding upriver, away from the feis.

I looked askance at Osian, who said only,

"She goes to the druid rath."

"Good riddance to her," I said, and set about the business of purchasing fish and bread, of selecting a place where we could hobble our horses and sit for our feast. We sat in a small circle and watched the people of Eire mingle around us.

"This is how our Lord must have felt," I said to the brothers, "when he went to Jerusalem with the twelve."

They nodded, their eyes wide, for most of them had never been far from Dichu's little rath in the north, and the festival was astonishing.

I watched it all and asked my Lord what he wished me to do.

The men and women of Eire were splendid, mounted on horseback in cloaks of many colors, riding here and there, up the concourses to the crest of the hill which towered above us, and down. From what I could see of the great stronghold of Tara, it was immense, with buildings abutting each other at the crest of the hill. The longest was a rectangular dwelling hundreds of feet in length. A cheer arose from the crest of the hill. Osian spoke.

"They are racing chariots, Padraig. And the dwelling you admire is the great banqueting hall. In my father's time, it held all the warriors of Eire, great Cormac and all his court, and all the poets and storytellers and bards of Eire."

He looked away across the plain and shook his head.

"What is it?" I asked him.

"Eire has shrunk since I left her," he said softly. "Look around you. Do you see any in Fenian cloaks? Do you see any of my size? Nay, none. Even the feis seems shrunken and small. I do not belong here, Padraig."

"Than your time must have been grand indeed, for to me and to my brethren, this feis is overwhelming."

The brothers nodded silently.

A group of women passed us on the way to the river. They were dressed like birds of brilliant plumage in gowns of blue and green. Their arms and necks were adorned with golden bracelets and torques. Their hair was braided and each braid was finished with a little ball of gold or silver, so that they clicked and made music when they walked.

They stared unabashedly at us in our brown homespun robes and at the huge old Fenian in our midst.

"Come ye from another country?" called one of the young women.

The brothers were staring, tongue-tied, so I answered.

"We do."

"Be ye traders then, or storytellers?"

I knew what the Lord wished of me then. I called back.

"We are storytellers. And on the morrow, we will tell a tale that Eire has never heard before."

They hurried off to the river in excitement then, speaking of us to their friends, turning and pointing in our direction.

I spoke to the brothers.

"In the way of Eire, everyone will know we are coming on the morrow."

They still stared about them and Breogan spoke.

"Padraig, perhaps it would be wise for us to camp a little apart from this place."

I saw the wisdom of his words immediately, for I would lose the dreaming brothers altogether unless I gathered them for prayer and told them what we must do. But as I stood and scanned the plain, tents and bothies, shouting children and mounted riders moved everywhere, as far as my eye could see.

Then Osian pointed across the river, where a hill rose up, opposite the Hill of Tara.

"That is a good place," he said softly. "My father and I camped there often when we came to Tara. The surface of the hill is flat. There is a spring and from the top of the hill, you can see Tara and all of the surrounding plain. It is called the Hill of Slaine."

When we had made camp, fed and watered the horses, I gathered the brothers around me and we prayed. I told them that on the morrow we would go among the people telling the stories of the Lord. We sat by our fire on the Hill of Slaine and watched the fires flicker on the plain and opposite, on the Great Hill of Tara.

Osian had been unusually quiet all day, but now he spoke.

"We will see these fires for two more nights, but on the fourth night of the feis, all fires will be extinguished here and on the great hill. For a moment, the world will be in darkness. Then the druids will light the great new year's fire and runners will take that fire from camp to camp along the plain. Twas a beautiful thing to see that fire blossom like stars along the ground."

I said nothing. An idea had lodged like a seed in my mind and, once rooted, it began to blossom like the great new year's fire of the druids.

15

repare ye the way of the Lord! Make straight his paths! For the Lord our God sends his blessing to the people of Eire. He is the Three-in-One, the One Who Comes. He is the Light of the world and his Light will fill the darkness. His is the Light that cannot be extinguished! Prepare ye the way of the Lord."

With Benin ringing the bell with all the strength his little arms could muster and the brothers riding at our flanks our chariot thundered onto the plain of Tara on the second day of the samhain feis.

I lifted the crozier that the blacksmith of Dichu had made me and shouted my message aloud to the people. I felt the joy of my Christ fill me and lift my voice, so that I was almost singing, my arms raised, filled with the joy of my love for him.

I am an unlettered man; this I have said. But when he speaks through me it is a wind, a light. The voice I lift is not mine, but the one that speaks in my head.

And they were hungry for his message, hungry, for they clustered around the little chariot, hundreds of them. Some druids gathered at the edge of the crowd; I saw them by their white robes, but no one did us harm. Once I thought I saw the druidess Ainfean from a distance, but it might have been the sun glinting from the red hair of another.

I told the story of his birth and of the strange star in the heavens and of the wise ones who came to bring him the riches of the ancient world. When I told of how the inn was full and the stable had to serve, a woman from the edge of the crowd raised her voice.

"We of Eire would have made room for the child and his mother; our hospitality is our law."

"And so you shall. For the people of Eire will light the light of Christ. They will bear his light to all these shores, carry it across the waters into the world. The light of the people of Eire will never be extinguished, for it is the Light of the One Who Comes."

I did not know what I said; it was often this way when I spoke of him. But they seemed to hear me for they murmured in agreement and listened to the tales and when we departed for the midday meal, they ran beside the chariot calling for the stories of my Lord until I promised to return.

Osian had declined to come with us, saying that he would remain on the hill with the dogs and horses. I knew that he did this because the sorrow of the changes in his country overwhelmed him. I once felt that way myself when I returned to my own country after six years of slavery, so I did not press him.

But I was surprised when we returned in joyous spirits from our morning to find Ainfean sitting with him, her face a grim mask.

"Leoghaire has heard of your activities. He confers with his druid Matha Mac Umotri. You and the brothers are in grave danger."

"Who is this Leoghaire?"

I knew, of course, that he was the king of Eire. I knew too that he was the son of Naill of the Nine Hostages, whose warriors had captured me and sold me into slavery so many years ago. I nursed a slow burn for Leoghaire of Eire, whose father had authored my captivity, but I did not wish Ainfean to know. I wished her to return to Tara and tell them my question instead.

The surprise on her face gratified me.

"You do not know the king of Eire?"

"What should I care for the kings of this world when I can know the one who made all worlds?"

She spread her hands.

"The kings of this world have power. You should not underestimate it. Even now Mac Umotri tells Leoghaire that your stories will undermine his rule, that your king will drive out all other kings, that nothing will be the same again."

I smiled pleasantly.

"These things are true."

She stood and braced her hands on her hips.

"This is what you want me to tell Leoghaire, that these things are true? I thought that you were daft at Sabhal Padraig. Now I know it to be so, Succatus. Use caution or all of your efforts here will be lost before they are begun."

I said nothing.

She looked at me in exasperation, then mounted her horse and rode away.

Osian watched me with a crooked smile.

"An interesting strategy, Padraig."

"What strategy is that?"

"I have known you now for seven turnings of the moon, long enough to know you are no man's fool. Yet you let her return to Tara with the message that you do not know the name of the king of Eire. Such a message is bound to spread. The people will be astonished; the king will be angry. His druids will feed that anger. Ainfean is correct when she warns you of danger."

I watched as Benin bent above the evening fire, helping Brother Longan to skewer a rabbit above the flame.

"I do not wish the brothers hurt."

"Then you should take her advice; proceed with caution. Be wise in the Great Hall of Tara. Give obeisance to the king. Be politic with his druids."

"My Lord was not politic. He was direct and true."

The corners of Osian's mouth twitched.

"So caution is not what you intend."

"Was Fionn a cautious man?"

"My father was wise. But had he given his word to do a thing, as you have done, no caution would have held him back. His word was his bond."

"I too am the servant of the Word."

Samhain morning dawned cold and crisp. At first light, I rode alone on horseback to the plains of Tara, ringing the little bell. When enough people had gathered around me, I spoke the message I had composed in my prayers.

"The people of Eire have known many gods. Some are gods of darkness. They feed on death and war; anger them and they will turn against you like a storm. Some are gods of light and laughter; if they are pleased with you, good fortune may come your way.

"But I bring you the unchanging God. My Lord will stand with those who love him. He will never abandon you; he will protect you with his strong right arm. You need not please him by your deeds or by your sacrifices; your love for him is gift enough. He will fill you with his spirit; his voice will sing in you. It is a voice that knows no fear.

"Tonight is samhain night. Tonight you fear the darkness that comes through the door of the world. But I tell you that tonight the Light that banishes all darkness will ignite in Eire. Tonight the fire of the Lord God will burn in the darkness. Tonight, the Light that can never be extinguished will be lit at the heart of Eire."

I left them and returned to the Hill of Slaine. While the brothers prepared the noonday meal and Osian told stories of the old days, I retreated to the far side of the hill, where I knelt and prayed to my God until the sweat ran from my body and my knees bled against the stones. And I did not rise until after darkness had fallen.

I came and sat among them then. They fell silent.

"We must gather wood," I said softly. "We will need a very great deal."

We gathered the wood in silence, none of the brothers speaking a word. Osian helped us, bringing back great armloads. When we had gathered all that we could find, we assembled it in the shape of a horn. It rose well above our heads, there at the crest of the Hill of Slaine.

We stood around it silently. Osian spoke first.

"I know what you plan, Padraig. This is a dangerous and foolhardy thing. But brave." His voice held an admiration that closed my throat. I swallowed hard.

"Brothers," I said softly. "We who serve the Lord must have courage. We must not be faint of heart. Tonight I ask you to light the Light at the heart of Eire. What I ask you to do will be dangerous; we will anger the kings and arouse the fear of the people. You need not stay with me if you are afraid; there will be no shame in leaving, for I love all of you well and would have no harm fall upon you.

"I give you permission to return to Sabhal Padraig, to hold it as a sanctuary for the Lord."

No one spoke. I looked at each of them, ten young men, little Benin. My heart turned over and I prayed to my Lord in the silence of my own heart.

Protect these thy servants, O Lord.

"He will protect us."

It was Benin who spoke. He lifted his hand into mine. I looked at him in awe, for I knew that he had heard the prayer in my heart and that the Voice had answered in his. I nodded, unable to speak.

Below us on the plains of Tara, the fires winked out one by one as we drew close to the turning hour. I prepared torches, handed one to each of the brothers. We watched the fire on the Great Hill of Tara.

It winked out.

Darkness. Stars and wind.

Now! said the Voice in my heart.

"Now!" I cried to the brothers.

We set our torches to the tower of wood. The flames rushed high into the night sky, sparks rushing toward the stars. Shouts and screams drifted up from the plain below, then the answering fire blazed, tardy, from the Hill of Tara.

We did not sleep. We sat in a circle near the fire, our hands linked. Over and over I whispered the words to the brothers.

"Yea, though I walk through the valley of death I will fear no evil. For thy rod and thy staff give me courage. You set a feast in the sight of my ene-mies. You anoint my head with oil. My cup overflows. Surely goodness and mercy will follow us all the days of our lives. We will dwell in the house of the Lord forever."

She crept into our camp only hours before dawn. Her white robe was soiled and dirty, her braid undone and sprouting twigs and sticks.

"Fool, Succat! What have you done?"

"I have lighted the fire of my Lord in Eire."

"You have insured your death and that of the brothers. The hill is guarded by all the warriors of Leoghaire. Let me at least get some of them away. Benin." She reached out her hand.

"How did you come here if the hill is guarded?"

"I am not without certain powers." She lifted a small bag from beneath her robe. "I have drugged the food of some. And some the wine. And some I have taken their sense of things behind my own eyes. They will wake as if from a dream and not remember. I have cleared a ragged path among them, but it is a thread only and it will not last long."

She regarded me with a pleading look.

"I know that you will not go. But at least let me save some of them. Osian will help me. At least Benin, Padraig."

I nodded.

"Yes, take the child and Osian. Brothers, again I say, any of you who wish may go. Go and carry the Lord with you into Eire."

But they remained silent, seated by the fire.

Benin put his hand in mine and smiled up at Ainfean.

"You must trust Padraig now. For he will ask his Lord to protect us and so it will be done."

I looked down at his sweet smiling face. Terror seized at my heart. What had I done? Oh, dear God, what had I done?

I knelt among them and prayed aloud.

"You who have spoken in me from the first. Father, Son, Spirit. Light at the heart of everything. Give me now the words that these your children may be safe. Keep them from harm for your Name's sake."

I knelt in silence. Slowly the brothers came to their knees around me. They linked hands in the circle, lifted my hands into theirs. No sound came; no Voice. Dawn pearled up on the horizon when I heard it faint, in my head, but coming, like a song, like the distant sound of chanting. I stood. I took up my crozier with its crooked stem and its head of bronze incised with the artwork of the smith of Sabhal Padraig. I held it above my head.

"Follow me, brothers," I said, softly.

"You will lead them to safety?" asked Ainfean.

"Nay," I answered. "I lead them to the Great Hall of Tara."

I started down the hill, the brothers in a line behind me. Ainfean and Osian watched our departure. The words which poured from me were not mine but His and I chanted them as we descended the hill.

> I arise today
> Mighty in strength;
> I have called upon the Trinity;
> I have invoked the Three,
> the Three-in-One.
> I proclaim the Oneness
> of the Creator of Creation.

We moved down the hill. I could see the soldiers of Leoghaire. They looked at us, through us. They did not move. I continued the chant, the brothers murmuring after me. I could hear Benin's voice, sweet behind me as he followed me down the hill.

> *I arise today*
> *strong in the birth of Christ,*
> *strong in his baptism,*
> *strong in his crucifixion,*
> *strong in his burial,*
> *his resurrection,*
> *his ascension.*

We reached the bottom of the hill. Still the soldiers of Leoghaire looked upwards as if awaiting our descent. We chanted on.

> *I arise today*
> *surrounded by cherubim,*
> *obedient to angels,*
> *protected by archangels.*
> *I hope in resurrection,*
> *strong in the prayers of the patriarchs,*
> *the predictions of prophets,*
> *the words of the Twelve,*
> *the innocence of virgins,*
> *the deeds of righteous men.*

We reached the river, poled the raft across unmolested. People on the plains of Tara built the morning fires, cooked stirabout in their pots. We passed among them unnoticed. My heart rejoiced.

> *I arise today*
> *strong on the arm of heaven.*
> *Light of sun,*
> *radiant moon,*
> *splendid fire,*
> *speed of lightning,*
> *swiftness of wind,*
> *depth of sea,*

strength of earth
are given me.

The Great Hill of Tara loomed above us and we started up the causeway. Now I could hear soldiers behind us, horses, chariots. They had discovered our disappearance from the Hill of Slaine, but here on the causeway to Tara we passed within arm's length of Leoghaire's soldiers and druids, yet none took notice of us. My heart swelled with gratitude.

I arise today
with God's strength to guide me.
God's might upholds me.
God's wisdom guides me.
The eye of God is before me;
the ear of God has heard me.
God's word speaks from me.
God's hand guards me.
The way of God is before me;
His shield protects me.
His host will save me
from the snares of devils,
from all temptation,
from all who wish me ill
afar and anear,
alone and in the multitude.

We reached the great banqueting hall of Tara and a path seemed to appear in the throng gathered within. I followed it, still chanting.

I summon today Your powers
to stand between me and evil,
to stand against cruel power
which oppose me body and soul,
against the curses of druids,
against the darkness of pagans,
against the laws of heretics,
against all heathen idolatry,

against women and smiths and wizards,
against all corrupting knowledge
that destroys the body and soul.

I confess that I thought of Ainfean with that last. Now we had reached the front of the great hall. I fell silent. I stood before Leoghaire the high king of Eire. He was seated on a dais at the front of the hall, flanked by his queen, his druids, poets and storytellers, yet none of them saw us until I ceased speaking.

Then he stood and the look on his face was one of utter terror.

"How have you come into this place?"

I answered in my strongest voice.

Christ shields me today
Against poison and burning,
Against drowning and wounding.
Christ with me, before me, behind me.
Christ in me, beneath me, above me.
Christ on my right,
Christ on my left.
Christ in the heart of every man who thinks of me,
in the mouth of everyone who speaks of me.
Christ in every eye that sees me,
Christ in every ear that hears me

I arise today
in the mighty strength of the Trinity,
in belief in the Three-in-One,
in the One Who Comes,
the Creator of Creation.

I stopped speaking. Utter silence fell over the hall. Beside Leoghaire, the druid Matha Mac Umotri stood, moved toward us.

At that moment, soldiers poured in behind us, shouting, their weapons raised.

Leoghaire raised his hand.

"How have they come into this hall? You were to take them at first light!"

The captain of Leoghaire's guard stepped forward.

"They did not leave the hill. We watched from darkness onward. Nothing left the hill but a herd of deer and one young fawn. Yet when we climbed the hill at morning, we found the remains of their camp, their chariots and horses, and no one there."

I gave a quick thanks that Osian and Ainfean had escaped them, raised my staff to Leoghaire and drummed it three times on the ground.

"We have chanted the song of the Lord. We have spoken his words aloud. He has protected us in his song. We bring that song to the people of Eire, for ours is the God who never fails."

"Seize them!" shouted Mac Umotri.

Soldiers surrounded us and my last conscious thought was to wrap little Benin in the protection of my arms.

I awoke in darkness. I could hear around me ragged breathing and faint murmurings and I sat up and rubbed the back of my head where a lump testified that someone had found it a fine target.

"Padraig?" said a voice from the darkness.

It was Breogan's voice.

"I am here. Where is Benin? Where are we?"

"Benin is not with us. We do not know where they have taken him. The rest of us are here with you. We are in a hut reserved for prisoners. It is at the edge of the hill. Darkness has fallen. You are not tied, Padraig, but the rest of us are bound hand and foot."

"How long was I unaware?"

"Darkness has fallen. You were struck on the head. Longan has a deep cut on his cheek. My arm is broken. But it is not the hand with which I write."

I laughed aloud, though ruefully.

"Brother, your sense of duty does you justice. Have we no fire or food?"

"They seem not to know what to do with us. They placed us here and left us. Perhaps they hope we will disappear as we did this morning. Padraig, was it we who appeared to them as deer on the hillside?"

"I know not. I know only that the Lord protected us and he will not abandon us now."

There was a soft scrabbling outside the hut and the sudden light of stars. A wind passed over us.

"Who comes?"

"It is I, Padraig. Benin."

Relief swept over me.

"Come to my voice, child."

He found me, placed a little hand in mine.

"They have not hurt you?"

"Padraig," he said, his voice reproving. "It is not the Eireann way to hurt a child."

"I am glad of that. Some of us did not fare as well."

"Leoghaire has reprimanded those who hurt you. It is against the law to hurt the person of a holy man or woman."

Now there was more noise outside the hut and the flap lifted aside. Ainfean stepped in accompanied by a torch-bearer, two women with food, an old man dressed all in white and a grey-haired crone carrying a deer-skin bag.

I blinked in the light and looked around me.

Our little company was battered and bruised. Breogan's arm stood out at an odd angle and Longan's face oozed dark red blood.

Ainfean gestured the old woman in Breogan's direction; she and the old man bent to Longan's face.

The old woman removed smooth flat sticks and a series of cloth strips from her bag. She lifted Breogan's arm in her hands and shook her head.

"It will have to be rebroken for the bone to set, boy. It will hurt."

She gestured to me.

"You. Come hold him from behind. Brace him against your chest and keep his good arm pinned to his side. It will try to lash out at me; the boy will not be able to stop it."

I crawled toward her but my head throbbed so badly that I had to stop for a moment and let a wave of sickness wash over me. Ainfean looked up.

"How bad is it, Succat?"

"Bad enough."

She nodded.

"It is only what you deserve."

I moved behind Breogan, leaned against the wall of the hut and braced him against me, pinning the other arm down.

"I am sorry for this, Padraig," he murmured.

"Nonsense," I said briskly. "You are my brother."

The woman took his arm. She lifted it slightly, positioned her hands. Suddenly she pulled and the bones of the arm made a snapping sound. Two of the brothers moaned aloud at the sound of it, but Breogan made no sound at all. His body sagged back against me and his head lolled to one side.

"Good," said the woman. "His soul is travelling. It will keep the pain apart from him for a while."

She bound the arm between the polished yew sticks, wound them around with linens. Breogan came to and moaned a little. The woman bent to her bag and brought out a little vial. She motioned to one of the food women, who brought her a cup of unwatered wine. The old woman poured the powder from the little bottle into the wine and brought the cup to Breogan's lips. He drank and leaned heavily against me.

"I cannot decide if that wretched horse was better or worse than this, Padraig."

Laughter moved around the circle of brothers.

"I bless you for your courage," I said to Breogan. I felt his breathing go deep and rhythmic. The old woman nodded.

"He will sleep now. He will have pain when he awakes, but it will diminish."

She helped me to lay him down on his back. I touched her aged hand.

She smiled, moved over to Longan and looked at the work that Ainfean and the old man had done.

"Good," she said. "But it is deep and must be sewn."

She brought out a slender needle of bone and threaded it with some kind of gut from her bag. She pierced the skin of Longan's face and I watched him blink back the tears from his eyes. My heart filled with love for these Hibernian brethren and I struggled to my knees and thanked God aloud for their strength and courage.

The old woman finished with her stitches. She rubbed a paste from her bag into the wound and watched Longan's face. In a moment, his eyes registered surprise.

"I can no longer feel the wound."

The woman nodded.

"The relief will be temporary, boy. You must clean it every day with fresh water. Put some of this paste on the wound each time you do."

She put the little bottle in his hand and stood as if to leave.

"Healer," I said, "I thank you for your care of my brothers."

"Only say a prayer to your God for me," she said softly. She slipped out of the hut.

Ainfean came over to me and put her hand on the back of my head.

"Ouch!" I pulled away.

She gestured to the old man and he knelt before me. His gray eyes looked long into mine. He lifted my hand. It grew warm and heavy and he lowered it to my lap.

"What do you do?" I asked. My voice sounded slow and watery.

He shook his head, placed the palm of his hand over the back of my head. The place grew warm and the pain left it; I felt the pain lift and go into his hand. He laid the hand palm up on his lap; it was red and swollen-looking, but as it rested there the redness left it and it returned to normal.

I touched the back of my head. The swelling was still there but the pain was not.

"Who are you?" I asked the old man.

Ainfean spoke for him.

"He is mute, Succat, but he has no need of voice. This is Coplait. He is an ollamh, a master druid. He was once my teacher. Now he is one of the teachers for the daughters of King Leoghaire."

I looked into the grey eyes of the old man; they were gentle and wise.

"Why are you here?" I asked. "I am no friend to druids."

The man's whole face laughed; it was extraordinary to see. His eyes crumpled into the laughter and his smile. He turned toward Ainfean and she nodded.

"That is most true," she said, nodding.

"He said nothing," I observed, but she shook her head.

"He said that you have not been well informed of druids."

"Tell him that I am grateful for the healing of my head. Tell him that I will repay him if I can, only that I cannot risk my Lord."

"Tell him yourself," said Ainfean. "I did not say that he could not hear."

The old man was regarding me closely again, with laughter in his eyes. I felt stupid for my mistake.

"I am sorry," I said softly. "The day has been most difficult."

"So it has," he said.

I heard him say it.

I looked at his mouth in astonishment.

His eyes laughed again.

"How did he do that?" I asked Ainfean.

She shook her head.

"It is beyond you, Succat. But Coplait wishes me to ask you if you will teach him the Faed Fiada."

"What is this? I do not know it." I spoke to her in irritation. "I am tired and do not need your druidry this night."

She laughed.

"It is the Deer's Cry, Succat. The chant you spoke when you walked from the Hill of Slaine to Tara."

"Who calls it this?"

"Everyone. It is all they talk of. The Faed Fiada, the Deer's Cry, the chant by which the One Who Comes protected Padraig and the brothers on the Hill of Tara."

We were fourteen days in captivity. In that time Longan's scar began to heal until he rubbed against it for its itch. Breogan's arm likewise diminished in pain and the lump on my head went away.

We were kept in the little hut, but on the third day we were given a fire. Each day we were fed and given time to perform the necessities. Each day Benin visited us, and Coplait, who brought his druid brother Mal. To them I taught the Faed Fiada.

Ainfean did not return and we heard nothing from Osian, so that I began to worry for his frail condition and his aged body.

On the morning of the fourteenth day Leoghaire sent women to remove our robes and breechclouts. They left us naked and shivering in the November air. I was angry, for I knew that the king had chosen women to shame and embarrass us and I was fairly certain that he had learned of our celibacy from Ainfean. Most painfully, my nakedness reminded me of my slavery, of the poking, prodding hands of Miliuc, my slavemaster, as he checked the muscles of my legs and arms, my teeth, as he laughed at what was then only my shriveled boyhood.

So I gritted my teeth when the woman pointed to my loincloth and stood proud in the body my Lord had given me, though by this time we had all begun to stink rather noticeably.

We had been sitting for nearly an hour when Ainfean arrived. She took in our naked condition, smiled easily and nodded.

"I was right enough that you needed to bathe," she said. She turned for the door. "Follow me to the bath hut."

The brothers remained seated and looked at me with pleading faces, so I stood and faced her. She regarded me directly and shamelessly and I had to think hard for my poor manhood not to show a reaction to her perusal. By her smile I could tell that she greatly wished my embarrassment. But my anger saved me, as it often did.

"If you wish to shame me, that is well. But you will not shame my brothers. Bring the water here if you wish them to bathe, for you will not parade them before all of Tara. You may have sold us into this captivity, but we will retain our humanity in spite of your efforts."

Her eyes looked surprised then, and something else.

"Is that what you think, Padraig? That it was I who put you here?"

I said nothing.

Her chest and face flushed, the red creeping slowly upward from the neck of her gown. She looked at me directly and her eyes blazed.

"I will have water brought to you," she said.

When we had bathed, we were given white robes to wear, then brought before Leoghaire in the Great Hall.

As we filed before the dais, no one rose or spoke. Only little Benin stepped forward, to smile at me sweetly and hand me a strange droopy bouquet of the three-leafed greens the Hibernians call seamrog. I clutched the wilted green circle as though it was the last growth of Earth I would ever see.

At the dais above us Leoghaire and his queen remained seated, as did his daughters Ethni and Fedelm. Mal and Coplait flanked the girls and Coplait's grey eyes smiled into mine.

I knew then that Leoghaire had given orders that no one was to acknowledge us in any way. We stood for a long time before that dais. And then a strange thing happened. I felt the little bouquet in my hand grow warm and the seamrogs seemed to lift their heads a little.

I looked up at Leoghaire and spoke.

"Great King of Eire!" I cried. "I know that you fear my God and the changes that he will bring, but I tell you that these changes will be gentle, like these green stems in my hand. For look where my God has prepared all of Eire for his coming. Your fields are filled with these green seamrogs; see how they speak the name of my Lord! For here the Father-Son-Spirit grow from one stem, three in one green and growing flower. Have you not already been prepared by my Lord in the threesome gods you have named? Is not three the sacred number of Eire?

"Look at my hand, Leoghaire. Look at it!"

He glanced unwillingly at the bouncing seamrog heads.

"See where the true God, the Three-in-One, the Father-Son-Spirit has carpeted all of Eire with his own name!"

Leoghaire stared, his face turning an apopletic shade of red.

From behind the High King, a man in the six colors of a poet stood. A murmur went through the crowd then; Leoghaire turned and glared at the man.

But he moved from the dais and stepped down before me.

"I am Dubtach, ollamh," he said softly. "Master poet of the Ard-Ri of Eire."

I nodded.

The master poet of the High King was a man of much power, second only to the King. This I knew and I knew as well that his word could kill a man or save him, stop a war or cause it to begin. So I waited in silence.

I had not long to wait before Dubtach spoke to the crowd.

"I will take baptism of the One Who Comes!" he cried.

Leoghaire groaned.

"Why have you chosen this?" I asked softly.

Dubtach smiled.

"I believe in the Word," he replied.

They tumbled after him then, Mal and Coplait, the druids and then Ethni and Fedelm, the daughters of Leoghaire. When he tried to stop them, Ethni placed her hand on her father's arm.

"You have told us to abide by the wisdom of our tutors, father. See where they take the baptism. We are women of Eire. We decide for our-selves. We choose the White Christ of Padraig."

Only Mac Umotri sat stony by Leoghaire's right hand. And Ainfean to his left. At last Leoghaire could bear no more.

"Halt!" He stood and raised his hand.

"Magonus Succatus Patricius, I give you permission to preach through-out Eire the doctrine of the new God, for I see that it will not be stopped. And I acknowledge with my poet that you preach it well. Only I forbid you

163

from ever returning again to the Hill of Tara, for I will not be baptized. I am a man of the old ways; they have served me well and I do not wish to be reminded that they will disappear as wind when you are finished."

"King," I cried triumphantly, "I need not return to Tara. For my Lord is among you now and his strong voice will continue the work that his servant has begun."

Then he returned to us our homespun robes and our chariots and horses, my crozier and Benin's bell.

We left with Benin ringing it in joy. On the plains of Tara people crowded around us for baptism, so many that we could not cross the river until nightfall; many clutched bouquets of the seamrogs in their hands.

We found Osian at the crossroad of the great northern and western roads. Though there was a good bruidhean there and an innkeeper known for a liberal hand with food and drink, Osian had built himself a bothy in the forest and was roasting a deer on a spit.

We were joyous as we approached him, singing and chanting snatches of the Faed Fiada, slapping each other on the back and recounting the words of Leoghaire and Dubtach.

He watched us in silence for a while.

"So you were successful."

"Glorious success. The Lord was with us!"

He nodded.

"I am happy for you then."

I regarded him.

"You do not sound it, old friend. You sound like a man about to attend his brother's burial."

Osian's smile was sad.

"Your victories are foretold, priest. They will come when they will come. It is inevitable. But as for me, each place you alter removes me further from the world I knew. My Eire is gone forever. Would that I were gone with it!"

"Do not speak so." I sat beside him near the fire. "You are my teacher. From you I have learned the ways of Eire, the art of storytelling. My victory here at Tara comes in part because I begin to see things in the way your people see them."

"So I am the agent of my own demise."

"Why did you come to me if you knew it would be so?"

"I did not know. I was in the far country with my wife, with Niamh of the Golden Hair. You cannot imagine how beautiful she was, Padraig. Or is. Though I think that I shall never see her again.

"I began to dream of Eire. Nightly I dreamt of my father and of Oscar, my son. I longed to hunt with them in the forests and tell stories by the evening campfires. At last I even dreamed of them by day. I told my wife and she said that I must come to Eire. She warned me that all would be changed, Padraig. She said that I would not find them here. But the longing would not let me go.

"So she gave me the strongest horse in Tir Nan Og and kissed me with tears in her eyes. Then three times she said to me,

"'My love, do not unhorse yourself in Eire. For if you do, we will never meet again.'

"Three times, Padraig. Yet when I saw you and the brothers, the strangeness of it overwhelmed me. That and the voice."

"What voice was that?"

"The one in my head. It said, 'Tell the tales to this one, Osian.' I felt myself slip from my saddle." He shook his head.

His sadness threatened to overwhelm him.

"Tell us of your wife," I said, thinking that his stories would cheer him. "Tell us of Tir Nan Og. Is it an island? Is it far from here?"

But Osian shook his head.

"I have no more stories. My storytelling is finished. I wish only to go into the forests of Eire now and die. Perhaps I can die remembering the days of hunting with my father in the forests around the Dun of the White Walls."

"I will take you there," I said. The thought surprised even me.

Osian looked up. His face showed some interest.

"To Almhuin? To the Dun of the White Walls?"

"Why not?" I said. "We cannot return to Sabhal Padraig now. We must sail while our ship is in the harbor. As my Lord once made a ship ready for me, he makes Eire ready for his name. We must carry that Name before us while the time is right."

Now that I had spoken the idea, I saw the sense of it.

"Breogan," I said. "Who is the most powerful chief in Eire after Leoghaire?"

Breogan shook his head, but Longan spoke.

"Angus of Cashel. He rules all of Munster; the chieftains give him their pledge."

"Then we must go to Munster. And so we shall. And upon our return we will take Osian to the stronghold of his father."

Osian slapped his knee. When he spoke, his voice had some of its old fervor.

"This is good strategy, Padraig. This is a plan to make a Fenian proud. In just this fashion my father bound all the chiefs of Eire to him when he took the chieftainship."

"So you have told me. So we will do."

Osian stayed my arm.

"Padraig. When we reach Almhuin, I will stay there. I will not return with you to Sabhal Padraig."

I looked at him quietly.

"If that is what you wish, Osian, that is what will be done. I owe you much."

"We feast then!" he called to the brothers. "And we give to Padraig the hero's portion, the haunch of deer."

I sat Benin beside me, but we had barely begun our feast when the woman rode up on her horse.

I stood to meet her.

She rode in among us and made to dismount, but I clutched her horse's reins.

"You see us before you dressed as men, unashamed, free despite your efforts."

She said nothing.

"Why have you come back among us, Ainfean?"

"You mistake . . ." she began, but I cut her off.

"I mistake nothing. You did not wish us to come to Tara, but we came. I wondered why you insisted on accompanying us, only to abandon us upon arrival. But you made yourself clear in time. You tried to frighten us away from lighting the fire of our Lord and you would have had us captured on the Hill of Slaine. You thought that our imprisonment would break our will; it did not. You thought that if you shamed us with our nakedness, the people would see us as fools. You thought that we would stand before Leoghaire as men humbled and afraid. So you believed that the people would not follow us. They would see our Lord as weak and powerless.

"You have failed in all your planning.

"I watched you sit beside Matha Mac Umotri. I watched your anger. How it must have shocked you when your own brethren joined us. And you, one of the few among them who would not take baptism."

Her face blenched as I spoke. By the time I finished, her lips were pressed tight together. In the firelight, her eyes looked wet and luminous.

"Well you might weep," I said, unable to stop my anger now that I had unloosed it. "For you deceived us and wounded us and your heart should be heavy with the weight of what you have done."

She looked at the brothers, but they regarded her in silence.

Only Benin tugged at my hand, crying,

"No, Padraig, no."

But though I knew that the woman had cared for him, I knew also that the truth must be spoken.

Through it all, Ainfean said nothing. She looked at Benin and shook her head. She wheeled her horse and rode away into the darkness.

Benin took to weeping when she had gone, but I knelt and gathered him in my arms.

"It will be well," I said gently. "We will care for you now. You will be one with the brothers of Sabhal Padraig."

But his little body shook with sobs; he gasped out his story between them.

"You do not understand, Padraig. I was with her when you were in the hut. I saw. When the brothers were wounded, she begged King Leoghaire for healers. Ainfean said that if the body of a druid was sacred in Eire, the druids of Christ must be sacred as well.

"Matha Mac Umotri wanted the warriors of Leoghaire to take your clothes and parade you naked in slave collars before the people. He said that they would see then that you were but weak, pale creatures and would turn from you. Ainfean pleaded for you. She spoke of the God Who Comes, of the prophecies the druids made of you in the time before you came. She asked that you be allowed to bathe and be given clean robes. Only when Coplait and Mal stood with her did Leoghaire relent. Ainfean said it was because he feared the wrath of his wife and daughters."

A ripple of uneasy laughter passed among the brothers. I knew what they felt for I felt it as well.

Shame. Hot as an iron.

But I spoke quickly before my heart could speak for me, as I so often did.

"You see with the eyes of a child," I said to Benin. "There are things you do not understand."

"I understand the truth, Abba," he answered simply.

When all of the brothers had fallen asleep beside the fire, I lay awake, the truth lodged in me like a stone. Ainfean had not betrayed us; I had betrayed her and I had done it with my fear. Fear of her druidry, fear of her influence in Eire. And yes, fear of my own longing. I admitted it to myself at last, there in the starlight. To myself and to my God. I longed for her, not as a convert, not as an ally. I ached for her as a man aches for a woman. And I hated her for my own longing.

When at last I slept, I dreamed a troubling dream. Miliuc, my slavemaster of long ago, stood over me. I was a shivering lad again, dressed in rags among the hounds.

"You will always be a slave," said Miliuc, smiling.

"I am not a slave now," I countered. "The boy you see before you is not the man."

"The boy I see before me burns with the fire of hatred for all things Eireann," he said. "That boy will always be my slave."

In the morning, I decided that we would go west, to the country of my slavery.

I know what you think to do."

Osian rode beside me. He had been silent for most of the morning, as had we all.

Only Benin sang in his sweet voice, snatches of sad songs. I envied him the heart of a child that need not bind its sorrow in silence. A thin frost crunched beneath our feet; I knew that we would have to travel quickly for winter would come, rainy and cold. We must return to Sabhal Padraig by then or winter elsewhere.

Still, my dream compelled me to Miliuc.

"I do not think it wise."

Osian broke my reverie.

"What is that?"

"You think to go to your old slavemaster and baptize him. You hope that the woman of your youth will be with him and that you can baptize her as well. You think that this will assuage your heart, close some wound you carry, but it will not."

"I follow a dream that sends me here. Surely that is something a Fenian can understand."

"You follow nothing. You run from your shame over Ainfean. She defended you with her voice and her life and you treated her most shamefully."

"What do you know of it? You were in the forest by your bothy fire. You do not know what she spoke or did."

"I know that the child speaks truth. And I read your fear."

"What fear is that?"

"She is a woman, strong and beautiful. You fear to let her into the little circle of your brothers."

"She is a druid."

"You were quick enough to welcome Mal and Coplait. You told me last night that Coplait is a good and wise old man. Her druidry has naught to do with this. Among my father's Fenians were many women. Caoilte's woman was a warrior herself, as were many. We of the Fenians treated each other with respect and love. Do you think that all of your new believers will come from the ranks of men?"

"There are women at Sabhal Padraig. The good sisters . . ."

"The good sisters. Have you looked at them, Padraig? They are women of great beauty, daughters of chiefs. You treat them as house servants, put them to sewing and kitchen labor. You fear the power of women."

"I fear no such thing. I see no power."

"You see it well enough and you fear to see it. The power of their beauty. The way they know instantly what we men must come to by many mistakes. The power to give life and bear it forth. The power to allure. You fear that you might once look at her truly and remember that you are a man."

"I remember always that I am a man."

"Faugh. Your Christ remembered; you do not."

I looked at him in surprise.

"Will you teach me of my Christ now, heathen?"

"You think that I have not listened to your tales? The mother Mary and the sisters Martha and Mary and the Magdalene. I have listened. He surrounded himself with the creatures; he listened to them and argued with them and feasted with them and kept them in his circle of friends. And when they were right, he did as they asked him to do. Ainfean has been naught but honest with you; your heart knows that. But you have not been honest with her. You cast her away because you fear to love her. You wound her for your own weakness and fear. This is not the way of a Fenian."

"You keep trying to make me into a Fenian! I am not. I am a rough priest, unlearned and afraid. There! I have said it! Does it make you glad, old Fenian?"

I rode away from him, stayed besided Breogan and Benin for the rest of the day. Though I knew it was childish to do so, I could not help myself.

*   *   *

171

"Shall I tell a story?"

The fire had died low and Breogan and I had cleared away the remains of supper. Though the night was cold, the bothies circled around the fire were warm enough and the brothers huddled in their blankets were ready for Osian to tell a tale.

Even I was glad to hear him offer; after his sorrow of the previous night I thought that he might never tell another. So I nodded in his direction when I should have told him no.

I should have known that he never told a tale without a purpose.

Fionn was always taking in the strays of the world. Men, women, children, dogs and horses, Fionn took them in and loved them all. For he was a man who believed that anyone could change if the opportunity was given them.

Now at that time there was a king of Lochlan named Colga. He was, as Norse kings always are, a wanderer and a warrior and he hungered to extend his lands beyond the borders of Lochlan.

So with a full complement of ships he sailed to the Ulaid coast of Eire and there set up a stronghold with hundreds of warriors. And he made preparation to battle for the kingship of Eire.

Soon the she-Fenians who guarded the towers and coast of Eire learned of the Norse incursion. They sent runners to Cormac Mac Art, who sent to Fionn at Almhuin. And Fionn saddled his men and rode hard to Tara.

By the time Fionn and King Cormac reached the men of Lochlan, the Fenians numbered in the thousands and the battle was a rout. Colga was killed and those men of Lochlan who were not killed escaped, wounded, to their ships and sailed away, leaving behind none but the bloody dead.

Or so the Fenians thought.

For there among the dead and dying Norsemen was a boy of some twelve years, his body pinned beneath a bigger man, but still alive.

Fionn had spent many months living among the Lochlanders, so he drew the boy out and spoke to him in his own tongue. When he turned to Cormac, his face was white with what he learned.

"This boy is Midac, son of Colga. He has seen his father slain today and this man who was his uncle fell shielding the boy with his body."

"Let us remove him from the carnage and take his measure," said Cormac.

So they took the boy from the battlefield, bathed him and dressed him in clean robes and fed him from their best provisions. The boy was polite and courteous in all things, but his speech was empty and cold.

Conan Maor of the evil tongue watched the boy for a time, then made his suggestion.

"Kill him. He'll be nothing but bloody trouble down the way, for his heart will seek vengeance for his father."

"It is not the way of Eire to harm the person of children," said Cormac Mac Art. He gestured to his wolves, who cavorted around him like puppies. "Even the wild ones of the forest may be tamed if they are treated with affection."

Fionn nodded.

"Our king speaks well. And since it was my grandson Oscar who slew this boy's father, we will take him into our household and raise him as one of our own."

"Oscar? You have not told me of this Oscar." I interrupted the story with my curiosity.

"He was my son, Padraig. The son of my first wife, who died in the bearing of him. He was most beloved of my father." His voice moved with sorrow. "I thought to see him here upon my return, though Niamh told me that it would not be so." He stared into the flames, silent. I was angry at myself for my interruption, feared that we would lose him again to his broodings.

"What of this Midac, Osian? Was he a good adopted son to Fionn?"

Osian made a snorting sound, returned to his tale.

So Midac returned to Almhuin with Fionn and the Fenians. He was trained in the arts of war with the finest warrior women and given tutelage by the wisest of druids. He grew up strong and handsome, invariably courteous and polite, but by his eighteenth year he was known by the name "The Cold One," for he never smiled and was never affectionate either to Fionn or to any of his Fenian brothers.

Now the warriors of Fionn brought up the matter in counsel.

"I warned you," said Conan Maor. "Six years ago. I told you that we should have killed him then, but you would not hear of it. Now look what problem is on your hands."

"That solves nothing, Maor," Fionn snapped. "He is a young man of great courtesy and strength and we must deal with him as he is now."

Caoilte Mac Ronan spoke then.

"He has come to his manhood. Give him lands and retainers of his own, only that they be far from Almhuin, where he will not cause harm among the Fenians."

"This is wise counsel, brother. Call him before us."

So Midac came before the Fenian counsel and Fionn stood and toasted the boy from his own cup.

"Midac, son of Colga, you have come into your manhood. I will give you now whatever land you wish and send with you horses and retainers, builders and brewers and whatever woman chooses to accompany you."

The young man nodded and spoke gravely.

"The Chief of the Fenians"—for he never called Fionn by his name—"is generous indeed. I will take the Isle of Kenri in the River Shannon and the three islets north of it."

Now the Fenians were surprised at the swiftness of the boy's response, for he had not been told that Fionn would grant him land. But Fionn had given his word.

"Done!" he said, and he toasted the boy again, then set the master of the household to assembling all that Midac would need.

When the boy had left the fian counsel, they burst out talking all at once.

"I like it not."

"I said before that we should not trust him."

"He spoke too soon. He planned it long before."

"Those lands would be a perfect stronghold. . . ."

But Fionn held up his hand.

"I see well the strategic value of those islands. They have access to the sea and they would hide any Lochlan ships the boy chose to invite. But I have given my word, and I will not be so suspicious of the boy. We dislike him because he is cold, but he is from the cold north country. Their ways are not as effusive as ours."

And for a while it seemed that Fionn was correct, for Midac built a good stronghold and lived there quietly for many years.

Though no woman would accompany him.

At last, Fionn and the Fenians decided to hunt one summer along the banks of the River Shannon. Fionn sent word to Midac that they would be hunting in his territory and Midac sent back a messenger that he would hold a feast in honor of the Fenians.

Fionn and his own fian arrived before the rest of the Fianna. On that day Midac rode out to greet them.

He had grown handsome, tall and golden-haired and he wore his cloak and helmet in the Norse way.

He was as courteous—and as cold—as he had ever been.

"I welcome you, chief of the Fenians, to my holdings. I have prepared a huge feast for you at my hostel, which I call the Hostel of the Quicken Trees for the beauty of its flaming red berry trees. I will be honored for you to follow me there."

Fionn and Goll Mac Morna and Conan Maor followed Midac down the hill, but Fionn sent Caoilte Mac Ronan to bring Osian and Dhiarmuid Ui Duibhne, who were coming behind with Ficna and Insa, two of Fionn's foster-sons, and a brave Fenian warrior named Fotla, blood father of Insa.

Now the Hostel of the Quicken Trees was beautiful indeed, a huge hall surrounded by flaming red trees the color of blood. It was set on an island in the middle of the river and the only access was a bridge over a little ford. Midac showed the Fenians proudly around his hostel, then showed them to seats in the banqueting hall and called to his servants.

"Bring mead and fruit for the chief of the Fenians and his men. They can refresh themselves while they wait for their company."

Immediately servants entered bearing large tankards of the sweet drink and platters heaped with fruit. Fionn, Goll and Conan Maor drank deep and sank their teeth into the sweet plums.

"You see," said Fionn, "we of Eire are accustomed to eating and singing and boasting. But Midac is most courteous in his quiet way."

"Perhaps," said Goll Mac Morna.

But Conan Maor only shook his head.

It was a few moments before they began to feel drowsy; Conan Maor spoke.

"It was a trap then."

"Do not say I told you so, Maor," said Fionn. "I cannot lift my arm to strike you, but if you say it, I will remember and strike you when I can."

He felt his body go limp and he rested his head on his arms.

Midac entered the room.

"So the great chief of the Fenians loses strength." He smiled. "At last. Did you think I would forget, Fenian? The look of my father's body crumpled on the ground?

175

The weight of my uncle upon me. The iron smell of the blood as it soaked through my garments? A Norseman never forgets. Blood demands blood. Even as you sit here, weak in all your limbs, I have ships hidden in the creeks and inlets of the River Shannon. I have gathered a fighting force on the Isle of Kenri. It has taken me years to plot this revenge, but now I will exact it.

"And I will begin by killing your son Osian and Mac Ronan and Ui Duibhne.

"Think of that while you sit here weaker than a child, chief of the Fenians. Think of how I am killing your Fenians while your legs go out from under you. Think of how I am sweeping across Eire when your piss spills from you unbidden and you lie in your own vomit and you cannot lift even your voice to assist them."

Midac swept from the room. Servants came behind him and extinguished all the lights and banked the fire. Darkness settled down upon the men.

Fionn spoke only one sentence before he lost consciousness.

"Never once in his life did he call me Fionn."

Meanwhile Ficna and Insa, the foster sons of Fionn, had ridden ahead when they heard Caoilte Mac Ronan's message, for they were hungry and anxious to join Fionn at the feast. They came to the hill overlooking the river and looked down upon the Hostel of the Quicken Trees.

"This cannot be the place," Ficna whispered, all his senses aware. "It is shrouded in darkness."

The two sat quietly for a moment watching the little ford that led to the island. There in the shadows they saw three men moving toward the ford. Ficna and Insa tied their horses and crept silently down the hill. The conversation of the three drifted up to them.

"Midac will kill you for this, for he wishes the head of Fionn for himself. But only after he has shown Fionn the head of his own son Osian."

"I care not for Midac. Who is he but an ungrateful boy? We are Lochlanders. Think of the bounty our king will shower upon us if we return with the head of Fionn Mac Cumhail!"

Ficna signalled to his brother.

"Ride back to Caoilte and the others. Warn them of what has befallen here. Fionn must be in danger in the hostel. I will try to hold these three off at the ford."

"Brother," said Insa. "Strength to your arms. If we meet not again here, we shall meet in Tir Nan Og." He climbed the hill toward the horses.

Ficna hurried down the hill and crossed the ford before the Lochlanders. He concealed himself behind one of the trees, then stood as a shadow when they tried to cross the little bridge.

"Who goes?" said one of the Lochlanders.

"I am Ficna, foster-son of Fionn Mac Cumhail. I know what you plan, but I will defend my foster-father with my life."

"Defend then, boy," said the Lochlander, laughing. "For it will be your last act."

Ficna ran at the speaker, his sword outstretched at the end of his arm. He thrust hard and caught the man in his heart, but before he could withdraw his sword, the other two were upon him, slashing his hand from his sword, then thrusting hard into the heart of the courageous boy.

Then the leader cut off the head of the Fenian youth and tied it to his belt. The remaining pair crossed the bridge to the Hostel of the Quicken Trees, but they found the door barred from within.

"Midac makes certain that the booty will be his."

"No matter," said the first Lochlander. "For we have the head of this Fenian and Midac is sure to give booty for this prize."

They returned across the ford and were walking back toward the Isle of Kenri when they encountered Insa, who had given the warning to Caoilte and the others and then ridden hard to help his brother.

In the darkness the Lochlanders mistook him for one of their own.

"We have a fine prize," cried the first Lochlander and he tossed the head of his brother to Insa.

"No!" cried Insa. "Brother, that I had been there to fight with you!"

Insa let out a sound like the howl of a beast, then struck out with his sword arm and cut down the man who had killed his brother, but the other escaped alone into the forest, running hard for the Isle of Kenri.

Now the others rode up: Caoilte and Osian, Fotla and Dhiarmuid Ui Duibhne. They saw Insa cradling the head of his brother and heard his tale. Ui Duibhne took charge.

"Osian," he cried. "Ride hard for the Fenians. Bring as many fians as you can find. For I see that a great battle will take place here. The rest of us will guard the ford against all comers and keep Fionn and the others safe."

Osian turned his horse and disappeared into darkness while Ui Duibhne, Mac Ronan, Fotla and the broken-hearted Insa returned to the isle of the Quicken Trees. They tried the only door of the hostel and found it barred, the hostel silent as a tomb. They stationed themselves to the right and left of the little ford and waited.

The night passed quietly enough. Toward morning a rustling came from the bracken at the other side of the river and in the dawnlight Midac appeared, accompanied by a few Lochlanders, including the man who had escaped from Insa the night before.

"I see nothing now," he said aloud, "but the body of the dead boy. But we will cross the ford and check that my prisoners are still within."

He gestured to two of his men, who proceeded across the little bridge. They had barely reached the other side when Insa leapt at them, killing one instantly with a thrust through the heart. Fotla leapt to help him and together they brought the second man down.

Now Midac gave a mighty shout and waved his whole company across the bridge, but because the ford was narrow and the river deep, they could cross only single file. The battle raged for more than two hours, with each man who crossed engaging with Mac Ronan or Ui Duibhne, Fotla or Insa.

At last, one of the Lochlanders got in a sweeping blow against Insa, who was tiring. The lad dropped to his knees, his lifeblood spilling in his hands. Fotla gave a huge cry and slashed out at the warrior, but the Lochlander crossing the bridge swung his sword and Fotla's head parted from its shoulders.

Caoilte Mac Ronan and Dhiarmuid Ui Duibhne were left alone to defend the ford!

Midac laughed aloud. He shouldered his horse across the little bridge and shouted to them.

"This is your last day, Fenians! You will die as my father and his warriors died. I will present your heads to Fionn Mac Cumhail before I claim his as my prize. And we of Lochlan will overrun the Fenians of Eire!"

A great shout went up from the Lochlanders.

They began to charge across the causeway and some of them threw themselves into the river and began to swim the cold water toward the little isle.

"I will see you in Tir Nan Og," Caoilte called to Ui Duibhne. The two stood back to back, ready to defend each other to the death.

Just then Osian came riding over the crest of the hill, the fian bands behind them. They raised the Fenian cry and drove their horses down the hillside into the fray with the Lochlanders.

Ui Duibhne seized the moment to heave his spear. It caught Midac in the heart and as the blood spilled forth, Midac looked up in surprise.

After that it was over in moments.

When the fighting was finished, the Fenians heard a low groaning from within the Hostel of the Quicken Trees. They surrounded the building and called to those inside.

Fionn answered weakly.

"It is a trap, Fenians."

The warriors outside the hostel laughed aloud.

"This news comes late," Osian called to his father.

"You must open the door," Osian called to Fionn. "It is barred from within."

But Fionn was still weaker than a child. He crawled on his hands and knees to the door and raised himself up by leaning on the wall. Even then he had to wait for his strength to return before he could lift the bar and then he allowed himself to topple to the floor. Then the Fenians raced in and dragged Fionn and Goll and Conan Maor into the sunshine.

But when Fionn saw that the battle had cost the lives of Insa, Fotla and Ficna, he wept and would not be comforted, taking the blame on himself for not understanding the character of Midac of Lochlan. He chanted the Dord Fionn, the battle chant of the Fianna. And the Fenians chanted with him all of that day into the evening until the forest rang with their sorrow.

No one spoke. The fire crackled and sent up a shower of sparks. Benin came to sit beside Osian and looked up at him quietly.

"Were you afraid?" he asked.

"I was afraid. And when it was over my heart was weighted with sorrow at the loss of my Fenian brothers. My father never forgave himself for thinking that Midac could change, for his certainty shed much Fenian blood." Osian looked pointedly at me, then turned his attention back to Benin.

"Shall I sing for you the part of the Dord Fionn that Fionn sang—the part for a fallen brother?"

Benin nodded.

Osian had no drum, but he beat with a stick on a hollow log and sang a dirge that I will remember all my days:

> Ta se ag dul as
> Ta se ag dul as
> He is fading away
> He is fading away
> Gone is our brother
> Gone from his fian.
> Chuaigh se an cnoc,
> Chuaigh se an cnoc,

He went over the hill
He went over the hill.
No more to the green fields,
No more to the sea,
No more to the mountains,
No more to the streams,
Leis fanacht,
Leis fanacht,
Tell him to wait,
Tell him to wait,
Ta an la ag imeacht,
Ta an la ag imeacht,
The day is passing,
The day is passing.

"Your story was not subtle," I said when the others slept.

"Nor did I intend for it to be. No good will come of your returning to your slavemaster."

"I hope for great good to come of it, Osian."

"As did my father," was all he said.

And I could not sleep that night for the Dord Fionn repeating itself in my dreams.

18

How strange it was to see the countryside of my slavery through the eyes of a free man. I did not remember, could not have known then, how my slavery had made each mountain and stream an obstacle, each forest an obstruction between that captured boy and home.

Now I saw the west country as if for the first time. It was beautiful, green and strong with rich forests and brooding high mountains wreathed in fog.

When we reached the wood of Foclut and the little cluster of huts there, I dismounted from the chariot.

A few curious people emerged from the huts and stared at us. An old woman approached; she peered closely at my face. Her face creased in a toothless smile and she nodded.

"You are the slave boy; I always thought you would return someday."

"Mother Mac Ferdiad. It was the people of Foclut Wood who called me back. In all the years of my slavery you were the only people who were kind to me."

"It was more than that, boy. The place had a hold over you even then."

"Tell the story, Padraig." Longan spoke from atop his horse. "Tell us of how the people of Foclut Wood called you back."

I smiled at him sadly, with his boy's face and eager air.

"There was more than just the calling back, brother. There was the coming here. That, I thought I would not survive."

"Then tell us that," said Osian. "And perhaps in the telling, you will vomit the bitterness from your heart and off your tongue." His voice was low and foreboding.

I looked at him a long time before I made answer.

"I will tell it, old man," I said. "I will tell it that you may know why I have come here."

The brothers dismounted then and circled me and many of the people of the little rath came and listened as well. I closed my eyes for a moment, remembering, though it took little enough, so fresh was the sight and sound of that day, so fresh the fear.

"I was sixteen years old. My father's villa was inland, his large one."

I looked around at the huts of mud and straw and smiled at the people.

"It had marble floors and silk curtains at the windows and there was heat in the winter from steaming water and pipes beneath the floors."

The people gasped.

"This is true, Padraig?" asked Longan, in a voice of childlike wonder.

"Just let him go on," Osian commanded.

"It is true," I said gently, to Longan, "but we owned another house as well, a little seaside dwelling where the estuary came in from the sea between the coasts of Eire and Britain. We would go there each summer, my family and that of my mother's sister. My cousin and I were there the summer of the trouble, wild young boys in our sixteenth year."

I closed my eyes for a moment, remembering my dear cousin's face. I dug my nails hard into the palms of my hands and continued.

"We were climbing the rocks high above the village when we saw their ships enter the estuary. At first we thought they were Norsemen, so great were their ships. But they lacked the dragon-prow, and the color of the sails was different. And then we knew they were Hibernians, slave-raiders, the ships of Niall of the Nine Hostages.

"We could have escaped them; we were that far above the village. But there was a girl. My cousin had his heart set for her. I told him that we should run for the forests and the hills, but he could not for thinking of her. Julia was her name; I remember it still. My cousin began to scramble down toward the village. I followed him.

"Oh God, oh God. We could see it all as we ran; the women running for the hills with their babies in their arms, the raiders chasing them, knocking them to the ground. We saw the men of the village fighting them off. I saw the arm of one fly loose into the air when he tried to save his wife with his bare arms, no weapon to hand. By the time we reached the water's edge, blood was everywhere. We slipped in it as we ran. I saw people that I knew, women with their children clutched to their breasts, screaming as they were separated from their husbands. The raiders had set fire to the huts closest to the water. The fire jumped like a living thing from dwelling to dwelling and blew windborn, like tongues of fire, through the air.

"The raiders had the girl Julia. We saw them dragging her toward one of their smaller boats, beached up on the shore. My cousin ran for her, screaming her name. I stood stupidly, paralyzed by all of it, unable to move. I saw my cousin stretch his arms toward her; I saw him throw his body against the raider who held her by the hair. The sword came up; the light from the fire made the blade gleam red. My cousin turned toward me then. His face was surprised; he held his entrails in his hands, spilling over his arms. But his look pleaded with me.

"That look set my feet free. I ran toward him screaming, took his bloody body before me like a battering ram, crashing us both into the raider. He released the girl's hair. My cousin dropped dead to the ground, his body taking me down beside him, and Julia moved toward us as if she were walking under water.

"'Run, Julia!' I screamed at her. 'Run!'

"She looked like a sleepwalker awaking and then she did run, heading toward the rocks, but it was too late for me. I felt the raider's hand lifting me by the hair, tearing at my tunic. My last sight was of the girl Julia standing atop the rocks."

I paused and closed my eyes, trying to will away from me the sight of my cousin's emptied body. When I continued, I spoke with my eyes closed that the brothers might not see my shame.

"I spent the voyage to Eire lying in my own vomit and urine. When we reached these shores, they herded us up like so many of the cattle you Hibernians are so proud of. We were stripped of our clothing; I remember the buyers fondling the breasts of the women. They did try to keep the mothers with the children; that was one grace. I learned later that they had found that the women made better slaves and workers if their children were not taken from them. Cursed Hibernians. Cursed, damned Hibernians.

"For myself, I was stripped naked."

I paused, remembering standing naked again before the druidess Ainfean. Hot shame rose up my cheeks.

"Miliuc examined my teeth and my legs as though he looked at the legs of a horse. He had me lift and chop wood and when he was convinced that I was strong and healthy, he traded me for two cattle, clapped a slave collar and a rough tunic on me and walked me across the width of Eire tied to the back of his cart.

"And I lived for six years in a stone hut with the wolfhounds of Miliuc."

When I opened my eyes, Longan was kneeling before me, tears streaming down his cheeks.

"You must forgive me, Padraig," he said.

"Forgive you? Why do you ask forgiveness?"

"You must forgive me for your enslavement."

"Nay brother, for you had nothing to do with it. And my enslavement brought me to the Lord God, for I was a godless, wild boy when I was young and did not know how to pray. I learned that here in my aloneness."

But Longan remained kneeling before me and Osian spoke.

"You have caused him to drink from the cup of your blame and your bitterness, when you should have poured that water on the ground."

I felt ashamed and said nothing.

Mother Mac Ferdiad spoke from the silent crowd.

"Tell us why you returned, boy."

I nodded.

"It was after I had escaped to my own people. I wanted never to return here again. Nay, it was more than that. I wanted to forget the place completely, never to think of it again.

"But I had not been long at home when I had a dream. In the dream a messenger came to me. Victoricus, he called himself. A Roman name. But he bore a letter from the people of Foclut Wood. And well I remembered you."

I patted the hand of the old woman.

"When I was most hungry and Miliuc would not feed me, it was the people of Foclut Wood who brought me food. When I was most lonely, I crept here in the darkness and sat by your fires and told what little I knew then of the Lord God.

"So it was fitting that the letter of my dream would come from you. Its message was simple.

"'We beseech thee, boy,' it said, 'come walk among us again.'

"I knew then that the Lord wanted me to return and I wept for I wished never to come here again.

"But I have returned. And I bear before me the Lord my God, who is the God of all forgiveness. In Him we will be one people. I will offer baptism to any who wish to receive it."

We baptized five in the small rath. In the morning, when we continued on our way to the rath of Miliuc, I turned to Osian.

"You see, old man," I said, triumphant, "all your forebodings were for naught. I have come to baptize my former slavemaster. I have come in forgiveness."

"I fear that your own bitterness will defeat you, Padraig."

"You are wrong. The Lord will give us a great victory here."

"Just what my father said to Conan Maor at the Hostel of the Quicken Trees."

But before I could frame a biting response, we came out of the forest and the rath of Miliuc came into view.

I had remembered the dun as huge, brooding over the hill above the sheep fields, but it was small and poor, smaller than our own rath at Sabhal Padraig.

The shabbiness of the place made me feel as a stranger to myself, as though my memories were too large for this poor, small place, but I drove the chariot up the hill to the rath with Benin ringing the bell. I reined in before the chief's hall and called Miliuc's name.

He emerged from his dwelling and left me speechless.

I had remembered him as a big man, but he was small and bulky, dark-eyed and almost bald. He raised his hand to shield his eyes and spoke to me.

"What do you wish, Talkenn?"

"Do you not know me?"

"I have no wish to know Christianizers. You are not welcome here."

A crowd had begun to gather and I spoke loud to the old chieftain.

"Nor did you welcome me when I was here before. I was the herder of your sheep and the caretaker of your dogs."

"You were my cumhal! That wretched Roman slave. You owe me, boy. You were my slave. You stole from me my property."

I laughed aloud at the logic, but answered him civilly.

"I stole from you myself, which you did not own. But I have come to make payment, Miliuc. I bring you richer repayment than you could ever imagine. I bring you my Lord, the Christ, the Three-in-One, the One Who Comes."

"You call that payment? I thought you a silent fool when you were a slave. You have grown up to full promise of that foolishness. I wish no god but the gods I have. You Christianizers ruin us. We were strong and fierce; you gentle us and make us good for nothing. You were better and more useful as a slave than you are in this ridiculous guise."

"Let me tell you of my Lord," I called. "He will take away your anger; he will give you a joy you have never known."

"I do not wish your joy. My anger is mine; I will not let you take it."

He turned and went into his dwelling; he emerged with his sword in hand.

"Come, boy. Give me back the life you took from me. Or get you gone."

He brandished the sword in the air.

I remembered his bluster, stood my ground, only placing Benin behind me in the chariot.

Miliuc stepped closer. He swung the sword and it whistled in the air.

From behind me Longan eased his horse forward.

"Cease!" he cried at Miliuc.

Miliuc looked at him in disdain.

"This is between slave and master. Stay out of it, Christian." He spat the word and shook his head at Longan.

"And a good Eireann boy too, I see. You should be ashamed for following the ways of this outlander slave."

"Padraig is my brother and my teacher," Longan called. "Hear him. He comes to bring you the forgiveness of the Lord."

Miliuc waved his a word in the direction of Longan's horse. The blade whirred, caught the light. The horse reared back in fear, kicking its forefeet into the air. Longan slid to the ground with a whoosh. All would have been well, but the horse had reared too far back. It kicked its feet wildly, trying to regain its balance, but it could not. It fell backward and landed hard upon Longan. Longan screamed in pain and was silent.

"No!" I cried.

I leapt from the chariot, rushed at the horse with both hands extended. The frightened horse scrambled back to his feet and shied away. Beneath him Longan lay crushed and barely breathing.

"Brother," I cried. I knelt next to him. His eyes were wide and terrified, but he could not speak.

I turned on Miliuc.

"Have you a healer? Bring a healer, for the love of God."

"I have no love of your God," he said. He turned and disappeared into his dwelling.

A woman knelt next to us. I remembered her as Miliuc's blood daughter. She leaned over Longan, listened to his breathing. She knelt back and looked directly into my eyes. She shook her head.

"No!" I howled it at the November sky. "Please God, no."

I turned toward Osian, who sat behind on horseback. His face moved in sorrow.

"Ainfean," I said. "She would have known. I should not have sent her away."

But he only shook his head.

I knelt back over the sweet young face then, with its fresh scar purchased in my service. Longan had gathered back his voice, but it came out as puffs of air.

"Tell me . . . of Heaven . . . Padraig."

"There will be no pain, no death. Our Lord will be there to greet you, brother. He will open his arms and take you in. He will surround you in light and warmth. 'Welcome,' he will say, 'good and faithful servant.' "

"Bless . . . me . . . Padraig."

I made the sign of blessing on his forehead. I lifted his hand in mine and kissed the young skin, pressed the back of the hand to my cheek. My tears streamed down, making a runnel in the place between his palm and my face.

"Do not . . . sorrow," he gasped. "I will . . . dwell . . ."

"In the house of the Lord," I finished for him.

"Yes," he nodded. "Tir Nan Og."

And he was gone.

I bent over his body, closed it in my arms.

"Padraig!" Breogan cried.

Miliuc rushed at us, two torches held aloft in his arms. He swung them in a wide arc, over my head, past Breogan and the gathered brothers.

"Here is what I think of your new God!" he cried. "For you shall not take me, slave boy. Nor will I see Eire change before me—transformed by a mewling Roman slave."

As he shouted, he touched the torches to the straw. The dwelling of Miliuc went up in a rush of flame. People screamed and ran from the rapid wall of heat and the licking flames. Miliuc turned toward me.

"Here's to your God, slave boy!"

He rushed into the fiery dwelling and was swallowed up by the licking tongues of flame.

I did not leave the body of Longan, though the heat rushed over me. I huddled over it, rocking with grief and shame. It was Osian who pulled me away, riding over me and leaning down from his horse to drag me by my robe through the dust. He deposited me unceremoniously at the edge of the hill and I curled in upon myself, turned away from the flame.

When the fire had died to embers, I reclaimed the ash-covered body of Longan. I carried him in my arms to the bottom of the hill, refusing the chariot or any horse. I walked beyond the hill to the woods line until I found the little stone clochan that had been my slave dwelling. There I turned to the brothers.

"This is a sacred place," I said to them. "For it was here that the Lord first spoke to me. Here we will bury our brother Longan."

We laid him out in the little hut and covered his body with boughs of pine. Over these we put rocks, piling them in a mound both deep and high, almost filling the clochan, that the wolves and carrion birds would not find his flesh.

I prayed the prayers for the dead and we chanted the twenty-third psalm. All night long we kept vigil there, until the first light of dawn, and then I bade the brothers to break the fast. For myself, I walked into the forest to the side of a stream that I remembered from my slavery. I knelt by the side of the water and let the sobs wrack my body.

I wept for brave young Longan, who had died in my defense. I wept for the slave boy of long ago and for the master consumed by fire. But most of all I wept in shame for my pride and stubbornness, for leading these boys into danger for my selfishness, for the wrongheaded way I had treated Ainfean and come to Miliuc and most of all for my hatred of Eire.

For I knew now that Osian was right, that even my great love of the Lord, even his Voice within me, had not erased the vengeance in my heart. And now these deaths were on my selfish soul.

"Forgive me, O God," I whispered. "Forgive your servant for his stubborn heart."

But I could feel no forgiveness moving in me and I bent above my hands and rocked in shame and agony.

I did not hear Osian come through the forest to find me, but when he put his arm about my shoulders I turned to him and wept as a child weeps in the arms of his father.

In the morning when I awoke, the foster-daughter of Miliuc was standing by my bed. She looked the same as she had looked when I was a poor slave boy. I sat up and ran my hands through my hair. I pressed the heels of my palms against my swollen eyes.

"From whence have you come?" I whispered.

"My foster-sister sent for me." She smiled, a gentle smile that my heart remembered. "You must not blame yourself, Padraig. Miliuc was a small and bitter man, always and at everything. But more than anything else, he nursed a hatred for you. He discovered what had happened between us and his anger was fearful to behold. He had wanted me for his own son, but when he found that I had lain with a slave boy, I was no longer worthy. He sent me back to my parents; had you not escaped, he would have killed you, Padraig, slowly, with starvation and cruelty.

"But you did escape and that was a great blow to his pride. He sent for brehons to speak him his rights under the law. He hired trackers, tried to have you followed, though they deemed it a great waste to search for a raggedy slave boy.

"Worst of all for Miliuc, his son Gosacht chose me for wife in spite of his father."

She smiled.

"Miliuc disowned him and hated me. More than anything else, he cursed you, Padraig. I believe he spent the rest of his life praying to every god he knew that he might have vengeance upon you."

"He has been victorious," I said quietly. "For he has taken from us the gentlest of brothers. But I cannot lay all of the blame at the feet of Miliuc. For I too wished vengeance on him. I nursed it in my heart for years, hid it in the guise of making Miliuc a Christian, but it was vengeance just the same."

"You are human, Padraig. He treated you most cruelly."

I took the hand she offered and pressed it to my forehead in gratitude.

I remembered the sweetness of her young breasts and my lips and the heat of my own breathing, a kind of fierce joy in the coupling with her. I kept my eyes closed until the heat of longing and need passed, but when I looked at her I saw that she knew.

"I owe you much," I whispered. "For this and for . . . before. I can offer you nothing but baptism, but that I offer with a full heart."

"I accept that offer."

I was humbled and could say nothing, bending my head before the constancy of her generosity. She spoke gently and held my hands between her own.

"The boy that I gave myself to carried within him a light, a light that I still do not think you see. I accept your baptism because I believe that light will be poured upon me."

That afternoon the people of Miliuc brought us food and drink. They stood awkwardly at the grave of Longan, where I prayed, and then the daughter of Miliuc and the women of the tribe brought forth their golden jewelry for his burial chamber. But I returned their jewels to them, saying only that the Lord wished of all of us the jewel of our spirit and nothing more.

Then the daughter of Miliuc spoke.

"Talkenn, we have heard of the Christ of whom you speak. We know that he is the One Who Comes. My foster-sister has taken the baptism. Now her husband, my brother, son of Miliuc, will take the baptism. As will my husband and I. As will many others of our village."

"Why?" I asked in surprise.

"My father spent all of his life in anger. But you said yesterday that yours is a gentle god, a god of joy. My father knew no such gods, but such a one might have healed him of his darkness."

Hope rose in me then like a spring breeze. I gathered those who wished the baptism and anointed them with water and oil. There at the grave of Longan, I asked my Lord that these who chose him be accounted to Longan's soul.

We did not stay at the rath of Miliuc, for I could bear it there no longer. We turned south for Munster and Angus of Cashel, but my heart was no longer in the journey. On the third day, I gathered the brothers around me.

"My brothers, I came to you a stubborn, prideful man. I believed that I knew all truth and that my way was the only way. My pride has cost us much. Osian warned me that it would be a fool's errand to return to Miliuc, but I would have my way. It is I who am responsible for the death of Longan. I am no longer worthy to lead you in the ways of the Lord, but you are more worthy than I. You must continue the work of the Lord alone."

They gathered around me, not speaking.

I understood their silence. Longan had been one of them. I was an outsider and I had been a harsh taskmaster.

I slipped from the chariot and gathered my little traveling bundle.

I knelt before Osian for a moment.

"We will not see each other again, old man, but I thank you for your wisdom and your stories. Forgive me, please, for my stubborn stranger's heart."

He smiled at me sadly. "I see nothing to forgive, Druid of Christ, but you must forgive yourself. That forgiveness will be much harder to come by, Padraig."

There was a mountain near the sea; I remembered it from my slave years. I had never climbed it then, but I had seen it once, its peak wreathed in fog. I wanted to disappear into that mist, to go up to the top of the mountain and wait there to die.

Had I climbed it as a younger man, or with a lighter heart, it might have seemed an adventure to me. But the way was stony and hard; the hide of my boots was shredded and my feet bleeding by the time I reached the summit.

Silence enshrouded the mountain top. The mist that I had seen from below was thick, like early spring rain, its color like cobwebs. It had a sound to it, that fog, that I will always remember, a whisper, as of something breathing. Now and again the shape of a stunted tree would emerge and disappear, startling me, then fading back into obscurity. No sound moved through the whisper of mist, no birdcalls from the plains and forests below, no wind from the distant sea.

I found a mossy patch of ground and knelt, but though I remained in that position for many hours, no prayer passed through me, no voice answered my unspoken call.

At last I lay down upon the bed of moss. The mist settled over me like a soft blanket and I slept. I dreamed of Ainfean. She was naked; her breasts were the breasts of a woman of middle years, large, no longer firm, but beautiful, comforting. Her hips were round and soft; I reached out my hand to touch her. She was so warm; I drew back as if I had been burned. She said nothing; only her eyes spoke and they contained no anger. I wanted her; I felt the rising strength of my need even in my dream, but when I tried to turn away, she was before me again.

"Look at me, Padraig," she said softly. I looked.

"You are beautiful." I stuttered it out.

"I am a woman of Eire. If you believe in your God, you must believe that this is what he has made, this and all that surrounds you."

"I am not strong enough," I said to the dream woman.

"When you are joyful, then you will be strong," she said softly.

"I will never be joyful in Eire," I answered, but she had vanished and I was left with the reminder of my longing.

When I awoke I was an old man. My robes were gray, as was my hair. My skin was filmy like a cobweb. It took me a moment to realize that the mist had aged me, but when I knew, I left it in place, for I felt that old, so old.

I sat up and leaned my back against a rock and waited. I did not know for what.

I do not think I consciously meant to fast. It was simply that I had no will to do otherwise. There were probably springs on the mountain, but I did not wish to look for them. My provisions were with the brothers, even now making their way toward Munster.

So I leaned there against that rock and did not eat or drink for many days. The mist-covered days passed into foggy nights. From time to time, I would tip to my side and sleep, but I did not follow a cycle of day and night. It no longer seemed necessary.

Once when I was awake in darkness, the fog cleared away. I could see all of the stars of the heavens; they made me wish to weep and I was glad when, after a few hours, the fog swirled in again and hid them from my sight.

On my third or fourth night on the mountain, for I did not know how much time had passed, I addressed Him.

"I did not wish to come here," I began, softly. "My mother begged me when I returned to my home. Begged me never to leave her again. She had lost me once to slavery; that was enough. And my father. The boy he got back from slavery was no longer his son; he was yours. Yours. It was not the same. He served you well, but he wanted a son who could keep his villa, marry and father many grandchildren. And what of me? Should I not have a woman to comfort me? Children for my old age? The sweet hills and rivers of my own country?

"But I came. Here am I in Eire. You will say that it took me too long to return. You see now why I waited so long. What good can come of me returning to a place I loathe? What good? You see what it has cost— the life of Longan, the unbaptized soul of the heathen Miliuc.

"I am a man in whom passions burn. When it is not rage, it is lust. When it is not indignation, it is wounded pride. I am neither strong nor holy, not enough of either for this work you have set before me. And these people. I cannot understand them. Their ways are strange. They look to me for something; I do not know what it is. I cannot give it.

"Let me go. Please let me go. I have planted a seed; let that be enough.

"I wish to die in my own country, among my own people."

There was no answer. I had expected none.

Days passed. I cannot say how many.

One morning an eagle made its way to the mountaintop. I heard it crying overhead. Later it landed on the rock above my head, and watched me with its strange, hooded eyes. For a time I thought that it meant to pluck out my eyes, to feast on them.

"You would feast on bitterness should you choose me."

The eagle cocked his head at me; his eye watched me quizzically.

I dropped over onto the moss and slept; when I awoke the eagle was gone, but the messenger was sitting opposite me. He was the same one who had lighted the candles in the chapel when Osian came. I recognized his white robe with the gold threading, his red hair.

I was too weak to greet him, but from my place on the moss I nodded.

"Victoricus. You have come for me," I said. My voice sounded dry and cracked, like the voice of an old man.

"I have," he said.

"I am glad of it." I had to swallow before I could speak more. "I no longer wish to dwell in this body."

"Leave it then," he said simply.

He held out both hands, palms up. I felt myself spiral up out of my eyes. I was standing beside him in the air then, looking down at the priest on the moss in his brown homespun. I felt a sadness for him. I looked at the messenger and he turned both hands over, palms down. Suddenly we were the eagle who had settled on my rock. We were soaring on the wind above the sea. Below me the water danced with light, and then the shores of my own home, of Britannae, rose up before my eyes. I swept downward, but a gust of wind lifted me and suddenly I was flying over Gaul.

"The distances are small from this vantage," I said to the messenger.

"They are small," he agreed.

Night fell suddenly. We were winging back above Eire; though it was dark, I could see Sabhal Padraig below me and Tara Hill. Little fires began to blossom on the land. As I watched them, they swept across the sea like tongues of foam, speeding toward Britannae and Gaul and even across the wide western sea where no one dwells.

"What flames are these that can cross water?" I asked the messenger.

"This is the fire you have lighted, Padraig. The fire of Christ."

I felt a strong downspiraling wind and then I was lying on the moss, looking at the messenger.

"Drink, Padraig," he said.

"There is no water," I protested.

"There is a spring, just there, beside the stone."

I looked and it was so, though I had not seen it before. I cupped my hand and drank over and over again. The water was sweet and cold. I pushed myself up and leaned against the stone.

"I am not strong enough for the work I have been sent to do," I said to the messenger.

"The Lord is strong for you."

"I am a stubborn, foolish, angry, lustful man and I cannot change."

"Just so, you are beloved."

"Look where my vengeance has cost the life of young Longan and of the unbaptised heathen."

"You need only ask forgiveness, Padraig."

"And I will never be Padraig."

The messenger said nothing. He opened his hand. In his palm there was a flashing green emerald, a blood red ruby, a smooth green stone that looked like the scales of a fish.

"I know these stones," I said. "These are the sacred stones of Eire. The ones from the tale of Osian."

The messenger closed his palm. I felt a weight in my own hand and opened it. The stones lay in my palm.

"We will meet again, Padraig," he said, smiling.

When I opened my eyes, I was leaning against the rock. My hands were empty and there was no spring beside the rock. But I was no longer thirsty. The mist had lifted from the mountains and from far below the smell of cooking food drifted toward me.

They rushed forward when I reached the bottom of the mountain. Even Osian, though he leaned on a stick and looked weak and weary, hobbled forward with joy in his visage. I knew how I must look. My beard had grown scraggly, black striped through with gray, and my hair was long, matted and dirty. I was emaciated and smelled rank, but their faces showed only relief and happiness.

"Why did you wait?" I asked them. "Why did you not continue on as I told you?"

"Of course we would not leave you," said Breogan.

"Brothers," I said, "I ask you to forgive me for the death of Longan."

"There is naught to forgive, Padraig, except for you to forgive yourself."

"That I cannot do."

"That you must do, brother, for we have loosed your sins and thus they are loosed you. This is what you have taught us. This is what the Lord would wish of you. Through us, you are forgiven."

"Besides," said Benin, slipping his hand into mine, "we love you, Padraig."

"Why would you say such a thing?"

Breogan laughed aloud:

"Because you are so much like us, Padraig."

19

The rock of Cashel, stronghold of Angus of Munster, soared more than a hundred feet above the plain, rocks jutting up at angles like the prows of many ships, cleaving a sea of trees and grass. The stronghold of Angus was composed of dwellings of stone, impressive against the sky.

Scouts had met us a day before our arrival. Although we were unsure of our reception, our fears were put to rest at once, for torches lighted the causeway and drummers and pipers led us up the hill and into the stronghold.

There Angus greeted us, his arms open wide.

"Welcome, Padraig and the brothers of the new Christ. We of Cashel are hungry for baptism."

"You know of us?"

"All Eire knows of you. We have prepared a feast in your honor! But first you will wish to bathe from the cold road and don better robes than these." He indicated our worn homespun.

The people of Angus had prepared hot herb-scented baths. For our arrival Angus had gathered silk tunics and winter cloaks lined with the warm fur of seals. We were given our own dwelling, with separate sleeping compartments for each of the brothers and three warm fires down the center of the hall.

And the feast that Angus set before us!

There was wild boar and roast haunch of deer. Salmon was wrapped in grasses from the sea and steamed with leeks and precious salt. There were whole loaves of brown and black bread with pots of honey in chased silver urns. Each brother was given his own goblet and they were filled and refilled with unwatered wine and ale. There were honey-cakes and berry cakes and steaming bowls of hot punch.

We were entertained with storytellers and poets. One of the poets had composed a rosc in our honor called "The Wandering Druids of Christ."

Angus was a huge man with a wild mane of red hair and a booming laugh that must have carried to the plain below each time he unleashed it.

When I had finished feasting and felt my head growing too light to tolerate much more mead, I took him aside.

"Why have you shown us so much hospitality?" I asked him. "Nowhere in Eire have we been better received."

Angus laughed aloud; the man seemed to be composed of sound and laughter.

"I am told that you bested old Leoghaire of Tara, that he knew not what to do with you and at last threw up his hands in desperation. Is this true?"

"In its essence," I answered, "though it was not come by as easily as that."

"No thing worth having is," he agreed and slapped me hard upon the shoulders. "But this is the way I see it. The druids of Leoghaire and the daughters of Leoghaire have come to you, as has his poet, Dubtach. You travel with this simple retinue, yet you are joined by an ancient Fenian most revered by all of us. People flock to your Christ, though you preach him as a simple man of peace. I am a man of politics, Padraig, but I am wise enough to see that something happens here which is larger than you in your homespun robes. So I choose the side of the new god for myself and for my people."

He nodded in self-satisfaction.

A part of me wanted to tell him that his motives for choosing my Lord should not be political, but the wiser part of me smiled and nodded back at him; Angus was the kind of man whom it was better to have on our side than against us. I trusted my Lord enough to know that he would work on Angus in his own time and in his own way. And I couldn't help but like the great chief.

At night, when the feasting was finished, Angus took to asking us for tales.

Osian obliged with the Fenian tales we loved so well, but then Angus asked me to tell the stories of the Christ as well. I obliged, telling of the Lord and often telling of Peter, the Rock of our Lord, who reminded me strongly of Angus of Cashel. Angus must have seen the resemblance too, for each time I told a story of Peter, he would slap me on the shoulder and cry out.

"I like this one of the twelve; this Peter was one of us."

By now, November had turned to December and we approached the solstice, when Christians on the continent had begun to remember the birth of Christ.

I decided to bring that custom here, so on the night of solstice, when the feast was finished and the people had gathered near the fire, I adopted my most solemn tone to tell the story of his birth

"Joseph and Mary were poor people," I began, "for Joseph was a carpenter."

"A good man who works with his hands," shouted Angus.

"Just so," I answered. I continued. "Now there was a king at that time who decided to count all the people of his realm. And he told them that they must all go to the cities of their birth. Joseph and Mary lived in Nazareth, but Joseph was from Bethlehem, so even though Mary was heavy with child, they had to make the long journey to be counted."

"Bad king," shouted Angus. "No thought for his people."

The people of Angus agreed vociferously.

The tale was taking a strange telling, but I went on.

"Now because they were poor, Joseph had to walk to Bethlehem, but he procured an ass for Mary that she might ride."

"An ass!" thundered Angus. "An ass for the poor lass and heavy with child."

"No good," he shouted. "We would have given her a chariot at least."

"And so you would," I said. "But there is more. For when they got to Bethlehem, there was no inn that was not full. No rooms in any of them. Joseph and Mary had to bed down in a stable."

At this, a gasp went up from the crowd. I held up my hands before Angus could say anything.

"I know, I know. Hospitality is the law of Eire. You would have put her up in a palace at least."

"My own home!" shouted Angus.

"'Tis true," his people yelled in support.

"But this was not Eire, and so Mary the mother of the Christ gave birth to him in a stable. She wrapped him in simple linens and because there was no bed, she laid him in the manager where the cows ate their straw. The breath of the animals kept him warm."

"Cattle people!" shouted Angus, who owned more cattle than any chief of Eire. "This is well indeed."

And the people set up a cheer for Christ among the cattle.

"There were shepherds as well," I said.

"As you have been, Padraig," cried Breogan from the crowd, getting into the spirit of this wild telling.

"As I have been," I said and I felt the great glory of the admission.

"They were watching their sheep when angels appeared above them and around them."

"What are angels?" someone called.

"Those of the Other," Osian answered from the doorway.

A gasp went up from the people. I let the answer pass.

"The angels were singing."

"As is only proper for the sidhe," said Angus. I had no idea what he meant, but I nodded.

"'Glory to God in the highest,' they sang. 'Peace on Earth, good will to mankind. For unto you this night,' I paused there, 'this night, is born a Savior. And he shall be called Wonder Counselor, the Prince of Peace.'"

The people were silent now, listening in awe.

"And the shepherds made their way to the stable and looked upon him and they knew. And they went out into the cities and towns and told the people that the Savior had come among them."

"How did they know?" someone called out.

"Come with me," I said to them.

I led them out the door of the great hall and into the darkness. The night was cold and clear; stars twinkled from the vault of heaven. A wind blew up from the plain below and climbed the hill, singing as it came. All else was silence.

"This was how they knew," I said, softly, into the great holiness. And the people nodded.

"Tomorrow I will take baptism of Padraig," Angus said to his people. "All who wish may join me."

I dressed in my fine new silk tunic and my sealskin robe. I carried the crozier our smith had made me and wore the warm new leggings that Angus had provided.

But Angus of Cashel arrived in a simple brown tunic and bare feet on the ice cold ground. I looked at him in astonishment.

"Your Christ was the simplest of men," he said quietly. "I can do him no less honor."

I have never been a respector of kings, but in that moment I became one.

"You are the wisest of men, Angus of Cashel," I told him.

We stood before the people and I faced him.

I rapped my crozier three times hard on the ground to begin and I felt it sink into the soft earth. Then I lifted the oil and water and anointed the head of Angus as I proceeded. Angus had a look of intense pain and stoic suffering on his face as we proceeded and I wondered at what cost he was giving up his old gods. But we completed our ceremony and I welcomed him with the clasp of arms.

He leaned forward and whispered to me.

"Is it finished yet?"

"It is," I answered, wondering at the need for secrecy.

"When is it appropriate for me to tend to the foot?"

I looked down and recoiled in horror. When I had thought to sink my crozier into the frozen earth, I had thrust with all my might. But I had stabbed it instead through the bare foot of Angus of Cashel!

"Good God, man!" I exploded. "Why did you not tell me?" I yanked the crozier up out of his foot.

He looked down to where the foot was now oozing bright red blood and then looked back up at me.

"Because I thought it was a required part of the ceremony," he said.

I wanted to say something unctious and apologetic, but I couldn't. I tried to hold my mouth still, but it trembled of its own accord, folding into a smile and then dissolving into laughter. I laughed so hard that I couldn't catch my breath, leaning on my crozier and letting gale after gale wash over me. The brothers who had been snickering around me convulsed as well.

Angus looked around our circle for a moment. I didn't want to hurt or offend him, though I thought it too late for that, so I put my hand on his arm. But I was too convulsed by laughter to say a word.

Realization dawned on him then and he gave the foot a rueful look.

"Well," he said, "I'm glad to know that Christianity won't be such a painful experience as that."

And then he laughed as well, throwing back his head and bellowing, clapping me on the shoulder all the while.

*   *   *

We wintered out with Angus; it was the happiest winter of my life.

Osian blossomed in his company, proclaiming him like the chiefs and Fenians of old. We spent the winter feasting, singing, telling tales. I grew fat at the feasts of Angus and learned at last how to really tell a story by his fire.

That was the winter I learned to be joyful. It was a feeling I had only known before in the company of my Lord and I thanked Him for bringing me here.

Toward the end of winter when cold days alternate with damp, four bedraggled and weary travelers arrived at the stronghold of Angus.

When he had led them in, warmed them and fed them as he always did, they stated their mission.

"We are druids of the Christ," stated a tall young man with copper hair, and that was obvious enough, for they wore the brown robes and tonsured hair that my brothers and I wore. "We come here seeking the Bishop, Abba Magonus Succatus Patricius."

Angus shook his head.

"I know of no such one."

"We have been told that such a one is among you."

I stepped forward then.

"I am that one," I said quietly.

"Good God, man!" Angus thundered. He had become most fond of that expression since his baptism. "What a strange and unruly chain of names. You were wise indeed to choose Padraig and stick to it."

"I did not so much choose it as it chose me. But you are right when you say it has stuck."

"And I like it well," he thundered slapping me on the shoulder.

I winced and turned to the new brothers, laughing.

"Be warned, brothers, that Angus of Cashel is hard on the shoulders of the druids of Christ."

"But not so hard as the priest is on the feet of the people," shouted Angus and we all broke into roaring laughter. The new brothers stared at us.

"Come then," I said, reaching out my arms to them. "Angus fattens us like cattle and makes sport of us the while, but if you think you can stand too much food and too much laughter, you are welcome to stay with the brothers of Sabhal Padraig."

But the four young men regarded us in confusion.

At last the first one spoke again.

"We have not come to stay with you. Indeed, we had no such intention at all. We are men of Eire, priests and brothers of the One Who Comes. I am Ciaran. These are my brothers Ibar, Ailbe and Declan. You are not what we expected, Abba."

"What did you expect?" I asked then, growing serious.

"We have heard reports of you," said Ciaran. "It is said that you stormed the stronghold of Tara, raising the ire of Leoghaire. Some of the tales say that you can disguise yourself and the brothers as a herd of deer, while others say that a chief of the west burned himself in fear at your coming. Some say that you travel with a druidess and a Fenian of old, while others say you are the cruelest of men. We have been told that you are fearsome and cold and that you force the Roman and Briton ways upon your brothers. We came here to do battle with you, for this is not the way we wish the Christ to come to our country. But we see now that we meet with you that these tales are not true."

"Nay," I said softly, "they are true enough, though they have grown some in the telling. But you see before you a man who is being re-shaped by his God, for the man who came to Eire is not the man of today. Nor is he yet the man he hopes to be. And if you will permit me, Ciaran, priest of Christ, I will make confession to you of my sins."

The young man's face moved from anger, through wonder and rested on surprise. It relaxed into a grin.

"It is true that our Lord is full of surprises, is it not, Padraig?"

"It is the truest thing that either of us will say."

But Declan would not be reconciled to me.

"He is not of us!" he cried. "He is not a man of Eire as we four are. It is only fitting that the men of Eire should bring the word of God to their own country."

"Hush, brother," said Ciaran, "for is he not our brother in Christ?"

But Declan shook his head stubbornly.

"I see what you do not. He looks down his Roman nose at we who are Eireann. He thinks himself better than all who surround him. He considers himself a Roman, and the only true purveyor of the Christ."

It was in some part true and I was shamed for it. I could say nothing. It was Osian who spoke for me.

"Padraig is more Eireann than he knows," he said softly. "Perhaps more than he will ever acknowledge even to himself. But he learns each day. He is a worthy teller to bring the tales of your God to Eire."

"See where the Fenian speaks for him," said Ciaran. "Now will you be satisfied?"

But Declan shook his head and set the line of his jaw.

And though the Hibernian brothers remained with us for the next month, and together we planned the route of Christ throughout Eire, and though Declan was warm and loving to Breogan and all of the brothers, he never once spoke to me directly, but only about me, and then only to disagree with any plan I made.

When April came and the buds began to appear on the trees and the warm wind moved over Eire from the sea, I grew restless to return to Sabhal Padraig and Osian began to long for the Dun of the White Walls.

So we bid our farewells to Angus and to our new brothers and we headed east. We did not know that we rode from joy into sorrow.

20

Yet when Artyr of Britannae left them, after my father had treated him so well and with such kindness, Artyr stole from Fionn his beloved hounds Bran and Sgeolan."

Osian was regaling us with yet another Fenian tale. For each of the days of the journey he had filled us full with tales, telling more and wilder stories as we grew nearer to the Dun of the White Walls.

"Go ahead," I said, encouraging him, glad at his obvious happiness. "How did Fionn get them back, for I know that he did so?"

"He did and more," said Osian, nodding happily.

Fionn followed the thieves to Britannae, the Fenians drawing up their warboats while the tracks from Artyr's men were still wet on the sand.

But now Fionn chose stealth to retrieve the dogs.

He and his Fenians disguised themselves as seamen. Dressed so, they came upon the encampment of Artyr and there Fionn saw his revenge. For not only were Bran and Sgeolan there, tied at the edge of the camp, but there also were the war horses of Artyr. These were not the shaggy ponies of Cymru, nor the small, fast horses of Eire. These were destriers, nineteen hands high, bred and trained to be ridden into battle, a beautiful pair, black and white, mare and stallion.

Thus disguised as seamen, Fionn and the men begged hospitality of the warriors and when the company were well into their cups and telling the much embellished *tale of how they had stolen the hounds of Fionn Mac Cumhail of Eire, Fionn seized upon Artyr and put his knife to the throat of the chief while Caoilte untied Bran and Sgeolan.*

"If you know so much about Fionn Mac Cumhail of Eire, you will know that his beloved dogs are as his brothers. You must pay an eric for this dishonor to my family."

"We have no eric," cried the warriors of Artyr. "We do not travel for gold."

"Choose something or your chief will pay my honor price with his life."

"Horses," sputtered Artyr.

"What say you?" said Fionn, but he did not loose his hold.

"Horses," Artyr repeated.

"A wise choice," Fionn answered.

So he mounted the great horses and rode them back to his boat with Bran and Sgeolan at his side. When they returned to Eire, those horses founded the line of the great war horses of Eire, which survive unto this day.

"Another good tale," I called to him, but he did not answer. I looked back and saw him staring into the distance.

"There, Padraig," he said. "Yon hill in the distance. Almhuin. The Dun of the White Walls."

Indeed the walls did seem to shine with an unearthly brilliance in the April light. As we came nearer, I saw that the whiteness came from thousands of tiny white stones set into the side of the hill.

"So that is how it came by its name."

He nodded.

"It was my father's idea. It was the way the ancient tombs along the Boanne were decorated, Padraig. My father liked the idea that he would be able to see it even from miles away, as we do today."

We drew closer and I felt my mouth fill with sawdust.

Once there had been a great causeway here. We could see its remnants stretching up the length of the hill, but parts of it had tumbled in, making narrow ravines along its length; the way was choked with weeds and vines.

Once too the top of the great hill had been palisaded with a high wooden wall. Here and there a section still stood, leaning crazily into the direction of the prevailing wind.

Osian seemed not to notice the disrepair. His face alight, he rode his horse up the causeway. That brave animal picked his way along between the gaps and growth with the courage of a mountain goat.

I leapt from my chariot and used my crozier to climb and jump my way up the long causeway. At the top of the hill I found Osian looking around in dismay.

It had been beautiful once, even I could see that. The remnants of a great banqueting hall still stood, thin ghostly reminders of former glory. Here and there a cedar post stood like a sentinel, still carved with spirals and braids, with woodland scenes of leaping deer and running hounds. The hunt of Fionn and his Fenians. The circles that had once been huts and smithies, bakeries and storage sheds were scattered about the hilltop, but there were no walls, no thatched roofs to shelter from the sky.

Osian changed before our eyes. He took in the circle, turning round and round like a dog who seeks a place to lie. At last he seemed to crumple into the ground, sitting down hard in just the place where he had been standing. He looked confused and began to speak to himself.

"So it is true then. They are gone. All gone. Until this moment I did not believe it. No descendants. No Fenians. The Fenians of Eire are dead. Now I will believe that the sky can fall. Now the sea can rise and swallow me."

I knelt before him.

"I am sorry, old man," I said softly. "I did not know it would be so."

He shook his head, said nothing.

I knew I had to get him off the hill.

"Come," I said softly. "We will ride a little way apart. We will make camp in the forest. Some hot food will do you well."

He shook his head.

"Here," he said. He would not move. Nor would he speak further.

So we hauled all of the equipment and horses up the great hill, only leaving the chariot at the bottom of the causeway. We used what wood we could find, tearing some of it from the palisades to make rude shelters. The brothers cut pine boughs from the nearby forest and brought them to the crest of the hill for walls and floors. We cooked our food and ate it and I tried to tell him stories to cheer him, but it was no use.

It was like being among ghosts there on the hill of Almhuin. I could feel them myself— Fionn, his white hair streaming, Caoilte Mac Ronan with his Fenian woman by his side, Goll Mac Morna with his single eye and Conan

Maor with his blistering tongue. I imagined Sabh here, wandering the wall, waiting for Fionn and my heart was heavy. Even the dogs felt the strangeness of the place, for they would not settle into sleep, but walked the perimeters of the great hill all night long. I wondered if they sensed their namesakes, Bran and Sgeolan.

We all knew how it was with the old man.

He would not lie down and sleep, but sat wrapped in his cloak, staring into the darkness, as if he half expected them to rise up from the ground around him.

We kept vigil with him, all of the brothers sitting in a silent circle. Even little Benin did not sleep, but sat by Osian's side, his eyes wide. I was reminded of the night before our Lord died, when the twelve could not keep vigil with him but slept instead and my heart swelled with love for these courageous Hibernian brothers, keeping vigil for their ancient friend.

At last I did the only thing I could think to do to recognize his sorrow. I chanted the Dord Fionn, the part for the lost comrades.

> Ta se ag dul as
> Ta se ag dul as
> He is fading away
> He is fading away
> Gone is our brother
> Gone from his fian.
> Chuaigh se an cnoc,
> Chuaigh se an cnoc,
> He went over the hill
> He went over the hill.
> No more to the green fields,
> No more to the sea,
> No more to the mountains,
> No more to the streams,
> Leis fanacht,
> Leis fanacht,
> Tell him to wait,
> Tell him to wait,
> Ta an la ag imeacht,

Ta an la ag imeacht,
The day is passing,
The day is passing.

By morning Osian was feverish, his eyes glazed.

Benin tried to rouse him, singing his sweetest songs, twining his hands into the old hands of Osian, trying to feed him breakfast as one would feed an infant, but to no avail. We rigged a kind of litter for him, lashing together poles from the palisaded walls. We tied it to his horse's saddle so that the horse could drag it. Osian did not protest when we rolled him onto the contraption, nor did he say a thing when we tied him down.

He shivered, though the day was warm and the brothers hurried to wrap him in our sealskin cloaks and to lift water to his lips as one would a dying man.

None of us said that of course, but we knew.

The heart of Osian had gone out of him there on the hill of Almhuin. He was dying and we were powerless to call him back.

Dragging him behind us, our progress slow and rocky, we made our way north to Sabhal Padraig. Each day Osian grew more withered and more remote. He began to talk to himself in the way of the very aged. He murmured names: Fionn, Caoilte, Niamh. Once when I bent above him with water, his face seemed to light with recognition and my heart leapt with hope.

"Oscar," he said, "Oscar my son. You have come for me."

"I am Padraig," I whispered, but he didn't even rouse himself to say that I had used the name I loathed.

When at last we neared Sabhal Padraig in the month of May, he was no more than a wizened shell. God forgive me, but I almost wished his death, that he be spared further sorrow.

And then we met the stranger on the road.

We were one day from our own rath. The spirits of the brothers had lifted at the sight of familiar roads and trees, for we had been gone from our home for seven turnings of the moon. Benin was singing a little song of home when the stranger appeared.

He was seated on a huge black horse some nineteen hands high. He did not dismount but sat facing us in the center of the road. He was a man in his middle years, handsome, with black hair and a ready smile, though there was something strange about him, something of the outlander. He wore a cloak of green and blue plaid.

He looked at me.

"You are Padraig," he said.

It was not a question.

He moved around to the side of Osian's litter. The expression which crossed his face was one of such pain that I put my hand out to him. But he shied his horse quickly away and did not dismount.

He spoke from atop the animal.

"Osian."

Osian's eyes blinked open and he looked up. I bent and pressed water to his lips. He sipped a little and made as if to sink back into a stupor. The stranger spoke again.

"Osian."

Osian turned his head, but the light was in his eyes. The stranger realized. He tightened his reins, but spoke to us first.

"Do not touch my horse or my person," he said. His voice was quiet, commanding.

We moved back with one accord.

He placed himself directly in Osian's line of sight.

The old man opened his eyes. He had not spoken for weeks, but now he croaked out a single word.

"Caoilte!"

The stranger swallowed hard once or twice. He nodded.

"I shall return," he said.

Without another word, he turned the great horse and galloped away toward the west, the direction that had brought us Longan's death so many months before.

Part Three

"After death, I may leave a bequest to
my brothers and sons."

–From the Confession of Patrick

21

"Of course it was not Caoilte Mac Ronan."

I hissed it to Breogan as we stood outside Osian's door.

"He is a long-dead Fenian. But I cannot say that to him. His health is too fragile. And it is all he talks of. Caoilte returning. He will not sleep. He has made us turn his sleeping platform toward the window and he watches day and night, out over the fields to the woods. Neither does he eat, saying only that it would waste time to do so. Brother, I know not what to do."

"Perhaps Ainfean . . ."

"Faugh. The druidess. But you know that she is gone from the rath. Benin has been to her dwelling, ran there as soon as we came to Sabhal Padraig. He says that her skins and powders and herbs are gone. Even her table. He has talked to everyone in the village; they said she left just after she returned from Tara Hill and none have heard from her since. And now most of them will not speak to me. Cursed woman. Cursed hill of Almhuin. Would that we had stayed with Angus of Cashel!"

Breogan said nothing, listened to me rail.

From Osian's chamber came a wheezing call.

"Padraig, see where a rider comes."

We rushed to his room. There was a rider, far off at the woods line, his green cloak billowing.

I squinted.

"It is too far for me to see."

"It is Caoilte."

As we watched, the rider swung his black horse and disappeared into the forest.

"Whoever it was is gone, old man."

"Why did he not take me on the road? Why did he say he would return? I cannot last much longer in this frame."

That much was true. Breogan and I eyed each other over the platform and nodded. Only a shadow of Osian remained. Thin and gaunt, most of his hair thready and gone, what had once been a huge, old man, late of years but strong in body, was a stalk of wheat now, thin and reedy, bent down by the winds of age. His breath was a wheeze. It was hard for him even to lift his head, so we had rolled skins and cloaks behind him that he might see out the window day and night.

"If this man is Caoilte," I shrugged at Breogan and spread my hands, made a sign for him to go along with what I was about to say. "If it is Caoilte, then perhaps he cannot take you with him because you are not finished here with us. Perhaps there is something you must do before you can leave us."

The old man stirred on his bed and said nothing. At last he sighed.

"I have thought this, though I did not wish to."

"If there is something you must do, then you cannot do it in that shriveled body, wasting for food and drink. You must let us feed you."

Again a long silence, followed by a sigh.

"Very well then. Bring stirabout. I will try to eat."

Outside in the hall, I clasped Breogan by the arms and punched him in the shoulders. He was grinning.

"It may not be Caoilte," I whispered, "but if it gets him to eat and restores his health, then well enough. This is the first interest he has shown since we left that wretched hill."

From Osian's chamber, he called out in a reedy voice.

"It was Caoilte, Padraig. And remember that you thought me a long-dead Fenian."

"Curse you, old man," I answered. "You have the ears of a deer."

"Of course," Osian called back.

By afternoon, some of the color had returned to his face and he was sitting up higher against his makeshift pillows, but he still would not allow us to move his sleeping platform.

So I sat in the window embrasure to talk with him.

"Are you happy now, Padraig?"

"I am. I do not wish you to die. Have we made your life so miserable here that you wish to leave us?"

Osian smiled, a small sad creasing of his mouth.

"I have not told you much of my son, Padraig. Of Oscar."

"You have not."

"He was a great warrior, a great hunter. The woman who was his mother, my wife, died in the birthing of him, so he was raised by his father and his grandfather. Together, the three of us were inseparable. But he was as much Fionn's son as he was mine, for Fionn loved him. When I left them, my father was an old man of some seventy years. I was a man upon your years. My son was a man in his twenties."

"Why do you tell me this now?"

"Because you remind me of them. Of Fionn and Oscar."

"I am no Fenian."

"You are, Padraig, though you will not say so. We were honorable men. We protected each other with our lives and when one of us died, we mourned that loss with the fullness of our heart."

I knew he referred to Longan and my heart ached for my young brother. I nodded.

"There was a light in us, Padraig. That light was Eire, the honor and safety of Eire, this green jewel in the sea. And there is a light in you as well. You have come here for your Christ; he shines through you despite your wrong-headedness and stubborn ways."

He chuckled.

"But Eire rises in you as well. I hear it in the sound of your tongue which becomes more Gaelic by the day. I see it in your love of the brothers, your fierce protection of Benin, the way you laugh more now than when I first knew you. They call you the druid of Christ, Padraig, but they are wrong, for you do not dispense the knowledge of Christ. You bring his fire. You are his warrior. You are the Fenian of your Christ.

"So I leave you because I do not belong in this time, nor do I belong any longer in this body. But I do not leave you for a fault of yours, for I love you well, boy."

I stared at him, dumbstruck, rooted to the window embrasure.

At last I stumbled to the side of his bed and knelt on the floor. I took the gnarled old hand in mine.

"Let me baptize you, father. Let me bring you the water of the white Christ, for I would be with you forever in his Kingdom."

"Nay, boy, for I cannot know if my father is there or my son. What of Caoilte and she of the golden hair? I must see them again. I cannot take your baptism. Not now. Not now. Perhaps one day."

He patted my hand gently.

"There is a story I must tell you. I have thought on this and I think it is perhaps the reason why Caoilte has not returned for me."

"Then tell it, if it will give you heartsease. Shall I bring Breogan and his tools? He has had much to do to assemble all the stories you told us during our journeys."

He sighed, a long sad weight of wind.

"Bring him," he said. "Though I do not like to think of this story being written down and passed along the generations."

I paused in the doorway.

"Why not?"

"You remember that I told you that my father had a light in him?"

"I have come to see that light as well. I pray blessings on your father."

Osian smiled.

"I have heard you call them out. I am glad of it. But you will remember too that I told you that there was only one time in his long life that I ever saw my father betray that light."

I held up my hand.

"Do not tell me a story that will make me think badly of Fionn. For I do not wish to know it."

But he shook his head.

"I think I must tell it, Padraig, for you carry that light in you and I would not have you betray it."

Now I sighed. Osian laughed.

"I told you once that you sighed like an Eireann."

"It is not the only bad habit I have acquired here."

"Bring Breogan," said Osian.

"Must all your tales have a purpose in the telling?"

Osian looked thoughtful at this.

"I did not intend them that way when I came here. In truth I knew not why I came. But they seem to have formed themselves that way, Padraig.

Your God moves between us like a weaver between the walls of a loom. It is most interesting. Lately I have thought on it much. It seems to me that the One Who Comes is here, between us."

I stood silent in the doorway.

He nodded, as if he was carrying on some internal conversation.

"Bring Breogan," he said. "It must be told."

After Sabh died, Fionn took no woman to wife, nor women to his bed. He contented himself with his son and his Fenians, with the business of Eire and the life of the forests. He was happy enough, but when almost twenty years went by and the boy Osian was a young man, the Fenians began to worry about Fionn.

"See where the boy is become a young man. He has eighteen years. He will go his way in the world and Fionn will be as lonely as he was when Sabh died." Goll Mac Morna spoke glumly and speared a piece of deer haunch with his knife.

From behind Caoilte Mac Ronan, his Fenian wife Aindir spoke teasingly.

"You are a man past your seventy-fifth year, Mac Morna. Why are you worrying on the subject of women?"

"Damn trouble the lot of 'em," said Conal Maor. "He's better without one."

"Trouble to one such as you," Caoilte's wife shot back. She kneaded hard at Caoilte's neck muscles.

"Ouch, woman. Will you kill me then with your anger at Maor? Fenians," Caoilte said quietly, "look where we argue among ourselves over Fionn's lack of a woman. It proves that it is much on our minds. Let us choose for him a woman we think would make a wife, then make the proposal to him. If he does not wish to have her, he will say no. We can do no more."

Aindir stopped rubbing Caoilte's shoulders.

"I have heard something interesting. Cormac Mac Art has a beautiful daughter, Grainne."

"I have seen her," said Caoilte. "She is indeed beautiful." He formed his hands in the shape of a woman. His wife boxed him on the side of the ear. Caoilte laughed aloud. He reached behind him and swung her onto his lap, tickling her.

"Ye sicken us with these displays," said Conan Maor. "Ye've been married thirty years. Ye should be past this foolishness."

"Leave them alone," grumbled Goll Mac Morna. "It goes soon enough. Let them enjoy themselves while they have each other. Besides, Fionn is younger than Caoilte by three years, so it proves my point."

"He's a man fast approaching his fifth decade," said Conan Maor. "What would the young daughter of Cormac wish with him?"

Aindir sat up and straightened her tunic. She exchanged a promising glance with Caoilte.

"Well, that's just it. I have heard that young men have made offers for her hand. Many have done so. She has declined them all. But Fionn is chief of the Fenians. In him she would win a prize."

"She would win a man past his prime years," said Conan Maor.

"Fionn is no such thing," protested Aindir. "He is strong and full of life. He rides each day with Osian. He can swim the lake faster than any Fenian among us, walk further and longer, disappear more silently into the forest. He is broad of shoulder, his legs are strong and he is . . . firm."

"You have been taking a great deal of notice of Fionn," Caoilte growled good-naturedly.

Aindir laughed.

"All women notice Fionn. Grainne will notice him. And a man that age knows how to love a woman well." Aindir leaned against Caoilte.

He seemed in a hurry to leave suddenly.

"It is settled then. We will present the idea to Fionn tomorrow night at supper. And now goodnight, brothers." He took Aindir's hand and they left the circle.

"Disgusting," said Conan Maor.

"I only wish it was me," grumbled Goll Mac Morna.

"What need I of wife?" Fionn took a deep draught of ale and grinned at the circle of Fenians. "Do you worry that I will lose one of my strengths if I do not use it?"

Caoilte laughed aloud.

"Nay, but look at Osian."

Fionn turned and looked at his son, who sat beside him. Osian was a muscular youth of eighteen years. Already women were beginning to notice him.

Fionn nodded.

"Let us offer him to Grainne, daughter of Cormac. He is a fine specimen."

But Osian laughed aloud and held up his hand.

"I would wish to choose my own woman. Or to let her choose me. The king's daughter is a difficult one. I have heard it said among the Fenians."

"Is she now?" said Fionn. "Well, let us go to Tara and have a look at her."

*   *   *

They feasted in the great banqueting hall at Tara. Grainne served the wine and Fionn watched her as she did so. She was beautiful indeed, her hair long and black, her skin milky white, her form strong and broad-shouldered. But she was not Sabh, and Fionn was not moved.

Grainne knew, of course, that Fionn was there to think of her as a bride choice. She had braided her hair and decorated it with balls of gold and silver. She wore her finest blue silk tunic and a cloak of spun wool embroidered with chasings of red and purple, green and gold.

But when she saw Fionn, she was disappointed, for he was a man past the fullness of manhood. She had turned down many suitors, waiting for just the right one. In fact, she was in her twenty-third year, for the number she had declined and she did not wish an old man to husband.

She deliberately bent low when she poured his wine, let her tunic slip forward. She watched Fionn's reaction. He looked, seemed to nod to himself, but that was all. This was not the reaction of a man besotted.

Fionn's reaction irritated Grainne, who saw herself as the most beautiful of women. She took herself to her chamber and sat with her women working embroidery, but she knotted the threads and tore at them with her teeth. Her women had learned to be wary of Grainne when she was in one of these moods, so they sat silent beside her in the chamber. At last she took herself to the hillside for a walk and there she saw Dhiarmuid Ui Duibhne.

Dhiarmuid was younger than Fionn by more than a decade, a man in his middle thirties. Among the Fenians, he was called "the love spot," for he had a small red birthmark like a strawberry high on his right cheek, just beneath his hairline. The Fenians liked to joke that it was that mark which led women to love him.

Dhiarmuid was handsome and strong and proud. He was broad-chested and tall, but his manners with women were courtly and gentle. He had had more of them than most of the Fenians assembled and none of those women wished him ill when their time together was over. But though many women loved Dhiarmuid, he gave his heart to none.

Grainne approached him through the dusk.

"I see by your cloak that you are a Fenian. Why are you not at the banquet?"

"I have just ridden in from the north," he said smiling pleasantly. "And now I am glad that I have done so."

"Why is that?"

"To spend just these few minutes in your beauty is worth the length of any ride."

It was Dhiarmuid's usual patter with women, but it assuaged the wounded pride of Grainne, who was still smarting over Fionn's disinterest. She laughed a low laugh and leaned toward him.

"Your tongue is as fine as the rest of you, Fenian."

Dhiarmuid laughed in delight for he was unaccustomed to a woman who could parry with him.

"My tongue would spend more time . . . praising your beauty."

"And is that all it does, Fenian? Praise?"

Quick as lightning his arm was around her, his mouth pressed to hers, his tongue darting against hers. She kissed him back full measure and when he stopped, she leaned against him laughing.

"Do they call you Quick-Tongue then?"

"Nay, they call me the Love Spot."

"Ah and what spot on you is made for love, Quick-Tongue?"

Dhiarmuid turned his cheek to her and laughed.

"It is this."

She traced her finger along the strawberry.

"I think it is not the only spot. Perhaps if you come to my chamber this night we can find those other parts of you that are made for love."

Dhiarmuid laughed aloud.

"You are quick," he said. "I like that well. But I promise you that I will be slow."

"I look forward to our time together then," said Grainne. And she left without telling him her name.

Meanwhile at the banquet, Fionn turned to Cormac Mac Art.

"Old friend, your daughter is beautiful indeed, but I do not think that she wishes me to husband. And in truth, my heart is full still with Sabh, whose memory never leaves me."

Cormac nodded.

"Only I ask that you go and talk to her yourself, Fionn. We have been friends for many years; I tell you honestly that my daughter is the most difficult of women. Her mother has been dead too long; she has had no woman's influence to shape her kindness. She has refused many suitors and has done so by telling them simply that I did not wish them for her. Can you imagine how many enemies this has made me? Men who are noble in birth, men who are warriors, who believed that I found them unworthy for my daughter! I have had to assuage much wounded pride and I would not have that between us."

Fionn laughed.

"You fear your own daughter!"

Cormac leaned close and whispered.

"In truth, I dislike her, Fionn. I am glad of your choice, for she would only bring you heartache."

After the banquet, Fionn went to the grianan, the sun hall of the women. Night had fallen and guttering torches led the way through the halls. Fionn spoke to one of the women.

"I seek Grainne, daughter of the high king."

The woman pointed at a doorway, but even as she did so, she shook her head at Fionn.

But Fionn knocked on the door and entered when she bade him to.

Grainne was naked to the waste, bathing her breasts with the water of sweet herbs. Her hair was damp from the steam and curled around her face, which was flushed in the firelight.

When she saw Fionn her eyes went wide, for she had expected Dhiarmuid Ui Duibhne. But she knew now that Fionn would not offer for her hand and she still smarted from his disinterest in her at the banquet. So she deliberately did not cover herself.

"Good evening, Fenian," she said, politely. She continued bathing and she was indeed beautiful, her breasts large, her shoulders broad. Fionn watched her quietly, unmoving. He had forgotten the look of a beautiful woman at her bath and it excited him.

She let him watch her.

"Will you help me at the bath, Fenian? It seems to interest you so."

Fionn stepped forward. He took the cloth from her hand and dipped it in the water. He squeezed the water over the tops of her breasts and watched the rivulets of it run along the white flesh. She did not move, but her nipples grew hard.

Something that had been asleep in Fionn for a long time awakened. He leaned down over those breasts and put his lips to them and swirled his tongue across the nipples. He thought for a moment of Liath.

"I did not think for you to bathe me with your tongue, Fenian," Grainne said. "But if that is what you wish."

She dropped her tunic and stood before him. Fionn was swollen and she reached her hand to his braichs and massaged gently.

"Have you come to tell me that you will offer for my hand, Fenian?"

Fionn nodded, inarticulate.

"Ah," she said, and she sounded disappointed. "Then this must wait until the morrow, for it is my duty as a woman of Eire to choose you with the marriage cup at the great feast."

She walked naked with Fionn to the doorway, leaned against him and kissed him full on the lips.

"On the morrow then," she said softly.

Fionn stumbled from her chamber. He did not see Dhiarmuid Ui Duibhne approaching from the other direction, nor did he see Dhiarmuid turn and go away when he saw Fionn emerge from Grainne's chamber.

Fionn hurried to Cormac's chamber and told him that he would offer for Grainne in marriage.

"She has bewitched you," said Cormac.

"She has," said Fionn, laughing. "And she has done it well, for I did not think to love another after Sabh, but it will be pleasure to learn to love your daughter."

"Very well then," said Cormac. "She must want you if she has done this thing, and it bodes well that the choice is hers. I will speak to her tomorrow and we will hold the feast in the evening."

In the morning, Cormac went to Grainne's chamber. She was embroidering with her women around her, and she did not look up when her father entered. She seemed in foul humor, slapping at the wrist of one of her serving women. Cormac watched her and felt the usual sensation rise up in him. She was beautiful, but cold, a woman too selfish for any other. He almost hated to see her mated to his friend. But Fionn had chosen.

"Fionn has spoken to me," Cormac began. He saw a small smile crease the corners of his daughter's mouth. "He offers for you in marriage. Will you have him?"

Grainne looked up. She waved her hand in the air the way one would wave at an insect in summer. She spoke nonchalantly.

"If he seems a worthy son-in-law for you, why then I guess he will do well enough."

"Do well enough? This is Fionn we speak of. He is chief of the Fenians of Eire and moreover, he has been my friend for thirty years. You will not shame him or my dishonor will fall on you. Do you hear me, daughter? You will choose for him or not, but you will not shame me!"

"I have said that I will choose for him," she said calmly, her head bent above her embroidery.

*   *   *

That night at the banquet Grainne entered the banqueting hall with the marriage goblet held high. She proceeded to Fionn directly, looked him in the eyes and smiled. Then she handed him the goblet and he drank deep. The marriage pledge was sealed.

Now Grainne turned to the company.

"I would celebrate with the company of Fionn," she cried aloud. She moved from one to another of the feasting guests, carrying the goblet. She bade her father drink deep and all of the Fenians.

Only she passed by Dhiarmuid Ui Duibhne, who blushed when she did so and felt great shame, for he had almost lain with the betrothed of Fionn. And even on that thought, he thought her beautiful and witty beyond most women he had met. Grainne met his eyes as she passed him and her eyes were accusing.

The betrothal feast broke up earlier than it should have for the merrymakers seemed unaccountably tired. Even Fionn kept yawning behind his hand and he wondered where his ardor of the night before had gone. At last he approached his betrothed and whispered in her ear.

"I am weary with this feasting and go to my chamber. Will you come to me?"

"By and by," she said softly.

After Fionn had left, Dhiarmuid Ui Duibhne stood to depart, but Grainne approached his table.

"I thought that we had a rendezvous, Fenian."

"I saw Fionn leaving your chamber. You did not tell me that you were to be his betrothed," Dhiarmuid accused her.

"I was not his betrothed. Nor would I be if you had come."

"What means this?" he whispered.

The few guests who still remained were looking at them strangely.

"I will come to you," said Grainne.

"That is not wise," said Dhiarmuid, but she was already drifting away, bidding good night to the retreating guests.

She came to him in the darkness, moving into his chamber like the scent of musky night flowers. She was dressed in her tunic and cloak and she carried a traveling bag.

Ui Duibhne sat up.

"What is this?"

"I will not be married to Fionn. He is an old man. Even now he snores in his cups. I am young and my blood sings. I would have it sing to you. I have come to ask you to take me away from here."

Ui Duibhne felt a stirring for her, but he shook his head.

"Fionn is more than just my leader. He is my friend. I will not betray him."

Grainne leaned in and kissed him on the lips but Ui Duibhne pushed her back.

"This I will not do."

"Then I put you under a geis."

Ui Duibhne sat up in terror.

"Do not do this thing. You will leave me no honor anywhere. I know my captain well. There will be nowhere in all of Eire that we will be able to hide from his wrath if you dishonor him so."

"I have put you under a geis, Fenian. Is that not your code? The Fenian who is put under honor bond by a woman must do as she asks or he is Fenian no longer."

Ui Duibhne fled from the chamber. He ran to the chamber of Osian, who was sleeping so heavily that he had difficulty rousing him. At last he awoke, but when he heard the story he shook his head.

"Do you love her, Dhiarmuid?"

"Yesterday I found her witty and interesting. Today I find her terrifying. I would rather break this geis and flee to Alba than to dishonor your father, who has been my friend and captain."

"I say to you that this woman is wrong for my father. She schemes and plots; she is dishonest. And there is the matter of the geis."

Now Dhiarmuid wept, for he knew that he had no choice.

"I will never eat with you again. I will never live at Almhuin or ride to hounds with Fionn or hunt with my Fenian brothers in the mountains of Slieve Bloom. I cannot bear this sorrow."

"I will be your friend always. I will try to reason with my father, to make him understand that he is better off without her."

"Will this work?"

"I do not know. Only get you gone with her, for I would not wish such a one upon my father."

They embraced then. Ui Duibhne saddled two horses and slipped from the gates of Tara into darkness. When they had ridden away from the hill and crossed the Boanne, he turned to her in anger.

"Would that they had awakened and killed me, for I do not wish to do this thing!"

"They would not awake," said Grainne proudly, "for I drugged their wine."

Ui Duibhne reined in and stared at her. He lifted his reins and would have struck her but for his vow. He dropped them and folded himself over his horse's neck. He let his body shake with weeping.

Now Grainne was moved by shame.

"I will make it up to you, Fenian," she said.

"There is nothing you could do to make up for this," he said. "Nothing you have to offer would heal the wound of ripping me away from my Fenian brothers."

Then Grainne was silent before his great anger, and respectful, for she had never met a man of honor like Dhiarmuid Ui Duibhne. Her heart began to think on that for the first time.

"Your father did nothing to dishonor himself. It was she who dishonored all of them."

"There is more, Padraig. Much more."

"You are weary from the telling. Rest and you can tell me more tomorrow. We are preparing a good beef stew for the evening meal and I will bring you brown bread and honey."

"You do not want me to tell it. For as much as you say that the figure we saw was not Caoilte, you know that it might be. And if I finish the telling, you fear that he will come and take me away."

"What of it?" I snapped. "I do not think he is Caoilte. I do think you are tired. And I am not ashamed to say that I do not wish you to go."

Osian chuckled.

"Ever quick to anger. You would have trembled before my father's anger that morning, Padraig. Even you. I told him what she had done, drugging the wine, forcing Ui Duibhne under geis. He would hear none of it. And Cormac. He was as angry himself. Together they assembled a war party and they went after them. And I rode with them, pleading all the way to both of them to let her go. But they were like old warhorses who did not know how to do aught but ride into battle. Fools!"

Ui Duibhne rode them as far to the west as their horses would take them. Deep in a wood he built them a dwelling with a dolmen at its center, two stones with a capstone. Around that he built a wall with four doors and there he sheltered them and fed her.

She was exhausted from the hard ride, but Ui Duibhne took no pity on her.

"This is the life you have chosen, daughter of Cormac. We will ride by day and hide by night. We will cook a meal in one place and eat it in another. We will have no bed to sleep in nor roof to shelter us. You will never marry or have children, nor see your father

or Tara again. You will lose your beauty and your grace and still we will be hunted like the deer and the hares. This is what you have chosen. I have no pity for your choice."

Now Grainne was afraid for the first time and she began to weep.

"What did you think?" snapped Ui Duibhne. "That Fionn would forget and that he and your father would hold a feast at Tara and toast us for our flight? Did you think that you would sleep with me and all would be well?"

Grainne looked up through tear-stained eyes.

"I did not think, Fenian. I see that now. I did not want Fionn, for he was old. You were young and beautiful. It seemed to me the way." Now she gathered herself together and spoke with dignity.

"But I understand that I have chosen this and I will not relent. I will follow you wherever you lead. I will learn to hunt and to build and I will never leave you even unto death, unless you wish it."

Ui Duibhne regarded her quietly.

"Perhaps you have some iron in you after all," he conceded. "Now eat, for we will depart of the morrow."

But the morning was too late, for we found them after nightfall and surrounded their dwelling. Fionn broke the group into four; each fian was posted at a doorway.

"We will capture them at first light," he said. "And Dhiarmuid will die by my hand."

"Only that you leave Grainne to mine," said Cormac grimly. "For she is a child without honor."

So it was agreed and the fians sat down to rest.

But in the middle of the night I heard a stirring from atop the rock which formed the center of the dwelling. Quietly, so as not to disturb Fionn and the Fenians, I climbed a tree and looked down upon the pair, asleep on the top of the rock. I saw right away that they slept apart; Ui Duibhne had hardened his heart toward the woman. From the tree around me, I broke off a few buds and twigs; I threw them down on the sleeping pair until Dhiarmuid awoke. He looked at me in the tree above him. I circled my finger and he looked around him at the clusters of Fenians. He nodded.

He awoke the woman with his hand over her mouth. When she saw me, her eyes went wide with fear, but Ui Duibhne let her to understand that I would help them. We had the woman remove her cloak and gown. Ui Duibhne wrapped them in his cloak and tossed the bundle up to me. Then they climbed the tree and we progressed from tree to tree until we were out of the range of the Fenians. When we climbed to the ground and she stood between us naked, I saw how beautiful the woman was and how she might bewitch many men. But I saw something more as well.

I saw that she had been infected with remorse and sorrow. Such sentiments are *necessary to being human, so I felt a kind of hope for her. I saw too that Ui Duibhne did not see it yet. His eyes were black with hatred for the woman.*

"Why have you done this?" she whispered.

"Because I love my father and because Ui Duibhne is my friend. I would have neither of them be harmed this day."

She nodded wordlessly. The two of them disappeared into the forest. Dawn was coming, so I made the call of a crow and soon many crows had flocked to the forest and were calling to each other. When the Fenians awoke and found Ui Duibhne and the woman gone and the glen filled with the calling of crows they took it to mean that Angus Og of the Other had helped his foster-son escape. Only Caoilte Mac Ronan suspected; I told him the truth when he asked me.

"Well done," he said. "For I would have no death of brothers today."

"It was a brave thing that you did."

"Nay, it was a desperate thing. I knew my father well. He could be angry for long times and hold grudges for years, but eventually he would come to shame at himself. I did not wish him to be shamed."

Osian waved his hand at Breogan, who nodded, gathered his tools and left.

"And so I see that you wish to speak to me of shame."

"You owe her your life; you treated her dishonorably. You cannot say that the shame does not sit on you."

"We speak of the druidess Ainfean."

"You knew that we would speak of her."

I nodded.

"I have been to search for her."

"Looking in her hut to verify the word of Benin is not a search, Padraig."

"I know that," I snapped at him. "I went to the rath of Dichu. No one has seen her. And I went to the fidnemid. It is summer green and still. No one has been there."

"So you returned here and searched no further."

"I thought it best to let it go. I believe that is what she wishes as well."

"Faugh! It is not what she wishes; it is the gift she gives you."

"What do you mean by this?"

"She is a woman who would be well for you, Padraig. She knows this; she knows that you know it as well. She is strong and truthful. She knows that you fear what you see in her. I do not understand this thing which you call celibacy, but she does. She stays from you that it may not be tested."

I turned and looked out the window. Far off at the treeline, a man in a green cloak was sitting astride a black horse. I blocked Osian's view with my body; the rider disappeared into the forest. I felt guilty for my action, so I spoke honestly.

"It would be tested with her."

"So it would. But I thought you believed that your Lord makes you strong. Instead, you wound the woman with your fear. My father let his dearest friend go into exile because he was dishonored by a woman. The rift between them was never healed. The woman Ainfean deserves to live at Sabhal Padraig with the others. She is a wise woman and she will be a strong voice for your Christ. If you are not too afraid to let her come to you."

"You are a hard taskmaster, old man," I said, shaking my head.

"The truth is a hard taskmaster, Padraig."

"I will go for her in the morning," I said, finally.

"Good. Then you may bring me my supper. And ask Benin to eat with us, Padraig. I would be with him while I can."

I shook my head in exasperation, but I did as he asked.

Who is this Angus Og of the tale you told? You said he was foster-father to Ui Duibhne? And what powers did he possess?"

We were seated around him with our bowls of stew and bread. He was too weak to come to the dining hall, but I thought that if a few of the brothers and some of the people of Sabhal Padraig came to eat with him it might cheer him. And it seemed to have done so, for he ate well and drank deeply of his ale. Benin had the seat of honor at the foot of Osian's bed, his legs curled under him. From beyond the window, the night wafted warm breezes over us. It was pleasant in the room and I smiled in contentment.

"Angus Og is of the Other."

"Who are these Other?"

"You do not know?" Our blacksmith boomed it at me, but Osian held up a hand to silence him and shook his head.

"The Other are the people called the Tuatha de Danaan. We call them the Other because they are the other ones who dwell in Eire. Sometimes we call them the sidhe."

"They dwell here? Why have I met none of them? I would offer them baptism."

Breogan cleared his throat and shifted in his chair.

"You know of them, brother? And you have not told me?"

"I know of them," Breogan answered. "But I have met none in my life."

"The Other are . . . shy," said Osian. Our blacksmith hooted with laughter. "They are shy," Osian insisted. "They do not like to live near the dwellings of men. They choose the hills and hollows of Eire."

"You have not mentioned them before."

"I have mentioned them in some of my stories."

"Which?"

"The story of how Fionn regained the captaincy of the Fianna."

"The goblin? He was of the sidhe? Is this what they are? Devil folk?"

"Nay. They are creatures like you and me, like all of us. But some of them are evil, as he was. Most of them are beautiful and good. They possess great powers."

"What powers? For the only true power belongs to the Lord our God."

"Not that kind of power," said Osian irritably. "Theirs are powers of music and laughter, of song and peace, of healing and great age."

"I have met a woman of the Other," Benin chirped up cheerfully.

"Have you now?" I said. "Perhaps the time has come to tell me of these Other, Osian."

"And perhaps it has not," said Osian.

I set my bowl down and crossed my arms. Osian looked at me.

"Oh very well. But I do not know that you are ready to hear it."

"Tell it anyway," I said.

Long ago, long before the race of people who dwell here now, there dwelled in Eire a people called the Tuatha de Danaan. Ah, but they were beautiful folk, the women fair as summer light, the men more tall, more fine than any Fenian.

Now the de Danaan were magical folk—not magical as we would think of magic in the conjuring of spells, but magical in the ways of beauty. For among them no war was waged; no quarrel raised. The de Danaan did not sicken, nor did they die until many years beyond the whispered years of men. The songs of the de Danaan were haunting, their feasts a celebration, their dwellings the places the earth made beautiful.

And thus they dwelled in Eire for many years and were untouched by sorrow.

One year many ships sailed into the harbors of Eire. These were the sons of Mil, come over the water from Iberia because they had heard of the fabled beauty of Eire. Among them was a poet named Amergin, a man known for his great power with words.

The sons of Mil came ashore in Eire. There they encountered the Tuatha de Danaan and they told the people that they would battle them for this sweet isle and banish them forever from its shores.

The Tuatha de Danaan begged for time to prepare themselves for battle, for they had been long out of practice, and the sons of Mil agreed. They returned to their ships and sailed away to the ninth wave and there they agreed to wait for three days.

Meanwhile the de Danaan were angry and afraid; Eire had been theirs since time out of mind. They could not leave her.

So they raised a fog at sea and the sons of Mil became lost in that fog. Some sailed away, never to be seen again, while others crashed on the rocks or ran aground. When the fog lifted, many of the nine sons of Mil were dead; those who remained vowed vengeance. They came ashore and hounded the Tuatha de Danaan to the Plains of Moytirra and there a great and terrible battle took place.

The de Danaan were defeated.

The sons of Mil declared that they would be banished from Eire, but a woman of the de Danaan stepped forward.

"Do not banish us!" she cried. "For if we leave this green and magical land, we will surely die. We will be gone from the memories of man, gone from their songs and stories. None will remember us more and we will be as the foam upon the sea."

Amergin the poet was moved by her plea.

"Warriors and brothers," he cried. "Let us be merciful in victory. Can we not share with these people the green hills of Eire?"

But the sons of Mil remembered their dead and hardened their hearts.

"We would not be reminded of those who cost our brothers their lives," they said.

Amergin made one more plea.

"Then give to these people the places other than those where the people of Mil will dwell. Give to them the caves and the hollows of the hills. Give them the winding streams and the trunks of ancient trees. Give to them the places beneath the water and the hidden clefts of the stony country."

The sons of Mil were persuaded and the people of the Tuatha de Danaan disappeared into the places they had been given. This is why we call them the Other, for they dwell in the other places, where men do not. This too is why poets are honored among us as no other, for the wisdom and mercy of Amergin saved the people of the Tuatha de Danaan, that their beauty and magic might forever linger here in Eire.

"It is a lovely fable," I said, nodding my approval.

"No fable," said Osian.

"This I do not believe. There are like stories in my country—fairies and elves."

"The sidhe are neither fairies nor elves. They are real; they dwell beside and around us, but their time does not move as our time moves. We do not see them. But they are watching us."

"You cannot believe this to be so."

"I can and I do. I know it to be so."

The old man was growing very agitated, shifting against his pillows and wheezing. I was afraid that his fragile health would turn for the worse, so I held up my hand.

"Very well, old friend." I turned toward Benin. "Child, you say that you have met a woman of the sidhe. Tell us that tale."

He answered seriously.

"No tale, Padraig. Only that she is my friend and has spoken to me all my life. She is small and beautiful and her hair is so white that it glows. Sometimes when I see her at night, I think that she gives off a light—a blue light."

I thought that his little woman of the sidhe sounded much like the accounts of angels that I have studied. Why should not a parentless boy have his own guardian? I smiled at Benin and ruffled his hair.

"As you say, Osian, there is much that I do not know."

"Faugh!" said Osian. "You placate me as an old one in his dotage. Leave me now. I would rest."

"Osian, it makes a lovely story. Why is it necessary that I believe it?"

"I told you you were not ready to hear it," he said.

But Benin, it seems, was not finished, for he piped up between us.

"The little woman of the Other came to me three nights ago, Padraig. She said that you are to be summoned."

"Summoned?"

"She said that one would come who would command you to Crom Cruach at Mag Sleacht."

"By the gods!" Osian exploded.

Two of the brothers crossed themselves.

"What is this Crom Cruach?" I asked, surprised by their reaction. The brothers sat in silence; Osian spoke at last.

"He is the voracious god, the one who hungers. Long ago in ancient Eire, he required that the people make sacrifice of one-third of all they possessed—their first born animals, their corn and milk and sometimes their children—that Crom Cruach might be satisfied. His great stone stands on the plain at Mag Sleacht, halfway between here and the stronghold of Leoghaire."

"Do you see?" I asked them. "Do you see why the true God comes here? He who requires no sacrifice of you. He who asks only your love. Stuff and nonsense! Crom Cruach indeed! I shall go to no such place, summons or no."

I shook my finger at Benin.

"Not that I believe in your little woman of the Other in the first place."

But my railings were interrupted by the appearance of our blacksmith, still in his forge apron, exuding heat and smoke. Behind him came a young man in the brown homespun and tonsured hair of one of the brothers.

"Abba Padraig," said the blacksmith, inclining his head respectfully. "The young brother seeks you."

"Welcome to Sabhal Padraig," I said to the youngster. I gestured to Breogan and the brothers. "You are welcome here among the brothers in Christ."

But the young man maintained a cold and distant demeanor, speaking only one sentence.

"Declan, priest of Eire, summons you to meet with him at Mag Sleacht in a fortnight's time."

And he would not speak more.

23

The morning dawned rainy and gray. I did not go to look for Ainfean, so I also did not go to Osian's chamber. Nor did I prepare to journey to Mag Sleacht, for the sullen young man who had delivered the message had refused food or lodging and disappeared into the summer twilight as suddenly as he had come. Though all that morning I kept thinking of Declan's summons, wondering at the meaning of it, then forcing it from my mind. What right had a minor Hibernian priest to summon me anywhere? I put his summons aside. I had the monastery to worry about. That and the old man. That was enough.

I was busy in the kitchen of the monastery when Benin came running to say that Osian wished me to come to him.

"Tell him I will come later."

"He said that you would say that. He said you are to come now."

"Who is abba of this place?" I muttered.

"You are, Padraig," said Benin. He smiled sweetly at me and I nodded in affirmation. "But is not Osian your friend?"

I looked at him sharply.

"Perhaps you are one of these Other he speaks of. There is far too wise a creature in a body of just ten years."

Benin laughed in delight.

"If you think I am wise, then surely it is true, for you are the wisest man I know."

"Ah, child," I said softly. I ruffled the top of his head. "Lead me to Osian."

He was sitting up against his pillows, watching the treeline. I came into his chamber, ready to be chastised, and angry that a withered ancient could make a man of more than forty years feel like a stripling boy. But he made no mention of my promise to look for Ainfean.

Instead he surprised me.

"The Other are the reason that my father had grey hair."

"Grey hair?" I did not think I could bear it if his mind went away in the way of the very old.

"Yes, my father's hair went grey at a somewhat young age."

"Did it?"

"Stop edging around me like I am a senile old fool! My father had an encounter with the Other. I wish to tell you the story."

"I do not particularly wish to hear it. These fables are entertaining, but I have business to attend to here at Sabhal Padraig. I prefer the stories of Fionn and the Fenians."

"Would you prefer that we discuss Ainfean?"

"Tell your story then. Miserable, intrusive old man."

A woman of the sidhe took a fancy to Fionn and offered for him in marriage.

"The sidhe?"

"The Other. I have told you this. I would continue."

She offered for him in marriage. She was beautiful, in the way of those people, fair, with eyes that changed color and hair of copper gold. But Fionn was still mourning his loss of Sabh and would have none of her. The woman of the Other was angry. So she spoke to her sisters and together they devised a plan by which they would take vengeance on Fionn.

Fionn, of course, knew none of this and so he went riding and hunting as he always had.

One day he was riding in the forest when he came to the shores of a beautiful lake. Beside the lake a woman was weeping. Fionn approached her.

"Why do you weep when the day is fine and the world around you is beautiful?"

The woman looked up at Fionn through light grey eyes.

"I weep for I have lost a thing most precious to me."

"What have you lost?"

"I was given a ring by my betrothed, ruby red, as red as the heart of his love for me. But I have dropped it into this water and alas, I cannot swim."

She looked toward the lake and Fionn saw that her eyes were as blue as the water. He took pity on the poor creature for her loss.

"I am a strong swimmer," he said. "Show me where you have lost this ring and I will try to find it for you."

So Fionn dived into the water and looked for the ring, but could find nothing. When he thought he must breathe or perish, he came to the surface to find the woman still weeping piteously.

"You were not able to find it, Fenian?"

"I was not. But if your betrothed loves you as he says, surely he will forgive you." The woman shook her head.

"He is dead, Fenian."

Then Fionn understood the depth of her grief and he dived again, but could not find the ring.

This time when he surfaced, the woman was staring intently at the water and her eyes were green, green as the grass which surrounded her.

She smiled.

"Alas, Fenian, you have tried well," she said. "It was all I had of him and now that it is gone, I no longer wish to live. But I thank you for your kindness."

Fionn did not wish for the woman to die, so he submerged once more. This time he stayed below the water for a very long time and at last he saw the gleam of gold from the mud at the bottom of the lake.

He surfaced triumphant with the ring, but before he could step from the water, the woman snatched the ring from his hand, dived into the lake over his head and disappeared beneath the surface. Now Fionn was afraid, for he knew that only a woman of the sidhe could do such a thing and he remembered the woman he had rejected. He pulled himself out of the water and lay on the bank, but his very limbs felt watery and he could not rise. He fell asleep there on the bank.

When he did not arrive back at the feasting hall, Caoilte Mac Ronan grew worried.

He gathered Fionn's hounds and some of the Fenians and together they went looking.

At last they came to the banks of a beautiful lake and there they found Fionn, lying on the shore. Caoilte approached him, but Fionn could not rise. He lay on the shore like a beached fish, his hair as white as fish bones.

Nor could he speak, but he kept pointing to the lake and at last Caoilte understood.

So he gathered the Fenians around him and they made a boat and put Fionn on it. In that boat, they sailed to a little island in the center of the lake, for on that island was a great hill. The Fenians knew that this would be one of the dwellings of the sidhe.

When they reached the hill they began to dig. All that day and into the night they dug. At last they came to a doorway hidden deep beneath the dirt of the hill. They flung open the door and there stood a beautiful woman, her hair copper-red, her eyes as grey as the dawning light. In her hand she held a cup.

She walked to Fionn and knelt before him. He recognized her as the woman of the Other who had offered for his hand. She spoke softly.

"This curse was cast upon you by my sister, for she was angry that you rejected me. But I bear you no such ill will. If you will only drink from my cup, I will restore your voice."

Now Fionn was wary, but he knew he had no choice. So he sipped from the cup and instantly he could speak.

"This was a cruel trick your sister played," he said. "For I expended all my strength to help her find her ring."

"It was," agreed the woman of the Other. "But if you will only sip from my cup, I will restore your strength to your limbs. For I bear you no ill will."

Again Fionn drank and little by little he felt the strength return to his legs and arms. Now he stood and faced the woman. She smiled gently at him and her eyes were the blue of the lake around her.

"Drink a third time, Fionn Mac Cumhail, and I will restore the whiteness of your hair to its former gold."

But Fionn looked at the woman and the outstretched cup and he shook his head.

"Your sister cursed me by three times asking me to dive to the bottom of the lake. If I drink three times from your cup I will be cursed as well, for I think it the marriage cup of the sidhe. I would keep my hair this color before I would marry one who tricks me here."

Now the woman threw the cup at Fionn and ran toward the hillside. Before any of the Fenians could catch her, she slipped through the door and bolted it behind her.

And Fionn's hair remained grey from that day until the end of his life.

Osian stopped speaking. We both sat silent.

"Well?" he said.

237

"I think it is as fine a way as any to explain why the hair goes grey. As for me, you see that I have tonsured mine, that the grey remain hidden beneath the collar of my robe." I laughed at my own joke, but it was uneasy laughter.

"You do not believe me," he said.

"It is a delightful tale. We will have Breogan write it down and read it to the people of Sabhal Padraig at the evening meal."

"That is not enough, Padraig," he said.

He leaned back against his wolf pelts, closed his eyes.

"You are weary," I said softly. "I will let you rest and I will send Breogan later with his tools."

Osian sighed. "I could hunt all day, Padraig. All day on horseback or on foot. And then feast and tell tales well into the night. My body cannot accustom itself to this being old. I will be glad to leave it."

I disliked when he talked so. I made my voice reasonable, soothing, the proper tone to adopt with the old and querulous.

"Age does that to all of us, Osian. We have spoken of your father's grey hair. Look at me. I am a man in the middle of my fourth decade, but look at these hands. Already they look like the claws of a bird. Imagine them when I am as old as you are." I held my hands with their crooked, aching fingers forward.

His eyes snapped open and regarded me. Intense, blue, angry.

"You do not believe me, Padraig!"

"Believe what?" I stepped backwards before the force of his anger.

"All of these tales of my father's life, of my life, and you do not believe me."

"I do believe the tales of his life, Osian. I have told you that. But this tale of his hair. It is a fireside tale merely. A diversion. Why is it so important to you that I believe this tale?"

"I am not an old man!" he snapped.

I said nothing, regarded his gnarled hands and thin grey hair. I did not wish to offend him. He shouted at me.

"I told you that I was young, young, until I came here to speak to you. And you do not believe me!"

"What will you have me believe? That you have been alive and young for nigh these two hundred years? I know that you are Osian. My messenger has told me that. I do not know how you came here. It is not for me to know. The Lord has sent you and that is enough. Let this tale of the Other stand as what it is—a diversion, an enjoyment for the brothers at the evening meal. Why do you constantly require belief of me?"

"You are unworthy!" Osian shouted, to someone, to no one, glancing wildly about the room as if he expected someone to respond. "You are unworthy of Eire!"

He struggled up from the wolf pelts, stood as if to walk away. His face grew flushed with the exertion and his breathing became rapid and shallow. His legs wobbled beneath him. Fear clutched at my heart.

"Nay," I cried, running to him. "Sit still, old man. I am sorry that I have vexed you so. You know how much I love your tales. Nay, more than that. You know how much love I have for you. Do not be angry with me. Why are you so angry now?"

Osian laughed, a rueful, tired sound. He leaned back against the wolf pelts, closed his eyes. He waved his hand at me the way one waves at summer insects.

"If I tell you, you will not believe it, Padraig. I am angry because I would tell you a story that you will not believe. I am angry with you because you will not go to look for the woman. I am angry because you have been called to the plain of Crom Cruach and you will not go. A man of Eire does not hide from challenges. You weary me with your foolish stubbornness. There is more beyond these monastery walls than your mind will ever envision. You like for the world to have rules and bindings and tidy borders. You are not yet wise enough to see the path that opens before you."

I turned for the door. I felt like a small boy.

"I am sorry I have angered you, old man. But remember that I am not a man of Eire. Your ways are not mine."

"Wait, Padraig." I turned back. His eyes were open and he was smiling suddenly in a merry, self-satisfied way.

"I have heard you speak often of angels and devils."

I saw the trap immediately, of course. I have studied theology with the best minds on the Continent. I have read the scriptures on demons and angels. I felt my irritation with him rise, that he had trapped me so neatly.

"I have said before that you argue like a sophist."

Osian grinned.

"It is no compliment, old man. But your people of the Other? They are not the same thing."

"How can you be sure?"

"I am sure. Angels dwelling in Eire! Faugh!"

"Where else would they dwell?"

I sputtered. He began to laugh loud and long and I gritted my teeth together at the sound.

"Demons I will believe," I said. "Demons in Eire seem obvious to me."

"Do you fear them? Is that why you do not go to Crom Cruach?"

"Fear? An old stone idol? What should I fear when I have my Lord to protect me? I need not answer the summons of a minor Hibernian priest. What right has he to summon me anywhere?"

"So you fear his summons more than Crom Cruach?"

I took a step toward him. "I have been summoned before! My superiors in Gaul summoned me. I stood before them abject while one who had been my friend betrayed my sins for all to hear. I have told you this! Do you recall? I will not be summoned by a stripling Hibernian."

I stopped suddenly. Osian was watching me intently.

"You are baiting me again." He nodded his head. "Why?"

"Because I know you. You burn with curiosity about the message of Declan, but you refuse to go. Part of you refuses to go out of pure Roman superiority and stubbornness. Part of you fears a summons that will expose your fear and hatred of Eire. And part of you refuses to go because you think that I will die while you are gone. The monastery will get on without you. I will get on without you. We will all be here when you return."

"You cannot know that."

"I know it. If it were my time to die, the sidhe would sing my death beyond the door."

"The sidhe again! No such creatures exist! And as for Declan, why should I answer the summons of a minor priest of Eire?"

"Because he considers you a minor Briton priest. Because he challenges you. Because perhaps you are not being summoned by Declan but to Crom Cruach. Crom Cruach is the darkness; he challenges the light. Would your God have you refuse this summons?"

"But we have had many victories. The word spreads throughout Eire. What if this boy Declan undoes all that?"

"Do you believe that your God wishes it to be undone?"

"I do not. But . . ."

"Well, if you think that is what your God requires, that you fade quietly out of sight, that you return to your country. . ."

"That is not what my God wishes!" It exploded from me before I could think.

"Ah," said Osian. "And have you ever considered, Padraig, that the woman who speaks to Benin may be one of the angels you are so fond of? That would make you twice summoned."

I turned my back so that he would not see that I had indeed thought it, but he read the answer in the set of my shoulders. Behind my back, he shouted aloud with laughter.

"I know you, Padraig. You will think about it. You will think about it all the rest of the day today. And you will consider it again tomorrow. And by the third day, you will be packing to depart."

I stormed out of the room to the sound of his laughter. And all the rest of that day, whenever I thought of the blessed angels and his damnable Others, of the voracious Crom Cruach and the summons of Declan, I cursed Osian's laughing soul.

But late that evening, I called Breogan to me and began preparations for a journey south.

24

I do not know what it was that I expected of Declan or of his summons. To speak truth, I thought little of it on the ride to Mag Sleacht, preoccupied as I was with my horse, surely the most stubborn and dangerous of all the creatures of God. And perhaps the stupidest.

Breogan and I had gone alone to Mag Sleacht, and then by horse, for the sake of speed. I had determined to go, to speak kindly to the reluctant Declan, and to return with all speed to Sabhal Padraig.

For I had no doubt that was what it would be—Declan's reluctance to have an outlander about the business of Christ in Eire.

But when we emerged onto Mag Sleacht, I knew that this would be the great battle of my work in Eire.

The plain itself was nothing, a flat outcropping, a field surrounded by trees and other fields. But Declan had assembled dozens of men there; as we rode among them, I could see the white robes of druids and the multicolored robes of some other rank.

"What are these?" I asked Breogan.

"They are brehons."

I shook my head, unfamiliar with the term.

"Keepers of the law, Padraig. In their memories are written every law of Eire and every case that has come before that law. They rule on land and cattle, on injury and honor prices, on slaves and freemen."

"Why are they here?"

Breogan was silent for a moment.

"It is possible that Declan has asked them to rule against your presence here in Eire."

"Against my presence! It is God who has sent me here, the Creator of all things."

"Our God is not spoken of in the laws of Eire."

I turned and looked at him. He was not smiling.

"Should they rule against me, that will mean nothing. Remember that we have defended our mission before our superiors in Gaul. You wrote the letter for me, Breogan! Remember how we explained each of our actions—the retinue with which we rode to Tara Hill, the gifts that we have paid to chieftains. All of these were accepted and vindicated. The bishops chose to keep me here. This is where I have been sent; this is where I shall stay."

"Then they will put you to death."

"To death!"

"That is probably why Declan chose this place for your meeting. It is the Plain of Prostration, the place where sacrifice is made that balance be restored in Eire."

"That is a heathen belief. Declan is a priest of Christianity."

"Surely you have come to see how the line between them more resembles a river than a road."

"Why are there druids here? They do not rule on the law."

"No," said Breogan. "But it is they who conduct all sacrifices."

He had only finished speaking when the stone of Crom Cruach loomed into view. I have seen the standing stones of Eire, the dolmens that Osian speaks of in his tales and the circles which are scattered about the plains. None of them had prepared me for the sight of the idol of Crom Cruach. It was the height of five men of Eire, perched each upon the shoulders of another. It was three times the width of any man and its feet were sunk deep into the earth, for as I later discovered the ground around it possessed a different sound, a sound perhaps like a drum.

Beside the great stone stood two smaller sentinels, dwarfed by the huge stone, though alone they would have been as the great stone circle in the south of Britannae.

All three stones were carved and incised so intricately that no space of even a handsbreadth remained. Spirals and circles spun crazily around knotwork and coils of braid that looked much like snakes, though there were none of those in Eire. The stick language that Osian called ogham ran up the right edge of the stone; I regretted that the ancient could not have come with us to translate it.

I refused to be frightened by a trinity of stones when my own Trinity traveled with me in my protection. I turned to Breogan.

"Those who did this were like the Romans, fine engineers indeed. And artisans. It is a pity that heathen believers used it for so foul a purpose."

But Breogan was crossing himself and his face looked pale and moist.

I chastised him.

"Brother, you cannot believe this foolishness about idols."

"I do not, Padraig, but I always believe in the cruelty that humans make possible. Look where Declan comes."

Declan approached us, flanked by six brehons in their multicolored robes. I determined to act civilly and smiled and nodded at him.

"Brother in Christ," I said. "It is pleasant indeed to see you again. What do you require of us that you have called us from our work at Sabhal Padraig?"

"Abba Magonus Succatus Patricius," he bowed formally in my direction and his speech was cordial. "We have made ready a dwelling and food to revive you from your journey. It is the way of Eire that hospitality precede all matters that men must decide. This, of course, you could not know. Will you partake with us?"

"We will partake with gratitude at the table of our brother Declan," I said.

It was not until we had eaten bread and honey, wild hare with leeks, berry cakes and milk and then been regaled with stories and song that Declan came to the business at hand. By then all the surface of my skin tingled with agitation, but I knew that he would expect just such a reaction, so I schooled myself to silence, to pleasant nods at the assembled company, to the small discussion of people and places that the Hibernians so favor. Only Breogan could sense my agitation and periodically I would see his head bent in a quick, fervent prayer.

At last Declan stood among the company.

"Brothers and brehons, we have among us a bishop of the Christ, a speaker for the One God. He is Abba Magonus Succatus Patricius of Britannae. We are honored by his visit."

He paused. A few in the crowd called their greetings. The atmosphere was friendly, as though I were a visiting dignitary. I kept still and waited.

"Magonus Succatus Patricius has worked tirelessly for the Three-in-One. He has spoken throughout Eire. He has baptized and brought many to the White Christ. Indeed, I was at the stronghold of Angus of Cashel in the past winter. There the bishop baptized the great chief and many of his clansmen."

Again the crowd made polite response. I remained quiet, perplexed by the way Declan spoke of me. Beside me Breogan hissed,

"He speaks the declaration of a hero. It is spoken before that hero departs for another place or dies—or is sacrificed."

Declan continued.

"We who are Christians in Eire will always be grateful to Magonus Succatus Patricius. Many among you are Christians, my brehon brothers. I ask that we acknowledge the Bishop of Britannae for the work he has done."

They stood then, shouting my praises, quaffing from their cups each time they called aloud one of the stories they had heard of me. I saluted them with my own cup and drank.

Now Declan came to the heart of the matter.

"But there are those in Eire, I among them—for I speak only truth before the bishop—who believe that it will divide Christianity in Eire if it be preached by an outlander. There are those of us who believe that the Word should be brought to Eire by those who know them best—by their own countrymen, who can explain the new religion in a way that those of Eire can understand and accept."

It was only what I myself had often thought, and I nodded unconsciously at the wisdom of his words.

"Therefore, brehons of Eire, I ask you to rule upon the Bishop of Britannae. Should he remain in Eire with us or should he return to his own country? I ask also that you consider the eric—the honor price that should be paid to Magonus Patricius should you return him to his own country. For he should return as a hero of Eire and in no other fashion."

"Here!" cried a few from the crowd. And, "Well said, Declan of Eire."

Suddenly there was a stir at the back of the room and Ciaran and Ibar burst in, but I had no time to greet my brothers whom I had met on Cashel, for they fell upon Declan in fury.

"Brother, what have you done?"

"Will you divide the brethren of Christ with your petty squabbles?"

"Have you brought the case before the law?"

Ciaran turned in my direction.

"Brother Padraig, I ask your forgiveness for this outrage."

One of the brehons stood then; I thought him the chief judge as he wore a hammered, moon-shaped collar of gold. He spoke.

"Declan of Eire has brought before us a clear case of the law. The Bishop Magonus Succatus Patricius of Britannae has brought word of the new God among us. Many have been baptized by his hand. But many others have been angered by his Roman ways, made fearful of the teaching he brings because he sometimes brings it harshly. Moreover, there are those who say that Magonus Patricius believes himself superior to those of Eire, believes us to be a rude and unlettered people. Should such a one be permitted the weight of such a great new endeavor? To balance these concerns, we have been told of the many fine teachings of the bishop, of the ways in which he uses the signs and symbols of Eire to teach the new God. Of this, many approve. Too, many believe that the presence of the ancient Fenian with this priest speaks of his fitness for Eire. We brehons will debate this case. We will examine the precedents throughout the great history of Eire. We will rule on the case of Magonus Succatus Patricius three days from this time."

I stood among them then. I did not know what to say, so I stood humbly for a moment, then spread my hands out with the palms up.

"Brehons and brothers. A man of the One God should never fear the truth, so I tell you that much of what has been spoken here is true. I came to Eire a proud and angry man. It was most difficult for me to return, for I had been a slave in your country; I carried with me a great bitterness for those years of my youth that had been taken from me.

"But I tell you that the Lord my God required that I return to you, and though I did so reluctantly, I would now be reluctant to part from this green country.

"You may rule on my case, brehons of Eire, but I can abide by your ruling only if the Lord my God abides by it as well. Should he rule that I must stay, then his will is the will that I will follow, come what may."

I left the chamber with Breogan, Ibar and Ciaran close behind me. The dwelling that Declan had erected for us was near to the great stone and stood apart from the other dwellings. As we approached our hut, I saw druids everywhere, but I did not see Mal or Coplait or any of those who had converted with us.

Then, as we neared the great stone, I saw a sight that froze my blood and caused my heart to knock against my ribs.

A circle of druids stood facing the stone. Blood covered the stone at the height of their heads. As they turned to face me, I could see that their faces were covered with blood and that for some the bones of their noses pro- truded, visible, from where the skin had been scraped away.

I cried aloud at their disfigurement.

"Breogan, what has befallen them?"

Ciaran answered.

"They worship Crom Cruach, Padraig. They worship him with their blood and their bone. They ask to be given the honor of making sacrifice in his name."

I slept not at all that night. I lay awake in the little wooden dwelling and lis- tened as the night sounds quieted, as brehons and druids went to their rest. When the encampment was still, I arose, donned my cloak and walked out to the stone of Crom Cruach.

I stood and looked a long time at the blood on that stone and though I felt no fear of heathen idols, I felt a great weight of sorrow.

I had come among these people and I had changed them. I had thought to change them for the good, to bring to them the great light of the Three- in-One. But what if I had indeed divided them? What if I broke and scat- tered them? To my shame, I realized that some part of me had hoped for that when I returned. Some part of me had hoped for vengeance against a people who had stolen away my life, not once but twice.

In the secret heart of me something wished, for just a moment, that the brehons would rule against me, would send me home. For though I might return defeated, I would go home. Home.

I closed my eyes. Benin's little face shown before me. What was it he had said? That I was the wisest man he knew. I laughed ruefully. I longed to ruffle the top of his head.

I thought of Breogan, bruised from the ride here, never leaving my side.

I remembered young Longan, who would see me again in Tir Nan Og. I thought of Ainfean, felt my face grow warm with shame at my mistreatment of her. I pictured each of the brothers, each of the people of Sabhal Padraig. And then I pictured Osian, the Fenian heart of Eire, who had given up everything to come to me.

Was I not responsible for them, for all of them, in the way that a father is responsible for the children he has taught and raised?

Something in me claimed more, more than responsibility for the people of Eire. I turned my mind toward the thought, unafraid for the first time, but before I could examine it, someone stepped from behind the great stone.

"Magonus Succatus . . ."

It was Declan.

"Brother . . ." I began, but he placed his hand over his mouth and motioned me behind the rock. I felt no fear, though I knew that my death gathered around my head.

We sat on the ground and leaned against the great stone. I laughed.

"Not so terrifying, brother. Old Crom Cruach."

"Terrifying enough, Abba, for there are forces here that I did not call to Mag Sleacht."

"What forces do you speak of?"

"The druids. I invited the brehons. Do you see, Magonus? Do you see? Eire must not be divided over the Christ. He must come to her gently as a bridegroom a bride. I wish you no harm. I want no harm to befall you. But these druids who have come are the dark ones. If the brehons rule against you, you must leave Eire immediately. You must. For if you do not, I fear that they will take your life."

I smiled sadly at him.

"You know that I must do as the Lord instructs, brother. He will bind me; he will loose me. No other law can speak to me."

Declan shook his head in exasperation.

"Nay, brother. These are the ones who serve the darkness. Do not discount it. They have power."

"I do not discount the darkness, Declan, for who can see the life of our Lord and not see how the evil ones fought against him? But what comes here will come. Neither of us can stop it now."

"I would not be a Judas, Magonus. I wish you no harm."

"I know that, Declan," I said softly. "But now it is out of our hands."

We sat silently for a time. When he spoke again, his voice was heavy.

"You are not angry with me." It was a statement.

"I am not," I said. "Much of what you said was true. Much of it. My heart thinks long on it this night."

We sat beside each other until the dawnlight began to seep across the plain. I stepped around the stone then and knelt, my back to the stone. I faced east, toward the rising light, away from Crom Cruach. Declan made to leave me, but I whispered to him softly.

"Will you pray with me, brother?"

He hesitated, but he knelt beside me. We were silent for a long time, until at last I whispered the only prayer I could think to pray.

"Choose for us Lord," I whispered. "Thy will be our will."

"Amen," said Declan.

When the druids came to Crom Cruach in the dawnlight, they found us kneeling there side by side.

I was afraid on that third morning, afraid with a deep fear that reached into my stomach and made my legs tremble beneath me like the legs of a yearling child.

But I bathed and knelt with Breogan, Ciaran and Ibar for prayers, then moved to the great hall for the ruling of the brehons. All of the assemblage was waiting, the brehons seated at a makeshift dais at the front of the room, the druids with their bloody, broken faces assembled along the wall like the grisly heads of Osian's ancient tales.

I stood before them quietly, but my heart beat within me like the bodhran beats at the great feis of Tara.

The chief brehon stood and addressed me.

"Abba Magonus Succatus Patricius of Bannaevum on Tiburnae in Britannae, we the brehons have reached a verdict on the case brought before us by Declan, priest of Eire. But before we pronounce that ruling, we give you the right of declamation, as is the custom in Eire. Will you speak?"

"I will."

I closed my eyes, whispered a prayer in my heart, opened them and looked steadily around the room.

"But understand that I speak not to you, but to my God."

Then I raised my palms and turned my head skyward.

"Father!" I cried. "You who are the Three-in-One, the Light, the Word. You who have been the light at the center of my being, hear me now. Decide for me, Oh Lord, for it is your will that I abide, your decision that will keep me here in Eire or return me to my own country. And as you will, so will I do, fearlessly and with a full heart."

I bent my head, for the tears had come unbidden from my eyes and streamed down my cheeks.

The sound began below me, deep below my feet. It sounded like the growling of a great beast. A murmur ran around the room. Outside there was a crack, a sound like lightning, then a deep basso rumbling, not so much like thunder as like mountains moving. Then the ground beneath my feet began to move! It heaved and fell, like the waves of the sea. I dropped to my knees and placed my palms on the cold earth floor. Some around me screamed; some tumbled to the floor.

The walls of the dwelling began to sway like trees in wind and the straw ceiling gave way and tumbled down on us, raining straw in wisps and bundles.

The room was filled now with terrified calls, incantations and screams.

Then one of the walls gave way and fell to the ground.

The earth stopped heaving, grew still.

I came to my feet and looked out to the plain through where the wall had once been.

Crom Cruach, the ancient stone, no longer stood. It lay facedown on the ground, the two sentinels stones tumbled over its back, like the bodies of two dead children over their sire.

After that, the hill was pandemonium.

Many of the druids fled the plain, disappearing into the trees. Others dropped before us and took baptism, as did many brehons.

As for me, I could say nothing. I made no speeches, spoke the words of baptism by rote. But inside me grew a surprising joy. The Lord had chosen for me. And he had chosen Eire.

25

I would tell you the story of Dhiarmuid and Grainne."

"You told me that one before my departure."

I said it pleasantly as I set his supper before him, but since my return from Crom Cruach, I had felt his mind slipping away and it saddened me.

I turned and looked toward the treeline, half expecting to see the rider in the green cloak. I was angry at myself for my own foolishness.

"He has not been today." Osian spoke from behind me. "Nor since you left. I have watched. But I think that he will come soon."

I sat down in the window embrasure.

Osian chuckled.

"You think that your great brown body will stop him from coming, priest?"

I sighed.

"Osian, I have only just returned and I am weary still. Why must you bait me today?"

"Because I know what you are thinking. You are thinking that I become foolish since your departure, that my mind has slipped its moorings and puts away to sea. You are wrong. I know what I am about. I have told you only part of the story of Dhiarmuid and Grainne. I would tell you the rest. I would know the end of my father's life, before the end of my own."

"You do not know how your father died?"

"I do not. Shall I tell you why that is so?"

"I will call Breogan."

"Nay, I wish to tell you the rest of this story alone."

I looked at him in surprise. He shook his head.

"It is a story of much sorrow."

"But you helped them to escape."

"That time, yes."

"There were other times?"

"Some time passed. I married and my wife died of the birthing of our son. Oscar. And Oscar grew. So perhaps five years passed. My father returned to his hunting and to caring for the business of Eire, but he cursed Ui Duibhne whenever anyone spoke of him.

"This put a rift between my father and me and between some of the other Fenians, for we argued that Dhiarmuid did only what he was honor bound to do."

"I agree with your father. Dhiarmuid could have said no."

"You do not understand the nature of a geis."

"Perhaps not, but I understand well enough the nature of being betrayed by a friend."

I thought of Declan, who had made confession to me there at Mag Sleacht. I had given him my forgiveness freely.

Osian nodded.

"You are right, Padraig. It was the wound of that. We all still loved Ui Duibhne, even my father. But the memory of him was as salt in that wound. Still, some years passed, as I said, and I thought the matter quiet and forgotten."

"What happened to stir it up again?"

Osian sighed.

"I will tell it," he said, "as a tale should be told."

Goll Mac Morna died. The Fenians mourned him greatly, but when the period of mourning was over, the nephews of Morna decided to renew their ancient feud with Clan na Bascna.

So they waged war on Fionn and his Fenians and they were defeated. The nephews of Morna and the soldiers who had fought with them were exiled to Alba for their disloyalty. But the warriors pined for Eire and at last they called Art Mac Morna to them.

"You must go to Fionn," they said. "You must offer him our sorrow and our apology. Ask him, nay, beg him, that we may return to Eire."

But Art Mac Morna shook his head.

"Fionn will never relent. For you know it is true that since Ui Duibhne stole the daughter of Cormac from him, Fionn forgives no betrayals. His heart has forgotten forgiveness; it grows hard."

"Then we must offer him something to buy back his favor," said the soldiers.

Now Art Mac Morna was a clever and devious man. When he had thought on the speeches of his soldiers for a time, he devised a plan.

He sent a message to Fionn, saying that he had heard in Alba that Dhiarmuid and Grainne had been living there in hiding, but that they had returned to Eire. This was not true, but Mac Morna reasoned that he could use this ruse with Fionn. And he was correct, for when Fionn received the message he agreed to a meeting with Art Mac Morna.

Mac Morna came to Almhuin alone. He went to his knee before Fionn and spoke in unctuous tones.

"Great Fenian, we were wrong to wage war against you and against your clan. For my uncle Goll Mac Morna would not have wished it so. I know that now."

Fionn snorted in disgust.

"You know only that you were defeated. You think to buy your way back into Eire. So cease this foolishness and make me your offer."

Art Mac Morna stood.

"Very well. I do not know where Ui Duibhne and the woman have gone, only that they have returned to Eire. I propose that we hire Clan Nevin."

Fionn regarded Mac Morna silently.

"Clan Nevin are the best trackers of the Fianna. But I could as well have hired them myself."

"But you could not have done what I propose to do, for in your heart I think you still love Ui Duibhne well."

"Make your proposal."

"I propose that when I find Dhiarmuid and Grainne I will slay them and bring you their heads for the unjust way you were betrayed."

"If you can do this thing," said Fionn, "then I will lift the sentence of banishment and allow you back into Eire."

But his heart was heavy and that afternoon he drew his fian to him.

"We will accompany Clan Nevin on this search," he said.

And so they rode out from Almhuin, filled with foreboding.

*   *   *

Far in the north of Eire, Dhiarmuid and Grainne had been living. For a time they had lived as the wild beasts do, sheltering in caves and the roots of trees.

What Dhiarmuid had said of Grainne became true. She lost her beauty, for she grew thin and colorless. He hair lost all its luster and because she had no combs with which to smooth and plait it, it swirled black and wild around her white face.

But she followed Dhiarmuid wherever he led and she learned to hunt and fish and build a bothy as well as any Fenian. Dhiarmuid gave her grudging respect, but not his love.

As they traveled longer together, she grew more silent, as did the laughing Dhiarmuid, until at last they traveled together without speech or song. Then, one evening of an autumn, a visitor joined them at their fire. He was a bard, a wizened little man who had traveled much and seen many things. They shared their supper with him in silence, but when the meal was finished the bard took out his clarsach, his traveling harp, and he sang to them of the Hill of Tara and of Cormac Mac Art. He sang songs of Fionn and the Fenians until at last Grainne could bear it no more and she began to weep.

The harpist ceased his singing and regarded her in astonishment.

"This is not the purpose of my songs," he said. "They are meant to bring joy and laughter."

But Grainne shook her head.

"I will never have joy or laughter again," she said. "Nor will I be beautiful. For the hard life in Eire has stripped me of all that I was. And I have only myself to blame."

Now the bard took pity on the couple and he thought long and hard.

"There is a tale," he said. "Though I do not know if it is true. But I have heard it often. They say there is a giant quicken tree deep in the forests of northern Eire. In that tree an evil one had built a dwelling in the high branches. There he guards the tree, for it is said that the berries are magical and that they will restore strength and beauty to any who eat of them."

Dhiarmuid shook his head.

"This is nonsense, bard. No such tree exists in Eire."

But the bard smiled at Dhiarmuid and spoke in a riddle.

"He who has nowhere to go, goes there quickly. But he who has a destination is there already, though he still be on the road."

And Dhiarmuid understood.

As for Grainne, her mind had seized upon the quicken berries and she could not let the thought go.

"If only we could find that tree," she said to Dhiarmuid. "I would be young again

and beautiful. Perhaps the tree would be magical. Perhaps it would shelter us where none could find us more and we could stop our wandering."

She dropped to her knees before Dhiarmuid.

"Fenian," she said. "I have cost you much, but I ask of you this one thing more. Only let us seek this tree and I will trouble you no further. You may leave me there and I will live alone happily, only that I might cease this wandering."

"The bard says that the tree is guarded by an evil giant," Dhiarmuid protested. But he was already gathering his cloak, for he too had tired of the life of a fugitive.

They journeyed to the north and those they asked told them in fear of the wood called Duirhos, from whence came strange howlings and sounds of a giant in his rage.

So they traveled into the wood. At its center, they found the great quicken tree, older and larger than any of its brethen, its branches weighted with red berries. Grainne ran to the tree to gather berries. She cupped them in her hand and stuffed them into her mouth, chewing fast so that the red juice ran down her chin and stained the already filthy front of her torn and wasted tunic. She waited and then turned to Dhiarmuid.

"What change do you see?"

He regarded her with disdain.

"I see no change, daughter of Cormac."

A little stream ran nearby. She ran to it and stared at her ragged reflection. She began to weep.

"The old bard lied, for these berries possess no magic power. Nor is the tree guarded by an evil giant."

But no sooner had she spoken than a great howling set up from the forest. A pack of wild dogs appeared from the trees and lined the stream opposite the weeping Grainne. She remained kneeling in terror.

"Back up to me," Ui Duibhne called from behind her. "For in one thing the bard did not lie. There is a dwelling high in the tree."

Grainne came to her feet slowly and backed to where he was standing. With one arm, he boosted her into the branches, and she began to climb, but it was too late for Ui Duibhne. The great dogs crossed the stream.

"Wolfhounds!" cried Dhiarmuid. "Gone wild and look at the size of them."

He held them at bay with the flashing of his sword, but they circled, snarling, big as ponies with their great teeth bared.

"So this is the giant who guards the tree," cried Dhiarmuid. "Come then and we will die fighting."

But from above him he heard a great cry and a crashing and Grainne came down among the dogs. She landed on her feet and continued the scream, turning like the spokes of a chariot wheel, her cloak and hair wheeling out around her. The dogs were terrified by the strange behavior, backed away snarling.

In that moment, Dhiarmuid espied the one who was their leader. He lifted his dagger from the belt at his waist and threw. The dog screamed in pain, then dropped to his side. The other dogs circled in a frenzy, then ran off into the forest.

Dhiarmuid dropped to his knee by the side of the dog.

"Bring water!" he cried.

"For the beast?" Grainne was incredulous.

"Bring water!" he cried again.

She ran to the stream and cupped what she could in her hands. She held it to the lips of the beast, who drank feebly.

"We will carry him to the stream," said Dhiarmuid.

Together they lifted the huge animal between them and carried him to the water. Gently, Dhiarmuid removed the dagger from the animal's side and let the icy water bathe the wound.

Grainne saw what he meant to do. She tore strips from her cloak and tunic. Together they bound the wound, then carried the animal to a soft, mossy place. Dhiarmuid went off and found a rabbit, which they fed to the animal by morsels. The dog whimpered and licked at the blood on their hands. And from that day forward the hound became their friend and traveling companion. And they were no longer bothered by the wild dogs of Duirhos.

At last Dhiarmuid spoke to her.

"Long ago I was put under a geis never to hunt a great boar, for such a one would bring my death. But today, I thought to die by the teeth of these dogs."

"It is fortunate then, that I fell from the tree," said Grainne.

"You did not fall."

"I lost my footing."

"You jumped."

She was silent for a moment.

"I asked you to give your life for me, Fenian. It was too much to ask, but I did not know it then. But I would not ask for your death."

He leaned forward and placed his bloodstained hand against her cheek.

"This was brave. Most brave."

She looked down.

"Fenian, I am not what I was. I am no longer beautiful and I am no longer proud.

But neither am I dishonest. What I am I will give to you, for you have given me more than I can ever repay."

"Ah but you are beautiful," said Dhiarmuid softly. "Now I see how beautiful you are."

He kissed her gently and that kiss folded their bodies together and that night they became husband and wife. And because they had learned to love each other through fierce trials, their love for each other was fierce and lasting.

And they named the dog Ior, which means Lasting, for he had brought that love between them.

"But this is a lovely story."

"I wish that I could say that it ended there, Padraig, but it does not. Shall I go on with the telling?"

I nodded, mesmerized.

Dhiarmuid and Grainne had not been living long in the dwelling of the quicken tree when the trackers of Clan Nevin found them. Art Mac Morna was with them and he claimed the right to Dhiarmuid Ui Duibhne's head.

So, like the fool he was, he climbed the quicken tree, where Dhiarmuid Ui Duibhne slew him and threw his traitor's body to the ground. Then Dhiarmuid climbed to the ground before Clan Nevin, where he addressed them.

"There are twelve of you here, but I will take some with me before I go."

The men of Clan Nevin drew their weapons and were ready to slay him when Grainne came up with great Ior by her side.

"What is this?" she cried in alarm, and she ran to stand beside Dhiarmuid with Ior between them.

"If you will slay him, you must slay me, for I will die by my husband's side."

Grainne had regained her beauty in the tenderness of Dhiarmuid Ui Duibhne, and the men of Clan Nevin could see the great love that had grown between them. They were loathe to destroy it, so the chief of the trackers' fian decided that they would return the body of Art Mac Morna to Fionn and tell him that Mac Morna had been slain by the wild dogs of the forest of Duirhos. To that end they left the body of Mac Morna deep in the forest where the dogs could find it. When they took it back to Fionn, it was torn and bloodied.

Now Fionn could see that the body had been torn by dogs, but he could also see the deep thrust of a sword wound. So he knelt to the body and drew in a deep breath.

"Dhiarmuid Ui Duibhne!" he shouted aloud. "The smell of him is all over the body. As is the smell of quicken trees. We are close now!" he cried in fierce vengeance. And he mounted his horse, with his Fenians following glumly behind.

At last they came to the great quicken tree. The Fenians expected a great battle, but instead Fionn took out his table and his camp stools and set up a game of fidchell beneath the tree.

"Osian," he called. "Come challenge me and see if you can win."

I sat opposite him while he baited the two of them and we played the game of fidchell. He won each move, of course, for my mind was so distracted that I could not concentrate on the game. At last my father spoke.

"If only Dhiarmuid Ui Duibhne were here, he would give you advice. For none could play the game as well as he."

A berry dropped out of the tree then. I moved my piece to match it. My father countered.

"Dhiarmuid Ui Duibhne must be in the tree above us," he said. "For that was a wise move."

"You are a fool if you think he would be in the tree playing chess with us," I said, as loud as I could.

Another berry dropped.

I matched it.

I won the game. When it was over, Ui Duibhne dropped from the tree and stood before my father.

The old man paused and was silent.

"What then?" I asked.

"You know, Padraig, I could swear, even now, even these many years gone, that they were glad to see each other. They looked at each other there by the tree and smiled."

"What happened then?" I insisted.

Grainne came down from the tree and stood between Dhiarmuid Ui Duibhne and Fionn Mac Cumhail. Fionn drew his sword.

"Grainne, daughter of Cormac, you have made a fool of me. Ui Duibhne of the Fenians, you have helped her to betray me. For this offense, both of you must die."

Dhiarmuid Ui Duibhne drew Grainne to him then. There before the Fenians and Fionn Mac Cumhail, he kissed her twice briefly and then once long and deep.

"*I do love thee, Fenian," she said aloud. "I am proud to die beside you.*"

He stopped again. His eyes had filled with tears.

"Did they die? Did he slay them?"

"He did not."

"Of this I am most glad. What stopped him?"

"I did, Padraig. I put my body between my father and the two of them. I said, 'Father, if you will do this you must kill me too.' He lowered his sword and his head.

"'That I am not willing to do,' he said.

"And he walked away.

"I think he was glad of it, Padraig. I think he was glad that I stopped him. But his pride would not let him say so. He did not speak to me for weeks after."

"Pride can make us foolish," I said softly.

He smiled at me.

"It can. It is perhaps harder to see in those we love because we do not like to think ill of them."

"What became of the two of them?"

Osian nodded.

"I will finish the tale, for I must. But do not interrupt me in the telling, Padraig, for I will not finish it else."

That night Angus Og came to the Fenian encampment. He was the foster father of Dhiarmuid Ui Duibhne, but he was of the de Danaan. He had the beautiful bearing of the Other and the sense one always has in their presence, a feeling of light. He spoke simply.

"*Fionn Mac Cumhail of the Fenians, we of the Other love you well. We have been your friends in Eire from the first. But Dhiarmuid Ui Duibhne is my foster-son, beloved of my heart.*

"*We of the Danaan say that this blood feud has gone far enough. All of you have done enough to wound the others. We say that it is time for a truce to be called. We*

259

have sent messengers to Cormac Mac Art at Tara. He will agree to put an end to his vengeance against his daughter if you will agree, great Fionn. What say you?"

Fionn stood and faced Angus Og.

"You speak well, man of the Other. My heart is weary with anger. I would return to Tara and spend the rest of my days with my son and my grandson."

Angus Og nodded.

"Then come forward, Dhiarmuid Ui Duibhne."

Dhiarmuid stepped forward from the shadowing trees and stood before Fionn. His face moved with sorrow, but he stood proud.

"This that I have done, I did because I was put under geis to do it. But I confess freely that now I love Grainne most deeply and would not be parted from her. In that I have betrayed you.

"In all else, I have been ever your friend, your companion in battle and your most loyal warrior.

"Therefore, I ask that dignity be granted me and she who is my wife. I ask that we be permitted to settle on my father's lands in the south of Eire. There I will dwell as a bo-aire, a cattle man. There we will live quietly and if we are blessed with children, I shall speak well of you with them.

"I do not ask to be accepted back into the band of Fenians, O Fionn, for I know that what has been broken between us can never be made whole again."

Here Ui Duibhne paused, turned his head and looked into the dark forest.

"Only know that I hold you still in great esteem and bear no enmity towards you."

Fionn faced Ui Duibhne.

"You have asked for your father's lands and these I grant you. They are yours by right. It is well that you have not asked to come back among us. . . ."

Suddenly Grainne stepped into the light.

"Captain of the Fenians," she said, cold but loud.

"It was I who commanded Ui Duibhne by geis to take me to the forest, and that I would do again, for I have no love of you. But Dhiarmuid Ui Duibhne I love well. If my life will purchase my husband's return to the Fianna, then I offer it here."

She swept Ui Duibhne's dagger from his belt and held it palm out to Fionn.

Silence claimed the clearing. It grew and brooded over us. Fionn's face worked.

"You are a worthier woman than I have thought you," he said at last. "I wish you long life and many children."

*   *   *

Thus, Dhiarmuid and Grainne moved to the south of Eire and many years passed.

Grainne bore four sons and one daughter. Oscar the son of Osian grew to manhood and came into his nineteenth year. Fionn resumed hunting and fishing in the forests of Eire and though he seldom spoke of Ui Duibhne, when he did so, it was with sorrow and not hatred in his tone.

Then, after so many years had passed, a traveler came from the south of Eire.

He was a bard, most aged, with a small traveling harp. When he had sung some songs, he stood among the Fenians and spoke his message.

"Fenians, I bring greetings from Grainne, daughter of Cormac. She has asked me to come among you and plead with you for her husband. For though their lives are wealthy and full, their children strong and handsome, Dhiarmuid Ui Duibhne dreams still of the days of hunting with the Fenians of Eire. Therefore, Grainne asks that you come to their holdings at Kesh-Carraigh, for a great feast and hunt. She asks that wounds of the past be buried."

"You should not have done this." Ui Duibhne threw his dagger on the table, tossed his cloak across the room.

"I thought to please you, husband."

"I know what you thought, but we will open the old wound. Fionn will see our great dun and our many cattle. He will see our fine children and our love for each other. Jealousy will rise in him."

"Do you think so little of him then?"

"I think most highly of him. But he is a man. And my heart is filled with foreboding at this feast."

Still when the Fenians came it was most joyous. For many days they feasted and hunted the green hills and forests of the south of Eire.

Fionn told tales of their father to the children of Ui Duibhne and the company laughed aloud.

Ui Duibhne took a particular liking to Oscar, the grandson of Fionn, proclaiming him much like his father. Oscar became his hunting companion for the time of the feast. A fortnight passed thus in happiness and Ui Duibhne grew more joyful as the days went by, reveling in the companionship of his Fenian brothers.

Then, on the last night before the feast, he heard dogs baying in the darkness, long after everyone slept. He awoke and Grainne sat up beside him.

"What is it, husband?"

"I heard the baying of hounds."

"I hear nothing. You have been too much at hunting these weeks. Go to sleep."

So Dhiarmuid laid back down and began to drift to sleep when he heard the sound again—the baying of hounds on the hunt. This time he did not tell Grainne, but lay awake listening. Just before dawn he heard the howling again and he rose and dressed and saddled his horse to follow. He took with him only the great, aged dog Ior.

He rode into the high mountains and there he found Fionn with Bran and Sgeolan.

"You have been hunting all night, for I have heard your hounds."

Fionn's face was flushed with excitement and he laughed.

"It is a great boar, brother. The biggest I have ever seen."

"You have called me brother."

Fionn looked up in surprise.

"So I have."

"Then let us hunt together."

But Fionn shook his head.

"I remember well your geis, Dhiarmuid. For if you hunt the great boar it will be your death."

"I have lived a death of separation from my Fenian brothers. These weeks have been joy to me, Fionn. I will hunt with you this day!"

So the two of them unleashed Bran and Sgeolan and Ior and the dogs bounded away through the underbrush, sniffing for the boar.

Now Fionn followed the sounds of Bran and Sgeolan while Dhiarmuid tracked after great Ior. At last Dhiarmuid came into a clearing and saw his hound keeping a great boar at bay. The boar was the size of a calf, with a vicious long horn. As soon as it saw Dhiarmuid enter the clearing, it turned upon him and charged.

Dhiarmuid threw his spear, but it clattered from the head of the boar and fell uselessly on the ground. The huge boar charged forward, bellowing in anger. It speared Dhiarmuid Ui Duibhne on its great horn. Ui Duibhne fell to the ground still locked in the embrace of the boar.

Now Ior attacked from behind, shaking at the neck of the great beast. The boar turned his head in the direction of the dog. Ui Duibhne drew his dagger and stabbed the boar through the heart. The pig dropped down beside him and died.

Dhiarmuid lifted himself from the great horn, but as soon as he was free his lifeblood spilled into his hands. Thus it was that Fionn, Oscar and Osian found him, kneeling in the clearing with his heart's blood spilling into his palms.

Oscar ran to him and laid him out on the ground, with Ui Duibhne's head in his lap.

"Grandfather," he cried out. "What is there to be done?"

"Nothing can be done," said Fionn. "For long ago this curse was put upon Ui Duibhne, that he would die on the horns of a boar. And so it has come to pass."

Oscar looked up in anger.

"You tricked him into this."

"Nay," said Ui Duibhne, "he did not. For I knew it was a boar we followed, but I wished to hunt with my captain once again. Only I ask that Fionn bring me water, for if I could drink once from his hands, I might yet live."

Now Fionn went to a nearby spring and he cupped water into his hands and he brought it back to the clearing. But when he saw them all looking upon him in accusation, he let the water spill from his hands.

"I tell you I had naught to do with his goring!" he cried.

"It is true," said Ui Duibhne.

"Grandfather," said Oscar, and his voice was low and threatening. "Bring him water from your hands."

Fionn returned to the spring and came back with his hands cupped. He knelt beside Ui Duibhne and bent over him.

"Why did you betray me?" he whispered.

The water trickled from his hands.

Ui Duibhne looked at him.

"I loved you ever, Fionn," he said clearly.

Fionn made a strangled cry. He leaped to his feet and ran to the well, filling his hands with water. He stumbled into the clearing and dropped to his knees beside Ui Duibhne. He brought the water the Dhiarmuid's lips, but it was too late. The light flickered out in Ui Duibhne's eyes and he died.

As the Fenians of Eire chanted the Dord Fionn, Fionn dropped over the body of Ui Duibhne and wept like a child.

Toward late afternoon, the Fenians made a litter of aspen branches and quicken bows. They carried Ui Duibhne home on these, with Fionn behind them leading poor wounded Ior.

Grainne saw them coming from over the hill. She ran from the dun and down to the body of Dhiarmuid. The Fenians laid him gently at her feet and she fell upon him weeping, pulling at her hair and scratching her arms. The Fenians stood silently around her. At last she came to her feet.

"Fionn Mac Cumhail," she cried. "You are responsible for the death of Dhiarmuid Ui Duibhne. I know not how, but I lay this death at your feet and at those of your family."

She pointed at Osian and Oscar.

"As for me and mine," she gathered her weeping children to her sides, "you are accursed of us forever. Never again will we speak your name without a curse to accompany it."

But Angus Og rode up among them then and dismounted. He was accompanied by several men of the Other and they circled the body of Dhiarmuid Ui Duibhne. As always with the Other, Ui Duibhne seemed then to be bathed in light.

"All of you are to blame here," said Angus, speaking in slow, measured tones.

He pointed to Grainne.

"For when you could have been honest, you lied."

He gestured to Fionn.

"And when you could have been forgiving, you hardened your heart."

And then he knelt beside his foster son.

"And when he could have been wise and found ways to talk to an answer, he followed instead an ancient, foolish path of honor."

He wept then, bending above the body of Dhiarmuid.

"So are you all punished," he said, slowly. "All punished."

He stood.

"You had him in life," he said to the assembled company. "Now we will take him in death."

They lifted the bier and rode away with the body of Dhiarmuid Ui Duibhne.

Fionn and the Fenians stood facing the weeping Grainne.

"Give me his hound," she commanded Fionn.

Fionn shook his head.

"What need have you of a hound?" he asked. "This hound fought for Ui Duibhne's life and now I will keep him with me."

Grainne rushed at Fionn and pounded her fists on his chest.

"This is Ior!" Grainne screamed. "Lasting. Do you hear me, Fionn? Lasting. This is Ior."

Osian lifted Grainne gently from Fionn's chest.

Oscar spoke low.

"Grandfather," he said softly. "Will you try to separate them even in death? Will the great leader of the Fenians shame himself over Ui Duibhne's dog?"

Fionn looked stricken then. He took to horse and left them and was not seen for many days. When he returned, he was old and tired. All the life had gone from his eyes.

We sat in silence for a long time after the telling. Osian was weeping and I let him do so, for my own heart was heavy.

"This is not a tale I will like to remember," I said at last.

"No," he said. "I left them soon after that, Padraig. Soon after. And I never saw either of them again."

He looked up at me with a pleading expression.

"I must know," he said urgently. "I must know what became of them. My father. My son. How did they die?"

"Who would know this?" I asked.

Osian shook his head.

"Caoilte. Caoilte would know."

I knew he spoke of the rider at the treeline. For once, I did not wound his aged heart.

"Tell me how to find him, Osian. I will go wherever you tell me. I will find him if it will give you heartsease."

He shook his head.

"I do not know. Only I think that where he is you could not go."

"Is there any one in Eire who would know?"

"The storytellers used to know. The poets and the seanchaies. Those who passed the stories down. But I think those times are gone. No one remembers us anymore. No one remembers."

A face filled my head suddenly and clearly.

"The old man!" I said aloud.

Osian smiled sadly.

"Tonight I cannot even argue with you, Padraig. For I am the most aged of men."

"No. No. The old man. Coplait. The druid of Tara Hill."

"What of him? You told me of him, but I was not with you."

"He knows. Coplait knows."

"Of my father? How do you know this?"

"I do not know," I said. "But sleep, Osian. I will leave you in Breogan's care. I will find Coplait for you if I have to search the length and breadth of Eire."

I found the brothers gathered in the dining hall, looking somber.

"He is dying, isn't he, Padraig?" asked Breogan.

"He is weak and sad. He tells tragic stories of his father and his son. He wishes to know how they died. I must find this out for him."

"How?"

"Remember the old man Coplait?"

Breogan nodded.

"He will know. I must find him. I will start at Tara Hill, for that is where he may be."

"He is not at Tara Hill." Benin spoke calmly from where he sat at the table, braiding a cross of straw.

"How do you know?"

"Because he is with Ainfean."

"And I suppose that you will tell me now that you have known where she has been all this time?"

Benin nodded.

"She dwells in the clochan by the Eastern sea."

"Why did you not tell me this?"

Benin looked up in surprise.

"You did not ask," he said.

26

Though I am no horseman, I rode through the darkness, ducking beneath branches and splashing through streams to come to the little dwelling.

It was a stone hut by the sea, small and corbelled, like a miniature church.

Though it was the middle of the night, she was standing outside waiting for me when I rode up.

I threw myself from the saddle and ran to her, clutching her upper arms.

"Osian is dying," I said.

"Yes."

"He wishes to know of the end of his father's life. It will give him heartsease. But none at Sabhal Padraig know. I thought of the old man. Wake him, Ainfean. Wake him."

"He is not with me."

"No. Oh no. But Benin said . . ."

"He was with me," she said calmly. "But he has departed."

"Then we must find him. Gather your things."

I released her arms, made for the little clochan.

"Succatus," she said softly. "My things are here beside me."

"You knew that I was coming?"

"I did not. But Coplait knew."

"Then where is he?"

"He has gone to Sabhal Padraig."

"How did he know?"

"Unlike you, he has a great stillness at his heart. Voices speak in that stillness."

I looked at her quietly, thought of the many things that I should say.

"There will be time at Sabhal Padraig," she said, as if I had spoken aloud.

I put her before me on the horse. I could smell the sea in her hair and peat fire in her cloak. The smell and feel of her made me dizzy; I rode as fast as I could toward Sabhal Padraig.

She did not speak at all.

When we reached the monastery, I could see candlelight guttering from Osian's window.

"They wake him. He has died," I said.

I lurched toward the monastery. She dropped her bundle and ran beside me.

All the brothers were there around him, Benin curled at the foot of his bed. Osian was sitting up and smiling in their midst. Beside him sat Coplait, his hand curled firmly over the aged hand of Osian.

"Damned, cursed Hibernians," I shouted. "No one ever tells me anything. Things happen here that should not happen. I will never understand this place. Never!"

Osian laughed.

"I am glad to see you as well, Padraig." He turned to Coplait. "Coplait greets you, his brother in Christ. He says that now you are here, we may begin."

Coplait signalled to Ainfean and she came and sat opposite him.

He placed his hands on either side of her head and looked quietly into her eyes. In a few moments her head came forward and rested against the forehead of the old man. They sat that way for some time while I fidgeted in the window embrasure. At last Ainfean gave a great sigh and opened her eyes.

"I will tell the tale," she said, "as Coplait has told it to me."

For a long time after the death of Dhiarmuid Ui Duibhne, Grainne, the daughter of Cormac, lived in the south and had no contact with any of the people of Fionn, nor would she speak with her father, great King Cormac. She raised her children with great hatred for Fionn Mac Cumhail and she grew bitter and lonely.

As for Fionn, his heart was heavy with grief and sorrow. His son Osian had left him and his grandson Oscar looked upon him with bitterness. Fionn went alone into the great forests of Eire and there he stayed for many months. He thought over his long life and he remembered the teachings of Finegas. And there in the green heart of Eire Fionn called upon the vision of his childhood. He placed his thumb firmly between his teeth and held it there. In the quiet center of his heart he prayed for guidance. And the vision came. He saw the world as one, suffused with light. Before him moved the faces of those he loved. Sabh. His son Osian and his grandson Oscar. Caoilte Mac Ronan. His mother and Bodhmall and Liath. Great Cormac. Goll Mac Morna.

The heart of Fionn broke with remorse and sorrow and was remade in that vision. And Fionn knew what he must do.

He went alone to the rath of Grainne in Kesh-Carraigh. He stood outside her walls and called her name. When she came forward, he knelt before her.

"We have brought each other much sorrow, wife of Ui Duibhne. But between us we brought more sorrow to Dhiarmuid, beloved of us both. I am here to make payment for that death.

"I will be your cumhal if you wish it, the dog of your household if you prefer. Whatever you need it will be done, for as long as it requires for us to make peace between us."

"Get thee gone," cried Grainne. "For there will never be peace between us as long as you are alive in Eire."

But Fionn would not depart. He built a bothy outside her walls and there he remained. He carried wood for the fires of her people and water for her dogs. He helped in the building of huts in the great rath and he taught the young men to ride.

The people of Kesh-Carraigh softened toward him for they said that Fionn of the great heart had returned to Eire.

But Grainne would not soften.

Then one night, the youngest child of Grainne, a boy of some five years, fell ill. The healer was called, but she could not stop the fever of the child.

"Go to Fionn Mac Cumhail," said the healer. "He will know where to take your child."

Grainne refused, but her daughter, who was nearing her womanhood, spoke to her.

"You are a woman of great pride, mother, but you are wrong in this. We your children have watched Fionn here at Kesh-Carraigh. He speaks no harsh word to any among us. He does the lowest work with a full heart. If you sacrifice our brother for your pride and anger, you do wrong by both our father and this Fenian."

Grainne looked long at the girl.

"I made the mistake of pride once before," she said humbly, and she donned her cloak.

At the bothy of Fionn, she stood in the firelight. He stood before her.

"My child is dying," she said simply.

Fionn ran with her to her dwelling. He lifted the feverish child to his chest and he prayed.

"Oh you gods! Take my life for the life of this child. Would that I could have done the same for Ui Duibhne."

He turned to Grainne.

"We must ride with him to Tara Hill. There Cormac houses the greatest healers of Eire."

Grainne made her choice then.

"You must ride with him, Fionn. I would only slow you down."

When Fionn returned weeks later with the healthy child, Grainne ran from her dwelling. She clasped the child to her and let tears of joy and sorrow stream down her face.

"I have wronged you, Fenian," she said. "Now and in the earlier time."

"We have both wronged Ui Duibhne," said Fionn.

They were married in a year's time. Fionn returned with Grainne and her children to Almhuin.

At first the Fenians were reluctant to accept her.

"Ui Duibhne was worth a thousand of her," grumbled Conan Maor.

But Caoilte Mac Ronan raised his hand.

"We will treat her with the respect that is due the wife of Fionn Mac Cumhail and the wife of our brother Dhiarmuid Ui Duibhne," he said.

And in time Grainne came to earn that respect, for though Fionn was a man in his seventies and she a woman in her forties, in the full blossom of her womanhood, she was a faithful and loving wife to Fionn and he a doting husband to her and father to her children.

Between them they kept the memory of Ui Duibhne alive.

*　　*　　*

Osian's face was shining when Ainfean finished the recitation.

"You have given me back my father," he proclaimed. "Full of honor, as I remembered him."

Coplait patted his hand and smiled.

Osian leaned back against his wolfskins.

"You must rest," I said, quietly.

He nodded.

"On the morrow, Padraig," he said. "On the morrow, I would tell you of Niamh of the Golden Hair. For we have very little time."

27

I have wronged you greatly."

I said it simply and directly.

"You have, Succat," she said.

I sighed. This would not be easy.

We were seated on the bench in the monastery garden. Dawn was an hour or two away and the night was still and quiet. Moonlight spilled on the plants and along the little stone walkway.

I sighed again.

She was silent.

"When I came here I did not understand the druids. . . ."

"Nor do you still," she snapped.

"Perhaps that is so," I said quietly. "There is much that I do not understand."

She turned her head toward me then, but I looked out over the garden.

"I thought that the druids were servants of darkness. I know now that that was wrong. I know that among them are teachers and healers, people of great wisdom. Many have been baptized in Christ as Coplait and Mal have done."

She said nothing.

"Nor do I understand women."

She expelled a quick breath.

"So say you?" Her voice was heavy with sarcasm.

"Ainfean, I try here. I try."

"Speak the truth simply, priest. You fear it, so you edge around it as moonlight edges these stones."

"Very well. I thought that you had ordered us arrested at Tara. I thought that you tried to stop the word of the Lord from coming to Eire. I thought that you had us stripped and shamed and held in chains. I thought that you conspired with Matha Mac Umotri. And I thought that you did all of this out of your deep hatred of me. I was wrong. I ask for your forgiveness."

"Well, this is simple enough. You have my forgiveness then."

I turned to look at her.

"Is it so easily said then?"

"Easily said, yes. The heart is another matter."

She was looking at me directly. Her eyes were grey in the moonlight.

"Your eyes change colors," I said. "It is a thing I have noticed."

The corner of her mouth twitched.

"Osian has been telling you stories of the Other."

"He has, but I do not believe them."

"I am flesh and blood, as you are, Succat."

"I know that."

"You fear that."

"Why should I fear that?"

Ainfean said nothing.

"Very well. I fear that."

Still she said nothing.

I stumbled on.

"You say that you are flesh and blood. It is a thing I notice. Do you think that I do not see the light in your hair, smell the flowers in it? Do you think I can ignore the whiteness of your skin? Your mouth twitches when you smile. It is precious to me. Precious. I have driven you from Sabhal Padraig and driven you from me, because I am a man. A man after all my striving. And I cannot drive it from me. I cannot! And I would not break my vow to my Lord for the sake of my weakness."

"You underestimate me, Padraig." She said it softly.

"Nay, I do not. For even sitting here beside you, the power of you over-whelms me and I must make fists of my hands not to take yours in mine."

"You underestimate my love for you."

I looked right at her then, my eyes wide.

"I know how you feel for me. It was there between us from the first day. It is how I feel for you as well. Padraig, your God does not wish for you not to be a man. You are a man that you may be human. But you have made a vow. I understand the nature of a vow. I am a druidess, Padraig. We too make vows and strive to keep them. Do you hold me so little worthy that you believe I would be the instrument of your guilt and sorrow?"

"I hold you more worthy than myself." I said it softly.

We sat quietly for a few minutes. When she spoke her voice was without accusation.

"You lean too much on your fear, Succat. You fear Eire; you fear that it will grow in you and that you will stay here forever."

"I fear it less now than when I came."

"But you should not fear it at all; you should dwell here in joy. Is that not what your Lord would wish you to do?"

"Before I came here . . ." I began, but I shook my head.

"I am not a joyful man, Ainfean."

"You are fierce. Joy is a close cousin to that fierceness."

I felt something rise in me then, something akin to heat and I spoke without measuring my words.

"I love you, Ainfean," I said simply. "I love the old man and the brothers and Benin and the people of Sabhal Padraig. I love old Fionn Mac Cumhail. I pray nightly for his soul. I did not know before. I never knew."

She smiled.

"Ah, Padraig," she said. "And now you do. See how your God has gifted you."

I nodded. It was a moment before I could speak to her again.

"I would have you take baptism, Ainfean. I would have you take the vows. I would have you be one of us, a druid of Christ, spreading his word in Eire."

"There are few priests among the women of your religion."

"There are few; I do not know if there will be more or fewer still. But there is no other place like Eire. Here the people will listen to your wisdom. You need not be a priest to speak of the Christ."

"And the sisters?" she asked.

"They must each do what they choose," I said. "For the women of Eire will choose in spite of me."

She laughed.

"You are learning well."

"Will you join us at Sabhal Padraig? I will hold you in my heart and never do you injury again."

She laughed aloud.

"That is a promise neither of us will keep, priest."

I shrugged.

"We can try."

"I must think on these things," she said softly. "I must go apart from you and pray."

"Only do not be gone too long." I looked back at Osian's window.

She nodded.

"It will not be long," she said. She left the garden. I sat on the bench and watched the moonlight shift against the stones. For a few moments it was silent and then I heard soft footsteps. Benin stood by my bench in his night-shirt and bare feet.

"He said that you were here, Padraig," he said. He yawned behind his hand.

"Breogan is still awake?"

"Oh no. They all sleep. Even Osian."

"Then who?"

"The Voice, Padraig. Sometimes it speaks to me and sometimes it sings."

"The Voice speaks in me as well. Or it did. When I was young. And sometimes before I came here. Not so much now."

"I know. It will come again when you are still and listening." He nodded. He sat beside me on the bench and put his slender hand in mine.

"Have you asked Ainfean to return to us?"

"I have. Did the Voice tell you that?"

"No," he said sleepily. He leaned his head on my shoulder. "I know that this is where she belongs."

"She may not think that, child. She may not return to us. I have been . . . unkind."

Benin sighed.

"She will return, Padraig."

I ruffled his hair.

"Such wisdom in so small a package."

"I am not wise, Padraig," he said in sleepy tones. "But the Voice is wise for me."

A strange howling went up from the woods beyond the treeline. It stopped and started again.

"Wolves," I said. "Or wolfhounds."

"Oh no," said Benin. "That is the people of the Other. They are singing for Osian."

"Singing for him?"

"Yes, he will leave us soon."

He began to sing then, matching the eerie song note for note. I shivered a little in the cool morning air.

"I do not believe in these Other. Nor should you."

Benin sighed again. I put my arm around him and he nestled against my shoulder.

"Perhaps it does not matter so much what we believe, Padraig," he said. "Perhaps it matters what God believes."

I looked down at him quietly.

"Perhaps," I said.

I sat still and quiet with the little boy tucked in the crook of my arm. Dawn light pearled across the wet lawn and misted the eastern sky. The sun rose. At first light, I heard the Voice speaking clear in me.

"I love thee well, Padraig," it said.

My heart rejoiced to hear it.

28

After Dhiarmuid died, nothing was the same. We hunted the mountains of Slieve Bloom and the forests around Almhuin, but the joy had gone from the hunt. There was no way to mend what had been lost.

It was on just such a hunt that she came for me. The day was fine and full of sunlight. We had been hunting beside Loch Lene, but we had stopped to eat in the warm sun. We saw her riding toward us along the shores of the water.

I remember that I stood.

It was not just that she was beautiful. Her hair was rose-gold, early copper, the color of autumn leaves just before they fall. She was in a white tunic and cloak, riding a white horse. It was as though she and the horse were one, for the reins lay slack on the back of the animal and he brought her toward us of his own accord.

I watched her; it seemed to me that she watched me as well.

When she drew close enough, I saw that her eyes were grey, then green, shifting to match her surroundings. The sunlight of the day cascaded from her hair, her dress, her arms.

She stopped before me and smiled.

"Osian," she said simply.

I nodded.

"You are of the Danaan." It seemed the most ordinary exchange, like a comment upon the weather.

"I am. I am Niamh. I have watched you long. You are a man of honor and courage. I have chosen you for husband. Though it is seldom permitted for those of us of the Other to marry with you, my father has given permission because he too has seen you and knows you to be, of the men of Eire, most honest.

"Therefore, Fenian, if you will choose me, I will take you to my country and we will live together in the Land of the Ever Young."

She sat her horse strong and proud, but I could see in her eyes that she was afraid. I knew that she feared I would decline.

But that I could not have done, for the moment I saw her my blood sang; my tongue became thick and my heart raced like thunder. I was young when I married the mother of Oscar. She was a lovely girl and sweet, but my affection for her was not one leaf trembling of what I felt with Niamh.

I walked to her horse and lifted her hand into mine.

It was not necessary to speak, for I felt that she already knew my heart.

She smiled and I smiled back at her.

I turned to my father and Oscar. Tears started up in my father's eyes.

"Come, let me hold you," he said. "For I think that we will not meet again."

"We will," I said. "I do not go to death, but to be married. Do not weep so. I will come back to hunt with you just as we have done."

But even as I said, it, I knew that it was not so, for those days of the Fenians were gone.

My father held me to him hard. He approached his seventieth year then, but he was strong; I could feel his grief through his arms.

He turned to the woman.

"Woman of the sidhe, love him well. For my son is a man of more honor and courage than I have been."

"We will live long and joyful lives, O Fionn," she said.

Oscar clasped arms with me in the Fenian way.

"Great joy, father," he said, seriously. Then he leaned in and whispered to me. "Would that she had chosen me."

I laughed aloud and clasped him hard to me.

I swung up on the saddle behind Niamh and we rode toward the west. Behind me I could hear my father chanting the Dord Fionn, slow and stately as a dirge.

Niamh sang to me of her country as we rode. Sometimes her voice was like wind over water, sometimes as flutes or doves. I never tired of her voice, for all the mysteries of the earth and sky were in it.

And oh the wonders we saw on our journey to the Land of the Ever Young.

We rode to the western sea. When I thought we would plunge into the waves, we rode above them, as pelicans do or gulls, so swift and light was the white steed of Niamh. When we had crossed the water, we came into a land where I had never been before. A fawn moved swiftly across our path, followed by a snow white hound with a red ear. Soon a maiden rode toward us on a brown steed. She held a golden apple in her right hand; the light gleamed from it as we passed. Close behind her rode a warrior on a white steed. He wore a mantle of golden silk and carried a sword of gold in his right hand.

"What is the meaning of these signs?" I asked her, but she shook her head.

"They are the portents of other times, of what has been and what is to come. They are not for us to understand, but for the greater ones."

All these I saw again when I returned to Eire, but I no more know what they mean now than I knew when I traveled across the water. There are more wonders in the wide world than we who are human can know.

So I was content to be silent and I rode behind Niamh in wonderment.

At last we reached the Land of the Ever Young. Oh, brothers, there is nothing I can say that will tell you of its great beauty. Only imagine the finest summer's day, with a sky of blue and billowing clouds. Picture the purest lake, cascading waterfalls of silver, bushes ripe with berries and forests full with living things.

And in that country they do not make war; nor do they grow ill or die. They do not grieve. In that country there is feasting, singing, laughter.

I married Niamh in that country, before the great assembly of the Danaan.

Not a day passed that my heart was not joyful in her presence.

I thought often of my father and Sabh, my mother, for just so it must have been between them. I weighed my father's loss against my own joy. How I loved her.

In the touch of her hand all weariness was healed, all sorrow. In her laughter I remained young.

We had three years together.

And yet I know now that it was not three years.

The dreams began suddenly. I was asleep beside her in the darkness when I heard the baying of Bran and Sgeolan. I sat up. She was awake immediately.

"What is it, Osian?" she whispered.

"My father's hounds," I said. "I heard them."

"You but dream," she said softly. She lifted her face above mine and the hair of fire cascaded around my face; I forgot all dreaming in the sweetness of her kiss.

Yet the next night I dreamed again. I was riding beside Oscar and Fionn in the mountains of Slieve Bloom. Fionn spoke.

"At last we are together again," he said. My heart leapt with the joy of hunting in Eire with my father and my son. I sat up.

Niamh awoke, but this time she did not comfort me. Instead, she looked into my face for a very long time, and her eyes were sad.

279

On the third night, I dreamed the strangest dream of all.

A man came to me. He was dressed in a druid's robe of white embroidered with gold. His hair was red.

"I do not know you," I said.

"Eire has need of you," was all he answered.

When I awoke that morning Niamh had my horse already saddled. She had packed for me a feast and strapped it to my horse's flank.

"Do not unhorse yourself in Eire," she said. "Or I fear that we will not meet again."

"I will return in three days time," I said. "Three days to see my father and my son. You must trust in my love for you."

But she shook her head.

"Husband, I know your love for me; it is not that I fear. You will find your country much changed. The change will bring you sorrow. And yet I know that you must go. Only do not unhorse yourself. Do not set foot upon the ground in Eire."

"Why not? What should I fear in my own country?"

"It will not be the country you remember, Osian. Time passes differently here among us."

She kissed me and folded herself into my arms. For a few moments she clung there like a frightened child. Though I had never seen her weep, her eyes were filled with tears.

"My love," she said. "My one true love."

As I rode to the east, she called out behind me.

"Do not set foot on the ground in Eire."

I know now why she said that. For you see before you an aged and withered man, but he who left her was young and strong.

I know too that it was not three years that I had with Niamh.

For when I returned to Eire my father and my son were dead. I fell into this body and into the monastery of Padraig of the Christ. And ever since that time I have wished for one moment with Niamh, one moment with Fionn or Oscar.

He was silent.

Breogan scratched at his papers. I watched the face of the old man.

"Padraig," he said softly, "think you that I shall ever see them again? Fionn my father, Oscar my son, Niamh my beloved. Are they lost to me forever?"

I did not know what to say.

"You do not believe in the Other. Even after all of the stories I have told, you do not believe."

I did not, but that was not what I said. For when I spoke, I surprised myself.

"I believe in a God who restores all things, Osian. All that has been lost to us will be restored. This is the gift of the Christ. Though life be lost and love and all that we hold dear, it will be given back to us again in him."

Osian's eyes lit up; his face was joyful.

"Padraig," he said, "O, Padraig. You are worthy after all. I will take baptism of you, druid of Christ."

I stared at him, incredulous. I had given up asking him, contented myself with praying daily for his heathen soul.

"Why have you decided this?"

"I have not. You have decided for me. For if that is the way of your God, then your God shall be mine."

I ran for my oil and water, set them up there in his room.

"Old man," I said when I had anointed him. "We shall be together in eternity."

Osian nodded.

"Together in the Land of the Ever Young."

"Tir Nan Og," Benin chirped from his perch at the foot of the bed.

My heart was too joyful to correct them.

29

Five days passed with no word from Ainfean. Osian grew weaker by the hour now, but he spoke daily of wanting to know of the death of his father and son.

On the morning of the sixth day, the rider appeared at the treeline. He lingered for a long time, his cloak lifting in the occasional breeze. At last I could bear it no more and I started toward him across the field. But I was halfway across when he wheeled the big black horse and disappeared into the woods.

His long appearance worried me.

We brought Coplait to Osian's chamber.

"Do you know the tale?" I asked him.

Coplait nodded.

"Can you tell it to him directly?"

Osian spoke from his bed.

"He cannot, Padraig. It takes great learning to be able to speak without words. I do not have the training."

"Then you could not work through me."

Coplait shook his head, but he smiled at me and patted my hand, I suppose to approve my willingness to try.

I brought him Breogan's tools then, his ink and parchments.

"If you can write it for me, I will read it to him," I said, but the old man made signs that he did not write.

"It is forbidden to the druids to write," said Osian.

Breogan nodded.

"Nothing can be written. It must all be passed down by memory."

I raised my arms in frustration.

"Damnable woman. How long could it take her to make up her mind?" Then I remembered that I had said to her that we would not wound each other so and I felt ashamed. I went to the chapel to pray.

I knelt in the drifting motes of sunlight and tried to clear my mind, but it buzzed like the hives of bees we had begun to keep.

I spoke aloud.

"He will leave us soon. I know that. The light in his body falters. I do not know how you sent him among us; perhaps Benin is right. Perhaps I do not need to know. Only know that my heart gives you gratitude for this gift."

I bent my head low over what I was about to ask.

"Father, hear my prayers for those he loves. His father and his son. The woman Niamh. The Fenians of his tales. I know not how to ask more, but I trust your answer."

"Padraig." She spoke softly from behind me. My heart leapt within me. I remained kneeling, turned in her direction. I knew as soon as I looked at her what choice she had made for her face was suffused with joy.

"He came to me, Padraig. Your messenger."

She came and knelt beside me.

"My messenger."

"He wore a druid robe, embroidered with gold. And his hair was red. He said that he was your friend. He looked like a man of the Other."

I looked up startled.

"Is that what they look like?"

"It is."

She smiled.

"I was in the clochan by the sea. I did not eat or sleep for many days and I wondered in my heart what I should do. When I arose at dawn he was sitting outside my door. He had bread and clear, cool spring water from a jar. I asked him his name.

"'I am the Victoricus, the messenger,' he said.

"'What message do you bring?' I asked him.

"'You need no message,' he said. 'For your heart has chosen for you already.'

" 'If that is true,' I said to him, 'then why are you here?'

"Then he did a strange thing.

"He laughed aloud and he looked up.

" 'Why *do* you always choose the difficult ones?' he said. He seemed to wait for an answer and then he nodded.

" 'You are strong of spirit, Ainfean,' he said. 'Your voice will be a strong voice for the Lord. Prepare yourself for a journey, for as the Lord has sent Padraig here to Eire, so he will send you with those who need you.' "

"What does this mean? On what journey will the Lord send you?"

"I do not know, Padraig. The messenger said this and I accepted it."

"What more did he say?"

"He broke a piece of the bread then and handed it to me. I ate it."

Her face colored.

"Padraig," she said. "Oh, Padraig. I have tasted of the salmon of knowledge."

We held her baptism in the chamber of Osian. Never has a stranger group assembled in the name of the Lord.

The people of Sabhal Padraig gathered, for she was their healer. Our smith still wore his fire-blackened apron from the forge. All of the brothers came as well. Old Coplait stood beside her, the two of them in their white druid robes. Osian sat propped against the pillows, his Fenian cloak up beneath his chin. Beside him the hounds of Dichu slobbered and made excited yipping sounds. Benin rang his little bell and we chanted the Faed Fiada, though I left off the part about women, smiths and wizards, seeing that all three were present in the chamber.

When we had anointed her, she took the vows to serve the Lord with her goods, her body and her spirit.

We raised her up among us and my heart rejoiced.

"Feast!" cried Dichu. "Feast! Osian, you must tell us a tale."

I knew that the old man was too weak and too far gone for tale-telling, so I held up my hand. But before I could protest, Osian spoke.

"Bring me a bodhran," he said. "For though I have no tale to tell, yet I have a poem of my father which I would give to the people of Sabhal Padraig."

Benin scrambled to find the goatskin drum from the village and Osian beat on it slow and deep. The thrumming filled the room with sound. Osian chanted his rosc.

Remember us, remember us.
We who are ancient of Eire.
By feast and firelight think on us,
for we are among you then.

When the deer starts from the hollow
we follow Fionn again.
If the battle rages,
chant for us the Dord Fionn.

When horses thunder at Almhuin,
when black crows call from the trees,
when wolves cry from wild Slieve Bloom,
remember Oscar, Fionn, Osian.

When the hulls of the barks toss the wave,
when the gull cries at Kesh Carraighe,
when the cattle low at Glen da Moil,
think on the Fenians of Eire.

When the hounds are baying in Duirhos wood,
when Bran cries at Cnoc-an-air,
when the stream sings over the stones,
Listen! For we will be there.

I will like to remember him that way always, drumming on the ancient drum, his voice strong, the green of his Fenian cloak around him. I will remember him thus.

In the morning, we gathered in his chamber. Ainfean was ready with the tale as Coplait had told it to her.

When Cormac Mac Art died, his son Cairbry became high king of Eire.

Cairbry was not the king that his father had been, nor did he hold the Fenians in high esteem, for he felt that they had too much power in Eire. Secretly, he looked for a way to destroy them.

That way came with Cairby's daughter Sgeimh Sholais. Sgeimh Sholais was a treasure. Her name meant Beauty of Light; it was a name that befitted her well. But Cairbry plighted her troth, without asking her, to a king from across the water. In truth, the daughter of Cairbry was in love with Fergus, a young warrior of the Fianna.

Now it was the custom at that time for the king to give the Fenians gold when one of royalty married. The Fenians knew of the love between Fergus and the daughter of Cairbry, so they sent the young man to claim the Fenian tribute, that he might spirit the daughter away among the Fenians.

But Cairbry knew as well and had been waiting for just such an opportunity.

When Fergus entered the hall to demand the tribute, Cairbry had his guards surround him. Before the surprised boy could even so much as look at his beloved he was thrust through the chest with a spear and dumped over the walls of Tara Hill.

His broken body fell onto the stone below.

Now Oscar vowed vengeance for his dead companion.

"Long did father and Cormac Mac Art share the protection of Eire," he cried. "But no more. For from this day forward the Fenians of Eire account themselves as servants of the land, but not her king."

Now some of the clans of Mac Morna had been nursing a long hatred for Fionn ever since Art Mac Morna was slain.

And these warriors took sides with Cairbry Mac Cormac. Cairbry swelled their numbers with his own warriors, with Lochlanders and hirelings until at last he brought to bear an army of ten thousand men against three thousand of the Fenian warriors of Eire.

The two armies met in the Battle of Gabhra.

For a time the battle went for the Fenians, for outnumbered as they were, they were the finest fighting men that Eire had ever known. No Lochlanders or hirelings could stand against them.

But eventually the numbers took their toll. One by one the Fenians fell beneath the sword.

At last, Oscar came face to face with Cairbry Mac Cormac.

"You will die," cried Oscar, "for you are a king without honor."

He thrust up with his sword and cleaved Cairbry Mac Cormac upon the blade, but Cairbry, falling backward, thrust up with his spear and caught Oscar just below his heart.

The Fenians bore Oscar back to Fionn, who directed the battle from the top of a rise. When Fionn saw Oscar, he dropped to his knees and howled at the sky. Oscar spoke to him with his last breath.

"Do not mourn for me, grandfather," he said. "For I have died as a Fenian should die."

Battle rage came over Fionn then. He lifted Good Striker in his aged hands and he rushed into the melee. He thrust hard left and right, cutting down many of the warriors of Cairbry, but at last he stood surrounded by an entire fian of his enemies.

He raised Good Striker above his head then.

"For Eire!" he cried.

And thus the chief of the Fenians died. And with him died the Fianna of Eire. For once Fionn was gone, the Fianna were united no more.

I feared the old man's reaction to the story, but when I looked at him he was smiling.

"It is well," he said. "For they died as heroes should die."

But we knew that these were his last days among us, and our sadness was not for the tale. We did not know then that we would lose more than just Osian.

I scented the trouble on the morning air before I heard or saw. There was a smell, as of burning. I rose from the pallet on the floor beside Osian's bed and gazed out over the village below. Two of our huts were afire!

And then, among them, I saw the flash of steel and heard the clang of weapons. Soldiers! Roman soldiers among us, for now I recognized the helmets and tunics, the bright breastplates of the Romans.

Confused, I ran toward the melee. Women and children ran everywhere, screaming, and the crackle of the fire and its heat roared above everyone. I saw a Roman sword cut down one of our men; he fell to the ground as his attacker seized his wife and threw her over his shoulder. He turned and raced for the sea.

It was then that I understood.

Slaves! They had come for slaves!

Breogan ran toward me from the monastery door, his robe thrown on in haste, his face a whitened mask.

"Padraig!" he called. "Our blacksmith holds one of them in the smithy."

I ran in the direction he pointed. Inside the smithy, our great blacksmith had bound one of the soldiers tight to a pillar with a great chain.

"Whose men are you?" I cried to the soldier in Latin.

He seemed surprised to hear his own tongue, answered me readily.

"We are the soldiers of Coroticus."

"You are my countrymen!" I screamed. "These are my people. Converts of the Christ."

The soldier shook his head in confusion.

"They are Hibernians," he said. "We took many as slaves before dawn. These are but the last few."

Fear ran through me, cold and watery. I ran out into the village. Men lay dead on the ground or walked confused among the huts. I circled in terror. Ainfean, Benin! I ran for their hut, burst through the doorway.

The little hut was empty, the tables overturned, the skulls of the ancestors scattered and broken on the ground.

"Breogan!" I ran into the yard. "Breogan, bring horses."

He appeared nearby, horses already at the ready. We mounted and rode toward the sea.

The sorrow that greeted us there shall stay with me for all my days. Most of the boats of Coroticus had already put out to sea. They had pulled beyond the ninth wave, turned toward Britain. I could hear the cries of the women and children drifting back toward me across the water. The last of the boats was pulling away from shore and I ran toward it, hitching up my robe, crying aloud.

"Coroticus! You, Coroticus!"

I ran into the water, up to my knees.

The leader looked up at me. He was a small, thickset man. His look of surprise at hearing his own tongue did not stop his shoulders from pulling at the oars. Before him, her arms sheltered tight around Benin, was Ainfean.

"Coroticus!" I cupped my hands around my mouth and called above the water and the wind. The little boat heaved and bobbed on the swells. "Hear me now. I am Magonus Succatus Patricius of Bannaevum on Tiburnae. I am your countryman. These are my people, the converts of the White Christ. They are not and cannot be your slaves. Return them to me now, or I will bring down upon you all the power of the Church."

Behind him, his boats pulled further away, the cries of my people lost on the wind. But Coroticus gave his oarsmen the command to pause in their rowing. I took in my breath, prayed. I saw him think for a moment, turn his head back toward his boats. Ainfean had turned to watch his face and she must have seen the decision at the same time that I saw it. I watched her yank the tunic from little Benin, lift him and throw him into the sea.

"Swim, Benin," she cried. "Swim for Padraig!"

His small white body began to thrash toward us through the waves and I pulled off my robe and began to run toward him.

Behind him, Ainfean stood suddenly and the little boat rocked. Coroticus released his own oars, clutched at her gown. She fell down between the gunwhales.

"Pull!" he cried to his oarsmen, and I saw the boat crest a wave and disappear into a trough.

I reached Benin and pulled him to me. He coughed and sputtered and I held him against my chest.

"Coroticus!" I bellowed it across the sea. "Coroticus. You damn your own soul if you take the people of Christ into slavery."

Now the rest of our village clattered up behind us, most on foot, Osian lying low on the floor of a chariot between the feet of our blacksmith. They gathered around me there in the breaking waves and two of our men formed a chair for Osian. Most of the boats of Coroticus had disappeared beyond our view and our villagers were calling and weeping.

Suddenly Ainfean stood again in the little boat, her feet braced apart. Coroticus reached for her, but she said something to him and he shrunk back, making the sign against the evil in the air.

I heard her voice come to me across the water. She was singing.

> I arise today,
> mighty in strength;
> I have called upon the Trinity;
> I have invoked the Three,
> the Three-in-One.
> I proclaim the Oneness
> of the Creator of Creation.

"Sing to her, Padraig!" cried Osian. "Sing! For she chants to you the Faed Fiada, the Deer's Cry. She tells you that she will protect your people. But only if you give her your strength for the journey."

And so I sang.

289

I arise today
strong on the arm of Heaven.
Light of sun,
radiant moon,
splendid fire,
speed of lightning,
swiftness of wind,
depth of sea,
strength of earth
are given me.

But I sang it clutching the child to my chest. And I sang it through the drumbeat of my sobs. My last view of Ainfean was of her white druid robe, billowing out in the sea wind, like wings above the water.

30

I denounce you as bloodthirsty barbarians, drowning in the blood of the innocents who have come to Christ. Nor will I call you my countrymen or number you among honorable Romans for this deed!"

Beside me at the table, Breogan scribbled down my angry words.

"It will not return them to you, Padraig." Osian spoke tiredly from the bed, his eyes never moving from the treeline.

"It will! I will send this letter to my superiors in Britain and in Gaul. I will send it to Coroticus and his soldiers! My words will bring them back to us!"

"For a fortnight you have worked at this letter by daylight and by lamplight. Yet did all of the words of your parents return you to them from your slavery in Eire?"

I sighed and pressed the heels of my hands against my swollen eyes. In all, we had lost six of our women and four of our children. Two of our men were dead and five wounded. And Ainfean. I had lost Ainfean.

Osian watched me sadly.

"Some of them will return as you returned, Padraig. In their own time, by their own means. Others will never return."

"I cannot bear it, Osian. My people. Our converts. Ainfean. My heart cannot bear this loss!"

"Yes," he said. "It can and it must."

I watched his face, burdened by its own losses and the great weight of his age, and my heart moved to pity for him.

"Come," I said. "We will go again to the garden."

He leaned heavily against me as we made our way through the cool halls of the monastery to the little stone bench by the garden wall. Each day this was our pilgrimage now, each day since the raiders had left us. And when each day passed into evening, we would carry Osian back to his chamber, no closer to his longing for all his vigil by the treeline.

We sat side by side on the bench. I drew up my knees and rested my head upon them, my heart too heavy to permit me to keep watch with him.

"They come for me, Padraig. She sings in the dark by the window."

"You hear the wind. Or the wolves. These last few nights I too heard them." I did not bother to raise my head.

The weight of his hand rested against my back, comforting.

"You have said that yours is a God who restores all things, Padraig. For this I took your baptism. And yet, in the depth of your sorrow, I think that you do not believe it."

I felt the shame burn up crimson in my face, but I could not make him answer. My heart was heavy with loss and I felt that my God was far from me.

Silent hours passed in the garden. The sunlight pressed against us, then moved aside. Evening shadows began to stretch across the field when Osian spoke.

"At last," he whispered. "At last. Padraig, see where they come."

At the treeline, a man and a woman were mounted, a riderless horse between them.

"I go to them, Padraig," Osian said. He stood, took one hesitant step, stumbled to the ground. I ran to him, lifted him against me like a frail child.

"I will take you to them." He shook his head, but I silenced him.

"Do not say me nay, old man. I will take you."

He smiled then, leaned against me.

He was sinewy and heavy, heavier than I would have guessed the frail old body to be. I stumbled a little against the hem of my brown robe. So we made our progress, slowly and awkwardly across the field to the edge of the woods, where they sat. The man seemed impassive, sitting his black mount silently, his blue and green plaid cloak drawn around him, his face immovable. In his hand he held the bridle of the riderless white horse which stood between them. I felt my anger rise at him. If this was Caoilte Mac Ronan, why did he not dismount, help his companion of old?

But oh the woman. She leaned forward in her saddle, stretched her arms toward Osian, moaned aloud to see him so weakened. And she was beautiful, more beautiful than all of Osian's describing. Her hair was the color of flame and it cascaded around her arms, her shoulders, her waist. Her skin was pale, so pale that she seemed to shine from within, as if a lamp illuminated her.

"Oh my love," she murmured. "Oh my dear love."

Osian stirred himself against me. "Niamh," he said, in the cracked voice of an old man. "Niamh, I return."

Behind us I could hear the people of Sabhal Padraig gathering, the brothers and the sisters, the people of our village.

I turned to them with my burden in my arms.

"Stay back," I called, though I knew not why.

When we reached the riders, I stood holding Osian before me like an offering. I spoke to the man.

"If you are Caoilte Mac Ronan, of whom Osian has told me, he has painted you in better colors. Dismount and help your comrade."

A great sorrow moved across his face and he shook his head.

"We cannot dismount, Padraig. We cannot. You should know."

Then I knew that the stern look on his face was at seeing his comrade so aged and disabled. Suddenly I was overwhelmed by the sacrifice that Osian had made to come to me. I felt his weight against me, his body so near death. The cry swelled from my chest and I hurled it against the vaulting blue of the sky.

"No! No! Dear Father, do not let him die! Give him back his life. Give it back!"

Caoilte urged his horse sideways.

"Quickly, Padraig, quickly. You must stand Osian here between his horse and mine."

"He is too weak. I fear he cannot stand. And he cannot mount, Caoilte. You can see that."

"Do not argue with me, priest! There is little time!"

Osian stirred himself against my chest.

"Do as he says, Padraig. Set me here between the horses, then turn and run. Run back across the field."

I lowered him gently. He leaned heavily against the side of the white horse. I stared for a moment into the intense blue of his eyes, then turned, gathered the hem of my robe and started loping awkwardly back across the field. In the distance I could see the brothers gathered at the low wall that separated the monastery garden from the wide field. I saw them watching behind me, heard their collective gasp. I saw Benin stretch out his hands, hope and joy on his child's face. I turned back then. I turned.

I tell you now that it was not a trick of the light, not the afternoon shadows, for I saw as clearly as I have ever seen anything in my life. Osian was mounted, his golden hair streaming in the breeze, his long plaid cloak billowing around his muscular, young body. He was a man in the full flower of his years, a man upon my own years. As I watched, he lifted Niamh's hand in his and kissed it gently and then he raised his arm, fist clenched, high above his head.

I knew then. I knew. That the God in whom I believe restores all things in their fullness. All things, all things, will be restored!

My own arm shot into the air, high above my head, fist clenched. I reveled in the tight feel of the muscles, in the strain on the shoulder, in the youth and beauty of the body and in the tears of hope and joy that cascaded, unashamed and untouched, down my cheeks.

Breogan came and stood next to me then, his own arm raised high. When I turned and smiled at him, he clapped his hand across my shoulder.

Then Benin was beside me and the brothers and sisters, the people of Sabhal Padraig.

Osian called to me across the field.

"I go to them. To Oscar and Fionn. I shall tell them that I have been with you, Magonus Succatus Patricius. I shall tell them all."

I began to laugh. My laughter tumbled and rolled across the field toward him.

"Do not tell them of Patricius," I called.

Osian stood high in his saddle then, his arm outstretched above his comrades. I felt the brothers gather close about me.

"What shall I tell them when they ask me where I have been?" Osian shouted. And he was laughing.

It came to me that the sky and the green earth and the dreaming people of Eire were mine and that I was theirs and that it would be so forever. The Voice whispered my name in the chambers of my heart and I called it aloud to Osian.

"Tell them you have been with Padraig!" I cried. "Tell them you have been with Padraig of Eire."

HISTORICAL BACKGROUND

We know little of Patrick, less of Osian.

The truth, what we might call objective history, is impossible to sort out in the cases of both men.

According to legend, Osian was the son of Fionn Mac Cumhail and Sabh, a woman who sometimes took the form of a deer as a result of a druid curse. Osian was raised by his mother in the forest until the druid forced her away from the boy. Later, he was discovered by Fionn, living in the forest as part of a wolf pack. Fionn brought him into civilization, taught him to speak, and eventually Osian became the poet and storyteller of the Fenians.

His name is variously spelled Oisian, Oisin, Ossian and Osian and pronounced O-sheen. I chose the latter spelling because it seemed closest to the true pronunciation for speakers of English.

Did Osian really exist?

I do not know.

If Fionn really existed, then surely Osian did as well.

Osian's father, Fionn Mac Cumhail (pronounced Finn Mac Cool) was the leader of the Fenian warriors of Ireland, who flourished in that country during the third century A.D. The Fenians were the standing army of King Cormac Mac Art. Their numbers are variously recorded as being between nine and twenty thousand strong. In the winter, these warriors billeted in the villages of Ireland; in summer they dwelled in the forests, living by hunting and fishing and sleeping in three-sided lean-tos called bothies.

A basic unit of the Fenians was the fian, which consisted of either six or twelve members. According to most records, the Fenians were divided into "battalions" of three thousand, each with its own captain, although Fionn eventually came to be the leader of all of the Fianna.

Scholars are divided on Fionn, with some saying that he is a mythical figure, the "son of the Light," like the mythical Celtic god Lugh, the "son of the Sun." Lugh, like Fionn, was a radiant youth who could do all things well and who regularly trafficked between this world and the spirit world.

Other scholars believe that Fionn was a real person and leader of the

Fenian army, a somewhat larger-than-life figure, whose exploits not only outlived him, but took on legendary and mythical proportions after his death.

I favor this latter opinion.

As for Patrick, he did, of course, really exist.

The problem is that he did not exist in as epic or fine a fashion as his early biographers would have later generations believe.

First of all, Patrician scholars cannot even agree on the dates of Patrick's arrival and death, some saying that he came to Ireland in 432 A.D. and died in 461 A.D. and others claiming that he came in 461 and died in 491.

It is true that Patrick spent his youth, from the ages of 16 to 22, as a slave in Ireland. Again, scholars cannot decide whether he was in the northeast, near Armagh, or in the west, in Mayo. The weight of scholarship holds with Mayo and, frankly, I chose it because it is where my own people are from.

The bare-bones facts of Patrick's life are these: he was the son of Calpornius, probably a Briton of Roman descent and a decurion in the Roman bureacracy. Patrick's grandfather Potitus had been a priest in the noncelibate Christian church and his father was a deacon. Patrick's family owned a villa and were probably what we would now call "upper middle class."

Prior to his enslavement, Patrick himself tells us that he was not a religious youth. The loneliness of his enslavement, tending sheep, surrounded by wolfhounds, led him to pray often and fervently and eventually led to the voice which spoke in his head for the rest of his life.

It is true that the Voice told Patrick when to escape from Ireland, that the youth returned home, and that in spite of visions and messages, he resisted returning to Ireland for eighteen years, when he was evidently sent by the hierarchy of the Romano-British Catholic church.

In his Confession, Patrick speaks of his brothers in Gaul, but it is not really clear if he ever did study on the continent or even if he ever visited there. It is true that his Latin is rough and ungrammatical and that, by and large, Patrick was an uneducated and not very erudite man.

This does not mean that he was not wise. Or that he did not become wise.

Of the events which occurred in this book, I have taken the liberty of selecting from both history and legend. It is probably not historical fact that Patrick set the fire on the Hill of Slaine. Legends say that he lit his blaze at the Pascal feast, which would have been sometime around Beltaine in the Celtic calendar (May 1). However, in the ancient Celtic calendar, the greatest feast of the year was samhain, what we now call Halloween. It was on that night that the old year's fire was extinguished and the new one lighted. Samhain was considered a very dangerous time for the forces of darkness, and thus would suit Patrick's purpose better.

It is probably also not historical fact that Patrick tried to convert his former slavemaster or that he ranged quite so far and wide across Ireland. In fact, many or all of the legends surrounding Patrick are just that. He probably did not drive the snakes from Ireland (largely because there were no snakes in Ireland) or destroy idols like Crom Cruach or create great signs and wonders. Most recently, Patrician scholars believe that Patrick spent the largest portion of his mission in Armagh, in the service of the Ulaid kings of that region. When their fortunes fell, Patrick's fell as well. In all likelihood, he spent the declining years of his mission near the sea in the area now called Downpatrick.

There must have been something about him, however, some quality that people could see or feel or relate to. Perhaps the light shining through him was more beautiful than the man himself, for his Confession and his Letter to Coroticus, the only two documents we have from his own hand, reveal a man largely uneducated, humble about his estate, yet stubbornly proud of his relationship with God, lacking in self-esteem, full of self-doubts and extremely defensive about his dealings with the Irish, his use of Church money, and the success of his mission.

It is that all-too-human frailty in his Confession and his Letter that I love most about Patrick.

Patrick did have problematical relationships with women. It seems from his Confession that they often offered him gifts of jewelry, the prized possession of the Celts, as well as gifts of another nature, which he says he resisted. His Confession and Letter are very brief; in that short space, he discusses the issue of women several times in each manuscript. In his Confession, he states that many of his converts were daughters of great chiefs who defied their fathers to come to him.

In his Confession, Patrick praises those women who choose chastity in the service of grace. In particular, he describes one of his converts as "a blessed Irishwoman of noble birth, beautiful, full-grown." He says of her that she came to him after six days of contemplation "for a particular reason." He does not specify what the reason was, but does tell us that she had made a decision to join his community and to select chastity in the service of Christ. He tells us how much his heart rejoiced at her decision.

In his Letter to Coroticus, Patrick is nearly incoherent with grief over the converted women and children of his flock who have been kidnapped and sold into slavery. In particular, he mentions a noble highborn woman convert whom it grieved him greatly to lose.

From these slender passages in the Confession and the Letter, I created the druidess, Ainfean. Not only did I wish to create a woman who would trouble Patrick in every way (as is only proper), but I wanted a voice to speak for the lost religion.

It is also true that in the ancient Church there were several women "priests," an occasional woman "bishop" and women who served as abbesses of huge monasteries, among them Bridget of Kildare and Patrick's contemporary St. Darerca.

Patrick confesses that he did commit one terrible sin in his youth, probably of a sexual nature, given the tone of his Confession, but we don't know what occurred. It is true that Patrick confessed his sin to a friend, who later betrayed him to Church officials, a betrayal which left Patrick hurt and bitter. According to his Confession, the sin took place when he was only fifteen. For the sake of drama, and perhaps for the sake of grace, I gave him a later "sin" with the foster daughter of his slavemaster. Patrick himself may not have considered this a sin; sexual behavior in the early Church was much less rigid than now.

As my first name is not a saint's name, Patrick is my baptismal name patron. I hope that I have spoken him as he was, and that he will understand in those places where I have not.

As to whether or not Osian ever came to Patrick and told him the Fenian tales, I cannot give a clear answer.

For me, the line between this world and the Other World grows increasingly blurred as I grow older.

As Patrick would say, all things are possible with the Word. All things.

And I believe him.

Bail O Dhia ar an obair.
Bless, O God, the work.

298

Selected Bibliography

Bamford, Christopher and William Parker Marsh. CELTIC CHRISTIAN-ITY: ECOLOGY AND HOLINESS. Mass: Lindisfarne Press, 1982.

Bellingham, David. CELTIC MYTHOLOGY. London: Quintet Publishing, 1990.

Cahill, Thomas. HOW THE IRISH SAVED CIVILIZATION. New York: Doubleday, 1995.

Caldecott, Moyra. WOMEN IN CELTIC MYTH. Rochester, Vermont: Destiny Books, 1988.

Chadwick, Nora. THE CELTS. New York: Penguin Books, 1971.

Cunliffe, Barry. THE CELTIC WORLD. New York: McGraw-Hill, 1979.

Delaney, Frank. THE CELTS. London: BBC Publications and Hodder & Stoughton Ltd., 1986.

————. LEGENDS OF THE CELTS. New York: Sterling Publishing, 1991.

de Paor, Liam. SAINT PATRICK'S WORLD. Dublin: Four Courts Press, 1993.

Dillon, Myles, ed. IRISH SAGAS. Edition 4. Dublin: Mercier Press, 1985.

Earl, Amanda, ed. A CELTIC FAMILY. East Sussex: Wayland, 1987.

Gantz, Jeffrey, trans. EARLY IRISH MYTHS AND SAGAS. New York: Dorset Press, 1985.

Glassie, Henry, ed. IRISH FOLK TALES. New York: Pantheon Books, 1985.

Green, Miranda J. DICTIONARY OF CELTIC MYTH AND LEGEND. London: Thames and Hudson, 1992.

————. THE WORLD OF THE DRUIDS. New York: Thames and Hudson, 1997.

Hoagland, Kathleen, ed. 1000 YEARS OF IRISH POETRY. Old Greenwich, Connecticut: The Devin-Adair Company, 1975.

Lynch, Patricia. KNIGHTS OF GOD: TALES AND LEGENDS OF THE IRISH SAINTS. New York: Holt, Rinehart & Winston, 1969.

MacManus, Seumas. THE STORY OF THE IRISH RACE. Old Greenwich, Connecticut: The Devin-Adair Company, 1921.

Markale, Jean. WOMEN OF THE CELTS. Rochester, Vermont: Inner Traditions Publishing, 1972.

Matthews, John, ed. A CELTIC READER: SELECTIONS FROM CELTIC LEGEND, SCHOLARSHIP AND STORY. Wellingborough: Aquarian Press, 1991.

————. FIONN MAC CUMHAILL: CHAMPION OF IRELAND. Illus. by James Field. Poole: Firebird Books, 1988.

McCaffrey, Kevin. THE ADVENTURES OF FIONN AND THE FIANNA. Dublin: Fitzwilliam Publishing Co., 1989.

————. DEIRDRE AND OTHER HEROINES OF CELTIC FOLKLORE. Dublin: Fitzwilliam Publishing, 1989.

McGarry, Mary. GREAT FOLK TALES OF OLD IRELAND. New York: Bell Publishing, 1972.

McMahon, Agnes, ed. THE CELTIC WAY OF LIFE. Dublin: O'Brien Educational, 1988.

Moscati, Sabatino, et al, eds. THE CELTS. New York: Rizzoli, 1991.

Neill, Kenneth. AN ILLUSTRATED HISTORY OF THE IRISH PEOPLE. Dublin: Gill and Macmillan, 1979.

Norton-Taylor, Duncan. THE CELTS. New York: Time-Life Books, 1974.

O'Faolain, Eileen. IRISH SAGAS AND FOLKTAKES. New York: Avenel Books, 1982.

O'Kelly, Michael J. EARLY IRELAND. Cambridge: Cambridge University Press, 1989.

Piggott, Stuart. THE DRUIDS. London: Thames and Hudson, 1985.

Powell, T. G. E. THE CELTS. London: Thames and Hudson, 1980.

Ranleigh, John. IRELAND: AN ILLUSTRATED HISTORY. New York: Oxford University Press, 1981.

Rayner, Lee J. LEGENDS OF THE KINGS OF IRELAND. Dublin: Mercier Press, 1988.

Rees, Alwyn and Brinley. CELTIC HERITAGE. London: Thames and Hudson, 1961.

Rolleston, T. W THE HIGH DEEDS OF FINN. New York: Lemma Publishers, 1973.

————. THE ADVENTURES OF FINN MAC CUMHAL. Dublin: Mercier Press, 1979.

Roy, James Charles. THE ROAD WET, THE WIND CLOSE: CELTIC IRELAND. Dublin: Gill and MacMillan, 1986.

Rutherford, Ward. CELTIC MYTHOLOGY. New York: Sterling Publishing, 1990.

Scherman, Katharine. THE FLOWERING OF IRELAND: SAINTS, SCHOLARS AND KINGS. Boston: Little Brown, 1981.

Sharkey, John. CELTIC MYSTERIES: THE ANCIENT RELIGION. London: Thames & Hudson, 1975.

Sjoestedt, Marie-Louise. GODS AND HEROES OF THE CELTS. Trans. by Myles Dillon. Berkeley, California: Turtle Island Foundation, 1982.

Smyth, Daragh. A GUIDE TO IRISH MYTHOLOGY. Dublin: Irish Academic Press, 1988.

Stewart, R. J. CELTIC GODS, CELTIC GODDESSES. London: Blandford, 1990.

Sutcliffe, Rosemary. THE HIGH DEEDS OF FINN MAC COOL. London: Puffin Books, 1967.

Van de Weyer, Robert. CELTIC FIRE: THE PASSIONATE RELIGIOUS VISION OF ANCIENT BRITAIN AND IRELAND. New York: Doubleday, 1990.

Yeats, W. B., ed. A TREASURY OF IRISH MYTH, LEGEND AND FOLK-LORE. New York: Crown Publishers, 1986.